ZONED FOR MURDER

By

Kait Carson

"Zoned for Murder"

Published by Mako Graphics, LLC

Copyright ©2011 by Kait Carson rev. 10/13

®Kait Carson

www.kaitcarson.com

DEDICATION

For Gary, who believed when no one else did, including me.

For the Gang of Six,

Starlight, Hutch, Elvis, Jazz, Fred, Zoe

and most of all Smokey Bear (1997-2008)

ACKNOWLEDGEMENTS

It takes many people to bring a book from idea to fruition. My first thanks go to Guppies, the Internet Chapter of Sisters in Crime. The water in the pond is always warm and supportive. Guppies gave me the best critique group a writer could hope for. To the women of Risky Business, Shirl, Pauline and Sand, you are amazing. This book would never have happened without you. Shirl Jensen, you stuck with Catherine through all eight drafts, always offering just the right touch to make her leap off the page. I owe Susan Schreyer, a debt of gratitude I can never repay. You are an incomparable copy editor who brought not only the story, but also the characters to life and kept me from embarrassing myself on more than one page. A special thank you to my friends, who were fascinated by the process of writing and willing to answer my endless questions and offer their expertise in the South Florida political process. Any errors are mine and mine alone. Finally, a special thank you to my family. To my husband for his loving support while I squirreled myself away at my computer for hours at a time surfacing only to ask for lessons in a different caliber. For his being willing to give me lessons in that caliber. And to the Gang of Six, my band of six cats who think my computer is home base and like nothing better snuggle while I type. For the parts of this book that were written in Maine, I couldn't have done this without you gathered at my feet like living slippers.

I long ago decided that if I were ever lucky enough to publish a book, I would donate 10% of the net profit to charity. 10% of the net profit of Zoned for Murder will be donated to PTSA at Design & Architecture Senior High School (DASH), Miami-Dade County Public Schools, Miami, Florida to help support a college scholarship for a student in the Architecture Department. I think Catherine Swope would be proud.

CHAPTER 1

"Order. I'll clear this room."

The tension in the commission meeting felt as thick and sticky as the Florida air outside. The sharp crack of Mayor Arnie Cunningham's gavel sliced through the escalating buzz of voices in the crowded room, reverberating like a rifle shot.

Ignoring the Mayor's attempt at control, the town meeting dissolved into a hurricane of angry shouts. Catherine Swope, senses on full alert, craned her neck to find the instigator. Her hand travelled to her hip, reflexively seeking her weapon. It wasn't there. Instead, her fingers grazed the puckered scar on her thigh.

A trickle of cold sweat dribbled a path down her spine. The acrid scent of rage mixed with fear filled her nostrils. Luis Alvarez, his head down and his cheeks deep crimson gripped both sides of the speaker's podium so firmly that his knuckles showed white while he waited for the Zoning Commissioner's decision about the variance. It was his last appeal. He'd begged for the variance, saying he faced foreclosure without it.

1

All around Catherine, people were in motion. Some squirmed in their seats, eyes wide, waiting for someone else to take action. Others were halfway out of their chairs, hands clenching and faces hardened. One man she didn't recognize cracked his knuckles, a smile playing at the corners of his mouth. The woman next to him slouched low in her chair and looked frantically from side to side. The whole room had the appearance of a wave gone bad at a football game. The late arrivals that lined the back of the meeting room shifted away from the walls and spilled into the aisles. All around Catherine individuals morphed into a mob and a familiar surge of adrenalin bubbled in her veins forcing her out of her seat and in the direction of the Commissioners' table.

Alarm and determination grew in equal measure with every step. Glancing over her shoulder through the shifting, her heart clenched. She no longer saw a clear pathway to the double doors of the lone exit, a relic of 1930's building codes and construction. The only hope of escape for the commissioners seated at the front of the room were the nearly floor to ceiling double hung windows that lined the walls. She prayed they weren't painted shut.

The zoning commissioner leaned toward the microphone as the roar of the crowd ebbed. In a voice honed by years as a criminal defense attorney, Gavin Jackman spoke slowly and evenly. "I'm sorry for your trouble, Luis." He made a sweeping gesture, waving his right arm over the restive crowd. "You are not alone in this crisis. Everyone's property values are plummeting. You admit bad refinancing choices. That's not this commission's fault. Building new bedrooms won't fix it either, and" -- he fanned the sheaf of papers he held in his hand and thumbed through them briefly. "Your neighbors don't seem to want that addition built. Therefore." The pause that followed seemed to hang in the air while Gavin neatly stacked the papers he held. "Variance denied. I will grant you one exception. You may appeal again in six months." He took off his glasses and pointed at the architectural drawing on the easel beside Luis. "But not with something that ugly." A sneer curled his lip.

Gavin's nasty words froze Catherine in her tracks where she stood midway down the aisle. The entire room seemed to catch its collective breath in shock.

"My God." A woman's soft voice broke the strange silence. For a moment, Catherine wasn't sure if it was a curse or a prayer. "That man needs to be impeached," growled a man's voice. Catherine was moving toward the commissioners' table when another man shouted, "You rock, Gavin!" And like a genie out of the bottle, the sound of jeers and oaths filled the air followed by the dry sound of folding chairs scraping rubber feet over the heart of pine floor as the group divided into pro and anti-Gavin forces. One chair smashed into the wall behind Gavin's head. A flash caught Catherine's eye and she ducked. Something came so close she heard a hissing noise as it flew over her. The group surged forward. The air filled with the sound of curses joined with shouts of pain as elbows rammed into stomachs, feet trod on toes and fists slammed into faces.

A man went down, screaming when his neighbors trampled him. Catherine struggled to reach him, but was helpless against the tide of humanity flowing against her. Gavin's supporters became undistinguishable from his foes as both groups battled to the commissioners' table Catherine winced as the edge of the table cut deeply into her as the crowd forced her forward. The tropical colors of summer clothes moved and danced in macabre patterns and the rocking movement of the floorboards beneath her feet brought nausea to her throat as the pressure of the table edge increased.

Shoving herself back from the table, she half-turned her body and hoisted herself up on the dais that held her prisoner. Her blood ran cold at the sight behind her. One man lay on the floor, blood running from a cut on his forehead. What looked like a small revolver flashed from the center of the writhing group of men, Catherine strained to identify the combatants, but couldn't find the hand holding the weapon again. Clenched fists and the sickening sound of flesh hitting flesh surrounded her as the room continued to divide and take sides for or against the zoning commissioner. The unmistakable smells of sweat, fear, and hatred wafted through the room. Dark spots clouded her vision as heat and the swirling crowds combined like a psychedelic soup. Gasping under the onslaught of a memory brought on by the sights and smells that surrounded her, she fought for control.

Arnie Cunningham bashed his Mayor's gavel repeatedly. The sound yanked Catherine out of her private hell and back to the present. Both of his fists wrapped around the wooden mallet like a weapon, he continued to bring it down on the wooden block like a crazed automaton. Catherine grabbed his shoulders from above and he struggled briefly, and then seemed to freeze. She took advantage of the moment to shove the man down and under the dais until only the scuffed toe of one of his shoes protruded beneath the white of the tablecloth. The rest of the six commissioners scurried after the Mayor.

The sounds of the melee were approaching deafening proportions. Once she assured herself there was nothing more she could do, she allowed herself a quick glance toward the front door. A movement her instincts identified as a threat caught her attention and she leapt to safety under the dais. The roundhouse punch she barely detected out of the corner of her eye came so close she felt a puff of air brush her cheek. Grateful for the scrape of the rough floor against her bare arms, she rolled and tucked the tablecloth closed behind her in one fluid motion. A bubble of pride rose in her chest. For the first time in a long time, she felt comfortable in her own skin.

The wet sound of flesh hitting flesh grew louder in the semi-darkness. Catherine peeked out at the chaos in the meeting hall from under the drape of the tablecloth. Unable to see an avenue of safe escape, she pulled her head back. Gratitude that her hiding place remained secure faded when a man's sneakered feet poked under the cloth. Mayor Cunningham moaned pitifully. Despite the cramped space, he lifted the gavel over his head in both hands. Catherine's stomach went into free-fall when a man's hand grasped the hem of the cloth.

She recognized the intruder as Mike Reardon, a Summer Hill lieutenant and her current boyfriend. She hadn't seen him in the crowd. Relief flooded through her.

Mike grasped Gavin's arm by the wrist and pulled him out exposing Catherine to view.

"What the hell are you doing under here?" Mike hissed at her, "This isn't your job. You could get hurt."

"Training. It kicked in before I could stop myself." The tension in her neck eased.

Mike's eyes bored into hers. For a brief moment, the rest of the room faded away and the world narrowed to the two of them. Catherine shivered, grateful for the concern she read in his eyes, but angry at the need to justify her actions to him.

"Catherine Swope?" Gavin spat out. "Why are you here? Is this about money?"

Mike's eyebrows arched a question. Before Catherine could frame a reply, two more off-duty officers joined the group. By unspoken agreement, Catherine and the three men formed a phalanx around the Commissioners and forced a path through the still roiling crowd to the exit. The uniformed officers, accustomed to obedience by virtue of their uniforms, seemed to grow taller as they barked orders to the crowd to stand back. Some in the meeting room stopped fighting to watch the commissioners parade past. Others took the partial lull as an opportunity to get in an extra punch. Clots of men and women shouting support of Gavin pushed forward to try to join the officers in protection. The group had gone no more than half-way when the double doors burst open and police, clad in the uniforms of at least three different agencies, poured in to help quell the riot.

Catherine's gaze slewed around the crowd automatically cataloguing who was near, identifying the individuals as friend or foe, assessing potential threats, watching the near distance for activity and the far distance for the unexpected. There was little to do to stop the hands thrusting into the heart of the group and swarming over the commissioners and officers like red ants. The sound or ripping cloth diverted her attention toward the man just behind her. A blow from the man next to her caught her in the solar plexus ripping the breath from her lungs and doubling her over. She lifted her head gasping for air in time to see a glob of spit strike Gavin on the cheek. Luis Alvarez shoved people aside and pressed toward them from the same direction that the spit had come from. Catherine struggled upright to tap Mike's shoulder and pointed.

Time slowed to milliseconds. Faces, too sharp and bright, emerged from the crowd and froze in time. In slow motion, Catherine watched and identified the faces and voices of the hecklers while she struggled to keep her breathing even. The loudest shouters were those rumored to be in the last stages of foreclosure, seeking someone else to blame for their own greed during boom. Small town life has no secrets. She looked around again at the twisted faces, but this time she felt compassion, and a flicker of understanding for the degree of hatred aimed at the zoning commissioner.

The flat of Mike's hand pushed hard on the exit door's brass bar, forcing the exit open. The humid outside air felt cool compared to the heat of the meeting hall as the group rushed out. Gavin's chest lifted as he took a deep breath and without a backward glance, moved in the direction of his car, tucking in the tatters of his shirttail as he walked.

When the officers went back inside, Catherine paused on the porch steps and took a deep breath over the dull ache from the blow, then another, and another. Throbbing strobes from the police cars bunched in front of the building made the cul de sac park look like a disco gone bad. Briefly, she toyed with the thought of going back into the fray. The pain in her stomach was oddly pleasurable, a symbol of a job well done.

The porch rocked with the footfalls of officers and the two men they bundled out of the Hall. Catherine lost sight of the small parade when they rounded the corner heading in the direction of police headquarters. One of the men, Catherine noted without surprise, was Luis Alvarez.

Mike escorted a frightened man to the porch. Spotting Catherine still standing there, he strode to her side. "Go home, Cathy, I need to know you're safe. This isn't your fight. Don't try playing cop again."

"It's habit, I guess." She looked him full in the face weighing her words. "It felt good and bad. I felt, I don't know, alive again." The realization surprised her.

His voice softened, "No. Don't even think it. You know how bad it can get, Kit Kat." He gently pushed back a strand of her still damp butter brown hair. "You were hurt enough before."

"Are you still coming by?" She hated the need she heard in her own voice.

Mike glanced from her to the meeting hall behind him. Shouts of the officers punctuated loud crashes. Catherine watched Mike's face lose all expression and harden into a mask. "Not tonight," he said through clenched teeth. "Sorry Cathy." He gathered her into a hard hug.

A wave of self-pity, followed quickly by anger, washed over her. She leaned her head briefly against his chest, forcing herself to stay silent.

Unable to watch him return to the fight, she twisted her neck to look at the clots of people gathering on the grassy median behind her. A familiar need gnawed at her gut. Clustering close to the porch stood a group of her friends.

"Let's gather the gang and have a ladies night out." Catherine announced when she jumped down to greet them. "I could use something cold." Sharp glances answered her, but the flashing kaleidoscope of reds and blues made them easy to ignore. "You stay put, I'll see if Susan or Vicki have made it to the door."

Catherine took the shallow steps two at a time and approached the double doors from an angle, keeping the protection of the thick log walls between her and the exit. Just as she reached the deck, the doors opened and a folding chair flew out.

CHAPTER 2

The early morning sunlight cut into her eyes like shards of glass. Her teeth felt fuzzy, like she'd been chewing on cotton balls. Damn. It's been a long time since I woke up feeling this bad.

Catherine swung her legs to the floor and her toes sunk into the soft fur of her German shepherd, Bullet. She wriggled them in his coat, grateful for his warmth. Her hand brushed the scar on her thigh and her stomach plummeted. Nausea mixed with self-loathing coursed through her. Vague snippets of the conversation at the Bistro came back in a kaleidoscope of images and voices. Scenes from the commission meeting coalesced into one Technicolor memory of standing on the commissioners' dais. The drinking was bad enough, acting like a cop at the commission meeting and liking it plunged her to a whole new level of hell. Was that what led to the drinking? The way I behaved at the commission meeting? Was I celebrating finding my purpose again?

The room swirled. She gripped the edge of the bed, steadying herself, and walked gingerly to

11

pull the curtains aside. "Never, never ever again. Drinking will not solve who I want to be when I grow up," she muttered. Unless I decide to be a drunk. Guilt mixed with a cold sweat and increased nausea accompanied the thought. Not an option.

Stumbling into the kitchen she started coffee hoping for a caffeine headache cure. The cold blast from the freezer helped ease the pain almost as much as the bag of peas she pressed to her head. How could a couple of beers make me feel this lousy? Was it only a couple? After the shooting, when her whole world seemed upside down, she resisted getting help. Now, she wished for someone to call.

Rearranging the cold bag on her forehead and centering the peas so they cooled her eyes, she visualized the group of women sitting around the restaurant table last night. Something important lurked just beyond the reach of her memory. She fought through the pain, trying to remember and failing miserably.

The gurgle of the pot and the heady smell of the rich brew assailed her nostrils. Testing the smell against the feeling in her stomach, she emerged from under the peas. Even the simple act of reaching for her mug caused pain. Her hand pressed against the countertop for balance and met the rough edges of her address book open to "J." Snippets of her complaints last night about Gavin owing her for dog sitting and getting what he deserved for stiffing her floated back.

Catherine's eyes rolled skyward, the movement causing more pain, as a hazy memory of her slurred phone message on Gavin Jackman's voice mail demanding payment returned. "Damn, damn, damn!" She muttered, slammed the book shut and slid it into the drawer. "Bullet," she said to the dog standing beside her, "next time Mommy heads for the phone for a little drunk dialing, put me under canine arrest."

The grandfather clock in the hallway chimed seven. Wishing she could crawl back to bed, she opened the doggie door, let Bullet out, and reached for her morning schedule. A hangover, she decided, is not an asset in the dog-walking business. The thought of breakfast brought bile to her throat. Instead, she opened the morning Metropolis to the local section and willed her eyes to focus.

A photo of Gavin Jackman leapt out at her under the headline 'Former Attorney In Sex Scandal.' "I don't believe it," she muttered. No way did the dry desiccated man she knew jibe with the man in the story. She glanced at the sidebar and read the contents of the victim's now five-year old confessional Affidavit claiming that Gavin never knew her true age. The body of the story implied Gavin and his law partners coerced the admission. One of those partners was now a Judge on the criminal bench, and the writers pointed out, up for re-election this year.

Catherine chewed her lip. Somebody really hates Gavin, to bring this up now.

The story, coming on the heels of the unexpected violence of last night's commission meeting, reeked of conspiracy, revenge, or maybe just bad timing. Local buzz, bolstered by Gavin's taking a job as a law professor, implied that the Jackmans were having trouble paying their second mortgage. Something like this could ruin the job and get him kicked off the commission. Someone was out for blood. Whoever it was, they must have a lot to gain. Why did she feel so guilty about own her call? Her drunken message seemed mild by comparison.

By the time Catherine walked her last canine client of the morning, the sun no longer cut into her eyes like knives and the incipient nausea released its hold on her stomach. Exercise always helped more than wallowing in shame and self-pity. Behind her, the rhythmic click of dog toenails on pavement made her look over her shoulder. Leaning down, she patted the little black and white Maltese on his leash and said, "Buster, let's wait for Amber and Topaz to catch up. I bet Aunt Nancy has something to say about last night."

Nancy fell in step with Catherine and looked her full in the face "Sorry I missed last night – it sounded like one heck of a brawl. Why do I always have to work and miss the party?"

A hot blush rose to Catherine's cheeks in response to the scrutiny.

"You didn't miss a thing, unless you like riots." She stooped and untangled Buster's leash from around Nancy's two Golden Retrievers. "Why are you home?" She shaded her eyes with her free hand. "Today's Wednesday."

"You feel all right?"

Catherine hid the quick spurt of anger behind a smile and avoided the question.

Over Nancy's shoulder, Catherine spied Meg Kent approaching at a jog. Glad for the opportunity to change the subject she said, "Oliver went to the hoosegow last night."

"Oliver Kent?" Nancy asked.

"The same. Gavin shot down Luis's variance and the natives got restless" Catherine jerked her chin in Meg's direction, "Here comes the explanation, or the excuse."

"Did you see this morning's paper?" Meg huffed and pulled her right leg behind her in a quad stretch. Catherine noticed the soles of her running shoes were barely marked.

"I hope he rots in jail. Didn't you work for him, Nancy?"

"How's Oliver, Meg?" Catherine asked. She wondered at the woman's focus on Gavin since the police had led her own husband away the night before.

Meg smirked and grabbed Catherine's arm drawing a growl from Buster. "Luis got arrested last night, not Oliver."

Catherine stared down at the intruding hand, shaking up and down as the woman jogged in place. It took all her control not to forcibly remove it finger by finger. Luis's arrest came as no surprise. He'd needed it, even if only to calm down. Catherine's gaze lifted inch by slow inch from the offending hand to Meg's eyes. They held an emotion Catherine identified as arrogance and quickly morphed to fear.

Meg pulled her hand away and saluted. Making a large arc in the roadway, she jogged back in the direction of her house.

"Luis got arrested? I thought you said Oliver." Nancy asked

Heat devils shimmering on the asphalt caused Catherine a brief spasm of queasiness while she considered what she'd seen in Meg's face and her answer. "Luis and Oliver both were frog-marched out the front door, I guess Luis ended up in the can and Oliver went home."

Nancy turned, watching Meg's departure. "There were rumors a while ago that Gavin and Meg were having an affair. I never believed it. That newspaper article is going to drag up a ton of dirt. I feel sorry for Ashley. Being married to Gavin can't be easy on a good day. Can you imagine it today?"

"I think Ashley is going to need some moral support. I'm going by after I take Buster home." Catherine said. "Want to come with me?"

"Don't personalize this, Cathy, it's not the same. You were a hero. You did the right thing."

The still raw memories of events after her shooting flooded back. Time dimmed none of the pain of her friends dwindling to one or two, even after the ruling that the shooting was justifiable. She was a cop, shot and under fire. She saved her own life and the lives of everyone on the street that day. Would she have pulled the trigger if she'd known the kid shooting at her was fourteen? Her fingers grazed the shiny edges of the scar on her thigh. "I know what living as a gossip target is like, Gavin

can swing for all I care. Ashley needs to know she
has support if she needs it."
***

Catherine paused, admiring the classic
mission style architecture of the Jackman home. She
loved her own art deco cottage, but the realtor she
had become after she left the force loved selling the
old Spanish styles with their quirky rooms and huge
windows. A flash of brown behind the fence caught
her eye.

"Hey Roscoe, what are you doing out?
Where are your mommy and daddy?" The chocolate
Doberman ran toward Catherine. His stub of a tail
pulled down flat against his rump, a string of drool
hung from his sleek mouth. He raced in frantic
circles, ran halfway to the detached garage and then
back to her at the gate.

A cold chill ran through Catherine, and she
quickly surveyed the yard. Nothing seemed wrong,
but a piece of last night's conversation clicked into
place. The zoning control officer mentioned
someone trying to kill her dogs — poison, some
kind of poison. God, if someone went after her
dogs…. Desperate to reach Roscoe, Catherine
yanked the gate latch open. Roscoe jumped up, his
front paws resting on her shoulders, his tail still flat
on his rump. She peered into his mouth relieved that
his gums and tongue were normally colored. The
dog dropped down, circled twice and pressed
himself against her leg.

Not poisoned. Scared.

Confused, Catherine let the dog push her up
the path to the front door. Her knock brought no

17

response, so she jiggled the handle and found it locked.

With the dog calmer, but still pressed to her side, she walked through the sprinkler damp grass to the back door. Holding her hands alongside her face and shielding her eyes, she peered into the breakfast room windows of the new addition.

"Nobody home, kiddo. How'd you get out?"

The dog looked at her and pawed open the back door.

Her hand automatically slid to her side seeking the butt of her weapon. The naked feel of her hipbone reminded her that the weapon belonged to another life. Catherine's body tensed. She was unarmed and without backup. She toed the door wide enough to slide inside. Her heart pounded and the hair on her arms prickled. The deep, almost velvet, silence of emptiness greeted her. Bobbing back and forth to peer around corners and through doors before entering, she looked for anything that seemed out of place. The sweet scent of several large bouquets of pink roses decorating the kitchen, living, and dining room nearly overcame her still-queasy stomach.

Exiting the house, she squatted on the back stoop and scratched Roscoe's ears. Her nose itched. Both Gavin's and Ashley's cars were in the driveway, she didn't see their old clunker, but they'd talked about selling it.

She ruffled Roscoe's fur beneath his chin while she considered her options. They never left the dog alone. The dog pulled away and ran toward the closed garage, stopping only to stare back at her.

Straightening with a sigh, she brushed off the back of her shorts and followed him.

The small decorative openings in the concrete garage window gave a limited view of dappled light and nothing more. Roscoe stood on his hind legs to paw the window, his claws leaving marks in the stucco. Cupping her hands around her eye only blurred the effect. Damn it, this is impossible. Anyone can be in there.

Catherine hugged the wall and edged around the garage to the back door. Her breath caught in her throat as she turned the knob. Keeping the protection of the building behind her, she eased open the door with her heel and swiveled her head around the door jamb, Her quick glance took in a freezer chest, refrigerator, kiln, jumble of boxes, kick wheel, and large cast iron double sink pushed up against the wall. A hard hit to the back of her knees nearly brought her down as she rotated to enter. Roscoe dashed past her.

An arched opening provided access from the storeroom area to the garage. Roscoe's throaty growl filtered back to her. Senses heightened, Catherine crept toward the direction of the sound.

"Damn!" The word came out on a hiss of breath. Simultaneously she reached for her cell phone.

CHAPTER 3

"Nine One One," her voice quavered and Catherine winced, "I'm in the garage at 14625 NE Sunshine Court in Summer Hill, The home owner is hanging." Sticky sweat from heat, adrenaline, or both, ran between her breasts.

"Say again?"

"I'm at 14625 NE Sunshine Court in Summer Hill. The homeowner is hanging from a rafter." Catherine spoke through gritted teeth.

"Help is on the way, dear. Stay on the line with me." The operator spoke in professionally soothing tones.

"Sorry, honey," Catherine muttered. Cop or not, her first priority was securing the scene. Roscoe could sniff, snort or shuffle away valuable information. Tucking the cell phone, line still open, into the pocket of her shorts, Catherine returned to the garage to corral the dog.

The 110-pound Doberman did not want to leave. Leaning back on his haunches he refused to move. His lip curled back exposing white fangs, a low threatening rumble sounded deep in his throat.

"Damn, I never thought I'd want to be heavier!" Catherine mumbled trying to ignore his growling. She pushed a damp strand of hair off her face and shoved again. One thing she'd learned dealing with animals, never let them smell your fear.

"Come on Roscoe, cooperate a little. Move!" Desperate, Catherine finally gripped him under his hips, lifted his hindquarters and half-pushed, half-walked the animal like a furry wheelbarrow through the workroom and out the door. A breath of air, sweetened by the scent of fresh cut grass, caressed her cheek like a reward. The normality of the day shocked her. Inside the garage hung a man who would never again smell fresh cut grass, or coffee, and life outside went on. The sound of a neighbor's lawnmower whirred monotonously.

Knowing that people in small towns have disaster radar, she glanced at her watch and calculated about eight minutes before the police arrived. The whir of the garden tractor grew louder, reminding her of the animosity between Gavin and his neighbors, Chris and Terry Payson. A brief memory of Terry grabbing for Gavin's shirt last night returned. Catherine searched her memory and didn't recall seeing Chris. Those chaotic scenes represented the last evening of Gavin's life. A wave of emotion washed over her. Did she miss something last night that resulted in Gavin's death?

Roscoe's feet scratched clods from the patch of earth near the garage bordering the Payson fence. The animal squatted as she watched. Her glance traveled up from Roscoe's 'emergency business' patch to the Paysons' kitchen window. Disgusted that the Jackmans encouraged Roscoe to crap right outside the Paysons kitchen, she reached for the shovel leaning against the outer wall of the garage. Shocked at her reaction, she dropped the tool. Now was not the time to scoop the poop.

Time seemed to stop as soon as she re-entered the garage. The Florida heat hadn't yet turned the enclosed space rancid with death's odor. Catherine brows knit together in concentration. The room looked pristine. An overturned cup that held pens, pencils, utility knives, and rulers spewed half underneath the workbench was the only item out of place. Nothing else, not even an oil spot marred the floor.

Gavin's left loafer had slid off and rested on its side in a damp spot beneath him. His naked foot pointed downward like a dancer's over the shoe. Pulling her client notebook and a stubby lotto pencil from her shorts pocket, Catherine quickly sketched the scene. He'd done it right, she acknowledged, noting the knot beneath his jaw to the left side, the lack of a struggle suggesting a broken neck.

"God rest your soul, Gavin." Catherine muttered. Not sure if it was a prayer or a plea. "I hope you find the peace in death that eluded you in life." Her head level with Gavin's knees, she tried putting herself in the mind of a man desperate enough to murder himself.

Without warning, his whole body convulsed, feet kicking out in grotesque angles. Catherine gasped. Gavin's right loafer flew from his foot and slammed into her chest.

"Son of a bitch!"

Adrenalin poured through her. Biting back a scream, she spun around. Sargent Billy LaMotta's bulk filled the doorway from the workroom.

"What the hell!" LaMotta said, racing toward the body and keying the microphone clipped to his shoulder epaulette. "Stat, get that meat wagon here stat! This guy ain't dead." His voice echoed off the walls as he shouted into the microphone fastened at his uniform shoulder.

"Didn't you check him for a pulse?" He growled at Catherine, shoving her aside. "Why the hell didn't you cut him down? What the hell is wrong with you?

"Billy, Billy." Catherine shouted back, grabbing Billy's arms. "He's dead. Believe me. He's dead. Look at his eyes! Look."

Catherine felt impaled by Billy's chocolate eyes. She saw his gaze slide from her to Gavin. The high color receded and the tension drained from his face.

"It was the jump. I hate it when they jump like that."

"I know, Billy..."

Sirens drowned out the rest of her words. The creaking wheels of a gurney squeaked a noisy approach.

Two paramedics zigzagged around Billy and Catherine as they raced to the body.

"Stop right there!" Catherine said, mustering as much authority into her voice as she could.

The women in grey uniforms marked with Metro Dade Fire Rescue in black letters across their backs nearly collided with each other as they halted in their tracks. "He's dead." Catherine continued, wishing Billy would say something, "Don't touch him. Wait for the M.E."

The taller of the two women, obviously in charge, glanced between Billy and Catherine, weighing the situation. She walked over to Gavin her gaze moving from ceiling to floor. "Eyes fixed and dilated. Skin cool to the touch, no obvious evidence of rigor, sphincters released." She turned to Billy, "He's dead. I'd rather wait for the ME to pronounce him. Do you want me to cut him down? Perform CPR while we wait?"

Sgt. LaMotta shook his head and clicked the button on his shoulder mike again. "Dispatch," He nodded to the paramedics. "I'm requesting the M.E. to the scene." Turning back to the paramedic, he said, "Do what you need…"

"Don't cut him down. Get in touch with Metro. We need their crime scene people too." Catherine and Billy jumped at the sound of Mike Reardon's voice.

"It's a suicide. Looks complete," Billy said. "Did you see the paper this morning?"

"After last night, don't jump to conclusions. Where's the wife? Any financial problems? What about the mortgage mess? And yes, I did see the paper this morning." The tall lieutenant commanded the room. "Catherine, where's Ashley? Catherine? Kit Kat?

"She isn't in the house." Catherine flushed when she saw a muscle jump cadence in Mike's cheek. A flicker of anger mixed with self-loathing lodged in her mind. She realized she'd contaminated more than one potential crime scene. "I found Roscoe outside... Susan mentioned threats last night. She's only the Zoning enforcement officer, if she got them...." Unable to stand still, she paced, and waved her arms as she spoke, her movements as disjointed as her words. The harder she tried to stand still, the faster she moved.

"Billy will call you later for a statement." Mike cut her short. "You'll be home?"

In the silence that followed his question, he caught at her elbow and guided her firmly away from the scene toward the back door. "Are you OK?" He asked softly.

Catherine nodded, unable to meet his eyes for fear that she would see the same contempt she felt for herself. She looked past him to the street and raked the fingers of her free hand through her hair. "Just stupid, sometimes." The soundtrack that played in her head screamed at her that while she was playing cop, she'd forgotten how to be a cop.

A large white RV style vehicle marked Crime Scene Investigation pulled up and parked on the swale next to the street. A white van painted with a gold laurel wreath on the side followed close behind. Catherine's eyes stung with unexpected tears as she recognized the mortuary van.

"I guess I'd better take Roscoe with me." Her words came out almost as a sigh. I saw a lead near the back door of the garage."

25

The hand holding her elbow tightened. "Don't touch anything, Cathy."

She flushed again and bit back a response. The warning in his tone was clear. She knew better, damn it. she was acting like an amateur.

CHAPTER 4

After the shade of the garage, it took Catherine a minute to distinguish individuals in the bright kaleidoscope of colors made by the clothing of the curious neighbors gathered in the street. Their chatter buzzed like the constant hum of bees seeking a new hive. Roscoe strained at his makeshift leash to drag her into the crowd, nearly pulling her off her feet. Expectant, avaricious, faces gathered in her field of vision and seemed to swell and grow in the heat.

Running a gauntlet of looky-lous made her stomach clench. She wanted to grab the dog and race to the shelter of the garage and Mike's concern. Reflexively she rolled the rope around her fist, drawing the excited dog closer to her side.

Chris Payson pushed his way through the crowd and stood in front of her. "Catherine, what's going on?"

Shaking her head, Catherine tried skirting around him on the grass. Even if she could find her voice, the thought of feeding the gossip frenzy sickened her. Besides, the police needed to make the first official announcement.

He moved to plant himself firmly in her path. "I have a right to know if there's been a crime next door to me."

Something in his pocket buzzed. Catherine watched him pull out his cell phone, a brief hope of escape blossomed, and she tried to step past him. He pivoted and blocked her path.

A red haze tinged the edges of her vision. Individual voices made their way to her ears, but she couldn't understand the words. For one sickening moment, she considered attacking him.

"OK people," Mike's voice boomed from behind her. "There's nothing to see here, move on."

Tossing a grateful look over her shoulder, Catherine took advantage of the diversion and moved past the knot of people by skirting the far side of the mortuary van. The distance gave clarity to the voices bubbling all around.

"Shut up, Oliver. Stop running your mouth." Meg Kent's voice broke through the general hubbub, her voice an octave higher than usual.

"He's dead, trust me," Chris Payson said.

Catherine froze in her tracks nearly tangling herself in Roscoe's rope. She looked back, trying to locate Payson and Meg Kent in the crowd. How could he know that? Whom was he talking to?

* * *

Exhaustion bowed Catherine's shoulders by the time she arrived at her front door. Thoughts whirled in her mind that she needed to get on paper before speculation blunted the sharp edges of fact.

Paddy Whack, her silver tiger cat lay sleeping curled in a tight ball in the center of her office chair. Unwilling to disturb him, Catherine fished a yellow pad out of her desk and walked back to the kitchen. It cost her two doggie treats to buy some peace, but she finally managed to get both Bullet and Roscoe to settle down so she could write her witness report. The techniques she learned in the police academy proved useful as she carefully avoided fleshing out the bare facts. Dropping her head to her hands, Catherine closed her eyes, visualized the scene, and then wrote what she saw. A familiar feeling in her gut told her she missed something. She dropped her head again intent on finding the missing piece of evidence. Gavin committed suicide, but something…The phone rang and she jumped.

"Cathy, are you all right?" Nancy's concern oozed through the phone. "I've left you two messages. I heard Gavin died, and you found him."

"Who called you?" Plucking the living room drapes back Cathy looked out. Traffic had increased on her quiet street since she'd arrived home.

"I'm worried about you. This must be hard."

"How do you know he died?" Catherine a deep silence engulfed her as every fiber in her body waited for a reply. Nancy, her mind screamed, not you. Don't let it be you. The intensity of the thought rocked her back on her heels. Was she missing something? Or was she trying too hard to re-validate her creds as a cop? Maybe Nancy was right this morning. But now she was personalizing Gavin's death, not Ashley's pain.

"Vicki saw them remove a body. She heard it was Gavin." Nancy paused for a few beats and then continued. "My boss called me, too. They were law partners before Phil got elected to the bench."

"How did you know I was there?"

After a stony silence, Nancy replied, "Vicki heard Meg tell Oliver something less than complimentary about you being there. Now, are we through with the bull dung and will you please tell me if you're all right?"

"Any death is hard to take. Doesn't matter, natural, homicide, suicide or accident, they're all difficult, but yeah, if you can put a name on the corpse...." Catherine's voice trailed off in a whisper. Sighing, she continued, "Feeling guilty doesn't help. I left him a nasty message last night."

"Well, you probably weren't the only one. How nasty?"

"I'm pretty sure I said things I'll regret. Damn, Nancy, I hate it when I backslide. I've worked so hard."

"Welcome to the human race. There's always next time."

"When do the next times run out?" Catherine's eyes burned with unshed tears. She shuddered. "Gotta go."

"Call me later. No, better, I'll come over tonight, I don't want you alone, girlfriend."

The call interrupted her train of thought. Catherine stared at the yellow legal pad trying to recapture what had bothered her. She re-read the notes and timeline, pulled from her pocket the sketch she'd made at the scene, stapled it to a new page and annotated it with the time, date and location. Her nose itched again, a sure sign she missed something. As she scratched, she compared the sketch to her description. They matched, but something was wrong. She went to make coffee and tried to put herself back in the Jackmans' house and garage, recalling every step of the way. Nothing new surfaced, but something danced in her memory, just outside her grasp. A double tap police-style knock on the door broke her concentration.

Sighing, she pulled the door open without a glance through the peephole. "Hey Billy. You running a double shift?"

"Most of my friends call me Sue." The tall slender woman bent and hugged Catherine. "Can I come in, or would you rather be alone?"

"I am so sorry, Sue. Mike said he was sending Billy over. I thought…" She studied her friend, noticing the red-rimmed eyes and the soft cap of light brown curls that now seemed untamed. "You were closer to him than anyone." Catherine led Sue to the kitchen table and put a cup of coffee in front of her. "I'm a little concerned that the entire town will know about Gavin's death before Ashley finds out. That stinks." The coffee maker hissed and spat as Catherine poured water into still warm chamber and she leaned against to counter to wait for it to brew.

Susan played with the coffee cup in her hands. "The suicide theory doesn't wash with me."

Catherine cradled her fresh cup in both hands and paced the kitchen. "What if Gavin knew about the story"

"How?"

"Ashley. She works for the paper." Sue opened her mouth. Catherine waved her hand to silence her. "Everyone has a breaking point."

"Bull." Susan answered. "Total and complete bull."

"Easier than facing the humiliation." Catherine found her copy of the newspaper. Opening it to the article about the Affidavit, she spread it on the kitchen table. "How about this theory? He and Ashley had a knockdown, drag out fight because of the article this morning and she left him. God knows, I would. So Gavin, being Gavin and never wrong —"

"Christ, Cathy, he's dead." Susan slammed her mug onto the table with enough force to slosh coffee over the rim.

Arching an eyebrow in reply, Catherine continued, "Gavin went into the garage and thought about last night, and the article, and believed everyone from the Village to Ashley hated him. Then in one massive moment of self-pity he got this great idea to make everyone's life easier and hung himself."

"No. Do you believe that?"

The question wasn't a surprise. Catherine considered how to phrase her reply without committing to one theory or another. In her heart of hearts, she did believe Gavin hung himself. But the lack of struggle, coupled with something she knew she saw and couldn't remember worried her. Maybe, just maybe, if she asked enough questions, something would surface. "I believe he died with a rope around his neck. I do believe that. There had to be a reason. Financial problems."

Susan shrugged. "I don't know. He wouldn't confide that in me. That's just a Village rumor."

"Sex? Another affair, maybe someone in the Village." Catherine poured another cup of coffee glancing up in time to see Sue roll her eyes skyward. She stared into the cup as if it held the secrets of the universe and fought down the images that floated up from her police past. Hanging is hard. No one goes willingly to their hanging and it takes a lot of strength to drag them. "Well then, which of our neighbors do you tap for a killer?"

"Why someone from the Village?" Susan's short, rounded, fingernail tapped the paper. "What about this woman's family?"

Catherine rolled this thought around in her mind. There were possibilities, but the timelines didn't work. Why wait this long?

Experience had taught Catherine that the best way to solve a problem was to give it space. If she couldn't shower away her confusion, then her second best way to cut her personal Gordian knots was to bake. The mindless act of measuring and mixing let her mind roam. Relieved to have decided on the perfect no course of action, Catherine reached into her cupboard for her mixer. She felt Susan's eyes on her. Bringing the ingredients to the table, she said, "Is that what Nick thinks? Has he heard anything?

"Just because my husband's a cop doesn't give him the inside track. If an irate neighbor's after members of the zoning board, he sure doesn't want me hanging in our garage because someone is on a vendetta."

"Sue," Catherine paused, and took a deep breath. "I know it's hard, but I was there." She took her friend's hand in hers. "I was a cop. Not many murders are hangings. It's too hard to do."

Both women looked up as Roscoe and Bullet raced for the door barking. Catherine grabbed the brownie pan from the counter-top, popped it into the oven, and chased after them. A hand on each canine's collar, she called over her shoulder to Susan. "Want a spare dog for protection when Nick's on duty? Guaranteed noise makers" She opened her door to Billy LaMotta.

The Sargent stood in the doorway, his chocolate brown eyes sweeping the room seeming to take in both dogs, now wagging their tails, and Sue sitting in the kitchen. A rhythmic snapping sound broke the silence. Catherine watched in fascination. Billy stood silently in the doorway and cracked each of knuckles by pressing down on the finger with his thumb in sequence going from index to pinkie repeatedly. With a start, she realized the man was nervous. The smell of fresh coffee and baking brownies reached her at the front door giving her an opening to end the strange, tense, standoff. "Coffee's on, Billy. Come on in." She released the dogs and nodded in the direction of the kitchen.

One foot poised over the threshold while Billy's other patent leather police approved oxford remained firmly planted on the top step. A faint blush painted the tips of his cheekbones and he withdrew his foot from the threshold to the step. He cleared his throat. "Catherine, this might be easier at the station."

"It's lot more comfortable here." Confused by his reluctance, she wondered if it was because of her relationship with Mike. Or if Mike wanted to interview her, but didn't want to do it here. As quickly as the thought crossed her mind, she discarded it. Mike was a professional. If he wanted to interview her, the venue wouldn't make any difference. This was a simple suicide. She was a witness. Nothing more. Any rookie could do this interview. So why was Billy so spooked?

Seemingly at a stalemate, he stood on the step while she held the door waiting to see if he would blink first. A parade of emotions raced across his face, and then he gave her a small, tight, smile.

"Besides, I just put in some of my brownies." She stepped aside and he entered, walking directly to the kitchen.

Billy nodded a greeting to Sue. While Catherine watched, he reached over the open newspaper and turned her legal pad around with the flat of two fingers until it faced in his direction. She could almost feel him absorbing the information. "Susan," he said. "Will you leave us alone? Give my best to Nick, and if the State police are hiring we may end up colleagues."

A spurt of anger brought color to Catherine's cheeks at Billy's high-handed actions. "Make me a list of neighbors. Anyone you can think of who had a grudge against Gavin, and why,"

Catherine whispered while walking her friend to the door.

Susan's tight hug warmed her. "That will be a long list," she murmured.

All of Catherine's attempts to bring a social patina to the meeting failed. Billy met simple questions with nods, or worse, grunts. Finally, the oven timer dinged and Catherine pulled the pan of hot brownies from the oven. Unable to stand the tension any longer, she cut into the too hot treat and set steaming chunks of brownie on plates to cool.

As if released from some sort of purgatory of silence, Billy mashed his brownie flat with a fork, turned it over a few times, and said, "I've got a lot of questions for you." He punctuated his words with the cracking of his knuckles.

Catherine cringed inwardly at the sound, glad she could cut it short by handing over her statement. "Anticipated, Billy." She handed him the pad he'd already looked at. Popping some now cool brownie crumbs into her mouth, she said, "There's something else though, I can't remember. Something I saw, I think."

Pushing the statement away with the tip of his index finger, Billy glanced away from her and cleared his throat. "We need to talk about your threats last night. And we need to know where Ashley Jackman is."

"Threats? You mean my call? OK, I get that, the call. But why ask me about Ashley?"

"You were there, in the house, and in the garage. You made threats. You know protocol, what we look for. And all the players in this game. You have knowledge that makes you dangerous to an investigation. If you decided to murder...."

"If I decided to...you think I'm..." she interrupted herself to gain control before she said anything more. Taking a deep breath, she continued calmly, "This was a suicide." She crossed her arms tightly over her chest to keep from fidgeting. The truth was she didn't remember what she said in her voice mail. Damn it, she was drunk. A cold feeling lodged in her stomach. Her head hurt from the effort of trying to remember the message. Did she make a threat? Damn. She was pissed, pissed off and piss faced, that much she remembered. But a threat? Think Catherine. Think like a cop. Let him fill the silence.

"You told Jackman if he didn't call you back last night, you'd be over in the morning. He owed you money."

"Dead people don't pay, do they?"

"How much money are we talking about?"

"Billy!" Her mouth was so dry she had to force the word out. She tried to swallow, but she had nothing to work with. She stumbled walking to the sink for a glass of water. Lifting it to her lips, she gulped it down.

"Catherine?"

She sighed, "I drank too much last night." She waved her hand in front of her face dismissively, but she couldn't force herself to face him. "No, I haven't taken up boozing again. I wish no one in this town knew my history. I guess..." She bit her lip. "Oh hell, no excuses. Gavin and Ashley owed me for the last three times I dog sat, about $150. I meant to say, I'd come over in the morning to get the money. Believe me, Billy, $150 is not enough to murder someone for."

"How much is?"

The glass slipped from her hand and shattered in the sink. Catherine's mind replayed her old interrogations. She knew her reactions played as guilty. She felt guilty. Not of murder, but of helping to make Gavin's last day unpleasant. The pounding of her heart was so loud in her ears that she almost couldn't hear her own thoughts. She turned and forced herself to stare directly into Billy's chocolate eyes, willing him to believe her. "I know this game too," she said, drawing out each word carefully. "Let me repeat. He hung himself and his neck looked broken. But even if he didn't, why am I the perpetrator du jour?" Her words picked up speed as she warmed to her subject. "The meeting last night got pretty heated. Then there's the paper this morning. That brings up another set of circumstances and motives. Could Ashley have murdered him?"

"Did you see any sign of a struggle and clean it up so we wouldn't find it?"

"Don't be stupid," she snapped. "Of course not."

Billy rose to go, taking her legal pad with him. "How would we know? You were the first one in the house, and on the scene." He lifted a stony face toward her. There was no mistaking the look. It was pure cop. "Don't leave town."

CHAPTER 5

Billy couldn't detain her unless he arrested her. His grandstanding irked Catherine. Did he think he was dealing with an idiot?

"Damn!" She kicked door shut behind him hard enough to rattle the glass in her front window. "What more do they want from me?" She shouted to the wood. Leaning her forehead against the door fear seeped through her. She expected thanks for preserving the scene and evicting the dog. She never expected suspicion.

She ticked off the events preceding finding Gavin's dead body. "Yep," she muttered as she pushed away from the door. "First I leave a message, and then I find the body. If it weren't for lousy luck, I'd have no luck at all."

She returned to the kitchen, and covered the remains of the brownies. Billy was fishing.

Feeling at loose ends, she snatched the phone from the counter and sprawled into the kitchen chair. Bullet's nails struck a familiar tattoo on the floor. He came to his mistress and laid his head in her lap. Absently, she leaned down and scratched him between the ears. Tapping the phone, she held against her lips, she decided she didn't want to talk to Mike. Whom else could she call?

There was no one. No one to call at all. A ball of pain built in her stomach and tears burned her eyes. The intensity of her isolation shocked her. The next times do run out. They just did. Rebuilding her life from the ashes of bridges burned during her drinking days was a hard, slow process. Too many excuses, too many accusations, too many people hurt trying to help. The walls were closing in and she couldn't breathe. She jumped up from the chair, slammed the phone back into its cradle, and grabbed her sneakers and two leashes. Whistling for the dogs, she set out for a run with Bullet and Roscoe.

"Ok, boys, let's work up a sweat! You guys should be able to run rings around me. Roscoe, stay in a straight line. No fair getting tangled with Bullet." Hearing his name, he looked back at his mistress, opened his mouth and smiled a Shepherd smile. "Mom needs a run, so be good."

As her sneakers ate up the miles, Catherine let her mind range over the realm of possibilities of who might have killed Gavin.

What made Billy so sure of murder? Was he yanking her chain for fouling the scene? Was it Gavin's role as commissioner? Given the havoc created by the economy, maybe someone believed his house languished on the market, or couldn't get what he thought it was worth because Gavin denied his requests. Losers always thought Gavin's decisions were arbitrary and vindictive. Winners always thought he was fair and even-handed. Did someone on that list decide to take revenge?

A lover?

Was he a pedophile? Did the newspaper get that part right?

Did the victim, her father, brother, current lover or spouse decide to wrest justice from the hands of an incompetent court system? Or was the story a shot across the bow by a jilted lover? A threat of more exposure to come? What else did Gavin Jackman have to hide?

Did the story even figure in his death? Who had enough pull to have it published? Why now? The story was old news.

Murder was always possible. Money, sex, and rage were the usual common denominators.

Had money problems, coupled with the story, driven him to kill himself? Cathy rolled that thought around in her mind. He struck her as too arrogant to kill himself. If it wasn't suicide, it had to be murder, but how do you get a man to his own hanging with no struggle? This wasn't some Clint Eastwood movie. This was real life.

Only one person fit the perfect storm of knowledge, access to the paper and motive. That was Ashley Jackman. And nobody could find her.

Stretching her legs against a park bench, she closed her eyes and saw a hanging man. A kid, the victim of a gang, killed as punishment for failing his initiation. That boy fought. The skin of his neck raw where he'd clawed it off trying to make room to breathe under the rope. Gavin's corpse showed none of that. Catherine stopped in mid-stretch as the thought hit her. It looked like someone hung a dead man. That made no sense. Or did he drug himself? Swallow enough what? Ativan? Valium? Sleeping pills? Did he even have any of those drugs? Were they strong enough to overcome the desire to breathe? She leaned into the stretch and admitted she had no idea.

Was Ashley a victim too? Dead? Kidnapped? Murdered?

Shaking her head, she pushed off again, her feet hitting the ground in a lulling cadence. Somewhere on the route, Roscoe took the lead and ran her back to the Jackman home. Jogging in place Catherine wiped the sweat from her face. The yellow house looked benign.

She wanted nothing more than to get back inside. To protect and serve was no longer her job description, but the instinct was so deeply ingrained she was powerless against it. The sun glinted off the glass waterfall that comprised the sunroom.

Realization came with the glare. Solve the crime; get an invitation back into the only family that matters. The brotherhood of blue.

The intensity of the yearning surprised Catherine. It didn't matter if she became a maverick. The only thing that mattered in the world of cops was the clearance rate. Success. Arrests. Convictions. As a civilian, she could play by different rules. Avenues closed in a standard investigation were available to her. She promised herself she'd make up for it later, once she was safely back in uniform.

"You're well dogged for a runner." Vicki's voice broke into her thoughts, calling from the yard across the street. "Come on over. The three of you look like you could use some water."

Shooting a smile at her friend, Catherine said, "I didn't expect to be here at all today. Now I'm here twice." Catherine followed her friend into the living room and paused at the front window. It looked directly at the Jackman house. "Vic, did you see anything? Cars parked in front? Ashley?" The two women and pair of dogs made their way back into the Florida room after a brief stop at the kitchen. "Why are you home?"

"I didn't want to try and get my car out on the street today, not through the crowd." Vicki blushed, "And I'm curious too. I've never been this close to a crime scene. Now I'm right across the street."

Tipping the glass to her lips, Catherine took a long sip. "I found Gavin." Over the rim of her glass, she saw her friend's eyes widen in shock.

"And?"

"That's it. Vick, I wish I knew more. I want to take another look." She leaned over and dealt with a shoelace to gain a minute to think. Hadn't Nancy told her Vicki already knew she was at the scene?

"Bad idea, Catherine. Really bad idea."

Cathy leaned back from the bench and studied the riot of flowering plants. Stucco bit against her bare shoulders and through her running singlet. Vicki's Florida room has begun its life as an outdoor porch. When Vicki moved in, her first design decision was to enclose the space with glass sliders and expand her square footage. She'd left the rough stucco walls, terrazzo covered slab, and she used the area to highlight her green thumb. "Something in that garage has a story to tell, I want to listen."

"So do the neighbors. I heard Oliver riding Luis about last night. A bunch more had nasty things to say about Gavin. This ain't your business."

"You have no idea, Vick."

***

Years of police work taught Catherine to walk the walk. Years of real estate sales after she left the force made her comfortable trying the doors on peoples' homes. If someone challenged her, she'd say she wanted to see Ashley, wanted to offer her condolences. Weak, but the best she had. A residue of fingerprint ink decorated the doorknob. "Damn," she muttered, "they've got me on all the doors. Well, I told them I went in the house."

Not finding the crime scene tape she expected, she considered her options. If she opened the door, it would be obvious to any tech that it happened after the dusting. Using her tee shirt for a glove would rub the ink off and be just as obvious. Deciding barehanded spoke of innocence, she grasped the door handle and tried to turn it. Locked. Looking down at her hand, she rubbed it along the side of her shorts and moved quickly to the rear garage door. Smudged fingerprint dust decorated the knob and there was a quarter inch space between the frame and the door.

Alarm bells sounded in her head. Feeling almost dizzy she slipped a sneakered toe into the tiny opening and nudged the door open wider. Silence greeted her. Moving forward on quiet feet, she entered the garage. A woman stood in the shadows. At first, Catherine thought it was Ashley. Before she could call out, the woman turned slightly exposing her profile to Catherine, extended a finger and, traced a line down from the corner Gavin's workbench halfway down the bench leg, squatting as she went. The dappled light entering through the decorative cutout window was sufficient for Catherine to recognize Gavin's next-door neighbor.

"Hello, Terry, did you lose something?" Catherine purred.

Terry's Payson's face twisted into a grimace. With strength that surprised Catherine, Terry shoved her hard to the ground and ran.

CHAPTER 6

Catherine crawled to the workbench and retrieved her cell phone from beneath the same corner Terry had examined so closely. Pulling herself up to a squatting position and rocking back on her heels, she studied the corner of the bench and ran her gaze down the leg following the line Terry's finger traced. Other than the dings and scrapes she expected to see, nothing stood out. A deep dent blunted the corner, but it was impossible to guess the age of mark. "Vick, did you hear that?" Catherine hissed into the speaker while she inspected the workbench, hoping for a witness to the strange meeting. Dead air sounded in her ear. Looking at the display, she saw the words 'no signal.' The phone had disconnected, either in its flight through the air or from the scourge of Summer Hill. Lousy cell service was rampant in the heavily treed community.

Still squatting, she slipped the phone back in her pocket, took out her notebook, picked up a pen from the floor and straightened. A sensation Catherine recognized as excitement coiled in the pit of her stomach. Taking a deep breath to steady herself, she let her pen fly across the page of the notebook she held in her hand, writing notes of the encounter while they were still fresh.

The image of Terry from last night – her face twisted with hate – floated back into Catherine's memory. Was the hate strong enough to commit murder? Was Terry strong enough to incapacitate Gavin? Kill him? The tender spot on Catherine's chest attested to the woman's strength.

She looked over the scene with new eyes, taking in every item on the workbench. What did Terry want? Then, narrowing her eyes, she pictured it the way she'd seen it that morning. Nothing seemed different. Was Terry just a looky-lou? Catherine's nose itched. Wishing for a flashlight, she examined the bench corner again, still seeing nothing out of the ordinary. Her gaze lifted to the rafter where Gavin's body had hung. She winced at the fresh chafe mark the rope left behind. Then she moved closer for a better look. The mark was in a single line, the wood didn't have a chewed appearance. No sign of a struggle. Her gaze went to the cleat on the wall that had held the other end of the rope. Everything was in a nice straight line. How does someone commit suicide by hanging and not struggle? His neck didn't look broken. He wasn't that lucky. Would Mike tell her if the Jackmans had drugs in the house?

Hair prickled on her neck. The sound of a soft footfall behind her brought her to her feet. She turned, muscles tense, ready to flee. Through the haze of adrenaline, it took her a moment to recognize Vicki creeping from the workroom into the garage area.

"I stayed on the phone until I got the disconnect recording. Let's get out of here." Vicki's gaze roamed around the garage finally focusing on the rafters overhead. "It creeps me out."

"Did you see Terry run out of here?"

"Terry! No way! Terry was here? No wonder you hung up." Grabbing her friend's arm, she pulled her out of the garage. "I'm not gonna be here when the cops arrive. Neither are you. They can talk to you at my house." Vicki's fingers bit deeply into Catherine's arm.

In the middle of the street, she paused and stared into Catherine's eyes. "You didn't call the cops, did you? What are you trying to prove? Anyone could have been in that garage. They could have killed you. Me, too, for that matter, going to look for you. Damn it Catherine" Vicki stalked off toward her front door. "Do what you want with your life, but don't put me in danger!" She threw over her shoulder.

The heat staining Catherine's cheeks had nothing to do with the Florida summer. "How can I call the police? Vick?" Catherine asked as she stepped into the cool house and the two friends headed to the kitchen.

"Easy, Cathy, dial 911, just like I'm going to do."

"No. I told you, I needed to find something there. Something I saw. Something I missed."

"Did you find it?"

Catherine shook her head. The whole exercise was pointless. Playing what she hoped was a trump card, Cathy said, "Vicki, you're forgetting, Terry's gotta worry about what I'm going to do about finding her there."

"So then do something. Call the cops."

Catherine let her gaze slide from the Jackmans' garage to the Payson house. Why was Terry there? Curiosity? Protecting herself or Chris? The feud between the two neighbors was well known.

"You're bleeding. You cut your elbow. Catherine what's so interesting about a simple, sad, suicide?

Whistling for the two dogs, Catherine clicked the leads on the collars and looked up at her friend. "The autopsy will tell the story."

She twisted her arm around and looked at her elbow. "Only a scrape. The Paysons hated Gavin; for thwarting most of their renovation requests." Catherine's gaze slewed in Vicki's direction hoping to see a reaction.

"Gleefully denying them from what I heard." Vicki broke in. "That's a motive for murder, Cath. And this isn't a murder. It's a suicide."

Catherine chewed her lip to keep silent. Billy's visit made her question that fact. The Paysons had motive, but was it enough and did they have the nerve? Chris struck her as still waters running deep. What brought Terry to the garage? Protecting her husband?

"Tell the cops, Cathy. At least tell Mike. It's not your job. You're the one taking all this personally."

Catherine threw back her head and laughed, but the accusation hit home. It was the second time someone told her she was personalizing the situation today. Three if she counted her self-accusation. "Oh Vicki, what is my job? I sure don't know any more." Leaning against the doorframe, she looked straight into her friend's eyes. "Face it; I've got nothing going on now. Once this is over, maybe I'll have some answers."

"Yeah, or maybe you'll be in jail for impersonating an officer or impeding an investigation! Call Mike!"

Sucking in a deep breath, Catherine said, "Why isn't someone looking for Ashley? That article this morning was tough stuff for a marriage to take. So, suicide works there, but so does Ashley killing Gavin."

"Catherine," Vicki said. "Ashley is what, a size 2, and this isn't murder."

"Hear me out." Catherine dropped the leashes, walked to the sink and ran water on a paper towel before applying it to her scraped elbow. Grimacing at the sting she continued, "Ashley could have gotten him in the garage. She's a black belt. We took karate lessons together. She's got the skills."

"You're living in some kind of fantasy. I am not covering for you Cathy. What you did, going over there, not calling the cops, that's obstruction."

"Ok." She said waving her hand, "I'll call Mike and talk to him. I hate the girl calls boy scenario; this real life, not some kind of cozy mystery novel." Her heart dropped as she watched her friend open the front door, turn, and walk away. "Did you hear me? Why are you walking away?"

Vicky stopped at the end of the hall and stretched an arm around the doorframe into her kitchen. Coming back with a cordless telephone, she walked down the hallway and handed it to Catherine. "Call him now. Be responsible."

Under Vicky's relentless gaze, Catherine dialed Mike's cell number and left a message to have him come over for dinner. Pressing the off button, she handed the phone back to her friend.

"Cathy, you need to play by the book. I don't want to be in the middle of this. When, or if, someone comes to speak with me. I'm going to tell them you went in."

* * *

Mike carried a small tray with some cheese, crackers and two wine glasses into the living room. "Here you go, girl." He said, handing one of the glasses to Catherine who sat on the floor, knees to her chest, her back propped against the couch. Wanting to avoid Bullet and Roscoe's inspection, he put the tray on the mantle.

She tried to see the 6'4" man as if it were the first time. His round face was handsome, in an odd pudgy way, and unmistakably etched with kindness. God, I'm lucky to have him in my life. Why do I always feel like I have to compete with him? She drank deeply then spat the liquid back into the glass. "Grape juice!"

Nudging her with his toe, Mike laughed and said "Yah, heard about last night too, that's the closest you'll get to wine from me."

"Great." She butt scooted over to the fireplace, hoisted herself erect, grabbed the cheese tray off the mantle and put it on the coffee table. "What's this?" She poked a cheese slice with the tip of her pinkie finger, and leaned back against the couch. "Plastic cheese to go with the fake wine?"

"Seriously, Kit Kat." Mike settled his bulk on the couch next to her seat on the floor. "It's stuff like that that puts you on the suspect list. Darlin'. You had too much to drink. You made a phone call. You wanted money. You made a threat. The guy turns up dead. He ticked off the events on his splayed fingers. What are you trying to do to yourself?"

The index finger he gently placed on her lips silenced her interruption, "Let me finish. Then you won't have to hear my penny lecture again. You keep telling me you're toying with the idea of going back on a police force, or back into real estate, or starting some other business." He picked up his glass, stood, and paced the floor in front of her. "You've been on reserves with the Marine Patrol since you quit North Pinehurst. You put in enough time to keep your certification current, do your range time and keep your shooting creds. Then you do something like this and blow your credibility"

"Mike, you don't…"

He squatted down in front of her and cut off her words with a kiss. "Let me finish." His Adam's apple worked.

"OK," she said in a small voice, "but I know where this is going."

"Doubtful, short stuff."

The flat of his fingers caressed her cheek as he stood. The tip of his tongue moistened his lips, and his head bobbed in a tight nod. Catherine's heart clenched. Mike's actions had all the hallmarks of a good-bye. He turned and walked away taking her breath with him. Her question to Nancy echoed in her thoughts. When do the next times run out? Tension coursed up the back of her neck. She didn't want the next times to run out with Mike. Not yet.

Finally, he positioned himself in front of the fireplace with a dog on either side and continued. "If you're looking for some kind of an epiphany, a great ah ha moment, then you're fooling yourself. You're interfering with an investigation. This isn't some golden opportunity that dropped into your lap to help you make up your mind. Cathy, you need to..."

The barking of the dogs drowned out the rest of his words. "Stay," he said, "I'll get the door."

"It's Nancy, she called earlier. Thank God. Anything to stop you from confusing yourself with my daddy. You're wasting your breath. Gavin died a suicide, so I can't be a suspect in anything. Right?" Catherine laughed at the look on Mike's face. "Billy was just being a pain in the ass."

While Mike's back was turned, she lifted his wine glass and took a sip. It tasted good, but not wonderful.

"Nance, pull up some floor and make yourself to home," Catherine said.

"Should I accept food and wine from a bona fide suspect? Is that why Dudley Do Right is here?" Nancy joked. "After all, you could be a serial killer."

"Not funny, Nancy." Catherine replied, wondering if Nancy would ever learn to like Mike. She leaned forward as Mike sat on the couch behind her and rubbed her back.

"Where did you get your information, Nancy?" Mike drawled the question in a way that made Catherine's pulse race.

"Mike," Catherine said twisting her body on the floor so she could look behind her to the couch, "Is this officially a murder investigation? Why the hell didn't you tell me?"

Looking slowly from Nancy to Catherine, Mike took a deep breath. For a brief moment, Catherine thought he was going to refuse to answer her. As soon as he spoke, she heard hesitation.

"All suicides are homicides. Somebody," he glanced at Nancy, "is making something of nothing." He gently moved Catherine forward, swung his legs behind her, and stood. The sound of dog nails clicked loudly as both Bullet and Roscoe inched closer to the coffee table. Mike picked up his empty glass and walked toward the kitchen.

"That's bullshit, Mike," Nancy said to his back.

"He had nothing to fall from. No chair, nothing," Mike replied turning back to the living room.

"Damn! That's it. That's what's missing. His feet. I kept looking at his feet. There was nothing near his feet." Catherine jumped up and paced around the room. The clacking sound of two dogs accompanied her. "Mike, it's not easy to hang someone…"

"There's no external evidence of a struggle. Not in the house or the garage that we saw unless, someone cleaned it up. But he's dead, Cathy. And you threatened…"

"To come over in the morning! Not to kill him! Catherine swung her right hand out in a sweeping motion. "Grasping at straws don't you think?"

Mike shrugged.

"Look, Kit Kat." He covered the distance between them in two steps. "Nobody will know anything until the ME finishes." He rolled his eyes in Nancy's direction. Catherine wasn't sure if he was trying to warn her to be quiet or accusing Nancy of having an agenda, but she was glad Nancy couldn't see the gesture.

"He might have jumped from his workbench." Catherine spread her hands wide. "There were pencils and stuff knocked over. The knot was good, not a noose but certainly large enough to be effective. Suicide makes a hell of a lot more sense than murder." Both dogs, picking up on her agitation, started barking. Walking to the curtains, Catherine pulled them aside and looked out. Turning back to face the room, she said, "Ashley?" A series of emotions played across Mike's face.

"We're looking for her." There's nothing to indicate abduction. We're checking the airlines. One of their cars is gone. We have an APB out."

"An all-points bulletin," Nancy gasped. "You think she killed her husband and drove a ten year old clunker on the lam even though she had a perfectly good Tahoe sitting in the driveway? Did anyone check with Oliver Kent? They both work at the paper. He's no fan of Gavin's, but I know Ashley and Oliver carpool sometimes."

Sensing a growing tension between Mike and Nancy and wanting to head off an argument, Catherine said, "Nance, did you know the kid? The file clerk in the newspaper story that Gavin slept with?"

"I never said Ashley's wanted for his murder, just questioning. Don't put words in my mouth, Nancy." Mike snapped.

Staring straight at Mike, Nancy responded, "Yes, sure, I knew her. We all did. Everyone in the firm. She was on a high school work/study program. She did my filing too."

Mike dropped into the oversized club chair across the coffee table from Nancy. He looked like a coiled spring. His chin rested in his hands, and his knees were splayed apart each supporting an elbow. The pulsing of a muscle in his jaw indicated the tight control he had over his emotions. "So he knew she was underage?"

"These kids are in high school but that doesn't mean they're under eighteen. She was a senior. It was nearing graduation."

Catherine looked at Nancy's face and saw something she couldn't identify. Almost secretiveness. Nothing registered on her mental bullshit meter. She looked up at Mike and tried to read his face. Despite their relationship, she couldn't tell if he believed Nancy.

"I, look, I mean, damn." Nancy put her glass down on the coffee table and said. "Mike, I know how you feel about Catherine, at least I think I do," she amended, "but there are some things I can't discuss."

"It's been in the papers." He reminded her.

"Yes, well, beyond that. Cathy, I'm sorry."

Catherine's protective antenna went up. Nancy was her best friend, their friendship a rock to both. If Catherine needed information from Nancy, she'd find a way to get it to her, and not compromise her ethics or her job. Mike was a newcomer to this party. He was out of line.

"Mike." Catherine interrupted "It sounds like you're threatening Nancy…"

The dogs barked. Bullet raced to the front door. Roscoe grabbing a hunk of cheese on his way.

Catherine glanced from Mike to Nancy as she strode to the door. The tension between them seemed palpable.

"You expecting anyone else?" Mike asked.

Shaking her head, Catherine looked out the front window "No cars." Catherine's jaw dropped to her chest. "My God."

CHAPTER 7

Ashley Jackman, her eyes red and her face swollen, stood in the open doorway.

Catherine gathered her into a hug. "I'm so sorry, Ashley," she murmured. The older woman seemed to melt into her arms. Catherine felt her shiver despite the sticky summer night.

"I'm sorry, Catherine, I wanted to... Oh, I'm sorry, I wouldn't have come if...I didn't knock...the dogs must have...Damn!" Ashley's shoulders wracked with sobs and tears flowed freely down her cheeks. "I'm sorry." She raked a tissue over her eyes. "I thought...oh, God."

Feelings of inadequacy washed over Catherine. Fumbling for words that expressed her feelings, but didn't sound trite, she finally settled on letting the dog take the lead. "I'm sure you know this kissy-face fellow." Roscoe jumped on his mistress, and washed her face with his tongue. "Come on in." She held the door open and stood aside.

Out of the corner of her eye, Catherine saw Mike turn away from Nancy and give his full attention to Ashley. His body morphed into a cop's watching stance and without saying a word, he became the focus of everyone's attention.

I miss the ability to command a room by virtue of my badge. Is this whole thing a power quest?

"Mrs. Jackman." Mike said. "I'm very sorry about your husband's death. We've been very worried about you too. Have you spoken with anyone at the station yet? Where have you been? When did you get back?"

Ashley pushed a wedge of her chocolate colored hair behind her ear, and lifted her swollen face to the officer. "Chicago," she mumbled. "I was in Chicago. I left this morning, business." She visibly struggled with control.

"When did you hear about your husband?" Mike's voice was soft and gentle. He looked at Catherine and gestured drinking a cup.

"My office." Her voice cracked. "They called, thank God, before I saw it on television."

"Television?"

Tears flowed again. Her voice brittle, she recited, 'Prominent Florida attorney commits suicide amidst accusations of underage sex scandal.'" She gulped, and then scowled at Mike. "They played that over and over and over while I waited in the frequent flyer lounge." Her voice caught. "I wanted to break the damn screen." She dropped her face into her hands and moaned.

Catherine shot a quick look at Mike willing him to understand her plea to stop further questioning. Instead, he reached into his back pocket for his ever-present notebook.

"Roscoe was gone. I figured you'd take him for us, Catherine. Oh, God, us. Listen to me, us." Ashley's voice caught in her throat and cracked. Taking a deep breath, she continued, "I came over to get him." Ashley scratched the dog between the ears as she spoke.

Catherine realized Ashley was so lost in grief it hadn't occurred to her yet to inquire into the details of her husband's death. Unless she already knew them. Catherine gave a quick shake of her head. No, this woman was not acting guilty.

"Mrs. Jackman," Mike said, "I'd appreciate it if we could speak privately. May I drive you home?"

Ignoring Mike's question, Ashley looked up and smiled a watery smile. She glanced at Catherine and Nancy and said, "I knew."

Swallowing hard Catherine asked. "Knew what?"

"About the affairs."

Catherine felt her heart drop to her stomach. "How long?"

Ashley leaned down, buried her face in Roscoe's neck and didn't answer at first. "I'd like the ride home, Mike, but I'd rather not talk to you now. Nancy, please give my regards to Phil. Can you ask him if...oh, no, sorry...I'm...oh...please, just give him my regards."

Nancy came over to face Ashley, and took both her hands in hers. "I know Judge Brandon would want me to express his sympathy. He and

Gavin were friends as well as partners. You know you have mine as well. Please, Ashley, if there is anything I can do…"

She smiled. "Yes, thank you. Talk to Phil for me, please I'd like him to give the eulogy, and I'd like to talk to him, but I don't want to impose. He's a Judge. I haven't seen him in a couple of…well, weeks now that I think about it." She rocked back on her heels, her fingers still gripping Roscoe's scruff. "He and Gavin spent time in the garage. Both of them came out covered in clay." She smiled. "Gavin loved throwing pottery. Did you know Phil taught him?"

"Ashley," Nancy said, "he'll call you. If I know Phil, he's already called you." She tossed a suspicious look in Mike's direction. "Why don't I take you home?"

Mike stepped over to the two women, putting his hand on Ashley's arm, he said, "I'll take care of that."

Ashley looked at Mike and then back to Catherine. She shrugged slightly as if to say, it has to come sometime.

"It's all right, Mrs. Jackman." Mike said softly. "I want to make sure you get home safely, and that no one is waiting for you."

Jerking her head back, Ashley said, "waiting for me. Who would be waiting for me?"

"Neighbors, the press, anyone. I'd rather see you settled at your home. I can arrange to have a policewoman stay with you. We can also step up patrols in front of your house."

Ashley pulled her arm away from Mike. "What are you talking about? A policewoman? I want very much to be alone, I want to talk to my lawyer, I want to be sure everything is in order and most of all." Her hands curled into tight fists. "I want my husband back."

"I'm sorry, Mrs. Jackman. Things got rough at the commission meeting yesterday. I don't want you bothered by anyone."

Sniffing Ashley said, "Yes, please take me home, but no, I don't want anyone to stay with me. And I certainly don't want anyone driving past my house at all hours."

Catherine watched the tall man and the short woman walk down her path to his car. He'd parked on the swale in front of the house not on the driveway. She felt more than saw Nancy approach her to stand at her side.

"Nancy," Catherine said, "what do you know about the Affidavit? The one in the paper?" Turning the deadbolt to lock the door she came back into the room and picked up her wineglass. "Your boss authored it didn't he?" Mike's revelations crystalized her misgivings about the scene. Catherine saw tiny holes appearing in the fabric of the suicide theory. She needed to find out more before she could figure out if the material was lace or rotted cotton. "Bullet, quiet." She called to the dog as he barked loudly and raced in circles. Suicide or murder? No matter how she looked at it, someone was trying to hold her responsible. How could she defend herself? All she was guilty of was a lapse in judgment and bad timing. She needed more information, and she needed it before anyone else got it in order to protect herself.

Leading the way to Catherine's Florida room, the pair of women walked through the brightly lit kitchen. Nancy stopped briefly at the doggie cookie jar, and fished out a cookie for the barking dog. She held it in the air, the dog sat and waited for the cookie to come to mouth level.

"You're stalling." Catherine said. "Phil sleep with her too?"

"No. I'm thinking," Nancy snapped. "Sorry." She ran her fingers through her cropped hair, letting it fall back over her forehead. "It was a long time ago. I don't remember much. Come to think of it, never really knew all that much. The partners can be a close-knit group. I remember Maggie's brother though. He was not someone you'd want to meet in a dark alley."

"Maggie?"

"The file clerk. Her brother Tomas called not too long ago. Just out of jail. He wanted to speak to the Judge." Nancy waved her hand at her friend. "I have no idea about what, or if Phil called him back. It was strange though. Up until then, I hadn't thought about Maggie for a long time. Now, it's in the paper."

"Ashley said affairs?" What do you know about that Nancy? Were they at the office?"

Glancing at her watch Nancy said, "I'd better go."

CHAPTER 8

Catherine stayed in the Florida room after Nancy left. Paddy Whack, her cat, sought refuge on the lounge chair next to her. Catherine picked the cat up, stroked her fur and considered what she knew. Mike's demeanor, the stand back/standoff quality emanating from him told her he didn't believe Gavin committed suicide. Ashley's admission of more than one affair created more questions. But hanging wasn't a woman's crime, it wasn't hardly anybody's crime. And this kind of hanging, one with no evidence of a struggle. It would take a lot of strength to pull that off.

Catherine tipped her head back to stare at the ceiling and project the vision she had etched in her brain. The soft Florida breeze played with the tendrils of her hair. Rough stucco, a relic of the days when the Florida room was a porch, caught at the loose strands. How do you hang someone and not leave evidence? No one goes willingly to their own hanging. Could it have been a sex thrill? Catherine curled her lip at the thought. She couldn't imagine it, at least not in the garage, and he'd been fully clothed. Maggie's brother was someone worthwhile considering, but then, so were half the people in town who hated Gavin. Still, hating someone and killing them were two different things. Who gains? Why, and what?

Then again, why not suicide? Gavin's finances may not have been so solid. And Ashley admitted leaving him the morning of his death. She said for business, was it? No doubt, the news story embarrassed both of them.

Catherine stood, stretched her arms over her head, decided to take Bullet out for a last walk before turning in. One thing she knew. No one could make a case stick against her.

Bullet came up alongside and nosed the cat, who responded with a swat. Cathy glanced at the clock. It was nearly two in the morning. "Ok, killer," she said to the dog, "no leash required tonight. Let's take a quick jog around the block."

Suiting word to action, Catherine laced on her running shoes, grabbed her key and strode out the door. Bullet raced on ahead setting the pace, then turned and ran back to the front of the house, his nose to the ground. Catherine jogged past the returning dog, softly calling to him as she did. In the darkness, she could barely make him out alongside her car. Running back she saw what he was sniffing. Her car sat on its rims. All four tires were flat.

Catherine stared at the tires. It smacked of a hate crime, personal and expensive. But who hated her that much? Terry? Catherine couldn't picture the woman flattening tires. Too dirty for her. Chris then? Why? Some kind of a warning? Go after my wife and there's more where this came from? Damn. She ran a finger along the bottom of the tire, the steel cords gaping from the slashed ends, and she shivered despite the heat. No matter what, someone was close to her house armed with a knife.

She stiffened, remembering Bullet's frantic barking earlier in the evening.

"Bullet, was this what you were trying to tell me?" she knelt down beside the dog and buried her face in his neck.

"Fool's paradise," she muttered. She remembered glancing out the window but with the interior lights on, she'd been unable to see anything. Catherine scoured her mind. Had she heard anything? She shook her head and got up from her crouch on the pavement. No, she decided, nothing.

Shivering again, she grabbed Bullet's scruff, and led the dog to the gate alongside her house. Her hand stopped in mid-way to the pull latch, wondering if someone lay in wait. Trusting in instinct, and Bullet's frantically wagging tail, she pulled the toggle and freed the gate lock. Still uncertain, she stood in the moonlight, peering into the dark recesses of the yard. Bullet began to run in circles. Catherine shut the gate and returned to the house. At the sound of Bullet's scratching, she unlatched the doggie door to let him back in after he was done. Peace of mind was worth having to scoop the poop.

Walking to the sliding glass doors of the Florida room, she leaned her head against the cool of the glass and felt the energy drain from her body.

A glance back at the clock indicated only fifteen minutes had passed since she'd left the house. It seemed like hours.

Once in bed she found it impossible to fall asleep. Every time she closed her eyes, visions of Gavin's body floated into view. Tossing and turning, she felt as if the bed was rejecting her. She got up twice to be sure she'd locked the doggie door after Bullet's return. Finally, she gave up on sleep and made herself some coffee.

While the coffee brewed, she went into her bedroom. Standing on tiptoe, she stretched her right arm back to the far corner of the top shelf. Her hand closed around the cold steel handle of the semi-automatic weapon and drew it forward. Groping further back on the shelf, she found ammunition and her cleaning kit. She took the gun to her office and sat down at her desk. She thumbed the button to release the magazine, pulled back the slide, checked that there were no rounds in the chamber and broke the weapon apart. Carefully inspecting the Glock, she cleaned and re-loaded it. Hefting it, the weight felt both familiar and alien. She took the weapon into the bedroom, and slipped it in the nightstand drawer.

Dawn tipped the eastern sky turning billowy clouds a soft orange pink color as she picked up the bedside phone and dialed Mike. "Hey there, sorry to wake you, but if I'm up, you're up." She tried to sound light. "Did you notice anything funny about my car last night? Like the fact the tires were flat and it sat on rims in the driveway?"

She pulled the phone away from her ear at his roar. Hurriedly she said, "Mike, calm down. No. No, Mike." Catherine swallowed hard. No way she wanted to have this conversation right now. The earpiece of the receiver felt slick with sweat. Unable to stay silent she drew a deep breath, "Mike, stop. Damn. If I were worried, I'd have called last night. This has to be a prank." She raked her hand through her hair. "Yeah. I'll be here, but give me a while I have dogs to walk." The corners of her mouth rose in a slight smile. "I know killer, me too," she whispered. For a brief moment, his parting words of affection warmed her. It wasn't until the receiver missed the charger cradle that she realized her hand was shaking. Mike's suggestion that the flat tires were no prank sank in with a vengeance. She'd known someone with a very sharp knife had been very close to her house, hearing it from Mike made it too real for comfort.

She was still gripping the handset as the phone rang again. Yanking it out of the cradle, she squared her shoulders, grateful that he was worried enough to call her right back, and said, "Hey, sailor, did you forget something?" It took her a minute to register who owned the voice on the other end of the line.

"Catherine, can I talk to you." Ashley said.

She glanced quickly at the clock. The lighted numbers read five forty-five.

"I don't know what's happening. My husband's" her voice broke, "dead. I feel like a suspect. You were a cop, you speak their language. Am I going nuts?"

"Ashley, you know that, well, Ashley…,"
Catherine hesitated unsure where to go with her
next statement. "Did you know I found Gavin?
That's how I got Roscoe." The silence on the end of
the line changed and deepened. For a moment,
Catherine thought Ashley might hang up. "I don't
want you to turn to me and then be blindsided."

"Why were you here?"

"The call," Catherine said simply. She heard
a sound it took her a minute to identify, a match
striking against a matchbook and the sound of
Ashley inhaling deeply and then exhaling.

"Can you believe it? I haven't smoked in
twenty years. I bought a pack at the airport. Damn
thing was $10.00."

Catherine waited for an answer to her
question.

"Yes," she said finally. "Mike told me you
found Gavin, maybe you can help me understand. I
feel so lost." Ashley's voice broke on the last word.

"Around ten, is that all right for you?

The clock chimed six. Damn, Mike was
coming over. Bullet needed his walk and she had
two other clients. Scrambling into a tank top and
shorts, she grabbed Bullet's leash. Both clients lived
close enough to walk with Bullet. Catherine looked
at the clock again. By walking all three dogs
together, she might be back before Mike arrived.
Catherine slid her feet into sandals and whistled for
her dog.

***

Midway through the walk Catherine heard
the urr urgah of an air horn. A backhoe approached

from behind her. Gathering the dogs closer she stepped onto the Kents' lawn. The backhoe operator sounded the horn again. Confused, Catherine looked around. Meg approached from inside the house, an annoyed look on her face.

"Get out of the way, he's coming in here." Meg made waving motions with her arm. Oliver appeared behind her and looked over the hedge at Catherine.

"Meg hates disruption. The backhoe operator is for us, he needs to get through the hedge opening we cut right where you're standing."

"Oh, sorry…I didn't realize...don't you hate septic systems?"

Catherine returned the dogs to their homes, staying long enough to feed and water each one. Looking at her watch, she cursed. If she didn't hurry, Mike would be gone, Chief was a stickler for attendance at roll call and Mike had to lead it. Gathering up Bullet's leash, she tried to jog back home. The sandals sliding around on her feet forced her to an impatient walk. The taillights of Mike's patrol unit flashed bright red as it slowed to turn down the street away from Catherine's house as she finally rounded the corner for home.

CHAPTER 9

While she waited for Ashley to open the door, Catherine reflected on the alienation she felt from the police. It wasn't personal. They were doing their job. Following the same protocol that she followed when she wore the colors. Whatever was going on in their investigation of Gavin's death wasn't open to her. Not unless Mike shared information, she kicked against the door riser, angry with herself for missing him by seconds. He couldn't expect her to ignore her investigative skills. She needed to know what he thought of the vandalism to her car, and why she was a target. Beads of sweat rimed born of her frustration rimmed her forehead. She brushed them away. My problem is I'm a hybrid. I want cop status and civilian freedom of investigation.

The wild haired, red-eyed, woman who opened the door at her knock barely resembled the pulled together Ashley she knew. Instinctively Catherine reached out and hugged her.

"Oh Catherine, I haven't had the nerve to go into the garage yet. I don't think I'll ever go in there again. I slept on the couch last night. I couldn't stand the thought of sleeping in our bed." Ashley made a sound that was half-way between a sob and a snort. "I kept hearing him, all night, he was everywhere."

Ashley's voice dropped to a whisper as she turned to lead the way into the sunroom. The temperature was easily approaching ninety degrees in the house. The humidity indoors was higher than outside. A trickle of sweat cut an itchy path from Catherine's hairline to her neck. Ashley stretched over the glass tabletop and picked up a fluffy robe. She was trembling, and she shoved one arm in, and then the next. Looking down she realized she'd put it on backwards, like a straightjacket. She tossed back her head and laughed, her laugh ending in gasping sobs. "I am so, so, sorry Catherine." She sobbed. "I shouldn't have asked you here. I'm not in shape to see anyone yet."

"Is there anyone I can call for you? A family member? Maybe a close friend? Anyone?"

Ashley shook her head and removed the robe, putting her arms in the sleeves correctly. Running a hand through her disheveled hair, she replied, "No. There really is no one. My family is in Chicago." She looked up at Catherine, her brown eyes swimming in unshed tears. "That's where I was, Chicago. City Ballet's there. I went to cover it. I was going to visit my sister, and..." her voice trailed off. Looking down at her hands, she said, "That doesn't matter, does it? Not now.

"What did you mean last night when you said you knew? What did you know, and did Gavin know you knew?"

The coffee Ashley held slopped over the rim of the hand thrown mug onto the table as she set it down in front of Catherine. Looking at the tan puddle, Ashley picked up the sash belt of her robe and blotted at it. "Oops," she giggled.

Catherine again looked at the older woman and wondered if she should call someone, a professional perhaps. She opened her mouth to ask as Ashley said,

"About the affairs, that's what I meant. I think I knew from the start. Not the who and why and wherefore, but I knew something happened. Gavin changed. And I knew. I, well, I had some issues going on then too." Ashley rolled the dirty sash belt into a fat cylinder as she spoke. "Then later, there were more, just closer to home." When he left the firm…I hoped it would change. It never did." She looked down at the rolled and plucked belt. "Let me shower and change. I want to show you something."

Catherine nodded, uncertain what else to do. She didn't want to leave the woman alone, and she had more questions than answers.

Ashley's arrow straight back disappeared in the direction of the other side of the house. The heat and humidity closed in making Catherine feel claustrophobic. She got up, whistled for Roscoe and took him out to the backyard to play.

The dog arced in mid-leap. He twisted his body, looked and ran back toward the house.

Catherine followed his trajectory and saw Ashley, her hair dripping from a shower, dressed neatly in jean shorts and a tank top, open the door into the sunroom. She held what looked like a sheaf of papers and a book in one hand while her other rested on the door handle. Catherine's heart broke for the woman. The dark circles under her eyes testified to a sleepless night.

It may have been a trick of light, but a quick movement from the Paysons house caught Catherine's eye. Giving the neighbor's house her full attention, she noticed the curtains over the back door move slightly.

Deciding not to upset Ashley with her suspicions, Catherine smiled brightly and made her way back to the house.

"I expect the neighbors have all been over, or tried to be," Catherine said. Wondering if she could steer the conversation into a discussion of the Paysons and their relationship.

"Vicki knocked this morning. Sue came by. That's about it. I...well, I wondered if anyone would come. Things were so bad at the last commission meeting. The town is totally out of control." Ashley twirled a piece of her wet hair around her finger. Her other hand still held the papers. "They didn't really know him. They knew the public him. The lawyer side. Not the real Gavin." Tears welled in her eyes. "Phil called. He's coming over later. I want him to...well, you know."

"Maybe you should show these to Phil first."

Ashley shook her head, sat down hard on the chair and put the papers down in front of her. She used both hands to tap the papers and straighten the edges and then, she rearranged them again. "When we first met," she continued, "I thought he was such a straight-laced prig." She looked at Catherine with a glint in her eye. "We almost didn't have a second date."

"What issues, Ashley?" Reading confusion in her eyes, she continued, "You said you had issues going on at the time Gavin had the affair."

Ashley grunted as she got up and walked toward the kitchen counter. Picking up a pink rose, she handed it to Catherine. "Breast cancer," she said simply. "I had surgery five years ago Tuesday."

Before Catherine thought of something comforting or appropriate to say Ashley blurted out, "It's back. It's back, and this horrible reminder of that stupid affair is back and Gavin, oh my precious Gavin, I want him back. Instead, I have to wait for Phil. Old faithful Phil." She spun around, ran for the kitchen sink, vomited and sobbed loudly. "I don't think I can go through this without Gavin."

Grasping the granite edge of the countertop, Ashley pulled herself upright and looked Catherine straight in the eye. "Help me, please Catherine, help me." She whimpered. "Phil was Gavin's friend. I want help from one of mine."

Catherine took a deep breath disliking Gavin even more for cheating on his sick wife. When Ashley asked her to come over to talk, she thought she might ask for advice because she wanted to know a cop's view, but to ask for help. That was a different matter. How could she help with the cancer issue? Halfway to the kitchen bar, Catherine drew a deep breath and said "Ashley, I'll take you to treatment, doctor's appointments, whatever you need, but about Gavin. Please, talk to the police, or Phil, not me. I can't help with Gavin."

"I'm embarrassed, Catherine. We're not great friends, you and I, but I trust you. You've always been fair, and upfront with how you feel about things. You used to be a cop, they'll listen to you."

"I'm a suspect, I found him." Catherine said. And an ex-cop with a drinking problem is the last person they will listen to.

"I looked in Gavin's journal last night. He's always kept one, it was in his desk, and I...What? Why are you looking at me that way?" Ashley's eyes became round as they looked up into Catherine's face. Catherine saw her own reflection in them and it frightened her. What possessed her to come here? Curiosity or a misguided sense of self? Was Vickie right? Was she confusing herself with a real cop? That made her a rogue. The thought was abhorrent.

Catherine shook her head as if to clear it. "Ashley, did Mike, or anyone, talk to you at all?

Ashley sat back and drummed her fingers on the stack of papers in front of her. She rose and went to the kitchen, opened a lower cupboard and removed a bottle of amber colored liquid. Holding it up toward Catherine she said, "Want some? It's 120-year-old cognac. Gavin's favorite. I, well, I think I need something in my coffee. We bought it on our honeymoon. We went to France."

Catherine had run road courses with fewer twists and turns than this conversation. Shaking her head in the negative, she watched Ashley pour a measure of the strong smelling liquid into her coffee cup, take a sip and hold it in her mouth. Her throat clenched as she swallowed.

"So, then, by helping me, you'll also be helping yourself. If you agree."

The calculation of the statement put Catherine on her guard. She deliberately didn't answer. She needed more information before she decided to commit herself.

"Why embarrassed, Ashley. Odd choice of words."

"I knew about the affair. We never discussed it. Seeing it in the paper made me feel naked. I know the exposure hurt him. It happened so long ago. He probably figured no one would ever find out. No one who didn't already know. He told me he felt sorry about it. He didn't say whom he felt sorry for. Him or me.

"What did he say when he saw the paper that morning?"

The distraught woman dropped heavily in a chair, pulled a cigarette from the pack and pushed it between her lips. She held it there, working it up and down as she thought. "That bastard."

"What?"

"That bastard." Ashley struck a match hard against the tab on the bottom of the pack and the smell of sulfur filled the room. "That's what he said." She leaned into the match and inhaled deeply. Her words came out on the exhale, "That bastard."

Catherine's mind worked overtime. Who, the publisher? Someone else. The person who leaked the article? The damn thing was years old. Why now? Who had motive and means to interest a publisher in an old scandal?

"Who, Ashley? Did he say who the bastard was?"

Her dark head tipped back against the chair. "Not to me. I wish he had."

"Were there other women Ashley? You said affairs."

Ashley pushed her hand back and forth in a dismissive gesture, and then pushed herself up and walked to the window.

Catherine watched the woman's back seem to slide into her hips and then straighten. Still looking into the back yard she said, "Ok, maybe. I heard rumors. I don't know. There's some stuff in his journal, but no names." She spun around to face Catherine. "And that's the truth." Jerking her head in the direction of the Payson house, she continued. "I think she started some rumors to cover for her husband. Made things sound worse than they were with Gavin. That bitch."

"Chris was having affairs?"

"Yeah, he likes married neighbors."

Catherine let the accusation hang in the air for a moment. "You Ashley? Are you one of the married neighbors Chris liked?"

"God! No. Not me. Others though. Meg for one. At least that was the rumor. Look Catherine, I never should have brought it up. What's the point of it? Who cares what goes on next door?

"When I left here yesterday, I intended to stay in Chicago. I told Gavin. Then I left. By the time I got to the airport, I knew I'd come back. I knew I'd forgive him, and I knew my pride shouldn't be the issue. Knew most of all that I needed him and his strength. Now and forever." Ashley looked Catherine full in the face and seemed to study her for a moment. "Whatever you might think, I loved my husband. And now, with that whole newspaper thing, he finally needed me too!"

She plucked a bit of cigarette paper from her lip and looked over her shoulder. Catherine read cunning in her narrowed eyes. "I could find out who planted the story. No one else could do that for him." The moment passed and tears spilled down Ashley's cheeks. "Did he kill himself?" She asked through clenched teeth. "If he did," her voice broke, "I did kill him."

"I'm sorry, I don't know. I didn't see a note." Catherine said gently. "I don't think one was found."

Catherine bit her lip. Mike told her he heard the ME's tech mention he felt a thick spot like a fresh bruise on Gavin's skull when he stabilized the head to cut him down. The ME would have the final word, but Catherine wished she had the nerve to ask Ashley if they had a fight.

Ashley shuffled back to the coffee table and lowered herself into a chair. With a tired gesture, she shoved the papers and book in front of her across the table to Catherine. "I don't know where the old ones are. Attic I guess, but he talks about the commission meeting and other stuff in here. Who said what and what he thought about it. You were there, but you weren't inside his mind. Did you see Terry spit at him?

"That was Terry?"

"He said so."

"Folded in the pages I found these e-mails. Most of 'em are threats. Some signed, some not, some vicious, some just complaining. From what I can piece together, he'd been trying to identify who sent the unsigned ones. He's got notes in there too, notes about zoning stuff and details about what they wanted and why he approved or disapproved their plans." She flipped through some of the papers. "Look," she shoved one at Catherine, "even notes about bribes." Her chin lifted in pride. "He turned down lots of money."

Ashley kept a grip on the journal when Catherine reached for it.

"What you won't find are the names of the people helped." She looked at Catherine, her eyes bright with unshed tears. "He made private loans to people to help them stay in their houses. Some didn't pay him back." Her voice broke. "The ARM on our mortgage is due to adjust this month. Big time." She ran her fingers through her still wet hair. "I know he was afraid we couldn't pay, that we'd lose the house. It's all here. Nothing is worth what it was. We were stupid. We thought it would go on forever." She opened a page and traced her husband's handwriting with her finger. Then she pushed the book at Catherine.

"Reading this last night made me feel closer to him. I hope he didn't kill himself. God help me, I

hope someone killed him. Otherwise I failed him."
She sobbed and stripped paper towels off a nearby
roll holding them to her face.

Catherine skimmed the handwritten journal
in front of her while Ashley composed herself.
"Ashley is there anything in here about an affair?
Do you know anything about the girl, the one in the
newspaper I mean? Well I guess she'd be a woman
now. Or her family?"

Ashley shook her head. "Young girl who
must have looked older. Gavin loved the law. He
wouldn't knowingly break it, not for sex. Sex, for a
man like Gavin, is too available. He's good-
looking." Her expression challenged Cathy to refute
her statement.

Finding no opposition, Ashley waived her
hand from side to side. "He was a partner in the
largest law firm in South Florida. A senior partner
at that. Women flocked to him." She made a noise
somewhere between a chuckle and a snort. "He had
no need to go after jail bait." Her lip curled on the
final words. "None of them did. Didn't stop them
though, did it? Why did he have to take the fall?"

She's still angry with him, Catherine
thought, and stored the image away for later
reference.

"Can I borrow these?"

"Sure, do you think he died for sex? Years-
ago sex?"

"I don't know, Ashley. I wish I did. If he did
die because of the sex, then something had to
change. Some reason to kill him now didn't exist
before. We just have to find it."

"It's pretty obvious, don't you think? The story in the paper. Somebody found out about it, gave it to the paper, the same paper I work for. Who would do that? How could anyone else in the Village find out?"

"Why do you think someone from the Village leaked the story? Why not the original players and her family? If someone here did go to the Metropolis, that's not a motive for murder, it's a motive to embarrass him. Very different from killing him?"

"Don't you get it," Ashley responded. "Someone knew him well enough to know he'd kill himself. They wouldn't have to do a thing. Those people from five years ago, they didn't know him at all. Maybe there was someone else, someone angry." Ashley grabbed Catherine's hand, pulling it toward her chest. At the same time, she shoved a sheaf of papers so hard they nearly fanned into Catherine's lap. "Here, look, it's all in here." She seemed desperate. She sobbed, washed her face with a tissue and said, "I'll find the old journals. Do you think they were blackmailing him?"

Nancy's words about Maggie's brother calling Phil floated into her head. "I promise. I'll look at them all. Ashley," Catherine softened her voice hoping to soften the blow. "You understand you're a suspect too, don't you?"

She reacted by pitching her head back, as if in response to a slap. "Me? I wasn't here. They can't be serious."

"Before you left." Catherine watched carefully for a reaction.

"I love him." She dropped her head into her hands. "I can't stand it if they think I hurt him. He's my husband, death doesn't change that." Silent tears ran down her face as she looked back at Catherine.

"Do you think there's life after death? I want to be with him!" Her tears continued to flow.

Nothing else Ashley had done moved Catherine the way her silent tears did. She gathered up the papers and journal and slid them into what looked like an interoffice envelope Ashley had on the bottom of the stack.

"Ok, Ashley, I'll take a look. If I think the police need any of this information, I'll have to turn it over to them."

"No." Ashley held out her hand and tried to snatch the envelope back. "If you're going to do that, give them back now."

Catherine struggled with her next words. She needed to see the documents for her own protection. "I'm a suspect too, Ashley. We're in this together."

CHAPTER 10

"Nancy, I don't get it." Catherine's legs hung over the edge of the porch swing in her back yard. A copy of the Miami Metropolis covered the ground around her. Her hand, holding sewing shears, described a circle in the air. "The more I look at the stuff, the more I'm convinced Gavin was murdered. And by an outsider. Did you have a chance to find out anything about the Affidavit?"

Lifting her head from the hammock, Nancy looked over at her friend.

Catherine saw her chew on her lower lip. A sure sign of Nancy's confusion. "Nance?"

"Cathy, it happened a long time ago."

She couldn't believe her ears. Nancy stonewalled her. "So, it's key to Gavin's death then. Or you think it is."

"Don't think for me, Cathy. You may not be right, and it's never easy for me to talk about work stuff. No matter how long it's been." She dropped her head back to the hammock and turned her face away.

The magnitude of the statement hit
Catherine like a blow to the stomach. From Nancy's
point of view, this was a confidential matter, she
might have to discuss it with Mike, it if came to an
investigation, but Catherine realized she was
imposing on friendship, and she had no right to
demand an answer. Understanding softened her
voice. "Nancy, I don't think someone in the Village
slashed my tires. Everyone here knows I usually run
or bike. Besides, you can't sneeze here without
forty people yelling 'God bless'. Then they run to
the phone and tell the neighborhood you have swine
flu or some other fate. Someone would see
something, and talk." Catherine got up, newspaper
falling to the floor with a rustling sound. Bullet
looked at her, and then put his head back on his
paws. She paced back and forth on the concrete pad.
"Vicki heard cars. She thought there was the usual
street traffic, but…"

"Catherine, you're running away with
yourself, and you're not making much sense."
Hearing resignation in her friend's voice, Catherine
turned and walked to the swing. She didn't want to
interrupt the moment by saying a word.

Nancy knifed her body over the edge of the
hammock, and reached down with her feet to steady
herself. She sighed deeply, got up and walked
toward the porch. "I'm telling you, I don't have a
lot of information."

Sitting down on the swing, Catherine
propped an elbow on her knee, her chin cupped in
her hand. She regarded Nancy, seated on the rise of
the porch, her legs tucked beneath her. "Who

decided to prepare an Affidavit, and why? Wasn't it more dangerous than leaving the situation alone? Hasn't this always been an opportunity for blackmail at the least, and embarrassment to the firm at the worst? Who knew about the affair? Did the girl's family get involved? How could a minor sign an Affidavit?"

"That's some list, Cathy. Are you done?"

"For starters, I'll make notes."

Nancy rolled her eyes at the sarcasm and said, "I may regret saying anything, but Phil drafted it. He and Gavin were friends until Gavin's death. Christ, they went to high school together. The partners wanted Gavin out. Moral turpitude is an anathema to law firms. Phil thought the Affidavit gave Gavin some protection if Maggie decided to bring charges. Only Phil, Gavin and Maggie knew about it. I typed it. Maggie had turned 18 by then. She hadn't been far off at the time the whole thing happened. That's it Cathy. I don't know anymore."

"Her brother? You said her brother called Phil not too long ago."

"Yeah, but that's all I know. Catherine, I really can't talk about this."

"And you remembered him, even though the whole thing happened five years ago, you remembered the brother's name?" Catherine pushed.

"Cathy, I love you like a sister, but I don't want to talk about this. Please try to understand. Phil called me last night." She waved her hand, stopping Catherine from interrupting. "He said he felt so bad about the newspaper and even worse that it caused Gavin's death. He's so worried. They were partners."

"Isn't Phil up for judicial re-election in November?"

"Yes, so what?"

"Why are you shutting me out?" Do you think Gavin committed suicide?" Catherine asked.

Nancy got up from the edge of the porch, and walked toward the back of the garden. Catherine didn't know if she would answer.

"No. I never saw it in him. People change though." Nancy finally replied. When she came back to the porch, her eyes were bright with unshed tears. "Do you think he was being blackmailed?"

Catherine's mind flashed back to the sheaf of papers Ashley entrusted to her. She hadn't mentioned them to Nancy. Right now, the envelope and journal were burning a hole on her desk where she'd left them when Nancy knocked on her door minutes after she'd returned from Ashley's house.

"Nance, how does someone go about leaking the Affidavit to the paper? It's so old. I'm surprised the paper cared enough to publish it. I doubt anyone from the Village knew about the affair.

"Except Ashley. Maybe." Nancy came to sit alongside Cathy on the swing.

"Why would she do it? It would embarrass her too."

"I don't know, Catherine. Maybe she just found it, maybe she wanted to hurt him but not be the messenger. Maybe he was carrying on with someone else, and she wanted to punch him, force his hand, give her an excuse to walk out. Don't forget, she works for the paper. She'd have access to the muckrakers."

"You said the brother called your boss before this hit."

"Yeah, but Phil's a judge, and the brother is a crim. That call could have been about anything from expungement to checking into a new trial. Who knows?"

"But Phil took the call? Catherine asked.

"I gave him the message." Nancy replied. The two women walked to the door. "The subject is closed Cathy. You're obsessed. This is my job you're playing with. I worked damn hard to get where I am, and in my business, it can all be over in a heartbeat."

Thoughts swirled in Catherine's mind as she watched Nancy walk down the street away from her house. Something was very wrong. She locked her door and turned for the bedroom that served as her office. If Ashley was on the level, the answer might be in the e-mails.

If she wasn't, then Catherine needed to know what Ashley wanted her to believe.

The envelope lay centered on her desk blotter where she left it, the leather journal making a bulge on top. Catherine's fingers itched with anticipation as she slid into her chair and gazed at the package, trying to imagine what secrets it held. Ashley said she read the journal, but Catherine was a trained observer. Years on the force taught her to connect the dots in ways a civilian would never imagine. She snorted, civilian. If Mike was right and Gavin was murdered; she was tampering with evidence if she opened the envelope. The thought made her sit back. In order to protect herself, she had to read the contents, but that bordered on obstruction.

She leaned forward and opened the envelope. The contents were all e-mails except for the journal. Taking a quick flip through, Catherine decided to arrange them by type, person and date. She stacked four piles, threats signed, threats unsigned, Mayor Cunningham and Sunny Side Bank. Tapping the envelope open, she spotted a scrap of paper scrap wedged into the bottom. Blowing into the envelope to open it wider, she groped inside and carefully pulled out what looked like a torn and crumpled bank balance inquiry, she smoothed it out and read the number, nearly one hundred thousand dollars, in a checking account dated last week. On the back, someone had scrawled "GJ pers." She laid it on top of the bank e-mails.

Paddy Whack jumped up on the desk and sat on the documents. "Ok, girl," Catherine said, "I don't need you reading this stuff now. Let Mom do it first." At the same time she picked up the cat and took her to the living room Bullet ran for the door. He wasn't barking, but his body language didn't suggest a trip to the great outdoors either. Catherine sidled over to living room window. She quickly glanced around the frame, bobbing her head and pivoting her torso quickly in true cop style and laughed. Reaching behind her, she thumbed the deadbolt off, opened the door and said. "I just cop looked a cop."

"Yah," Mike said, "and I saw you." He tousled her dark blonde hair, he stepped back, cupping her chin in his hand and lifted her face to his. "What's wrong Kit Kat? You're eyes are the color of amber. You're trying to hide something."

Catherine shrugged, "I need a friend, not a cop friend. I need to bounce some stuff off you, but." She raised her hand to stifle whatever he'd opened his mouth to say. "I don't want to put you in that position. You're probably in enough trouble knowing me."

Mike took her hand and led her over to the couch. Bullet sat down in front of him and put a paw on his knee. "Cathy, listen to me. I am your friend, and a lot more, I hope. You've worn the colors. You know the tightrope. I can't make you talk to me, and I can't tell you I won't use what you tell me. I've never lied to you, not about anything, and I sure as heck won't lie about this."

Catherine studied her hands. She could just make out the beginning of sunspots on them. Fleetingly it crossed her mind that she needed to make up her mind about Mike too. He'd asked her to marry him, twice, the last time on her birthday. Dilemmas like this kept her from saying yes. It wasn't the first time she had information he wanted. She sighed deeply. "I guess I need to know what's going on before I decide. Can you tell me?"

Rising from the couch, Mike paced back and forth across the room. She heard the rustle of his jeans and the click of his boot heels. Bullet paced behind him, staying close enough to touch the tall man's hand. "OK, official word, suicide."

"M.E. report came back?"

He shook his head. "Next week, probably. Cunningham filed a request through the Police Commissioner for us to stand down. Thom says he's satisfied with the suicide theory, and the problems the M.E. brought up could be bruises from the Commission meeting. There's been some talk of spousal abuse too." Breaking eye contact, he said, "Did you know Ashley is a black belt? I understand that the unexplained throat bruises are consistent with chokeholds."

Catherine pulled her lower lip out with her thumb and index finger. "We were in the dojo together after I quit the force. She's good. Well, I'm off the hook then. Why don't I feel relieved?" She saw indecision on Mike's face.

"There's more." Mike walked over and embraced Catherine. She buried her face in the hollow of his arm. "He's pushing to get you charged with abetting and obstructing."

"Abetting what? Obstructing what? I found him. That's the total of my involvement! "

"Cunningham and Simms are trying to say you pushed Gavin over the edge when you threatened him. That you argued with him."

"And what, tossed a rope over a beam and around his neck and he stood there and let me? Hello, that's total crap. Not, not crap, that's total....Oh, I don't even have a word for it."

"No, your fight was the last straw. Between the Affidavit, money problems, Ashley leaving him…"

"So she did leave him?"

"We don't know, not in the traditional sense. She'd gone to Chicago, who really knows when, why or for how long. We're getting the records. "Anyway, Cunningham thinks, based on your phone message, that you were the last straw. He says you met him in the morning and threatened to badmouth him in the Village and sue him in small claims court."

"I didn't but that's a pretty lame argument to make, and how is that abetting or obstructing."

"Leaving him after he made serious threats to suicide."

"Bull, I have no obligation to call someone because he makes stupid threats."

"Then he did?"

"Whose side are you on? I never saw him alive. Not after the Commission meeting."

Catherine raked her hand through her hair. She wanted to pull it out by the roots and throw it in his face. This cop game would drive you nuts and she walked right into it with her eyes open. He's asked her a loaded question, and she gave the wrong answer. She knew anything she said could turn against her.

"You had a higher duty because of your training. Cunningham says you went back after your argument. You found Gavin hanging and staged the scene to look like murder."

Catherine took a step back, her heart clenched in her chest. She'd known she'd be a suspect, but she hadn't figured they'd concoct a scenario. "I thought they'd exclude me immediately." She whispered. "They really believe that? They'll say we fought and I hung him if the ME finds bruises." Tears bit the back of her eyes. "What did I do that makes them think this? Either way, I fall. Murder or manslaughter. I killed him or I left him after he threatened to kill himself. This sucks."

Mike rubbed his hands over her shoulders and down her arms. He grasped her hands and pulled them both to his lips. "Oh, Kit Kat. I love you. You need to know the worst that can happen. We'll get through this, but you have to be prepared." He gathered her into a hard hug.

God, if only this hadn't happened. I really could love this man.

"You sure picked a lousy night to tie one on and get mouthy. By the way, were you at Ashley's today?"

Startled, Cathy nodded her head. Back in cop mode, she followed the thought to its likely conclusion. "Co-conspirators? They think Ashley and I worked this out between us?"

"What was in the envelope you took out of there, Cathy?"

"Something else is going on here, isn't it? Something you're not sharing with me."

At Mike's silence, she sighed deeply, and said, "You'll let me know as soon as you're sure of things?" When he nodded she continued, "I'll show you." Taking his hand, she led him to her office and pointed at the desk. Then she gathered up the documents and journal and replaced them in the envelope. "Chief is right about one thing. Someone hated Gavin."

Lowering his bulk into the desk chair, Mike reached for a stack. "That's in these papers."

"I don't know. I sorted the papers, but I haven't read them. Ashley gave these to me in confidence. I told her that if they were important to the investigation, I'd have let you know about them. But I don't know that yet." The wood floor bit into her knees as she knelt alongside the chair. "Let me look through them first. I gave my word."

She watched the play of emotions chase each other across his broad face. "There's a journal too…" Catherine searched for words. "Let me look at them first. I promise I'll share them if they are pertinent." The skin of her forehead tightened. How many promises was she going to make and break in a few short hours? She took the stack from his hand and laid it on the desk. "Besides, if they've determined that Gavin committed suicide, I can't see what official interest you could possibly have in this stuff."

Mike rocked back in the chair. He half turned and ran his finger down Catherine's thigh. She shivered as sparks ran through her.

"That's the official word." He said quietly. "I don't think it's the final word." He picked up the envelope, stuffed the loose papers in and walked from the room.

"Then who? Mike." Catherine raced after him, stumbling over Bullet, and catching herself against the wall. "Come back here, you can't take those. Mike, I promised. Damn!"

"I'm sorry, Cathy. It's evidence. I don't know who, not yet. I meant what I said. I'll share information."

She thought she saw a hint of sorrow in his eyes as she regained her balance, but the door clicked closed before she reached him. Catherine picked up one of Bullet's chew bones laying on the floor and threw it with all her might at the door.

CHAPTER 11

The Payson house loomed before her like some kind of malevolent beast. The closer she got to the front door, the bigger the house seemed to grow. Her heartbeat increased as memories of her last encounter with Terry flooded back, and Catherine rubbed the still sore spot on her chest and wondered why she had to be the one to ask the questions.

"What do you want?" Chris Payson stood in his doorway, his chin jutting forward and one hand firmly on the jamb. His eyes glittered with dislike.

"Just a couple of minutes. I'd like to speak with you. And Terry if she's home," Catherine said.

Mike's comment about abetting stuck in her craw. There was no way she saw Gavin alive. No way had she aided him in committing suicide, not even by leaving after he threatened to kill himself. Someone had to have seen something that morning. Why not the next door neighbors? If the Paysons saw someone going to the Jackmans'…

Catherine's memory returned to finding Terry in the Jackman garage. Unless the Paysons were in the garage.

The door swung toward the latch. Catherine shoved her foot in the opening. The pressure increased on her toes. She held firm. The force stopped. "Wait here."

Reluctant to remove her foot, she stayed with her nose practically pressed to the mahogany of the door. "Terry." Catherine heard Chris yell in a falsetto voice. "Ms. Swope's at the door." She struggled to make full sentences of the disjointed word that followed muffled by distance, the bulk of the door, the cacophony of Chris's heavy steps moving deeper into the house, and the quick slap of someone's open back shoes against a wooden floor.

"That's BS...after information...." Terry's voice responded.

"She's a wannabe...in the garage...." Chris replied

The voices and the footsteps got clearer, and louder as they neared the door.

"Maybe I wanted to make sure the bastard was dead," Terry said.

"Where were you?" Chris's voice had a pleading note. "When I got up..."

"Don't do this Chris." Tinny chords, sounding like a bad rendition of Mission Impossible broke into the argument.

"God, will you change that ring tone," Terry said, "Answer the damn thing, I'll let the bitch in."

Catherine pulled her head sharply away from the door wondering how much of the exchange was for her benefit.

The image of Terry's furious face at the commission meeting floated back in Catherine's mind. She didn't remember seeing Chris at the meeting. Where was Terry the morning Gavin died? Where was Chris, and did he have an alibi? She shelved her questions for future consideration and pasted on her brightest smile as Terry yanked open the door.

"Oh, hi Arnie," Chris spoke into the phone and turned his back away from the door.

Terry raised one eyebrow, glanced at Catherine standing in the doorway, smiled, and crooked a finger directing her to follow as she led the way into a room around the corner and away from Chris's conversation.

Catherine deliberately stepped on the lace of one of her running shoes pulling it undone. As she approached the dividing wall between the two rooms, she dropped to her knee and retied the lace. From her vantage point in the threshold, she saw Terry lower herself into a deep club chair and light a cigarette with practiced ease from the butt end of the one she held.

"I'm in here, Catherine. Not in the living room." The woman's voice was breathy, talking on an exhale, "I guess this is about the garage."

"No, I'm happy to listen, though, if you want to talk about why you were there." She remained standing in the doorway, reluctant to risk missing more of Chris's conversation with the Mayor.

Chris's voice pitched high interrupting his wife's response. "Me! Sure. Yeah. I'd love it. Talk about sweet revenge, Arnie." Her stomach tightened in frustration as Chris's voice dropped to a near whisper. The words "Hank Simms" and "money" floated back to her, but she couldn't get a handle on the context.

"Now, Catherine." Chris trotted around her in a wide semi-circle, like a football player making a run for the end zone, and spiked the phone onto the charger next to his wife. "What do you want? Is this a social call or do you like hanging out in my neighborhood?"

A shaft of sun broke through the clouds bathing the room in light bright enough to bleach the color. Squinting against the onslaught Catherine said, "I wondered if you happened to see anything at the Jackmans' the other morning."

"The day you found him hanging? Besides you playing hide and seek?" Chris sneered. He too flopped down in a chair and lit a cigarette.

She glanced between the Paysons needing to know what they knew. Frustration built and she could feel the start of a migraine building just over her left eye. Their body language was clear. They were enjoying not telling her anything. Chris blew a stream of smoke in her direction. Behind the cloud, she saw a look on his face she understood. He wanted power. To get anything from him, she had to give something. She had to make them allies. "The night before Gavin died, I got drunk. I called him and left a not-so-nice message that the cops consider a threat. It wasn't." She dropped her face to her hands and rubbed her palms on her temples. She looked into Terry's face from across the room where she still stood against the doorjamb. "I really need your help."

Catherine held her breath and watched Terry and Chris exchange a look of such intensity she almost felt the communication between them.

Terry broke the silence first. "I heard the ME thinks he might have had a fight before he died. Did you fight with him?"

The statement took Catherine by surprise. Her thoughts whirled with the names of people who had access to the information of Gavin's bruises. Who had told the Paysons? Or did anyone? Was this some kind of test to see how much she knew? Catherine felt her features morph into her bland cop face and she shook her head. "No. I never saw him alive."

"That was why I went into the garage." Terry continued, her eyes narrowing as she glanced in Chris's direction. "I wanted to see for myself what happened. Where it happened."

She wanted to see if Chris fought with Gavin and if there was any evidence. Maybe this wasn't the first time Terry cleaned up Chris's messes.

Husband and wife exchanged another long look. Terry stubbed out her cigarette. "I heard Ashley leave. She took the old clunker. What about you, Chris? What did you hear that morning?"

Catherine bit her lip. There had to be more. She was reluctant to press these two. They had motive and means. Especially knowing Gavin was alone in the house. The Payson Florida room looked out at the Jackman house. From where she stood, Catherine had a clear view of the walk to the front door, the gate and the driveway.

"Were you and Chris both home all morning?"

Terry's lashes fell to shutter her eyes. She pulled herself up from the chair.

"Where else would I be that early in the morning, in jail with Luis?"

Chris's head whipped around to stare at his wife. If Catherine had any doubts about the subject of the argument she'd overheard at the time she arrived, she didn't now.

"What about you Chris? Did you hear anyone?" She walked over to the windowed wall of the Florida room. "You've got quite a view here." In the reflection, she saw Chris shake his head never taking his eyes from his wife.

"That view gives me heartburn. I try to avoid it," He said.

"What about when you were outside mowing?"

"You can't hear anything over the mower. I didn't see anyone. Just you. I saw you in the yard with the dog. That's all we know, Catherine." Chris shot a quick look at Terry. "Good luck with the police."

Terry struck another match, held it to her cigarette and inhaled deeply. "Cherchez les femmes.

101

Look for the women," she said. And blew out a long plume of smoke.

Walking home, Catherine's stomach churned as she replayed the conversation. Every time Catherine went to the Jackman house, she'd noticed activity at the Payson curtains. It was inconceivable that they didn't see someone. What did Chris get so excited about when Arnie called? Was "Arnie" Arnie Cunningham the mayor? What little Catherine heard of the conversation pointed in that direction. Besides, she couldn't think of another Arnie in the Village that fit the context of the rest of the names. What about Simms? Was Chris looking for a job? Was Cunningham offering one? Gavin's maybe? And what did Terry's parting comment mean? Look for what women?

The sight of Mike, sitting on her front steps, brought her up short. She jogged the last few yards to her house torn between wanting his opinion on her visit with the Paysons and wondering if he'd found something in the papers he'd hijacked from her house.

"Hey big fellow." She leaned down and kissed him firmly on the lips.

Rising, he tousled her hair. "Didn't want to let myself in Kit Kat. Wasn't sure the water temperature would be good."

Catherine felt herself melt into that space just under his shoulder. Even with the butt of his service revolver prodding her in the breast, the rational part of her knew she'd come home. She wondered why the competitive part of her fought so hard to keep from admitting it, and if her two sides would finally make peace with each other. "You're always welcome. Can we talk for a minute?"

Bullet's greeting nearly knocked them both back outside. Managing to break away, Catherine clapped her hands and ran for the back door. The dog followed. When she returned Mike was standing in front of the mantle, his hands braced, looking down into the empty firebox.

Coming up behind him, Catherine ran a hand down his back feeling the tension gathered in his neck and shoulders. She massaged his neck. "More trouble?"

He straightened and picked up one of the knick knacks that decorated the space and rolled it between his hands.

She wasn't used to seeing Mike fidget. He paced across the floor, looked down at his hand, paced back to the fireplace and returned the ceramic dog he'd picked up. He paused, looked at her and nodded. "There's been talk, really quiet talk, that money's missing."

"From Gavin's account? Maybe Ashley took it. If she knew about the Affidavit, she might have planned to leave Gavin, took the money and then leaked the Affidavit."

"No, from the Village." He looked down and seemed to study the floor. "Cunningham thinks Gavin skimmed from the account. Apparently, Gavin and Hank had signature power and Hank claims he rarely signed anything. They're getting the records." She knew Mike was risking his job sharing the information with her. A wave of love for the tall man washed over her, but right now, she was afraid to trust him with her information in return.

"So Gavin suicided to avoid jail time?" Catherine's mind shot back to the conversation she overheard at the Paysons' and the pieces clicked into place.

Before she could find the words to tell him about her visit to the Paysons, he continued, "I think the official story is going to be something like that." He turned and held her at arm's length. "The ending I heard is the violence at the meeting and then your call threating him later that night pushed him over the edge."

Catherine sat down on the coffee table, her hands reaching for his strong grip to keep steady. Her pulse roared in her ears. No matter how much she denied it, she knew in her heart of hearts that she blamed herself for having a part in Gavin's death. Her rational mind railed against the thought, but it didn't matter. On some level, she believed her drunken call was responsible.

CHAPTER 12

A few hours later, balancing a cup of coffee and a bowl of tuna in each hand, Catherine headed for the porch. She kicked open the door when leaning her back against it failed to work.

Attracted by the heady scent of the tuna, Paddy Whack purred and threaded her way around Catherine's legs. When Catherine's cell phone and doorbell rang simultaneously, the cat bolted for safety under the couch. Placing the bowl on the chair and the coffee on the floor, she reached for the phone holstered at her hip and walked slowly toward the front door. Lunch and time to think about Mike's news, not interruptions, headed her priority list.

Susan stood on the stoop. Her teeth worrying a hangnail a crumpled piece of paper in her other hand.

"Nancy's on the phone." Catherine greeted the code enforcement officer. "Friendly or professional?"

Susan grimaced. "Betrayer. Nick would kill me." She said mentioning her police officer husband. "Look at this." She handed the paper to Catherine, who glanced down and wrinkled her brow. "Can you put Nance on speaker on that thing?" She pointed to the cell phone. "I think I could use some of her practical advice."

"Nance," Catherine began.

"I heard. Hi, Susan. Yes, put me on speaker, Cathy."

Catherine led the way back into the kitchen, pushed a button on the side of her cell phone and set it in the little Adirondack chair holder she'd bought so she'd have a fighting chance of finding the phone regularly.

"Nance, Sue just handed me a paper that nominates Luis Alvarez, Chris Payson and Meg Kent for interim Zoning Commissioner." She looked up at Susan, "I thought the remaining commissioners appointed someone to fill a vacant term. We need a special election?"

Susan responded, "No, but the nominations should have been made in an open special meeting, then floor nominations could be taken. This doesn't give anyone else a chance."

"Sounds like plain old business as usual in the good ole boy network of the Village," Nancy said.

"Yeah, I know. I was thinking about Dannie Gutierrez," Susan said. "She called me yesterday, wanted know what the process was to fill Gavin's seat. She was so embarrassed she didn't want to ask a commissioner, but she wanted to be on the Commission so badly."

"She talked to Vicki and me too, I told her to call you," Catherine said. Damn, she'd be so good too, she knows everything in this Village, and she's fair."

"So, I'll call and nominate her," Nancy said. Make them add her to the list. Why not? Problem solved."

"Thanks Nance," Susan said. "That's not my problem. Cunningham's insisting that Gavin's death is suicide. Worse, he's blaming you, Cathy, for causing it. Well, you, the commission meeting, and the story in the paper, but you were the match that lit the flame. Nobody's gone public yet. But Nick says that's what the official story is going to be.

By the time Susan finished her story the silence on the phone grew to deafening proportions. Catherine ground her teeth. She hadn't digested Mike's more detailed version yet. Hearing a similar story from Susan forced the knot in her stomach higher in the chest. A few of the details were different, but overall, the stories matched. Cunningham was framing Catherine for a suicide. One step better than framing her for a murder, but she could defend herself from a murder charge.

"Catherine?" Nancy prodded her. "Did you hear Susan? Cunningham wants you to stick to what you do best. Dog walking. He's telling people that your drunken accusations caused Gavin to take his own life."

"That's stupid. I won't even discuss it." The only thing she could add to the discussion at this point was more speculation. Something was very wrong. Why was Cunningham rushing to a verdict in advance of the ME report? Maybe she was wrong. Maybe Gavin's death was a murder after all.

"It borders on slander, Catherine. If he keeps it up, you need a lawyer. Let Mike know."

Catherine's face reddened. "What can he do if there's no crime? I can handle this myself. Payson must have called him and moaned because I talked to them. It'll blow over."

Susan rose from her seat at the table, walked to her friend's side, and grasped her arm so she and Catherine faced each other. "Catherine, Cunningham said he'd stop you if you didn't stop yourself. He's told Mike he'd better rein you in, or he can forget any promotion. Catherine, listen to me." Susan shook her friend lightly. "He really wants you off the case. Take it seriously!"

She wanted to defend herself, but she had no adversary. Not here in this group. Mike definitely hadn't mentioned Cunningham threatening his job. Her heart cracked a bit, he didn't deserve that.

Her mind spun to Ashley. She'd promised her she'd help her clear Gavin's name. Then she let Mike take the information Ashley entrusted to her. Shaking her head like Bullet after a swim, Catherine's gaze bored into Sue. "It makes no sense," Catherine said, "Suze, you must have heard wrong."

"No. I heard right. He spoke very clearly. He's got Hank calling the Village attorney. He wants to know if they can get some kind of restraining order against you."

Nancy's sharp intake of breath was so loud that both Susan and Catherine grabbed for the cell phone.

"He has no grounds for an RO. None. This is Florida! You need at least two acts of violence or stalking for a non-domestic. Cathy, you know the criteria. Damn, on a Friday, too. Of course, it figures."

Catherine jumped to her feet and paced the length of the kitchen. Mentally she reviewed each action she'd taken since she found Gavin hanging. Except for sneaking back into the garage and house the day of Gavin's death, she'd done nothing wrong. She shuddered, recalling her interview with Terry and Chris. Even money said Chris's caller was the Mayor. Had to be. Where did the money figure in? Salary? Were the Paysons that hard up for money? Was that why they were so rabid about their renovations? Renovations Catherine remembered Gavin denied.

Susan looked at her watch then back at her friend. "I don't want Nick to know about this. It's bad enough I might be losing my job." She smiled ruefully. "I figure that's a given if any of the three likely suspects gets voted in."

"Hello," Nancy's voice sounded from the cell phone.

Catherine picked up the phone from its cradle and snapped off the speaker option. "Sue has to go. You called me. What's up – a little late." Catherine hoped her voice held the levity she didn't feel. Her mind was spinning so fast she felt dizzy.

109

"Phil saw Gavin a couple of days before his death."

Waiting for more, Catherine held her silence. Finally, she said, "Nance, Ashley told us that."

"Yeah. But she didn't tell us Gavin was depressed, depressed enough to worry Phil."

"Did he say why?"

"Who, Phil? No, not to me. But he told me he was sorry he'd told Gavin that Tomas called, and why. Said he didn't think he needed to hear that."

"Hold on Nance. I need some timelines here. When did Phil tell Gavin about Tomas, when he saw him or before?"

"Cathy, I'm sorry, I...."

Nancy's voice trailed off and Catherine gritted her teeth. She couldn't let her stop now. She had to know what Tomas wanted.

     * * *

Catherine barely felt the heat as she walked her charges later that afternoon. Nancy's story didn't make sense. Why would an on-parole convict call a criminal court Judge to ask if his sister could sue for sexual harassment? Sue whom? The firm? Gavin? Phil? How did this tie in to the story in the paper? Why would the paper even care about a five-year old peccadillo?

Approaching the park in the center of the Village, Catherine ignored the No Dogs sign and walked to the water fountain at the back of the recreation center. Bending over to take a drink, she caught a movement out of the corner of her eye. Buster made a warning noise in his throat.

Catherine lifted her head and choked, violently spewing the water she'd tried to swallow. Billy LaMotta stood behind her, his ticket book already out of his pocket.

Deciding not to argue, Catherine accepted the ticket for violating the dog ordinance. The coincidence had Catherine wondering if his shift orders including watching her.

Instead of going home after she returned the dogs, Catherine wandered to a bench under a large banyan tree in one of the Village's woodsy medians. On top of everything else, people in the Village were avoiding her. More than once, neighbors answered her greetings with turned backs. Somehow, finding Gavin's body made her a pariah.

She leaned over, picked up a stick and sketched aimlessly in the sand next to her sneakers. While her hand made abstract movements, her thoughts replayed her earlier conversation with Nancy. Rita, Gavin's former secretary, wanted a meeting on Monday. From the way Nancy sounded, she didn't like the whole situation. What kind of information could the woman add to the sod story? Or was she just another vulture looking to pick the bones of a tragedy?

CHAPTER 13

With Mike on duty, Nancy busy with other friends, and Sue and Nick off to the Keys, the weekend hung heavy on Catherine's hands. Unable to quiet the questions swirling in her mind, she called Mike and asked him about Cunningham's threats to get a restraining order. He shut her down, refusing to say anything about the investigation or Cunningham. The time between morning and afternoon dog walks stretched endlessly and the walls of isolation closed in on her.

Torn between a soul deep tiredness and a pity party threatening to pull her to the liquor cabinet, she sat in front of her computer. An e-mail from Mike, sent after her call, confirmed that the ME's report on Gavin's death was still pending. Something about the phrasing struck her though. Did he mean pending or undetermined. Did they have the death certificate and were they opting to sit on it? Catherine's blood boiled as she read Mike's odd suggestion that the Summer Hill force was adequate to investigate a suicide or a murder if it came to that, without her assistance. Anger built in

her like magma building in volcano. How dare
Mike question her investigative skills? Oh sure, if
she called him on it, he'd probably say he was just
trying to keep her out of trouble, but she knew the
truth. She could read between the lines. She'd paid
her dues, damn it. Even got commendations for it.
Tension coiled in her neck and shoulders and she
rotated her head in an attempt to loosen her
muscles. How could he do this now, just when
she'd decided to let him into her life?

"Sit on it Reardon." Catherine muttered.
"I'm just as much of an investigator as you are. No
one's gonna lay Gavin's death at my door. Not if I
can help it. I'm not guilty, of murder or causing a
suicide."

Pulling up a search engine, Catherine typed
in the words "Miami-Dade, foreclosures." The sheer
number of listings shocked her. She scrolled down
address after address of residents all in the process
of losing their homes. Fifty-six addresses in her
immediate neighborhood alone, some in the early
stages, some ready for public sale. The news caught
her by surprise. Despite a successful career in real
estate during the heady days of the boom, she'd
pulled out of the profession when prices rose to
insane heights. She didn't want to be part of the
inevitable tragedy she saw all around her. Sighing
deeply, she printed the list, pulled and printed the
minutes of the last year's commission meetings.

By the time she finished color coding and
cross-referencing the addresses and zoning requests
on a Village street map, she realized that the fifty-
six foreclosures represented twenty-one zoning or

variance requests and Gavin denied twelve. Cunningham's name was on both lists. Early stages in the foreclosure process though, so there could be a mistake.

Hot pink sticky flags indicating denied variances nearly covered the map. Catherine rocked back on her haunches and studied the color patterns. When her cell phone sounded its familiar salsa ring indicating Mike on the line, she shot up from the floor and nearly doubled over in response to the sudden crick in her back.

Her hand groped on the table for the device. Finding it, she flipped the phone open and brought it to her ear. "Mike. Where are you?"

"Just turning down your street. Feel like lunch?"

"Sure, but I'm cooking. I've got something to show you. And by the way, you are pissing me off with your attitude."

"Oh, I love it when you make me feel welcome!"

She opened the door to find Mike standing outside, an interoffice envelope in his hand. "Kept the e-mails, but the journal is in here." He thrust it at her.

"Do you have a copy?"

He shook his head and lifted her off the floor. He kissed her as her legs wrapped around his waist.

"Put me down you brute, your gun is biting into my thigh!"

He laughed and lowered her. "And I thought you liked me for my big gun. What did you want to show me? I'm figuring we're having sandwiches for lunch. I'm starving so I'm hoping you can show me while we eat. And why are you angry with me?" He lowered her to the floor but didn't let her out of his grasp. One large hand reached out and brushed the hair from her forehead as he gazed into her eyes. "There were folks in the office at the time you called. I couldn't talk."

"Sandwiches are in the office," she replied, holding his gaze. She turned and he followed her into the office.

Mike sat at the desk, a mile high turkey club on his plate. She pointed to the map at his feet.

"See all those stickies?"

"Hard to miss." He said around the sandwich in his mouth.

"Pink are denied variances, green are granted, and purple are houses in foreclosure. The color combinations speak for themselves."

Mike whistled. "So, it looks like a lot of people had reason to at least be angry with Gavin Jackman."

"Yeah, and at least twelve probably hated him. Maybe even Arnie Cunningham. That's him, right there, pink and purple."

"Christ!"

Catherine waited for Mike to ask about other residents. The silence rolled on and became uncomfortable. "I guess I'm not the crappy investigator you seem to think I am." Catherine finally broke the silence. "So, any of this in the journal?"

"I never suggested you were a crappy investigator. Far from it."

"Yeah, right."

Mike put the remains of his sandwich down in his plate. "You may find this hard to believe, but I am trying to protect you." He turned his gaze away from her, toward the far window. "Something is going on here that I don't understand, and I don't want you caught in the middle."

The harsh tone of his voice had the same impact as a slap in the face. Catherine instinctively bobbed her head back. To buy time while she considered the implications of his words she said, "You never answered my question about what was in the journal."

"Most of what we read was personal, no depression, no fear, more arrogance.

"Arrogance?"

"Yeah, he reported stuff like the commission meeting, but the tone of the writing. More "me" versus them and "me" wins."

Mike leaned down and lifted the folder of minutes of the meetings. He looked at Catherine, returned the folder to the floor and said, "So what else are you looking into?"

Something in his tone made her competitive side rear up on its hind legs and back away from him. Was she opening up another new avenue for his investigation? So far, she'd only shared what she absolutely needed to. She wasn't buying the protection angle. Well, maybe, at least insofar as he was trying to keep her from becoming the number one suspect, but she was a cop once, she knew the only way to be cleared was to be considered. Did he think she lost her edge over the years? Was he using her because she had access to sources he didn't? No, that wasn't Mike, he was by the book. What then? "Nothing, I was just curious, about the variance requests." Now was not the time to tell him about the meeting with Gavin's secretary.

"Keep it that way Kit Kat. This." He waved his hand. "Is all very interesting, and irrelevant."

Her hands curled into fists at her side. She wanted to kick him – where it hurt for being so blind. But that would hurt both of them when she forgave him. And she knew she'd forgive him. First the dismissive e-mail, now this. If this man cared half as much as he pretended, he'd support her, not…not what? Or was he supporting her? He told her about the missing money. Was that the missing link? Was she looking in the wrong direction? Catherine tried and failed to separate her emotions. Mike was right. She was too close to the situation. In her experience, sometimes that could be a good thing.

* * * *

Catherine moved quickly to disobey Mike's quasi order to stand down before the situation changed. She knew that the last straw event, no matter how trivial, often triggered suicide. She couldn't shake the feeling that her call did trigger Gavin's death. Maybe Cunningham and company were right after all. Then again, who else was in the running? She needed a gossip source. The best one she could think of was Dannie. The woman collected local information like a velvet dress

117

collects lint. The curly haired Nicaraguan immigrant had a hankering for politics Latin style and since she arrived in Summer Hill, she'd wanted nothing more than to become a commissioner. If it drew breath in Summer Hill. Dannie knew about it. More than that though, she was a loyal friend, warm and loving, with ethics that could not be compromised. Catherine knew she could trust anything Dannie told her. She also knew Dannie's best qualities set her up to fail in local politics.

Would Dannie's omission from the list to fill Gavin's seat make her angry enough to point a finger?

Lacing on her running shoes, Catherine set out in a light summer drizzle to clear her mind and plot some strategy.

CHAPTER 14

The next morning dawned hot and sticky. She found herself looking forward to meeting Nancy and Gavin's ex-secretary, Rita, for lunch downtown. She slipped her feet into cool sandals, glanced at her reflection in the mirror, and walked out the door to get to her appointment.

Rita looked completely different from Catherine's idea of Gavin's secretary. She'd expected a thirty-something fashionista. Instead, she saw vanilla pudding with red hair. A woman past middle age, and built one circle on top of the other, like a snowman. The sly look in her eye and contemptuous half smile curling her lips reminded Catherine of the kinds of woman she'd met before. The one who looked out for themselves, used others to the maximum, sucked them dry and never looked back. Main-chancers she'd called them, always after the one big score at someone else's expense, and generally after someone else's husband in the bargain.

Since the lunch was Nancy's treat, she suggested The River Fish Grill a restaurant known for outside dining, great food, and reasonable prices. Rita made it clear, no al fresco for her. She wanted to sit down inside, out of the heat, with a view. In short, she wanted a pricy lunch in a "see and be seen venue" and she wanted it on her terms. The muscles in Catherine's neck tightened with frustration as the three women walked to the People Mover for the ride across the river. She shot a slant-eyed look at Nancy who responded with a shrug and a quick shake of her head. Why, Catherine wondered, didn't Rita meet them in the lobby of The Palm Towers Hotel if that's where she wanted to go? What was her reason for this trip back and forth over the river? She rolled her neck to try to ease the building tension as the trio entered the glass-encased lobby restaurant overlooking the Miami River, Rita strutting in the lead. Catherine watched in growing amazement as the redhead rejected the first two tables the maître d' lead them to, finally accepting one with a window view.

The sunlight slanted through the wine glass Rita held in front of her as she examined the color. The swirling liquid cast ruby shadows on the tablecloth. "Be glad you don't still work in that hell hole." She tipped the glass to her lips, slugged down the entire contents, and then nodded to the waiter. "It's good," and held out her glass for a fill up. "They work us to nubs, won't pay overtime and complain constantly about the quality of our jobs."

A blush the color of the wine tinged Nancy's cheeks. "Rita, law firms were always that way."

"Yeah, so they say. I work for the senior partner, and his freaking family, and his two squally kids, and still have to deal with two other shareholders and an associate, and…" She drained her glass and refilled it immediately, her glance touching on Catherine as she did. "But you are right. It's always been that way. It's been a bad day, I'm working to fix it. What's up with you?"

Nancy daubed her lips with a napkin.

"Wouldn't you know it?" Rita waved her fork toward the window of the restaurant." My ship finally comes in and I'm at lunch!"

Catherine and Nancy looked at the large yacht making its way down the Miami River. Catherine's face split in her first genuine smile since the three sat down. Rita had an agenda. There were rumors that the firm was closing. Could part of her exit strategy be cutting a deal by leaking the Affidavit? Was she smart enough to use the release of old news as her opening salvo? How much was the rest of her information worth to the firm? Or did they call her bluff?

Shading her eyes against the glare, Catherine said, "I love the way the sun hits the water. Looks like diamonds."

"You better have diamonds if you own that boat." Rita replied.

"Rita." Nancy cleared her throat, "You mentioned some phone calls, about Gavin. Recent ones. What were they about?"

The secretary studied the bit of lettuce speared on her fork and grimaced. "Nancy, you know I can't say too much." She cut her eyes to Catherine, labeling her an outsider in the small, private, club she and Nancy shared.

Nancy's face grew hard. Catherine watched her body language change as she morphed from friend and former co-worker into the Judge's Secretary.

Wanting to avoid a scene, Catherine broke in. "Rita, I've been to the courthouse. Nobody filed a lawsuit, there's no confidentiality issue here. We all read the story. Of course, if the calls were about something else…" Catherine let her voice trail away hoping the woman would answer the unasked question.

Seeing Rita's lips narrow into a thin, tight line, Catherine tried an appeal to the woman's vanity. "You worked for Gavin for a long time. He respected and liked you. You have the inside track on so many things that might help us understand why he did what he did. The suicide, I mean. Can you tell me about him?"

Rita's lips relaxed into a slight smile. Her eyes took on the avid appearance of someone hungry to hear more about themselves. Catherine raised her hand to stem any response. "I don't want you to do, say, or tell me anything that makes you uncomfortable"

The color in Rita's cheeks nearly matched her hair. Catherine glanced over at Nancy. She didn't like it much when folks got so red in the face. Made her think she'd need to use her CPR training. Rita carefully set her fork down and nudged it into alignment with the rest of the cutlery. Her breath came in shallow gasps and she lifted her face to Nancy, "You didn't even have the decency to tell me they forced Gavin out. I won't forgive you for that. Now you want information from me. Screw you!"

Nancy reeled back. Catherine gasped and wondered about the real purpose of this meeting. She was sure Nancy said she'd heard from Rita, not called her. There had to be a payoff here someplace.

"I took the first call from that guy at the Metropolis," Rita picked up her knife and plunged it into a tomato causing it to squirt its juice on the tablecloth. "I looked like a moron. Sorry you missed the amusement of seeing me chase around trying to figure out what hell would be in the paper. All I kept thinking was how you screwed me back then. You and your senior partner boss." Her face wrinkled into an exaggerated moue and she pitched her voice several octaves higher. "Sorry, I should say the "Judge." He needs to kiss my butt that I'm not talking about him. I tried to call Gavin. Left him a message to call—"

"Did he call you?" Catherine interrupted.

Rita gave Catherine a look that made her want to duck. "No, he did not." She separated each word as if Catherine were too stupid to understand.

Rita glanced toward the entrance to the restaurant. Catherine saw a look in the woman's eyes she couldn't identify, almost glee. Following the glance, she watched the maître d', frantically look from patron to patron. A burly man at the door tried to shove him aside. The maître d' grabbed the lectern and managed to keep his footing.

Without warning, Rita pushed her chair back and strode toward the altercation. She took the burly man by the arm and led him back in the direction of the women.

The redhead's face looked triumphant. "Juan Rivera." Directing a pointed look at Nancy, she continued, "Maggie's husband."

Nancy appeared to crumble. She put a hand over her face. "Oh, God."

"Nance? What's going on?" Catherine swiveled her head between Nancy, Juan and Rita. Her body tensed and her senses went to high alert. Rivera's stance indicated trouble.

"Why the hell don't you leave my family alone?" Rivera's meaty fist slammed into the table causing cutlery and glasses to jump. Out of the corner of her eye, Catherine saw the maître de speaking into a phone. She hoped he had a hot line to security.

"Mr. Rivera…" Catherine began.

The large man wheeled on her. "I don't wanna hear no crap about money. That's past. No money. Gone, done, over." He grasped Catherine's wrist. Spotting something in his waistband, she reversed his hold and brought his arm behind his back. Her other hand patted the cell phone he wore.

"What money?" She whispered in his ear hoping he couldn't hear relief in her voice that she hadn't found a gun. "Were you blackmailing Gavin?" He moaned as she increased the pressure in response to his struggle. He might be big, but she had control. "Severance." He sputtered. "She got severance just because she worked in the files don't mean she don't get severance."

"How much severance? How long did it go on?" Catherine interrupted.

"None of your ..." His lowered brow nearly concealed his eyes. Nostrils flaring, he continued through clenched teeth, "Nobody is gonna tell me I took what wasn't mine."

Two men in dark suits approached the table interrupting Juan's reply. They sidled up to Catherine. She released her hold. Rivera lowered his eyes when he saw the men. "I'm leaving. I made a mistake." He mumbled. One of the guards raised an eyebrow to the three women. Catherine responded with a slight nod and looked at Nancy.

"Yes, a mistake." Nancy responded hastily.

The two guards each took an elbow. As they lead Juan away, he turned and glared over his shoulder. "You better pray she don't leave me."

"Can you explain how he knew we'd be here?" Catherine's fingers itched to grab Rita and shake the smirk off her face.

"I don't know. You should have asked him." Coolly picking up her purse and striding away from the table, she looked back and said, "Amazing what's in the files, isn't it. Remember me to Phil."

CHAPTER 15

The metallic taste of adrenalin filled
Catherine's mouth and she took a deep swallow
from her water glass "Well, that was interesting."
Nancy nodded. She looked miserable.
Clearly, she neither expected Juan's visit nor
recognized the man. Why had Rita told him about
the meeting? Granted the woman was angry with
Nancy, but did the anger sprout from some new
perceived affront or old jealousy.

As soon as they left the restaurant, the wet,
sticky heat of Miami enshrouded them. Catherine
blinked, blinded by the sunlight. Standing on the top
of the stairs, the two women debated the merits of
walking or taking the short track elevated people
mover to Nancy's office. Deciding the heat on the
platform would be worse than the heat of a walk,
they headed to Flagler Street on foot. Catherine's
bare feet squished in her sandals on the climb up the
courthouse steps. She blew her bangs away as she
walked through a security portal. The steel security
frames seemed almost sacrilegious in the 1920s
building.

Catherine looked up at the ceiling of the rotunda supported by restored columns featuring art deco frescos. "Magnificent. I haven't been here since the scaffolds came off." She raised her head and sniffed in the air thinking it smelled of power and old paper in equal parts. "You're lucky to work here, Nance. In here you can believe the law lives and justice can be served."

Nancy snorted. "Right, as if the law has anything to do with justice."

Eschewing the creaky old elevator, Catherine and Nancy mounted the steps to her office on the third floor. The building boasted a rabbit warren of corridors and old-time bubbled glass doors still bearing the partially scraped off gilt painted names of their original occupants. New occupants' names were on brass plaques attached by stick on tape.

Plopping into the visitor's chair, Catherine watched Nancy pick up messages, shuffle files and glance through her inbox. "What do you think, Nance? Rita contacted him?"

There were tears in Nancy's eyes when she finally looked up. Catherine rose and put her arms around her friend. "Tell me, Nance. What's up? If you know anything, you need to tell me or Phil or Mike, someone. That guy left today because we were in public. He's dangerous. If he's after you, well…" Catherine gestured to the office door. "If he came here, you'd have no place to go. You have no exit."

Drawing in a ragged breath, Nancy sifted through a large stack of files sitting next to her desk. Thumbing the tabs, she pulled out one near the bottom. Silently she handed it to Catherine. "I could lose my job for this. Hell, I could lose the ability to get any job in the law biz for this."

Catherine glanced down at the legal sized file folder she held in her hand. The peeling paper label had yellowed with age. It bore the title 'Lopez Matter – GLJ." She shot a questioning look across the desk.

"Maggie Lopez, she was a Lopez then, GLJ is Gavin. Every attorney uses three initials."

"Can I…"

"No!" You can look at it here, but it stays here. And if anyone comes to the door, you think of some way to hide that file. You're right. He's dangerous. I didn't know how dangerous."

"You told him?" Catherine breathed. "You called Maggie's husband? Why? How do you know him?"

"No. I never knew any of Maggie's family. Rita was pissed. You have to understand law firms. It's all pecking orders and the secretary status comes from the boss. Short form is - she's jealous. She thinks she should have known about the affair when it happened. What worries me is what she found on computers or in some hard file." She concentrated on her fingernail scraping the edge of a file folder on her desk. "She had to get information from somewhere," she mumbled.

Nancy's eyes didn't rise to meet her friends. Spots of high color appeared on her cheeks and she continued, "Phil and Gavin were friends since they were in high school together. Phil arranged Gavin's departure story. Ashley had breast cancer, Gavin wanted to be with her. Rita came back and the firm reassigned her. To two junior associates. Those phone calls she says she got from someone at the paper before Gavin died. God knows what anger they dredged up."

It didn't sound like much to Catherine, but Nancy was right. The politics of a law firm were a mystery to her. From what little she knew, Phil had the clout to force the firm to march lockstep with Gavin's departure cover story. Hell, it even managed to make him sympathetic.

"Could she kill Gavin?"

"I don't know. She was embarrassed."

"What is it with law firms and embarrassment? Do they have some kind of course in law school? Death by embarrassment? I don't get it!"

"You gotta be there. Anyway, the information about this is available if you know how to look, and you have the right password. That's how you get this file."

"Does she? Have the right password?"

"I don't know. She works for the senior partner now. A guy also rumored to have had a fling with a file clerk. If there's another Affidavit out there, well…"

Catherine read the file in silence, wondering what other cover-ups might exist. "I feel sorry for him."

"Who, Gavin?"

Nodding, she handed the file back to her friend. "Yeah, it's pretty clear he didn't know her age. Essentially, the partners railroaded him. One big problem though. The only address in here is her parents' house. If Rita called Juan, she didn't get the information from here. I wonder where Maggie lives now?"

Catherine watched Nancy, reading her face as she considered and discarded various options. Nancy needed to make this decision on her own. Catherine didn't want to pressure her. Nancy went into the Judge's chambers. She came out and thrust a slip of paper at Catherine.

"Phil said you could give me information?" Disbelief sounded loudly to Catherine's own ears.

"He's not here today. He has access to probation files. I used it to get Tomas's probation information. It lists family info."

"Redlands, this address is in the Redlands. That's high priced real estate. Someone is doing well if they can afford a Redlands address." Catherine said. She walked behind Nancy, squatted down and picked up the file folder she'd replaced. "The old address is Little Havana, just off Calle Ocho, judging by the house number."

"All these years," Nancy said, "and I still can't get used to hearing Eighth Street in Spanish."

"Nancy, where'd they move the recording office? I want to get a Deed history on Maggie's old house, There may be a trail. Do you think Rita would bother doing the legwork?"

Nancy looked up at her friend. "I gotta tell you, the Rita who showed up at lunch bore no resemblance to the Rita I knew. I don't know how far she'd go."

CHAPTER 16

"Yah, Mike, what's up?" Catherine whispered into her cell phone, wincing as she realized she sat right under one of the Public Records Recording Office's no cell phone signs. Despite the air conditioning, beads of sweat moistened her forehead. She held her silence, using the time to gather her thoughts after he finished reading. The preliminary autopsy report made it clear. Gavin was alive when the knot on the noose tightened and strangled him to death. Catherine shuddered at the thought. She squeezed her eyes shut to close out the image of his death

"So it was suicide."

"Probably not, Catherine." Mike responded. "There were signs of oxygen deprivation in his brain before he died. Small bleeds.

"Well, he hung himself, that's reasonable. There were ligature marks?"

The scrape of a beard in her ear told her Mike nodded his agreement. "Yeah they were there too. But these were different. More like choking. The bruising was straight across the front of the neck. And there was that bruise on his skull, no broken skin, but some swelling. Odds are he was either unconscious or too dazed to fight back."

The stuff the tech mentioned. The stuff the Paysons knew about. A chill that didn't come from the air conditioning passed over her. "Why are you telling me this?" She breathed into the phone. Silence so deep she thought he hung up on her greeted her question. After a few beats, his voice sounded softly in her ear.

"It's the only way I know to protect you."

The spasm that shook her fingers as the multiple implications of his words sunk in nearly made her drop the phone. "Then you think it was murder." Bile rose to the back of Catherine's throat. Someone hated Gavin Jackman enough to murder him, and the police lost precious time concentrating on their suicide theory.

"Looks that way. Report's not final, tox screen still outstanding. Either way, official manner of death on the ME's report has to be listed as undetermined."

"Official? The Death Certificate will show the manner to death as undetermined?"

"Kit Kat. Nothing is official until it's filed, but what else?"

What else was; Billy had to let up on his surveillance. What else was Cunningham couldn't implicate her for driving Gavin to suicide anymore. What else was somebody she might know was a murderer. What else was somebody Gavin Jackman knew was a murderer. What else was...What else was also she could no longer deny were Mike's feelings for her. Sharing this news could be job ending for him. Damn him, she wasn't ready for him to care this much. She wasn't ready to care back that much.

Frustration made her dig deeper into the records. Her chest tightened with excitement when she discovered the trail she sought. Maggie sold her parents' house after her mother died. Juan joined in the Deed. So, they were married then, but the Deed had no seller's addresses. Two hundred Juan Rivera's came up when she searched under that name. No Maggie Rivera owned property in the county. Acid burned in Catherine's stomach. Then she keyed in Magalie Lopez. Bingo, Magalie Lopez and Juan Rivera owned a home in the Redlands. Catherine scribbled down the address, compared it to the one Nancy gave her, and pulled her car keys out of her pocket glad that she'd moved her car from the Courthouse parking lot where she'd left it when she met Nancy for lunch.

She stared at the blank computer screen for a few more minutes wondering if she had missed anything. She plugged Maggie's brother, Tomas Lopez's name into the Public Records search engine and found nothing. Then she plugged in Gavin's name. He had three mortgages on his house. Pulling up the recorded documents, she discovered two of the mortgages were the 'interest only" variety. She printed the financial information pages and scanned them hoping for some insight. The mortgages were due to balloon. Did Gavin have mortgage insurance that would pay if he died? She couldn't find a record. The last recorded item startled her. It was a

Promissory Note. Gavin loaned Hank Simms $50,000. The due date was last month. Did this explain the $50,000 deposit record she'd found stuffed in the bottom of the envelope Ashley gave her?

Catherine felt isolated. She wanted to call someone, share the information and her intention to interview Maggie, but she couldn't involve anyone else. Nancy and Mike would both veto the idea. She briefly considered calling Ashley, trying to find out about the mortgages and Promissory Note. Her heart went out to her. Ashley might be relieved of the survivor guilt of Gavin's suicide, but she probably faced the scrutiny of being considered a murder suspect. Or did she? What did the ballooning mortgages say about Gavin's death? Could it have been a suicide after all? Catherine shook her head. No, don't go down that road again. Not after Mike's call. It's a dead horse.

Now that she had a few minutes to think about it, her removal from the suspect list felt good. She doubted even Arnie Cunningham could be sufficiently paranoid to believe she killed Gavin by simultaneously holding, hitting, and hanging him. Argued with him, maybe, fought with him, well, Cunningham could believe that too, but killed him. Nope. Not likely. Unless Cunningham was covering for himself. Damn Cunningham, that was a thought.

* * *

During the drive to the Redlands, Catherine tried to plan her strategy. Despite the tension twisting her stomach into knots, she enjoyed the scenery. The Redlands represented the last remaining bastion of country left in South Florida. Gentleman farms dotted the landscape. Idly, Catherine wondered how Maggie and Juan afforded the neighborhood. Juan hadn't looked too prosperous.

Catherine checked the address again. She could hardly believe her eyes. In the midst of the surrounding luxury, she stared at a tiny house that looked like it had started life as a trailer. She judged the fenced area at about a half-acre, huge by Miami standards, tiny for the Redlands. Children's toys littered the weedy front yard. A propane tank and old style metal children's swing set decorated the backyard. Given current area zoning, she knew the Riveras were stuck. They didn't have enough land to tear down and re-build. Selling to a neighbor represented their only hope of recouping the investment.

Catherine left her car parked on the grass in front of the neighbor's house. Good, no car, Juan's probably not here. She approached the house cautiously hearing the sound of playing children through the open windows. Someone was home. She offered up a silent prayer that she'd find Maggie, not her brother Tomas or a babysitter.

The door flung open before she knocked. "Hi there, little guy." Catherine said to the child on the other side. He looked about two years old. His diaper sagged dangerously under the weight of what smelled like a full load. Catherine struggled not to wrinkle her nose.

"Carlito, get over here, now." A woman's voice called from inside. "I don't have the strength to chase you… Oh, I'm sorry," The woman stopped short and wiped sweat off her forehead with the back of her arm. "Can I help you?"

Catherine forced herself to put her hand down to restrain young Carlito before he could bolt out the door. She only hoped his body wasn't as dirty as his diaper. "Hi, Maggie," Catherine directed the child into his mother's waiting hands. "I'm Catherine Swope. If you have a minute, I'd like to talk to you about Gavin Jackman."

The woman grabbed the child. "I don't have anything to say."

Before Maggie could slam the door in her face, Catherine inserted her foot. "Just for a few seconds. I'm not a cop. I'm a friend of Gavin's, and I'm trying to understand what happened. Five years ago and now."

Maggie seemed to briefly consider her options, glance around her, and then sag visibly. She turned and walked away from the door taking the soiled child with her. "Got kids?" She asked.

Catherine followed her into the house. "No." Two other children followed her progress from in front of the living room couch. Toys, in various states of disrepair, seemed to cover every surface.

The woman laughed bitterly, "At two you either have them trained or they try to hold on to everything, and I mean everything. I'll be right back, have a seat in the kitchen. It will be nice to talk to an adult for a change."

While she waited for Maggie to finish with the child, she looked around the room. An old Formica table, probably worth more than the house given the retro craze, sat in the far end of the kitchen. Cupboards many decorated with decals, lined the far wall. In contrast to the rest of the house, the kitchen appeared spotless.

Maggie wore a long sleeve shirt when she returned to the kitchen. The house had no air conditioning. Or if it did, Maggie didn't use it. Refusing an offer of coffee, Catherine said, "I know you worked for Gavin, and I guess I, and most of Miami, know you had an affair with him."

Maggie leaned back in her chair. Her eyes took on a far-away look. "Everything seemed possible then. It only happened once. I'd gone to him for help, my mother; she had problems, one thing led to another, Stupid, stupid, stupid." Maggie shook her head.

"How did you get caught?"

"I never really knew for sure." Maggie unconsciously pushed up her long sleeves revealing faint bruises on her forearms. "I think someone saw us. That's what Gavin said. I know those lawyers watched me like a hawk after that. And the office administrator." Maggie rolled her eyes. "Every time I turned around, she was behind me. I kept the job for another two months, 'till I graduated from High School. I got credits for it, easier than going to class." Looking down at her arms, Maggie shrugged. "Kids, it's amazing I haven't broken something chasing after them."

Catherine studied Maggie's face carefully. She noticed concealer covering one side of her face extending to beneath her eye. Taking a deep breath, she held her silence and waited for the younger woman to fill it.

Maggie stood up, opened the refrigerator and pulled out some chicken. She busied herself chopping an onion and mixing marinade. When she turned back to Catherine, her eyes were red.

"Did your husband know about Gavin?" Catherine broke her silence.

"No, not then. We were dating, back then. My brother Tomas told him. My husband…"

"Maggie, if he's hurting you…" Catherine held up her hand to stop the protest forming on Maggie's lips. "There's help, Maggie." Catherine's voice broke unexpectedly. "You can be safe."

Large tears rolled down Maggie's face leaving concealer free streaks on her bruised cheeks. "Oh God, you don't understand."

"What are you teaching your kids if you put up with violence?" Catherine stood, crossed the room and grasped Maggie's hand in her own. "Get help. If he harms you, he can harm his children."

"No, it's not like that."

Catherine looked down at her hand, uncertain what solace she could offer the crying woman. She hugged her tightly and released her. Maggie sobbed, tears flowing freely down her face. "It's Tomas, not Juan. Tomas knew. I told Tomas, we were close, then, still are. He's my big brother." Maggie sobbed harder. "After I left the firm, he called Mr. Jackman. He wanted money."

"Did Gavin pay?" Catherine asked.

"I think so, but I think he stopped when Tomas went to jail. He's out now." Her voice rose to a high keen "But that's not what I mean. Tomas did this, not falling, not the door, not Juan. Tomas. Because I wouldn't call Mr. Jackman for him. But he's my brother."

Catherine drew in a sharp breath. It all made sense, Tomas called Phil. To find out information about Gavin, or did he already know of Phil's authorship of the Affidavit. Did he threaten him? Try to blackmail him? Had Tomas managed to find Gavin, threatened the release of the Affidavit to embarrass him, and force him to restart the payments? Given Gavin's money problems, he may have decided to play the odds that either Tomas was bluffing, a story that old wouldn't interest the paper. Did Tomas or Juan confront Gavin after the story hit the paper? A confrontation that got out of hand?

Maggie wiped her eyes with the back of her hand further smearing her makeup. "You have to go. Juan will be home soon."

"And your brother? Does your husband know what he did to you?"

Maggie shook her head. "No," she whispered, "Juan would kill him. I told him I took the kids out on the bikes near the canal and I fell."

"He believed that?"

Maggie shrugged and looked at the clock. "Maybe." She whispered. "I've always been clumsy."

"Is Tomas staying here?"

"Sometimes. He..."A look of panic crossed Maggie's face as she heard a car door slam.

Catherine glanced out the window to see a new model compact car parked outside and Juan

139

striding toward the door. Maggie had the look of a cornered animal.

"Oh, God," she moaned. "You have to leave now. He can't find you here." She tried to shove Catherine out the back door as the sound of the front door slamming open echoed in the small kitchen.

Juan started to close the distance between the living room and the kitchen. Catherine felt impaled by his eyes. "You bitch. What are you doing here?" He lunged for Catherine.

CHAPTER 17

Heart pounding, Catherine groped a slippery palm for the knob behind her back. Torn between defending Maggie and escaping, Maggie managed to intercept Juan before he entered the kitchen.

"Let her go." She screamed. Juan pushed his wife out of his way and continued for the rear door. Maggie's interception bought Catherine enough time to turn the knob and open the door. Maggie reeled against the wall. Catherine reconsidered her decision that Maggie was in less danger if she left. Before she could retrace her steps and in the split second before Juan gained the door, Catherine saw him turn his head and return to his wife. Through the open door she heard him cry out, "Mags, oh Mags, I'm sorry."

Catherine raced for her car. Juan had a nasty temper, but after hearing the concern in his voice, she couldn't see him hurting his wife. She felt grateful for that at least. He seemed genuinely concerned. Did he know about Tomas's abuse? Did he believe Maggie's excuse? Where did all of this

141

fit with the divorce Tomas told Phil about? Was Thomas shaking Phil down?

# # #

Rush hour traffic slowed to a halt near the airport. Catherine drummed her fingers on the steering wheel willing it to clear. Sun devils danced on the pavement between the bumper-to-bumper lanes. She tipped the air conditioning ducts directing the outflow to her face.

She didn't have any client dogs to walk tonight, but at this rate, Bullet would have his legs crossed by the time she got home. She fumbled in her handbag for her cell phone. Not finding it she groped carefully under the seat. Then she remembered. She'd tossed it in the glove box before she'd left the car at Maggie's. She hadn't wanted to risk any interruptions.

"Damn," Catherine said aloud. She glanced at the display before she dialed and saw the message symbol flashing. Pushing the message button, she heard Mike's voice. 'The State auditor can't account for approximately one million dollars. Rumor is some Village money ended up in Gavin's accounts.'

Mike's hunch was right. A million dollars was a lot of motive. Who could have known about the theft, and the deposit? How had the Paysons' heard? Or had they heard. Chris and the mayor didn't have to be discussing Village money. Yeah, sure, Catherine, and maybe Gavin loaned Chris money and then again, pigs could fly. A mental image of Chris's face on a flying pig tickled her funny bone and she smiled. Could Cunningham be

involved too? A way to save his house? Pay Gavin
back? Frustration that Mike was sharing this
information so freely twisted in her chest. As fast as
the thought reared its head, Catherine shoved it
down.

Her car crept along at less than five miles an
hour, but her brain was flying. Was Gavin a
scapegoat in the story? He was conveniently dead,
and he couldn't defend himself, from a charge of
embezzlement. Catherine's nose itched violently.
Find out who had the most to gain, and lose. That's
what Mike should be doing. Why Gavin? Could he
have taken money without Cunningham knowing
about it? Possible. Without Hank Simms knowing?
Impossible.

Hank Simms. Catherine rolled over what
little she knew of the man in her mind. Recently
divorced, it was rumored his wife took him for a
bundle leaving him little more than the mortgaged-
to-the-roofline house he lived in. Did he get a loan
from Gavin too? Odd that Simms managed to keep
such a low profile in a town of gossips. He'd been
on the commission as long as Catherine lived in
Summer Hill.

The information she'd uncovered about
Cunningham's foreclosure put him in the running
for embezzlement. Then again, Gavin was in similar
straits. But did Cunningham know? What Catherine
couldn't figure out was why either Cunningham or
Simms would want to kill Gavin. Unless he
discovered the theft. As an ex-lawyer, would he feel
a need to blow the whistle? Or had he participated

in it and got scruples at the last minute. They all needed cash.

Holding the phone in her hand and tapping it against the steering wheel, she debated calling Mike immediately, both for information and to walk Bullet. Deciding he'd said all he would on the phone and not wanting to answer his questions herself, she called Nancy for the favor and briefed her quickly about the meeting with Maggie.

By the time she got home, Catherine wanted dinner and a bath and not necessarily in that order. The heady scent of basil and garlic greeted her as soon as she opened the door. Nancy, wrapped in an apron came around the corner from the kitchen.

"Hey there, girl. I made dinner. Now I want details for my trouble. Speak!" Bullet barked at the command and the two friends laughed. Nodding her head in the direction of the back yard Nancy continued, "He's outside, I took him for a nice long walk. Boy is the neighborhood buzzing."

Catherine raised a questioning eyebrow.

"The usual Village gossip. Gavin's murder, you and Ashley lead the pack for suspects."

"What! Me! How did I get included? How did word get out so fast?"

"You doubt the grapevine now! What did you expect? Susan called me today, so did Dannie, Meg called her." Nancy licked sauce from her thumb. "You and Ashley were friendly before, now you're buddy-buddy. That translates into guilt. You're trying to keep on top of the evidence so you can frame someone else. And don't forget." She wagged a wooden spoon at her, "You found the body!"

Catherine shook her head in disbelief.

"Yeah, amazing. The CSI effect. What happened to the suicide theory everyone loved" Not for the first time, Catherine wondered who the hell was leaking information, and why. What did someone have to gain, or hide? It had to be someone on the Commission. "The tox screens still aren't in." Kicking off her shoes, she made her way to the kitchen and opened the fridge. She scanned the contents, pulled out a wine bottle and held it aloft. "Want some?" Nancy held out her glass for a refill. "What else is on the Village telegraph?"

Sipping deeply, Nancy dropped pasta into the boiling water. "Don't you want to know how you did it?" She asked.

"No. I can make up my own fantasies."

Nancy shrugged and tapped a spoon on the side of the pot. "Ok, let's see, what else. Someone's starting a petition to recall Susan. They plan to bring it up at the next Commission meeting. Meg wondered if she could buy Ashley's potter's wheel instead of buying a new one for the studio she wants. Dannie's angry she hasn't been included in the nominations for Gavin's seat. Someone else wants to bring up speeding and traffic problems again. With Gavin gone it seems some people think maybe the Commission will vote to close some roads. Do you need more?"

Catherine groaned. "No, I get the picture. Any idea who the 'some ones' are? Never mind, it doesn't matter. Let's eat. We can solve the problems of the world later."

After Nancy left, Catherine took her coffee out to the back porch. The air was heavy with humidity and heat lightening played across the sky rolling among the black clouds illuminating their edges like the tips of angel wings. She hadn't wanted to share Mike's news with Nancy. Not yet anyway, not until she had the full story. Walking into the kitchen, she reached for the phone to call Mike and noticed the message light flashing.

Cursing under her breath, she dialed the voice mail number and waited for the message to begin. Ashley couldn't get anyone to cover the Russian Ballet's premier performance. She'd gone to work hoping to take her mind off Gavin's death. Could Catherine look after Roscoe? Catherine rolled her neck to ease the tension. The story sounded weird to her but then, everyone deals with grief differently. She looked at the clock. After ten, Ashley wouldn't be home for a few more hours. The message time stamp said she'd called around three in the afternoon, the same time Catherine was in the Redlands at Maggie's.

Catherine pulled on her sneakers, grabbed her cell phone and headed out the door. She hadn't gotten to the end of her walkway when thunder sounded and the sky opened up, letting loose a full-fledged summer gully washer. Racing for her door she called Bullet in from the backyard, fastened the dog door, pulled her raincoat off its peg and headed back out to rescue Roscoe.

The puddles squished beneath her sneakers. Water ran between her toes and Catherine wished she'd changed to rain boots. She struggled to lift the water soaked flowerpot to pull out the key; glad Ashley hadn't moved it after Gavin's death. Through the door she heard Roscoe whining. Poor puppy, he needed a walk and dinner.

She leashed the dog and led him into the storm. Rain beat so hard against her face that she pulled her head as far back into the hood as she could get it. Lacking sidewalks, she walked the dog along the grass swale side of the road through the driving rain. He startled and pulled with each thunder crash. Catherine tried to coax him into doing his business, but as soon as he'd begin to circle thunder broke his concentration. Trudging through ankle deep puddles, Catherine decided to head the dog in the direction of home. Maybe the storm would abate after she fed him. Through the pounding of the rain and the crashing of the thunder, Catherine heard the sucking noise of tires on wet road approaching from behind. To avoid the inevitable splash when the car stopped at the intersection, Catherine pulled the dog further onto the grass. Even in rain this bad, the stripes on her reflective jacket would be visible.

Catherine couldn't believe her ears, rather than slowing for the stop sign, the car sounded like it was accelerating. She tried to turn her head to get a better look. Her hood, the headlights and the driving rain obscured her vision. She screamed as the car veered off the road, aiming directly for her, and Roscoe. Acting instinctively, she threw herself onto the wet grass, pulled the wet dog off his feet and rolled with him away from the danger. She lifted her head and looked over her shoulder. The car, headlights dark, missed her by inches, sped past the stop sign and continued south.

In the dark and the rain, Catherine couldn't get a good description. Pulling herself up off the dog, she fished in her inside pocket for her cell phone. Her hands trembled as she punched in Mike's home number. It took all of her control to tell him what happened without breaking into sobs. She finally agreed to take Roscoe to Ashley's and wait for Mike there. Rising, she tried to wipe the mud off her legs. Feeling a tug on the leash, she saw Roscoe circle and successfully complete his business. "So," she muttered, "it scared it out of you!"

Through the torrent, Catherine saw Mike pull up at Ashley's house. She hoped the rain streaming down her face from her saturated hair would help hide her tears. Mike held her off at arm's length and stared deeply into her eyes before he pulled her close into a tight hug. He took the key from her hand and opened the door. "Are you all right?"

Catherine felt herself slump against him. "I think so. I don't know. Adrenaline is still pumping." She winced as she leaned down to unhook Roscoe's leash. Freeing the dog with one hand she rubbed her hip with the other. "I must have landed on something. Boy, this is tender."

"Hospital tender?

She shook her head. "No, big, black, bruise tender."

Mike shoved his pocket notebook and a pen into her hand. "Write down everything you remember. I'll take care of feeding Roscoe."

She opened her mouth to protest. The look on his face told her not to bother. Unzipping her raincoat, she took a seat in the breakfast room and started to write. She was so engrossed that the sound of Ashley's greeting caused her to emit a squeaky scream. She looked up sheepishly, embarrassed by her reaction and tossed the little notebook to Mike. "It's no good. Between the rain, the dark and the headlights going off and on, I didn't see enough. All I'm sure of is the car was compact. No color, no tag, no make, no model, not even a basic description of the driver, I don't know if it was a male or a female."

"What happened?" Ashley asked. A hint of hysteria in her voice.

Not wanting to upset the woman further Catherine said, "Are you all right, Ashley? Today must have been horrible for you. It's too soon for you to go back to work."

Ashley sighed, folded herself into the chair next to Catherine and lit a cigarette. "I've had better. I don't get it, Catherine. Why in God's name would someone want to kill Gavin?" She lay her head back against the headrest and stared at the ceiling. "I don't understand," she whispered.

Catherine sucked in her breath, so someone did get in touch with Ashley. Before or after she went to the ballet?

149

Taking a deep drag, she continued, "I've spent the whole afternoon trying to move fast enough to outrun that question." Tears stood out in Ashley's eyes as she looked from Catherine to Mike. "Catherine, I'm sorry. I appreciate what you did, but can I ask you and Mike to leave?"

Trying not to limp as she walked to the door, Catherine hugged Ashley and followed Mike to his pickup. She struggled to lift herself up on the running board and into the seat. Mike came around, and lifted her in. His lips brushed hers as he reached around her to fasten the seatbelt. She threw her arms around him and kissed him hard. "Thanks, sailor." She quipped. "I needed that."

Mike settled himself into the seat next to her and started the engine. He left the car in park and looked at her in the dim light of the dashboard. "It could have been an accident you know. The rain, wet roads, the car could have hit a puddle and gone into a skid."

"It's cleared up. Let's go see what the tire tracks look like."

Mike parked on the roadway not wanting to compromise any evidence. He shone his light down on the grass next to the pavement.

If the car had skidded, Catherine knew wet roadway wouldn't hold marks, grass and mud might.

"Here it is." He said.

Catherine climbed painfully down from the passenger side and hobbled over to where Mike squatted. The mud held deep gouges. "Small tire tread. This looks pretty controlled to me."

She tapped his shoulder. "How do you explain the lights on and off if it wasn't deliberate?"

Mike's eyes seemed to soften when he looked up. "Catherine, you know as well as I do they could have hit the smart stick struggling to regain control of the car. Either that or your mind could have been playing tricks in the rain and dark."

"Do you believe that?" She asked quietly.

Mike straightened, switched off the flashlight, lifted Catherine in his arms and took her back to the passenger seat. He climbed into the driver's seat and turned to look at her. "No. I don't believe that. I don't think you were targeted either. I do think someone tried to scare you. Catherine, I'm staying the night tonight."

"No, Mike. Thanks for the vote of confidence. I have Bullet. If it was deliberate, it was opportunistic. No one, me included, knew I'd be taking Roscoe for a walk tonight."

"Except Ashley." He said.

CHAPTER 18

Catherine kissed Mike good night, then closed and double locked her front door behind him. He had checked the house and back yard as soon as they came in. So why did she feel so uneasy now that he was gone. Laying in her bath, she jumped every time the air conditioner cycled on. Finally giving up the attempt to soak her troubles away, Catherine climbed out of the tub and toweled off.

Bullet, sensing her discomfort, padded along at her side. Catherine finally went to her bedroom, opened her nightstand drawer, removed her Glock and headed for the enclosed back porch.

She opened the doggie door to let Bullet into the yard and despite the air conditioning, opened a window to let in the sweet scent of the angel trumpet plant. She took a deep breath of the heavy night air, then shut the window and flipped the locks closed. Still uncomfortable, she sat at the porch table, positioned the weapon in front of her and stared at it. She hated guns. Always had. Even in the days she wore one strapped at her hip. As far as she was concerned, they were a means to an end.

A necessary evil of her prior job. Rage bubbled through her at the thought that she had to consider arming herself again. It felt like a huge violation. Picking up the weapon, she held it in her right hand, and with her left pulled sharply back on the slide and watched a round snap cleanly into the chamber. Maybe she should go back to selling real estate. It seemed safer.

The attempted hit and run drove questions she wanted to ask Mike out of her mind. Now she wished he had stayed. She wanted to think about something else.

      * * *

The morning dawned hot and steamy. Catherine grimaced as she swung her legs out of bed. Lifting the tee shirt she'd slept in, she looked at her hip. The bruise had deepened to a purple so dark it almost looked black. She took a fist full of Bullet's scruff in her hand and used his bulk to pull herself to a standing position. Keeping her hand on the dog's neck, she took a step, giving the bruised leg her weight. The pain didn't seem too bad.

"Well, old boy, it doesn't look like we're running this morning. How about taking a nice long walk after mom showers to work the kinks out of mom's battered body?"

Dressed in loose running clothes, she grabbed Bullet's leash and her camera. She retraced her route from the night before wanting to take photos of any evidence the rain might have left. Mike's remark about Ashley knowing she'd be walking Roscoe upset her. The more she thought about it, the more sense it made. The timing threw her. She usually walked Roscoe earlier, but if Ashley were watching, it was possible for her to pull off the hit and run. What car did Ashley have last night? Had Ashley been involved in Gavin's death? Even if she had been, Catherine couldn't figure out why she'd try to hurt her, or Roscoe.

As she rounded the corner and approached the median where the accident happened, Catherine spotted her friend Dannie talking with Meg and Susan. The three women gathered near where Catherine remembered the tire tracks should be.

"Hey, what's with the limp?" Dannie asked. She gave her friend a hug. "You feel all right?"

Catherine nodded and looked at the ground under her feet, trying to make out a clear impression of the tire marks. "I'm fine. Got tangled in a dog leash and fell. I'm just a little sore."

"People drive like crazies around here. Especially in bad storms." Meg said. "Someone should do something about it. A little traffic enforcement maybe? Instead of worrying about paint colors."

Susan rolled her eyes. "How's the septic construction coming along?" She asked Meg.

"It's a mess. We're going to move it from the back yard to the front. We have the permits for it. Don't worry."

"When did you get those?" Susan asked. "I haven't seen them. I figured you were doing emergency work, and you'd apply as soon as you had firm plans."

Meg blushed deeply. "Oh, we got them before, for the pool house. I'm thinking we'll pour a

slab out back for a patio. I'd love to do some tiles for the patio. Does Ashley have a kiln too?"
Turning her attention to Catherine she said, "What do you think about the murder theory?"

Weighing her words carefully, uncertain if Meg sought Mike's information Catherine responded, "I thought it was suicide. I'm not sure the police are looking in the right direction if they think something else."

"I'm sure there's no doubt now. Thom told Oliver they're going to arrest Ashley. Did you hear, Gavin was ready to file for divorce before he died?

Dannie's sharp intake of breath caused the three women to look in her direction. "Thom told Oliver? Thom the Police Commissioner told Oliver? Why?"

Susan shot a hand out to grab Dannie's arm. "Dannie. Let it go, it's gossip."

"Gossip!" Meg hissed. "I don't think so. Things are going to be changing around here. And I mean for the better. You wait and see." Meg stalked down the street toward her house.

"Whoa, what was that all about?" Catherine asked. Dannie shrugged, but looked embarrassed. "Her knickers are in a knot. Her hubby's not commissioner yet. And I might be." She bared her teeth in a tight smile. "If the gods are good."

I'm mosquito bait standing here." Susan said, swatting at a buzzing insect. "Let's walk."

"Suze, what's going on?" Catherine asked again.

"I'm what's going on," Dannie said. "And Susan. Meg's pissed that I'm giving her, and the rest of them, a run for their money."

"How does that involve Susan?"

"Cunningham put me on probation. Any more complaints from anyone, and I'm out."

Catherine jerked to a stop. "What? That's stupid. Your job practically requires people to complain about you."

"That's politics" She shrugged." Well, I gotta go. Gotta annoy more people before they fire me. Talk to you later."

"Congrats Dannie on making the list. How will they choose Gavin's successor?"

"A debate and some open discussion. Then the commissioners choose the interim. How did you really fall?"

"Like I said, I got tangled up."

Catherine left Dannie in front of the younger woman's house and walked Bullet back in the direction of the tire marks. The thick grass now obscured whatever the footprints had left intact. Not two feet away from the end of the flattened grass stood a brass sprinkler head. Just looking at it made Catherine's hip throb.

Catherine slowly walked her dog back home. As she turned onto her street, she saw a patrol car sat in front of her house. Her heart pounding she ran as best she could toward her front porch. As she drew closer, she heard her burglar alarm wailing. Forgetting her pain, she sprinted toward the door. Racing into the house, she unclipped Bullet's leash allowing him to run ahead of her. Catherine veered off toward the hallway to check the alarm control panel.

"Mike! What's the zone number? Where's the breach? How did you know?" Catherine called out, seeing him in front of the panel.

The tall man turned and faced her, pink colored his cheeks. "I forgot the code. What's the code? I let myself in. Damn, I'll get the phone, it's gotta be the alarm company. You turn off the noise before someone calls the cops."

Catherine heard Mike give the code word to the caller as she punched in the numbers and silenced the alarm. Laughing, she joined Mike in the kitchen. "It's your birthday, idiot."

"No, not for a couple of..." He smacked himself on the forehead. "And I punched yours in. Twice!"

"And for the record, you are the cops!"

She poured and held out a cup of coffee to him. He took it, put it on the counter and held her at arm's length. "How's the hip?"

"Stiff, sore, but I'll live. I landed on a sprinkler." She sat at the kitchen table. "I'm scared, for you. Cunningham is out to get me. You're an easy way for him to do it. What I don't get is why he wants me so bad. What did I ever do to him?"

Mike pulled out the kitchen chair and turned it backwards to straddle it. Catherine hated the posture. She knew he did it when he wanted to hide something. He must have seen the look on her face. He rose and reversed the chair. Sitting at the table, he cradled the coffee mug between his hands and blew over the top. "You look good for it. You and Ashley."

"My motive?"

"Rage."

"What happened to the suicide theory? I don't buy the story in the paper as motive either."

"Won't fly with the ME. Not with the blow to the head. Not without more evidence."

"You said the investigation was still open."

Nodding, he took a sip of his coffee. "You think he hit himself in the head, then jumped up to pull the noose over his head and was killed by the drop? Come on Catherine. Think!"

"You think. Who says I was the first in that garage? Anyone could have moved a chair."

"So, there was a chair?"

Catherine stood and strode across the room. "You know what I mean Mike! Don't play cop with me!"

"Occupational hazard."

Mike came up behind and wrapped his arms around Catherine. She felt herself stiffen at the contact.

"He never clawed at the rope. He had to be out when they hung him."

"They? Did you see someone else there, Mike?"

He spun her around. "No, but I can't see one person doing it."

"Not unless he did it himself. He broke his neck. You told me that yourself."

"It's an investigation, Catherine. That's why it's called an investigation. We'll know in the end."

She pulled away from his grasp and sat down again. Picking up her own mug she held it in both hands and pressed the warm pottery to her forehead. Mike sat across from her. She read caution in his eyes.

"You're not the only one on the rage motive list."

"Ashley?"

"Yeah, and for the kid in the Affidavit, and for half the village, and for anyone else he had an affair with."

"My, my, my. I'm glad to see you're narrowing the suspect pool. What about the missing money? That should add a few more names."

Mike blanched. "Catherine, don't tell anyone about money missing." He placed a hand on each of her shoulders. "No one. Do you hear me?"

"It could be a motive if Gavin's involved."

"How?"

"It could tie to the affidavit, Mike." Catherine's fingers folded her lower lip and tucked it behind her top teeth.

"I can see your thinking pose, but I can't follow your thoughts."

"Maggie's brother blackmailed Gavin, and Gavin paid." She looked at Mike. He wore his expressionless cop face. Debating whether to continue she took a deep breath and told him about her visit to Maggie's house the day before. Mike listened, pulled out his notebook and began asking questions.

"What kind of car does Juan drive?"

Catherine slammed down her coffee mug with enough intensity to spill some of the liquid. "A compact Japanese job," she said. Her mind flashed back to the small car that tried to run her over.

"Do you think…"she began. "No, how would he know I'd be walking a dog."

"Maybe he didn't, maybe it was dumb luck. I'm going to turn this information over. I have to." Mike looked down at the table and tapped his pencil against his notebook. "I've been taken off the investigation."

"What!" She exploded. "You're the lieutenant. They can't take you off the investigation!"

"They can, and they did. Thom convinced Chief I might be tainted. I'm off the investigation and at a desk for the duration."

Catherine felt her stomach fall to her knees. This could ruin him, and it was her fault. She got up and stood behind him, massaging his neck. "I'm sorry." She whispered.

"Yeah, me too." He shrugged. "Someone targeted you last night. I think you know something you don't realize you know. I don't think outsiders are involved."

"Ashley?"

"She had motive, means and opportunity, both with Gavin and your accident last night."

Catherine turned the idea over in her mind. It didn't feel right.

"No. She'd never hurt Roscoe."

She studied his face, looking for a clue to his real feelings. Was he on a fishing expedition? "Did you hear Gavin was ready to file for divorce?

He drew his head back as if she slapped him. "No way."

The look on his face confirmed his surprise. What did that do to Ashley's motive?

CHAPTER 19

"Why don't you get into a hot tub after I leave? Might ease those aches." He strode across the kitchen and planted a kiss on the top of her head. "And Catherine, don't open it to anyone. I have a key. No one else needs to be here."

Catherine rolled her neck in response. "Yeah, a bath sounds like a good idea." She watched him walk around the low kitchen island where she sat and head for the front door. "Mike," she began ---.

He turned and looked at her. The subtle metamorphosis to cop had begun. Not the time to mention her feelings.

"What's up?" He asked.

"Just thanks."

He nodded, "I checked the doors and windows, and you're secure. I'll set the alarm on my way out, too."

Catherine listened to the sound of the key turning the deadbolt lock. A sense of peace came over her, and she realized she felt safer. She wondered whether it was the sound of the lock turning or the fact that Mike had a key. "Not now, Catherine girl." She mumbled to herself. "Don't confuse love and security. You did that once before."

With an effort of will, she pulled her mind from her past to the present and her aching hip. Clearly, news of Gavin's murder hit the town telegraph almost as soon as the ME's preliminary report had hit Chief's desk. Someone in a place of power had a big mouth. Where was the payoff?

There were subtle changes in the way Catherine's neighbors treated her once the news hit the street. More neighbors talked to her. They were looking for information, but at least they were talking.

Bullet dropped his head in her lap. His cold nose rested against her thigh. Catherine looked into his chocolate brown eyes and scratched him behind both ears. "I didn't realize how much I want these folks to like me, big boy. Wonder if they'll turn again when they realize Cunningham still likes me for the perp! What do you think? Did he do it? Did Aunt Ashley do it?"

The dog vigorously shook his head and Catherine laughed.. "No, me either. I'm favoring someone else. I'm liking our ex-con Tomas for the actor. You too?"

The dog yawned.

"Ok, Bullet, don't share your thoughts. Mama's going for a hot bath."

The sound of Bullet barking filtered over the whine of the hair dryer. Switching off the machine and cinching the belt of her robe tighter around her waist, she padded on bare feet to the window alongside the door. Holding her breath, Catherine lifted a corner of the curtain and peered out. Ashley, her face blotched and her eyes swollen, stood on the front steps. Ignoring Mike's advice, Catherine swung the door open wide and ushered the upset woman inside.

"Catherine, I'm so sorry for the way I behaved last night." Her voice caught in her throat nearly ending in a sob. "I, well, I'd had enough. I didn't stop to think. I felt like you and Mike were interrogating me." Ashley fished in her handbag, pulled out a crumpled tissue, daubed her eyes and rubbed the red spot under her nose. "You guys were pussycats compared to the real thing."

"You've been questioned?" Catherine asked, and led the way out to the enclosed porch stopping in the kitchen long enough to pour two coffees. Bullet raced ahead pushed open the doggie door and ran out to the back yard. Catherine lifted Paddy Whack off the loveseat and set her on the cool tile.

Ashley settled herself in the loveseat, blew on her coffee and said, "The simplest things sound so bad." Tears welled in her eyes as she looked up. "I feel, I don't know," she paused as if searching for a word, "dirty, I guess."

"Who interviewed you?"

"Chief. LaMotta took notes, I don't know why. They taped the whole thing."

Catherine turned the information over in her mind while she tried to figure out how to phrase the next question. "Did they call you to come in, or did they come for you?"

"Does it matter?" Ashley asked wearily.

Catherine opened her mouth to reply that letting her come in by herself was better as Ashley continued, "They came. Probably thought I'd be too upset to drive. Damn, what if I lose my job? LaMotta said they'd questioned my boss. They wanted to know why I decided to leave town."

"I really doubt they'll fire you for being questioned by the police." Catherine took a sip of her coffee and wondered why hot liquids in Florida's heat somehow cooled her off in the summer.

"Catherine, what if they do? I need the job." Her voice broke again.

"Do you have a lawyer? Don't talk to them again without one."

"That's what Phil says too."

"You called him??

"No. He came by after Gavin died." Ashley rolled the coffee mug between her hands and stared into it. "He wanted to see the garage for himself."

The sun slanted through the window illuminating Ashley's face. It looked ravaged. Catherine searched for a way to work the loans she'd discovered into the conversation. No opening gambit came to mind. The information was too specific. The questions seemed too cold. Right now it seemed better, kinder, to let the woman lead the conversation.

"They took Gavin's computer," Ashley said. They had a warrant. Mine too." Ashley's voice seemed flat. She'd switched almost to autopilot.

"Chief asked about the e-mails Gavin got." She looked up and met Catherine's eyes.

Wincing, Catherine understood. Reaching out to grasp Ashley's hand, Catherine said, "I'm sorry Ashley. I meant to tell you I discussed them with Mike." She searched the woman's face and saw only resignation there. "Anyone who made threats to Gavin is a suspect. They need the machines to see if they can trace the anonymous ones."

"My machine?"

"To eliminate you."

Ashley opened her handbag again and pulled out some paper. Carefully smoothing out the folds, she pushed the sheets across to Catherine. "I found these this morning in the workshop. I don't know what they mean. Do whatever you want with them."

Catherine looked down at e-mailed deposit advice confirmations.

"These for your account?"

"No. Gavin's. I found a file with bank records for a personal account I never knew about." She blushed bright red. "Maybe our marriage was tanking, I don't know. I didn't think so. Believe me. The bank won't let me touch the money because he's dead."

"Two fifty-thousand dollar deposits a week before Gavin died," Catherine said. Excitement shot through her. "That's a heck of a lot of money." Could this be proof of embezzlement? Was Gavin on the take?

Ashley sat back in the loveseat and crossed her legs. She pulled her handbag onto her lap.

Unzipping a side pocket, she pulled out another paper. Without unfolding it, she tapped it on her knuckles as if trying to decide what to do. Then she handed it to Catherine.

Slowly unfolding the sheet Catherine read aloud "Interbank transfer, $50,000 Village of Summer Hill to customer account. Is this his salary?" Catherine looked up sharply. Ashley seemed to age before her eyes. Did you give this to the police?"

"No. No way. Gavin received five thousand a year from the Village. That was all he'd take. Some of the others took real salaries, but not Gavin. This has to be a mistake. It's bad enough they think I killed Gavin. I don't want them thinking he was a thief."

"I thought commissioners got a salary. It's in the budget we vote on every year."

"Yeah. Gavin refused it." The coffee cup hit the table with a clunk. "He gets a partnership income from the firm. I should say got." She sniffled. "He didn't plan on dying. It dies with him. A payment was due the end of this month."

So that was how he planned to pay the loans. Must be a lot of money.

"It wasn't a lot, but it was enough for us to live on." Ashley continued as if she read Catherine's mind. "At least until the stock market disaster." Unshed tears glittered in her eyes. "Why am I telling you this?"

A perfect storm of financial disaster. The timing of the deposit to his death stunk. With Gavin's stocks in free fall and his payments coming due – what better way to cover his debts than to take a no interest loan from the Village. He had power of signature on the accounts. The finance commissioner was traveling. Gavin was the secondary signature, payroll due, talk about temptation. As Ashley said, he didn't plan on dying. The whole thing could have seemed like a great idea for a short-term loan.

"Where did you find these exactly?"

Ashley burst into tears. "In the file cabinet in the garage workshop. I'd forgotten about it. I wanted to open the kiln. It's next to the kiln. I pulled it open and found the banking information and a bunch of other stuff, mostly from Gavin's law firm days. Old stuff, except for this.

"I opened the kiln then. Oh, God, I found a face jug. Gavin made me a face jug every year for my birthday. My present, he left me a present." Sobbing uncontrollably, she said, "Chief told me to get an attorney. You were right. You told me I needed one."

Exasperation colored Catherine's voice. Hadn't they had this conversation already? "I thought you already had an attorney."

"No, why did you think that? I didn't kill my husband."

Still seated next to Ashley, her arm around her shoulders Catherine said, "No, Ashley, they may suspect you now, but that's just cop speak for look to the one who finds the body and look to the spouse. I found the body. I'm still a suspect, too. You will be also for a while. It's basic Cop 101. I wish I could tell you not to worry, but with no evidence, they can't do much."

Ashley leaned her head back against the love seat and closed her eyes. "I'm so tired, Catherine. I don't know if I'm rational anymore. Chemotherapy wasn't this grueling the first time"

Sympathy shot through Catherine's veins like hot fire. This woman has enough to deal with. Who says you never get more than you can handle.

The two sat in silence. Catherine trying to will some of her physical strength into the tired woman.

"You'll still help me Catherine?" Ashley asked. "I don't trust the police, not in this town. Will you still help me?"

Rising from the loveseat, Catherine paced the length of the room. Something felt wrong. She couldn't bring herself to believe Ashley killed Gavin, but something about the woman didn't gel. Maybe it was from the cancer or the chemo. Catherine didn't know enough about either to make a judgment.

"Yes, Ashley. I'll still help you"

Catherine walked Ashley to the door. As she reached for the knob, Ashley touched her arm.

"Chief said they had some questions for you too."

CHAPTER 20

In her dream, Catherine ran through a wood, racing toward the sound of incessant pounding. Her breathing came fast, her heart pounding so hard she swore she could see it pumping through her chest. Water, she must be near water or rain, something sticky covered her face. Reaching out a hand, she felt, fur. The pounding sounded again, this time more insistent. Catherine's eyes sprung open to see Bullet's face in front of hers, his tongue in mid-extension and heading for her face.

Leaping from the bed in one fluid motion she winced as her feet hit the floor. Rubbing the bruise on her hip, she let her hand wander further down her thigh to rub the scar. She grabbed a robe and half ran, half hopped for the front door. Anger rose when the grandfather clock in her living room chimed seven times.

Ripping open the door, her heated words died on her lips. Billy LaMotta stood outside. Her blood turned cold as anger changed to fear. She clutched the doorjamb, sent up a silent prayer for strength and managed to say, "Mike? Did something happen to Mike?"

Billy stood on the front porch. His hand and arm raised, ready to pound on the door again. His face fell at her question. "No. Mike's fine. I didn't mean to...I mean... Catherine, you need to come with me."

"Excuse me? It's seven o' freaking clock in the morning. What are you talking about?"

In response to her question, Billy drew himself up straight. His face hardened. "I don't need your attitude. Get dressed. We need you to come to the station."

Catherine looked over his shoulder to the patrol car in the street. Beyond that, she saw the curtains on the house across the street shake as they fell back into place. Great. Welcome to gossip central - again.

Clutching the edges of her robe, she forced her spine as straight as possible gathering her dignity around her like a cloak. Swinging the door wide, she stood aside and invited the officer in. "Please have a seat, I'll need a few minutes," she said formally. She waited until he sat and then walked down the hall to her bedroom. "Billy, what the hell is this all about?" She called over her shoulder. "Why couldn't you call me to come in like a normal person? Did you think I was going to run?" She dressed in the silence that followed, grateful that he hadn't followed her into the bedroom despite her directions. She knew if she were under arrest, he'd be in her doorway making sure she didn't bolt.

She walked past him on her way to the kitchen to take care of Bullet. Lifting a finger for Billy to wait a minute, she opened the doggie door for Bullet to go into the back yard. Then she flipped the switch on the coffee pot, figuring she'd have just enough time to brew some to take with her. Billy made no effort to stop her or hurry her along. He followed her to the kitchen and stood in the doorway, his face impassive. The quiet of his stance concerned her. She realized she wasn't afraid, more confused.

The two walked out the front door together. Catherine paused near the front passenger door of the patrol unit, and then reached for the door. Without looking at Billy, she got into the front seat and shut the door behind her. He opened his mouth, shrugged, and walked to the driver side door. His silence, as he drove to the police station, was as thick and sticky as the morning air.

Chief waited in the conference room that served as an interrogation room. He sat against the wall, looking at the door, a tape recorder and legal pad in front of him. The legs of the chair sounded as loud as a shot as they hit the floor. Chief stood, extended his hand and said, "Thank you for coming, Catherine."

For the second time this morning, Catherine felt fear. Whatever this was about it wasn't a game. Reining in her emotions, she nodded tightly and took the seat next to Chief. She watched the two men exchange a glance. Billy sat opposite her, neither man asked her to move to the less powerful seat, the one with its back to the door.

Thumbing on the tape recorder, Chief recited the names of each party present, the date and time. Then he looked at Catherine and said, "You're here to answer some questions pertaining to the death of Gavin Jackman. You are not under arrest, you may stop this interview at any time and leave if you so desire."

Her mouth went dry. She licked her lips, nodded and silently cursed herself for forgetting her carefully made travel cup of coffee in her kitchen.

Repeatedly, Catherine responded to the same questions. She wanted to scream out that she'd answered these questions before, when Billy came to her house and now she was answering them again. Unable to bear the constant repetition, the chair scraped under her as she pushed it back from the table and then slammed it home. "Damn it Chief. I've told you a hundred times, and that's only today, that I called and left the message on the Jackmans' machine. I was drunk. I admit it." Heat rushed to her face and she shoved a fist in her mouth. Damn it Catherine, sit down and stay down. You are not an amateur.

Pulling the chair back out from the table, she spun it around and sat resting her arms on the back. She hated the pose when others did it, but she truly needed the support and she didn't want to look weak by slumping on her arms on the table. Spacing out her words she said, "I did not mean the message as a threat. I doubt anyone at the Jackmans took it as one. I meant I would come in the morning to get my money."

"Or."

"Or what, Chief."

"Catherine, we know you were there."

"Damn straight you do. I called in the death, hard to do if I wasn't there!" She washed her face with her hands wondering how long this would go on covering the same ground.

"Why did you hit him?"

"The only hand I laid on him was to make sure he was dead."

"That's not true, Catherine. We know you were there, we know you were there for a while before you called it in, and we know you hit him."

Catherine looked from one man to the other. She saw no softness in their eyes. Nothing to indicate they were fishing for information. They knew something, and it pointed to her.

"I never touched him, not in any harmful way."

"What did you and Ashley Jackman talk about the day after her husband's murder?"

"What do you think we talked about? I offered my sympathy."

"And she gave you private information about her husband?"

"You know what she gave me, I gave it to Mike."

"Did you plan it together?"

Catherine opened her mouth and shut it quickly. She saw Billy make a note on the legal pad while he stared at her. She'd been about to respond no. She knew she couldn't let her guard down. A no response only opened the door to further questions, about how she planned it and if she planned it alone. I have to stop thinking like a civilian and start thinking like a cop.

She stood and walked around the tiny room, using the time to gather her thoughts. When she sat again, she was all business, and all law enforcement.

Chief and Billy sensed the difference in her and let the question lie unanswered. After a few more perfunctory questions, Chief stood and thanked her for coming.

Refusing Billy's offer of a ride home, Catherine took a favorite running route that led her to the banks of the canal that formed the eastern boundary of the Village. Now that she was back in cop mode, she recalled the questions Chief asked. Recalled them and turned them on their side hoping to reveal the evidence the police had and hoped to uncover from her. She knew from the technique that they were looking for something specific. What did the police know that they thought she knew too? What corroboration were they trying to get from her? Would tonight's Commission Meeting hold any answers, or just bring more questions.

CHAPTER 21

Mayor Cunningham's gavel crashed down, calling the standing room only meeting to elect an interim Zoning Commissioner to order. Catherine ducked her head and shouldered her way down the row between the closely packed chairs in the direction of the empty seat Dannie and Sue held for her. The atmosphere in the Village Hall seemed to border on frenetic even before the meeting started.

Dannie clutched a fist full of index cards. She smiled weakly at Catherine. "My speech," she whispered.

The Mayor glared in Dannie's direction and slammed his gavel once again.

"Order, this meeting will come to order." Cunningham looked out over the crowd. A slight smile played at the corner of his mouth.

He's enjoying this! Catherine thought. Big fishy in tiny pond may find himself devoured by a shark. Her experience this morning at the hands of the police made her wonder if he was, in fact, the shark. Someone struck Gavin. She pictured Arnie Cunningham's gavel as the weapon.

"I think this is going to get really interesting." Sue whispered to Catherine out of the corner of her mouth. "I refused to let Nick come. He'd feel honor bound to defend me."

Catherine raised her eyebrows in question. "Defend you from what?"

"Oh, I think after they decide on a Zoning Commissioner, they're going to decide I need firing."

"No way, Suze. They can't replace you. No one else would be crazy enough to take the job!"

"We'll see." Susan shrugged her shoulders.

The plastic seat stuck uncomfortably to Catherine's bare thighs. She crossed her legs at the ankle, careful to avoid kicking Luis Alvarez's seatback. Also nominated for Gavin's position, he sat directly in front of her. Rosita sat alongside her husband. Next to the Alvarezes, in the same row, the Kents and the Paysons sat. Meg and Chris, both nominees for Zoning Commissioner, looked over their speeches.

Nudging Catherine, Dannie swept her hand in a gesture meant to take in the three rivals to her desired seat. "Look at them, all together like little ducks. You'd think it would kill them to have saved a seat for me."

Catherine chuckled. "Ah, Dannie, you wouldn't have taken it, would you?"

Dannie shook her head vigorously, her hair standing in a halo of soft curls. "No way. You're right about that." She smiled.

The undercurrent of voices finally died down. Cunningham stood. Sweat beads shining on his bald head. He rubbed a handkerchief over it. From his position in the center of the dais, he looked from side to side at his fellow commissioners. He cleared his throat loudly and said, "I wanted the Village attorney to read the part of the Charter that speaks to filling a vacancy in the Commission. Unfortunately, he couldn't make it tonight." The mayor inhaled, causing a high-pitched whine to shrill from the sound system. Wincing he continued, "I have copies of the Charter here if anyone wants to see. The Charter says, "the Commissioners can appoint a successor without special election if the vacancy occurs within six months of a regularly scheduled election."

The meeting room erupted into what sounded like a loud roar. In response, the Mayor slammed his gavel down over and over again. The harder he slammed the mallet, the louder the audience became. Catherine saw the Mayor nod in the direction of the police commissioner. Thom fingered his cell phone and spoke into it like a two-way radio. The back door burst open admitting a phalanx of five uniformed Summer Hill police officers.

Catherine craned her neck. She didn't see Mike's tall form among the men who took positions at either side of the dais or behind the Mayor. The two remaining officers stood at the back door. "Hey Dannie, have you read the Charter?" Catherine asked.

The dark-haired woman nodded in response.

"What about Alvarez's arrest? Does that disqualify him?"

Dannie's liquid brown eyes bored into Catherine's blue ones. "Great question. I have no idea but if he's appointed, I'll bring it up for sure."

The Mayor waited until the five officers were in place before he slammed the gavel one more time. Raising his voice, he said, "If you would let me finish, please."

The room quieted. Whether because of the Mayor's plea or the presence of the officers, Catherine wasn't sure. Cunningham's eyes seemed to take in each individual in the audience before he continued.

"Rather than exercise our right to appoint the replacement of our choosing, we've decided to allow nominations. Luis Alvarez, Chris Payson, Oliver, sorry, not Oliver, he declined, Meg Kent, and Dannie Gutierrez all accepted nominations."

"Accepted," Dannie hissed. "Like they would have nominated me if Nancy didn't call and point out a few things to them."

Catherine lay what she hoped was a calming hand on her friend's leg.

"Each nominee will offer a five minute speech detailing their qualifications. There will be a question and answer period from the floor and bearing the nominees presentations in mind, the Commission will make its appointment." Slamming the gavel again, the Mayor continued, "I demand order throughout the presentations and discussion."

The first three candidates give what sounded like interchangeable speeches. The Village needed a Zoning Commissioner who would listen to the Villagers and approve or disapprove plans and designs based not on personal taste but on the Village Codes. Catherine tuned the words out after the first one and listened to the emotions.

Her frequent glances at her seat neighbor Dannie only increased her respect for the woman. Dannie gave her full attention to each of the candidates, making small notes in the margin of her index cards. Catherine knew Dannie could sometimes be overbearing, but for the first time she thought Dannie might be the perfect candidate for the job. Nudging her friend before she got up to speak, Catherine said, "Knock 'em dead girl. You got my vote for what it's worth."

Dannie smiled quickly, rose and went to the podium. She was in the process of adjusting the mike for her short stature when Mayor Cunningham interrupted. "Do you have something to add here Ms. Gutierrez, or are you simply going to repeat what we've already heard?"

Catherine's attention instantly went to battle stations. She couldn't believe he intended to dismiss Dannie without hearing her.

The tap of Dannie's index cards against the wood of the podium sounded like a rifle shot. "Mr. Mayor, with respect, I believe you said each candidate would have five minutes. I'd like mine, if you don't mind. And I believe you'll find that Robert's Rules of Order…"

"These speeches are a gift. They're not about the Rules of Order, with which, I'm very familiar, thank you. If you read the Charter, you'd find the Commissioners have the right to appoint without input from anyone, including the candidates."

"Mayor," the Public Works Commissioner and only other woman on the panel began. "I'd like to hear what she has to say."

"Shut the woman up!" An unidentified man shouted from the rear of the meeting hall.

"Which one?" Called back someone else.

"Both. Who cares?"

Feeling trapped in a rerun of the Commission Meeting from the night before Gavin died, Catherine craned her neck to try and identify the speakers.

"I'm not here to extol or condemn the past Zoning Commissioner. I'm here to tell you what I will do if I'm appointed." Dannie tried again to get her five minutes.

"Time." Hank Simms, the finance director called. "Thank you Ms. Gutierrez, if you would please stand down, we'll commence our discussion."

Anger bubbled in Catherine's veins. The plastic seat made sucking sounds as she pushed herself up and walked to the stand alongside her friend. Dannie's liquid eyes swam with tears. Knowing what she was about to do could ignite the crowd, Catherine tapped on the mike for attention and said, "I believe you said the floor would be open to questions after the presentations? I'd like to ask what Ms. Gutierrez has to say."

The crowd in the meeting hall erupted. It was impossible to determine who called for debate and who called for getting on with it. Catherine looked behind her, trying to see if anyone had started throwing punches. The officers called in earlier by the Police Commissioner looked in Thom's direction, waiting for instruction.

The gavel banged frantically. "You are out of order, Ms. Swope. I'm going to request the Sergeant-at-Arms to remove you."

Her mouth dropped open in disbelief. She was out of order?

Billy LaMotta rose from his place behind the Commissioners and strode toward Catherine. She looked into his face and wasn't sure if she saw amusement or compassion. The Commissioners nodded their heads close together, clearly ratifying a decision they had already arrived at. Billy, uncertain what to do since Catherine stopped talking, and in the absence of further orders, stood alongside the Commissioners' table next to his fellow officers. His hand rested ominously near his gun belt.

Mayor Cunningham's head turned toward Billy, then Catherine. He shook his head slightly and Billy retreated behind the Commissioners again. "We have arrived at a decision. Our appointment is Luis Alvarez who will serve the balance of Gavin Jackman's term until our regular elections take place in November." He banged his gavel again, and looking directly at Luis said, "Do you accept."

Luis rose from his seat and walked to the podium. Once there he elbowed Dannie aside and pushed Catherine with a hand on the small of her back.

Enraged, Catherine dug in and refused to move. "No!" She shouted. "No way, no how, this stinks."

"Listen, you two-bit cop wannabe, get away from the podium." Hank Simms, the Finance Commissioner, hissed. "If you keep conducting a private investigation..."

"Hold on Hank." Thom interrupted, "You're out of line, if anyone is going to discuss this, it should be me."

The Mayor's gavel slammed again. "Mr. Alvarez has the floor, I believe."

"Move, bitch." Luis's voice, amped by the mike carried to the back of the room.

Catherine felt a large arm encircle her shoulders. Startled, she looked up into Mike's red face. She hadn't seen him come in to the meeting room. Glancing behind him, she saw Ashley looking frightened. Mike, still holding Catherine, wedged himself between the podium and Luis Alvarez. "Let me be clear about two things." Mike began. "This isn't the forum to discuss Catherine, and any information she may or may not have. At no time is it appropriate to attack a citizen in a public forum. Thom," Mike nodded at the Police Commissioner, "if you want to discuss this with me further, I'm available during my shift." Mike turned and led Catherine gently away from the front of the meeting room. Fear that Mike's actions had terminated his law enforcement career competed with Catherine's pride in his unexpected public defense of her.

Dannie pushed her way back to the podium and grabbed the mike stem. Speaking directly into it she said, "Mr. Police Commissioner, have you checked the Charter about Mr. Alvarez's pending charges for disorderly conduct at the last commission meeting? I haven't seen the charges dropped." She backed away and turned for her seat in the silence that followed her question.

Red faced, Luis resumed his place at the podium. "Err, well, I've been told only felonies disqualified me. I have no felonies. The Chief assured me he dropped the charges." Luis turned and smirked in the direction of the rear of the meeting room. "Now, on to business, first of all, I accept the appointment and am proud to be asked. Secondly, I believe that the services of Susan Faraday are terminated effective tonight."

"No!" Ashley's voice shouted out. "You can't do that!" Her voice was slurred, whether from drink or exhaustion, Catherine didn't know.

"Yes, actually. I can."

"I second the termination." Hank Simms announced from the commissioners' table. "From a budget standpoint, I believe having sworn officers and a code officer who is not a sworn officer is not cost effective."

"My officers are spread thin enough now." Thom protested. "I don't see how Chief can spare one for code enforcement!"

Mayor Cunningham sat back in his chair, his long fingers caressing the wooden head of his gavel, and appeared to wait for the debate to end. Finally, he slammed the mallet on its well-worn block and announced, "Susan Faraday is terminated. The position of Code Enforcement will be an unpaid appointment as it was in the past. I appoint Terry Payson."

Ashley slid to the floor in a faint.

CHAPTER 22

Grateful for the cool air and quiet of her house after the raucous scene of the commission meeting, Catherine leaned her head against Mike's shoulder as the two sat on the couch in her living room. She propped her feet up on the coffee table and idly traced the outline of his hand where it lay across her stomach.

"Did you know Ashley's cancer came back?" Mike asked.

Too tired to answer, Catherine nodded. "She told me the other day. She's getting chemo again."

She felt Mike's body stiffen under her head. "That gives her more motive you know."

"Tell that to Chief."

Kissing the top of her head, Mike wrapped his arms around Catherine and nuzzled her. "I'm sorry, Cathy, but you knew it was coming."

She twisted around so she could see his face. "No, Mike. I didn't know it was coming. Maybe you should have warned me. How the hell do you think Ashley or I lifted Gavin and dropped the noose around his neck?" Heat flooded her cheeks.

Anger spiked her heart rate. He was Summer Hill's only lieutenant, off the case or not, he knew the schedule. Why didn't he warn her? Planting a hand on his thigh, she pushed away from him. His arms tightened around her and she fell back in defeat. "Do you think Ashley and I worked together?" "Do I think it? No. Do others? I don't know. Catherine, stop this rogue investigation before it destroys us. I'm helping you all that I can. You have to trust me."

"Screw it, Mike, just screw it." This time she managed to break away. She strode to the mantle and picked up the antique dog, using it to scratch the sudden itch on her nose. "You are pissed at me because I am being accused of murder."

Mike ate the distance between them in two strides. He freed the dog from her grasp and replaced it. Then, leaning against the mantle with one arm on either side, he trapped her where she stood. "First, no one is accusing you of anything. Second, you have no jurisdiction. Third, if you continue to investigate, you are forcing Chief to fight back. Fourth, you don't want a murderer to get away because you taint an investigation." He spun Catherine around in his arms. "I love you Kit Kat, let me do my job. Let the force do its job I'm not saying stay out of it, I'm saying work with me and let me work with you, don't be a rogue. You are creating more questions than you resolve. It will hurt you in the end."

Unable to sustain her anger, Catherine let her head fall against his chest. He easily lifted her off the ground and dropped her into his lap as he

187

took a seat on the couch. She nestled in his arms too tired to argue any longer. She heard his words, but she still felt she had to prove herself. Scratching her nose again, she let her thoughts skip from one event to another. Who else, she wondered, had a reason to want Gavin dead? The more she learned about the money missing from the Village accounts, the more she thought the murder tied to the money, and that could only point to Simms. Her eyes felt heavy. She sighed and resolved to follow the money. And that meant Cunningham's loan repayment, a place Mike couldn't go. Could Cunningham sign checks? Maybe he leaked the Affidavit too. Gavin and Arnie were close friends once, but close enough for Gavin to confide that he was all but fired from his firm? She didn't know.

"Bullet's scratching. Did you open his doggie door?"

Catherine shook her head in reply. "I didn't want to forget to lock it." She put a hand down on the couch and levered herself upright.

Mike patted her thigh. "You stay. I'll let him in."

Catherine chewed her lip while she waited for man and dog to return. Sprawled out with her legs extended and her head cocked back on the couch she decided Mike needed a nudge in the money direction too, kind of like a test. When Mike returned she said, "About the missing money…"

A look of frustration crossed his face. He sat on the coffee table and placed one large hand on each of her knees. "Do I want to hear this, Kit Kat?"

She lifted her head, looked him dead in the eye and responded, "Probably not, but you're the one who wants me to stop my, what did you call it, rogue investigation. Well I have a copy of an automatic deposit notice and a copy of a bank statement from immediately before Gavin died."

Mike's silence held a waiting quality. Catherine recognized it from her days as a cop. It meant continue at the same time it withheld judgment or encouragement. This was the kind of silence people found hard to resist filling, generally to their detriment. Nodding hard, Catherine said, "Two fifty thousand deposits, from Summer Hill."

"Joint account?"

Ducking her head, Catherine realized the implication of her next words. If it was joint, then Gavin wasn't hiding anything. A solo account meant private funds. "Not joint."

Sighing deeply Mike stood and said, "And you're going to give me the documents? I'm not risking my career with an ethics charge. Especially after I told you about the missing money. Kit Kat, how long have you known about this?"

Catherine hated seeing the disappointment in his face and the thought that she put his job in jeopardy. She knew Mike well enough to know that he loved being a cop, for all the right reasons. "I'm not sure what the documents mean. I need some time. You've been straight with me. I'm trying to be straight with you. They may mean nothing."

"Or they may provide a reason for murder."

"How?"

"You know the answer to that, Catherine."

"I told you, Cunningham's house is in the foreclosure process. But did you know that he borrowed $50,000 from Gavin. One of these can be a repayment."

Mike's head snapped around. She had his full attention now. "Where are you going with that?"

Silently she mulled over the reasons that made sense. Someone wanted in on the take or the deposit was a mistake, and Gavin's murder a way to silence him. Maybe Gavin was guilty, and took the money to pay his mortgages. Someone found out he was skimming, confronted him, offered to overlook the fraud and he died in the argument. Then again, maybe Cunningham repaid Gavin with Village funds, and Gavin found out and Cunningham killed him rather than be blackmailed. None of it worked for Catherine. Tomas and Juan, the criminal and the blackmailer. Yep, that worked sort of. If Gavin had a private account all along, that's where he'd take the blackmail money from. "The Village Commissioners are all over me like the Keystone Cops. I want to know why no one is looking at the Rivera/Lopez clan."

"Evidence. In the end, it all comes down to evidence, or in their case, lack of evidence. There is nothing to tie them. Go to bed, Catherine, we'll talk about this tomorrow." Mike leaned down and kissed Catherine.

"Umm, sure you won't stay?" She asked and licked her lips.

"I'll lock up behind me."

CHAPTER 23

Bullet's frantic barking woke Catherine. Her hand groped toward the nightstand holding her Glock. Glass broke before her hand found the weapon. A dazzle of fireworks exploded behind her eyes and she felt herself swirling down a long dark tunnel to oblivion accompanied by the wail of sirens.

Her head throbbed. Squinting in the bright light she raised a hand to her forehead and gingerly patted a bandage covering her right temple. She thought she was dreaming. Her last memory was languidly floating just before she fell asleep.

"Don't get up. The paramedics will be back in a few moments to take you to the hospital."

Two Mikes danced in Catherine's field of vision. They zoomed in and out, fading to blurs and then almost sharpened to focus. A wave of nausea washed over her. Unable to help herself she leaned over the side of the bed and vomited on the floor. "Oh, God." Rubbing her mouth with the edge of her pillowcase, she tried to make a coherent sentence, but only disjointed words came out. Even the simple act of thinking brought white-hot stabs of pain, and worse, more nausea. Nothing made any sense.

"Nancy," Mike called. "Bring a couple of wet towels. It's ok Kit Kat. You probably have a concussion. Do you know what happened?"

"Nancy, here?" Catherine tried to ask.

"What do you remember?" Mike asked as he wiped her face and dropped a wet towel to the hardwood floor to cover the mess.

"What time?" She croaked, wondering why her throat seemed so dry.

Trying to get through the pain was like running in a corn maze. High walls stood at every turning and she wasn't sure it was worth the effort. Her eyes felt gritty under the weight of her lids. The soft edges of oblivion tugged at her, but something — "Bullet? He barked!" She struggled upright. Mike strong-armed her back onto the bed. His blurry faces looked worried.

"Oh, Bullet!" Catherine moaned.

"He'll be fine. Flying glass cut him. One of my guys is taking him to the all night vet. I had a hell of a time getting him to leave your side. He actually growled at me."

Catherine felt a faint smile crease her face as her eyes closed. "Somebody loves me," she croaked.

"Don't let her go to sleep," Nancy said.

Mike tapped her on the nose. Annoyed, she tried to brush him away. "Glock," she shouted. "Where?"

"I have it Kit Kat, don't worry, nobody took your weapon."

Squeaking gurney wheels announced the paramedics' arrival in the hall. Catherine futilely begged Mike to send them away. Still struggling with a kaleidoscope of memories, she asked, "What happened?" The wheels turned into her bedroom.

The Mikes got up and spoke to the paramedics. They left the gurney and went back down the hall. For the first time Catherine realized Nancy sat on a chair at other side of her bed. She tried to shake her head to make both images of her friend focus into one. The movement only served to bring more nausea. Catherine swallowed hard to keep from getting sick again. "Nance," she whispered. "Tell me."

Nancy looked up at Mike. Her face hardened. Through the fog, Catherine realized whatever happened, Nancy held Mike responsible.

Do you have any memory of tonight, Catherine? Anything at all?

She sucked in a deep breath. Closing her eyes to stop the double vision and to shut out the bright light, she said, "Bullet barking, glass breaking, fireworks, sirens, no, maybe the alarm. That's it until just now. What did happen?"

"You're sounding better. You're speaking in sentences." Nancy said.

Catherine smiled weakly, "Still hurts like hell."

"Yeah, I bet. You've got little cuts all over too. They'll get the glass out at the hospital." Mike said.

Reaching a hand in Nancy's direction Catherine said, "The alarm company called you?"

"No, your neighbor did. Good thing we have no secrets in this little town," Nancy said. Mike got here at the same time I did. I don't know how he knew."

"Heard on the police band that a 911 report of a nuisance alarm at your house came in. I didn't get here soon enough though. I didn't see anyone. Just brick on the floor near your bed. Must have bounced off your hard head! Get some rest, Catherine, and do what the doctors tell you. Nancy is going to follow you to the hospital."

"Not you?"

Mike shook his head. "I want to look around." His face softened and he took her hand. "I'll be there as soon as I can. I promise."

"You should've stayed when I asked you." Catherine teased.

"Oh, sure, so I could have gotten hit in the head. You're sleeping on my side!"

Catherine stuck her tongue out at Mike as paramedics loaded her onto the gurney. A cop, caught in mid-stride coming in the direction of her bedroom stood aside as they wheeled her past. Over the squeak of the wheels, she heard someone tell Mike they'd found a man size shoe print and a flattened cigarette butt in the soft earth under the bedroom window.

Her head splitting with pain, she begged the paramedics to run silent. The wail of the siren turned her stomach. What she didn't tell them was it also interfered with what little thought process she had through the pain. The fear she felt tonight made her consider listening to Mike and giving up her investigation. Why didn't the alarm company call her? Or Nancy if they couldn't reach her.

She remembered locking her side gates. A shoe print under her window meant someone had gotten in her back yard. Her locked back yard. What, she wondered, would have happened if Bullet hadn't barked and the alarm gone off?

* * *

The next morning Mike and Nancy arrived together at the hospital to take her home. Catherine, face covered with tiny steristrips would have leapt into their arms if the nurse hadn't insisted she stay in the wheelchair until the hospital door closed behind her at the curb. Her discharge instructions were the size of a phone book, but right now, Catherine didn't care. She wanted her own bed, her own house and Bullet. Her feet tapped on the footpads of the wheelchair in anticipation. She still had a headache, but her mind felt clear. No concussion according to the MRI. She had a large goose egg bump and a bruise extending below her hairline. She figured she'd give Mikhail Gorbachev a run for his money if she went bald in the next few weeks. Sometime during the night, she realized the brick could be a weapon of opportunity. She'd edged her back flower garden with bricks set up in a saw-toothed pattern. Had someone used one of her own bricks in the attack against her?

As Mike's pick-up pulled into Catherine's driveway Bullet's face appeared at the window, his tongue hanging out in true German Shepherd smile style, a multitude of shaved bald spots and small bandages dappled his coat. Mike put a restraining hand on her to keep her from leaping out of the vehicle. "Catherine, Bullet is doing really, really well. He does have a large gash on his left hind leg. The vet says it looks far worse than it is. He'll be fine. She stitched him up and he has to take it easy for the next two weeks. And she specifically said that bandage better stay clean. She wants to see him day after tomorrow to check on the healing."

Guilt washed over her. It was her fault the dog was hurt. If she had listened to Mike and stopped investigating Gavin's murder, none of this would have happened. "I'll make sure he has the life of Riley. No runs, just sedate walks around the back and in the yard."

"He's gonna hate that, you know." Nancy said.

Laughing, Catherine agreed. She took two steps toward the house at the same time a car pulled up and stopped in front of her house.

Putting his bulk between Catherine and the tall man that approached, Mike thrust out an arm in 'stop there' fashion. "What do you want?" Hc demanded.

"Catherine Swope." The man said looking past Mike. "Are you Catherine Swope?"

Catherine nodded.

The man opened his jacket. She saw a badge hanging on his belt. Bile rose in her throat. He pulled out a sheaf of papers.

"You've been served."

CHAPTER 24

Nancy snatched the Complaint from Catherine's hand. Unfolding it, she scanned the document while Mike opened the front door with his key and ushered Catherine in.

"The Riveras are suing you." Nancy announced. "They're claiming you harassed Maggie causing the death of their unborn child. They also claim defamation of character. It's a civil suit, honey," Nancy stroked Catherine's arm gently, "for amounts in excess of $15,000."

The blood drained from Catherine's body. Weakly she slumped on the couch, reaching down with a hand to try to calm her dog's exuberant greeting. "Baby? I caused her to lose a baby. Defamation of character? I asked her some questions, that's all I did. Juan burst in screaming. He pushed her and she fell. She had bruises. She said her brother hit her. Maybe Juan did. I don't know."

"Maybe, but none of that matters. What does matter is you need a lawyer, and you need one fast. You have to respond within twenty days." Nancy morphed from friend to legal advisor in a heartbeat. "Let me ask Phil about an attorney for you. He's coming by later. Said he wanted to check up on Ashley. This isn't in his court. The number is Judge Vest's. You'd think they'd go for wrongful death if they wanted recovery for a miscarriage."

"Oh, God." Catherine covered her face and shuddered. Without thinking about it, she rubbed the scar on her thigh. The family of the boy she killed filed a wrongful death suit against her. The Judge dismissed the case after hearing witness testimony and viewing the tape of the shooting from the parking lot camera. Catherine began to tremble and couldn't stop.

Mike wrapped a consoling arm around her. "Nancy, stop speculating." He said in a warning tone of voice. "I'll call my brother. He'll handle the case.

Catherine looked up in time to see a flash of anger cross Nancy's face. She managed to catch her eye to keep her from responding.

"Kit Kat," Mike swept her up in his arms. "I think it's time you got in bed."

"The bedroom is clean!" Cathcrine said looking around.

"Yep, Nancy took care of cleaning it up and getting rid of the glass. You're safe here, Cathy. I'm not leaving." He leaned down and kissed her on the top of her head. "Get some sleep."

"Mike, Nancy didn't mean anything. I'm too sensitive."

"And you're too nosy. Why the hell did you go to that woman's house?" He bit the words so harshly he ended with a cough. "It's done, we can't change it." He frowned.

Catherine watched Mike stalk out of the room. She'd never heard that particular tone of voice from him. He was angry, but she couldn't change what she'd done.

She tossed restlessly in her bed unable to find a comfortable position. Her cuts might be small but they throbbed and stung. She kept imagining she felt shards of glass digging into her. When she threw back the covers to look, she didn't see any glass. Her eyes finally grew heavy, and she thought sleep would finally overtake her, but the doorbell pealed.

Throwing off the sheet, she sat up on the side of the bed. Relieved that the room didn't spin, she shuffled her feet over the wood floor looking for her slippers. She remembered they'd been at the side of her bed when the brick flew through the window. Gratefully, she realized Mike or Nancy had thrown the shoes out before she put her feet into glass-filled slippers.

Padding barefoot into the living room, she saw Mike standing at the open front door. "Thanks, Mayor, I'll let her know you stopped by."

"What was that all about?" It amused her that Mike jumped at the sound of her voice.

"God, Catherine, make some noise next time." He emitted a deep chuckle as he spoke. "A girl could get shot that way!"

"Not if the boy knew to identify before he pulled the trigger." She wagged a finger in his direction. "What did Cunningham want? And where's Nancy?"

"Nance left right after you went to bed. She didn't want to miss her boss. I think Cunningham wanted to cover his tracks. He said he wanted you to know how appalled the entire Commission was about what happened to you." Mike sat on the couch and patted the space beside him. "Feeling better?"

Catherine sat down and curled her legs beneath her, pitching herself so the injured part of her back didn't make contact with the leather of the sofa. "Yeah, couldn't sleep. No messages?"

She saw a look she couldn't identify race across Mike's face. Knowing she'd learn more if she kept silent than if she pressed, she waited.

"The phone company is scheduled for later today."

"Scheduled for what?"

"Restore phone service. Someone disconnected your phone from the outside box. That's why the alarm company never called Nancy. The alarm company didn't get the alarm call."

Catherine felt chilled. She pulled her robe closer. "So, I guess that means we can write off random vandals. Someone actually wanted in here."

"Maybe, or maybe they wanted to scare you."

"How does that figure, Mike?"

"Well, if they disconnected the phone…"

"They were disconnecting my calling ability until I got to my cell. It doesn't mean they knew about the alarm. Besides, the audible alarm still went off, the only thing the alarm couldn't do was call the cops or the alarm company."

"Maybe. Don't think about it now.

"This place has been Grand Central Station. I'm surprised the doorbell didn't pull you out of the bedroom before this." He shot a knowing look her way.

Catherine gulped. She hadn't heard a thing until the Mayor came. Normally a light sleeper, sleeping through the sounds of doorbells and knocking upset her. Especially since she didn't remember sleeping at all.

"There's a ton of food in the kitchen." Mike continued. "I've been taking donations all morning." Ted's coming by later to pick up the Complaint. He says not to worry. These folks are looking for money. When you showed up at their door, they figured you were their personal Prize Patrol."

"Great, I feel like hell on horseback and you want me to meet with your brother?"

He lifted the corner of her hair and looked at the darkening bruise. "You look good to me. Oh, Nancy said no criminal case has been filed."

"Criminal! You and Nancy think they might file a criminal charge!"

"Kit Kat, they could file a stalking complaint or, if what you suspect about the bruises is true, they can claim you got physical. She probably has some fresh marks after her altercation with her husband. And if she did lose a child…"

"Shit."

He took her chin in his hand and turned her face toward him. Catherine thought his eyes would bore a hole in her head. "Listen to me Catherine. Do not, and I repeat, do not, ever try to play cop again. You really overstepped and look where it's gotten you."

For the second time that day, Catherine heard a hard edge to his voice. Shaken to the core she nodded her head. He was already risking his job keeping her in the loop.

He released her chin and she said, "Mike, one thing I can't give up. Ashley needs help. Let me help you help her. She no more killed Gavin than I did."

"That's good to hear, since both of you are high on the suspect list. I have to admit, you've fallen to a distant second recently from what I've heard. With everyone except Cunningham, that is. And since he came by to see how you were, maybe that's changed too."

"Why did Cunningham come over? Why the whole commission?" Catherine knew she had no friends there, never tried to cultivate any. Did they want to see for themselves if she'd been scared off? The thought made her bite the inside of her cheek. Scared off from what, she wondered.

Mike's hand covered hers. Catherine felt lost in his huge paw.

"Kit Kat, investigating on your own is not a good idea. You're not winning friends."

"Do you think that's why I was attacked? Do you think the same person who tried to run me over did this? Who do you think killed Gavin?"

"I don't know. Not yet. But you can't keep putting yourself at risk. You have to promise me." His eyes showed only concern.

Catherine's cell phone rang at the same time as the doorbell chimed. Mike got up to open the door and tossed Catherine's cell phone to her from the end table. She caught it in mid-flight waving hello to Ashley with one hand and pressing the phone to her ear with the other. A woman's voice responded to her hello with a hissed, "Back off bitch." The phone clattered to the floor from her nerveless fingers.

Both Ashley and Mike rushed to her side. Catherine felt a cold sweat dapple her forehead. Mike grabbed for the phone and shouted into it, hoping for an open connection. Picking up his own phone, he dialed quickly. "Can we get a Celnet trace? No, not on my phone." He gave Catherine's cell phone information and clicked off.

The microwave dinged and Ashley came out of the kitchen carrying a mug. Handing it to Catherine she said, "Chamomile tea, drink it. Catherine, I can't put you through this. I appreciate everything, but I'm begging you. Leave it alone. I'll be fine." Her eyes slid away from Catherine's. "Besides, Phil says you're hurting my case. You're making me look guilty by not leaving this to the police."

Catherine looked from Ashley to Mike. She read concern in both their faces. Catherine wanted to scream out, can't you see this is about me! They're after my dog and me. Someone is coming after me.

Mike was right. She wasn't a cop. Not anymore and that gave her freedom to investigate outside the box. So far, he'd shared bits of the investigation with her, but she had no guarantees that he would continue. She would share what she discovered and be grateful for what he shared, but she wouldn't stop. She couldn't afford to. Gavin's murder seemed more a symptom than the disease. She felt like she was trying to swim through molasses. Too much was going on and there were too many factions involved. What could the Commission have to do with the Affidavit and what could the Ramirezes have to do with embezzlement? For that matter, did Gavin have anything to do with the embezzlement? And why, given all of that, would anyone try to come after her?

"No." She responded. "It's personal, and I'm in."

Mike's face fell before he could school his emotions.

CHAPTER 25

Bullet's nails made a familiar click clack sound on the front stoop. Catherine lifted her eyes from the book in her lap, looked out the living room window and saw Bullet's tail swishing back and forth. Mike's key scraped in the lock and Bullet rushed in, covering his mistress's face in doggie kisses.

"What's the matter, Mike?" She asked, pointing to the cell phone he held in his large hand. The flip earphone remained open as if he intended to continue a conversation.

Mike sat down on the end of the couch lifting Catherine's feet and settling them on his lap.

"You are not going to believe this."

Catherine closed the book in her lap and gave the man her full attention.

"Chief called me. He wants an all-available officers meeting tonight at eight. Cunningham insists Gavin died by his own hand."

"What!" A stabbing pain in Catherine's back stopped her as she tried to sit up. Gingerly settling back she said, "In light of the ME's conclusions,

Cunningham is still trying to sell his suicide theory? Didn't anyone tell him that dog won't hunt?" She adjusted the pillows again. "Did something new happen?"

"There's no death certificate — yet." Mike gently put her feet back up on the couch and walked to the mantle. Picking up a figurine, he turned it over in his hands.

Catherine carefully managed to lever her back away from the couch without aggravating too many of her cuts. She carefully walked to stand alongside Mike, took the dog statue from his hands and replaced it on the mantle. "Antique," she said. Placing her hands on either side of his face, she tipped his head down until she looked directly into his blue eyes. "That's old news. How does Chief explain this sudden change of heart? Christ, Mike." Every muscle in her body telegraphed danger to her tired brain, and Catherine fought the urge to ball her hands into tight fists.

Pulling in a deep breath, Mike said, "Gavin and someone unknown had an altercation. Yada, yada, yada. Same story, different day, different interpretation, but…it matches the ME report. And this part is key. Gavin went into his garage and hanged himself because of a combination of embarrassment, guilt, fear and frustration. So, although persons unknown may have contributed to his death, Gavin died by his own hand." His eyes bored into hers with so much intensity that for a moment Catherine thought he was trying to hypnotize her.

Turning away, Catherine walked over to the end table near the couch trying to order her thoughts before she commented. Picking up a bowl of potpourri, she stirred it with her finger, bringing up the scent. Still holding the bowl, she moved back to where Mike stood. "Since when does Chief take his orders from Cunningham? Does the investigative evidence support it?"

"No. At least not the evidence I know about. But I've been out of it. So, maybe. If something new came up. It's good news for you and Ashley, though..."

The pain of shrugging her shoulders caused Catherine to wince. "So was the last result you called me about, Mike. Remember. For me at least. I was in the clear then too."

A cloud of concern darkened Mike's blue eyes and he continued, "Chief's calling off the investigation. This time I think it will stick. Unless something shows in the tox screen." He showed his frustration by slamming one fist into the other. "With the ME's report specifying no support for a homicide, he has no place else to go."

"Where's justice for Gavin?"

"Case closed, Kit Kat. It's going to be official in a few days" Mike strode over and gripped the edge of the mantle. He leaned against it a few times as if he were doing shoulder presses. Then he swiveled his head to look at Catherine. "In some ways, that's the most elegant solution. Solves a lot of problems."

"What's the deal with the tox screen? Why wait. Was he drugged?"

207

Shrugging, Mike said, "There were a lot of drugs in the house, sleeping pills, anti-depressants, some heavy duty pain pills. Two empty vials were in the bathroom trash, a vicodin and a valium. Both filled within the past two weeks."

Catherine's head reeled. This was news. Her thoughts chased each other so quickly she thought she'd get dizzy trying to catch them. Returning to the couch, she sat with both feet firmly planted on the floor. "I feel like I'm drunk." She muttered.

Mike stopped in mid-stride. "Did you just say you wanted to get drunk?" He demanded. The look on his face was comical if she didn't believe he'd repeated what he thought she said.

"No, duck, I said I feel like I am drunk. I remember this feeling, trying so hard to steady myself that I trip over my own feet. This can't be happening. Mike. It solves nothing and you know it."

Mike sat down heavily on the couch beside Catherine. "Ok, I have to leave here in fifteen minutes for the meeting. Make your case, Cathy. You know Chief runs a clean investigation. He wouldn't do this if he didn't believe it."

Catherine carefully closed the book she'd left spine open on the arm of the couch and laid it on the end table beside her. Lifting her hand with five fingers extended she pushed her index finger down and said. "Cunningham came here and apologized. Why? What was he sorry about? He certainly couldn't speak for the Village or the Commission. He had something up his sleeve. And he owed Gavin money"

Pushing down her middle finger she said, "My business, such as it is, has gone to hell in a hand basket. Someone tried to run me down while I had a dog in my charge. People, including old customers, have called to cancel my services. Gavin committing suicide does not explain why someone tried to run me over."

Pushing down her ring finger she said, "Claiming Gavin's suicided does not clear me or Ashley in anyone's eyes except the Commission. This Village has a long memory, and they'll remember something happened long after they've forgotten the details. I'll never get my reputation back, neither will Ashley. Has anyone looked at all the people who flat out hated Gavin? Talk about a field ripe for the picking. You're missing the point, he enjoyed creating strife."

Pushing down her pinky finger she continued, "Why did someone try to brain me if Gavin committed suicide? Did someone want me dead, or want in my house for some reason? That brick incident was no accident. Someone was in my locked backyard. Whoever it was disconnected my telephone to disable my alarm. I don't believe that was random. Hell, most of the people who haven't spoken to me since I found Gavin have told me how shocked they are. OK, I know most of them are looking for more information but still. If Gavin died by his own hand, no one had to go to that extreme.

Finally pushing down her thumb she said, "The missing money. This whole fantasy is geared to point the finger at Gavin, who can't defend himself. Cunningham is having money problems.

He can sign on Village checks. So can Simms. Has anyone checked them out? Seems to me, suicide is an easy out. A cop out."

Mike sat silent for a moment and stared at Catherine. She knew he would process the information and turn the puzzle pieces around in his mind to see how he put them together. She saw him look up at the ceiling, then out the window and finally meet her eyes. "You're forgetting something, Cathy. You're forgetting your own theory that what's happened to you is not coming from inside the Village, but from outside, Maggie and her family."

"So, you think they're behind all of this? What about the money that's missing? Why come after me? Who has the most to lose?"

"That's right, who has the most to lose?" He replied. "You do. Gavin's gone and the Affidavit is public knowledge, there's no reason to think anyone would pay blackmail money. If Gavin ever did. I'm not so sure about that. Catherine, I've got to go."

"Why do I have the most to lose, I've already lost."

Mike raked a hand through his hair. "You're losing your business, and you haven't decided what to do to replace it. Your amateur investigation lost you any chance of serving on Summer Hill's force if that's what you wanted. You've pissed off a hell of a lot of neighbors, and you've certainly pissed off Maggie and her family. They're suing you so you stand to lose even more. Cash only, I'll grant you, but still, no matter how you look at it, you lose. I love you Kit Kat, but you really went out on a limb on this one. And it broke." Leaning over to kiss her, Mike ran his hand over her face and ended lifting her chin so her eyes met his. "You gonna be OK while I'm gone?"

"Yeah. And Mike, I'd appreciate it if you called later, but I want to be alone tonight. If you're right, I'm in no danger." Catherine saw Mike hesitate, it was clear from the play of emotions she saw chase over his face that he wanted to argue.

Finally, he turned and walked to the door. "I'm a phone call away, Kit Kat, and I'm going to have the patrols stepped up past the house." He raised a hand to cut off her protest. "Take your choice, me or the patrols."

Sighing, she nodded her agreement.

Unable to find a comfortable spot, Catherine shook one of the pain pills out of the bottle the emergency room doctor had insisted she take. A cozy warmth stole over her as the pill took effect.

Unable to concentrate on her book, Catherine picked up that day's Miami Metropolis. Idly flipping pages, she scanned the paper to see if the vandalism at her house made the news. Not finding anything, she continued to flip through the pages. A full-page story by Oliver Kent caught her eye. He'd written about how to landscape around a pool and pool house for privacy, shade and sun. She noticed the pool house pictured looked like the one Gavin Jackman denied him a zoning approval for. Skimming the article, she wondered what would happen to those plans with Luis Alvarez occupying the job.

211

Catherine tossed the paper aside. Her thoughts turned to Ashley. How would the closing of the case affect her? She'd always wonder why her husband committed suicide. An overwhelming feeling of sorrow for the other woman washed over her. Ashley's second battle against breast cancer was just beginning, and she'd have to deal with the questions about her husband's death as well. Reaching for the phone, Catherine dialed her number. The phone rang into voice mail and Catherine hung up.

* * *

The sound of a ringing telephone woke Catherine from a drugged semi-sleep. Stumbling from her sofa to the kitchen, she picked up the phone. The dial tone sounded in her ear. Checking the caller ID, she was surprised to see Oliver Kent's number displayed. She waited a few minutes and picked up her phone again, hearing the familiar stutter tone indicating she had a message she dialed in her code.

"Hi Catherine, it's Meg. I wondered if you'd do us a favor. We're going out of town next weekend. Could we get you to sit with Pugsley? Give us a call. Oh, did Oliver call you? He wants to do an interview with you for the Metropolis magazine section, something about second careers. Well, let us know."

Amused, Catherine put the phone down. The Kents never used her services before. Now that she'd lost most of her business, they wanted her to watch their dog. "What do you think about that,

Bullet?" She fondled her dog's head. "Do you want to make a new friend?"

Catherine dialed the Kents' number. Oliver picked up on the third ring. "Hi Catherine, good to hear your voice. Will you be able to help us with Pugsley?"

"I'm not sure I'll be up and around as early as this weekend. I'm still not feeling great. Can I confirm or renege later on? In the meantime, if you need to get someone lined up, I understand. By the way, you know my gardening skills are hardly worthy of a story."

"Oh, didn't Meg tell you? It's not about gardening. I want to get out of the daily grind of newspapers and start freelancing. I thought your experience, two careers down, and moonlighting as an investigator while you look for a third, would make a great freelance article. Since Gavin committed suicide, I'm curious about how your investigation dovetailed with the police.

CHAPTER 26

Insistent knocking and Bullet's frantic barking woke Catherine from a sound sleep. She fumbled for her slippers and struggled into her robe. Glancing down at her feet, she laughed out loud. Mike had replaced the glass-encrusted ones with a new pair sporting dog heads on the toes.

Stumbling to the front door, she pulled aside the curtain. Oliver Kent stood under the shelter of the porch overhang. Details of last night's telephone call and her agreement to an interview filtered through the fog in her brain. Grabbing Bullet's collar with one hand she muttered a curse and shot the deadbolt back with the other.

"Oliver, I'm sorry, I totally forgot. Give me a minute to let Bullet out the back and wash the sleep devils from my eyes." Her voice sounded husky. The hangover effect of the pain pill concealed the frustration she felt. She pressed the door closed and heard his footfalls following behind her. Vaguely, she remembered him telling her Gavin committed suicide. An emotion somewhere between caution and fear prickled the hairs on the back of her neck. Why did he say that? Wasn't the rest of the town was still buzzing about murder?

Oliver and Catherine settled on her back porch with two mugs and a pot of coffee between them. Oliver pulled out a slender pen and dropped it. "I can't find my favorite interview pen. I think not having my good pen affects my writing. Isn't that stupid?"

Catherine sat back and listened. Still lethargic from the drug, she wondered where the interview was going and when it would start. Tired and sore, with a throbbing headache, she let him dither at his own pace.

After a cup of coffee, and what seemed like hours of chitchat, Oliver opened his notebook and asked questions about the transition from cop to Realtor to dog walker. Lulled by the ordinariness of the questions, she answered without much thought.

"What did you think at the time you found Gavin's body?"

Startled at the sudden transition, from her first dog walk clients to death, Catherine replied, "Nothing. I didn't think anything. I called 911, reverted to police mode, took mental notes and got Roscoe out of the area."

"What kind of mental notes? Was anything out of the ordinary?"

"A man hanging in a garage is not ordinary."

"Describe the scene. Just as you saw it. What happened next? Walk me through your world."

Uncomfortable, Catherine looked at Oliver and then down at the tiny cuts that covered her hands. "I think my career choices are more germane to your article than the death."

"Did you know it was a suicide? Was it one? What do you think?" He pressed.

"I don't think anything. Except that it was an awful day for Gavin and Ashley. I'm uncomfortable talking about specifics with you, or anyone for that matter." Catherine responded with more heat than she intended.

"Ok, I understand. I used to cover the Courthouse beat before I started the garden and landscape column. I know things are not always as they seem. You investigated on your own; at least that's what Thom said. Do you share everything with your boyfriend? What's that like, investigating independently? Did Mike give you leads? Ask you do stuff the real cops can't without jeopardizing the investigation? That he can't?"

Catherine got up and opened the doggie door to let Bullet back into the porch. "I think it's time for you to go, Oliver."

"Why? It's old news. Gavin committed suicide. I mentioned this last night. You didn't object then. What are you hiding?"

Not wanting to follow Oliver's train of thought any further down the track, Catherine slanted him a look through half-closed eyes. "Let's get back on topic."

By the time Oliver left, Catherine was exhausted. She felt raw, violated and, extremely nauseous.

Picking up the phone, she dialed Mike's number. "Hey guy, I think I did something stupid." Quickly she brought Mike up to date about her interview with Oliver and asked him to come over for lunch. Looking at the clock, she counted off the ten minutes until he arrived, during which she returned to the porch and continued to fight off nausea, before she heard his key in the door.

"You look awful. Stay here." He pulled up an ottoman on the porch and lifted her legs. "Let me make you some tea. Are you as sick as you look? Is this from talking to Oliver?"

Fighting down another round of nausea, Catherine shook her head. "No, I took one of those pain pills. I think this is the hangover effect. Oliver was OK, I guess, until he started pushing about Gavin. And whether or not I was working for you." A cold sweat broke out along her hairline. "Can you bring me a damp dishcloth or something?" She called back over her shoulder.

Carefully placing a mug of tea on the end table, Mike handed Catherine a damp washcloth. "Oliver is probably just being a busybody. I wouldn't worry too much about him."

Catherine draped the washcloth over her forehead and eyes. Then she lifted a corner up to uncover one eye. "He knew about Gavin's death being an official suicide. He mentioned it yesterday when he called." A shadow flitted over Mike's round face and then cleared.

"His wife is a commissioner now," Mike said. He smoothed the corner of the washcloth back into place. "Your color is better. Ted's coming by.

217

He wants to ask you some questions about you and Maggie. I told him we'd all go out to lunch afterward. Let's see how you feel."

Catherine gritted her teeth and removed the washcloth. The thought of speaking with an attorney, even Mike's brother, was distasteful. She pushed herself to her feet, took her tea, and moved to the living room. Thinking back over the events that led up to the abortive interview, from Juan's appearance at lunch culminating with her last sight of him in his own house, Catherine knew her actions failed the 'reasonable' test. Would that mythical reasonable person have gone to the home of an enraged man and confronted his pregnant wife? No, the legally reasonable person would have called the proper authorities, or done nothing.

"Are you OK?" Mike asked.

"Did Ted say anything about how the case looked?" The summer heat closed in on her. She turned up the air conditioner and stirred the potpourri in the bowl on her mantel. Overcome with nausea again, she raced for the bathroom and this time, retched helplessly into the bowl.

Mike came in and helped her up. He wet a washcloth and wiped her face. "Better?" At her nod, Mike bent, and helped her shuffle off to the bedroom.

"Get some sleep."

"What about Ted?"

He's a lawyer. He'll be there for you."

"Yeah, but what does he think?"

"That the whole thing is bogus. And he wondered if the attempted break-in meant the

Riveras were upping the ante, trying to get you to settle."

Turning her head to look out the newly replaced window, Catherine saw Bullet, wrapped in his bandage, lying in the sun. "Won't work" she mumbled. "If they wanted something, they'd let me know who they were."

"The day's young, Kit Kat."

"What's the point?"

"Money. Gavin isn't paying them anymore."

"Do you believe he killed himself?"

"You have to leave this alone now. It's dangerous for you. Give it up."

"Mike, I can't." She groaned, struggling to fight back another round of nausea. You know Ashley didn't do it. You know I didn't do it. We both know someone did. Why are you buying into this? The evidence doesn't support it."

"Cathy, you're sick. Let's leave this alone."

"No. Talk to me."

He sat on the edge of the bed and laid a hand over her forehead. "You're sweating."

"I'm freezing." She held up an arm and displayed goose bumps. "Why did you change your mind?

"Gut feeling. Face it, Cathy, not that many people get murdered, but people do kill themselves for all kinds of half-baked reasons. Gavin hated to be embarrassed. You could see that in the Commission meetings."

"No struggle, Mike. He didn't fight the rope. I can't make that work. Who hangs himself and doesn't try to get out of it before the end"

"I know. That does bother me, and I believe the tox screen will answer that. But even if it doesn't, Kit Kat. He hit his head. He could have blacked out." He brushed her hair off her forehead with a gentle hand. "If you look at the evidence, the hard evidence, it's pretty clear it was a suicide."

"What about the threats? The e-mails and who knows, maybe phone calls too."

"Zoning people get those all the time. Susan gets them, and her husband is a cop." Mike dropped his face to his hands. "Did any of the e-mails talk about money?"

Catherine shook her head. "Nope, they were garden variety "we're gonna getchas."" She lifted her fingers and hooked them into quotation marks in the air to emphasis her point. "You have them. But we know that Gavin was walking a financial tightrope."

"Chief knows about the deposits so that dog won't hunt as a motive for murder. The Village attorney had a stack of papers a foot high on the investigation. The State auditor found discrepancies of more than a million dollars."

"Gavin only had a hundred thousand, Mike. Those deposits were recent, and Chief knows now, but nobody knew then. Where's the rest?"

"A hundred thousand we know about, Kit Kat, and maybe $50,000 of that was Cunningham's, as you pointed out. Not so much out of more than a million for a motive."

"Mike, if I get the rest of the records from Ashley, if I find out there's been bribes paid to Tomas and/or Juan, if I find out if there's been other deposits into Gavin's account, can you get a warrant to investigate where the funds came from?"

"Sure, if it ties to the open investigation, but what's the point."

"I don't know. If that much money is missing, and Gavin only recently got some of it, could it have been by mistake. Could this whole suicide by embarrassment be a cover up for someone trying to hide his or her involvement? Gavin was many things, but I think he had ethics. Could the embezzler have murdered Gavin because Gavin blew the whistle on him? Or suspected he would, and murder seemed the better option to inquiry and investigation?"

"You're grasping at straws, Cathy. And if Gavin's death was a suicide and tied to the missing money, then who's coming after you?"

"Maybe the two aren't related. Maybe I'm a target because I stuck my nose into the Riveras business. Or maybe, someone knows I have Gavin's bank records. Did you tell anyone?"

Mike shook his head. "About the records? No. You're concealing evidence. I can't afford to know that."

Catherine winced at his choice of words.

"There's nothing left to investigate. It's over. I think you're right. Whoever targeted you came from outside the Village. It all started after you went to the Redlands. Now get some rest. I'll wake you when Ted gets here." He pulled a crocheted comforter over her, tucked it under her chin, and walked to the door. Before he entered the hall, he turned and said, "If you stop to think about it, some of your cases are probably getting out of jail about now. This could be a grudge."

His words struck Catherine with the force of a physical blow. The daily dangers she'd lived with for so long rarely crossed her mind in the years after she'd turned in her badge. On some level, she knew the danger never went away. But she'd never considered someone coming after her once she was no longer a cop. She ran an inventory of the cases she recalled. Two stood out as possibilities. Catherine shivered at the thought. She'd have to call her old Chief.

*　*　*

The meeting with Ted took longer than Catherine thought possible. She had to ask him to repeat everything he said two or three times before he finally suggested they might want to meet another day. Completely exhausted, Catherine closed the door behind Ted and Mike, glad to see them go. She wanted privacy and she wanted to think, and she wanted to get warm.

Wishing she could settle into a bath, she filled the bathroom basin and plunged her hand in. She wanted to wash the day away. If thc cuts didn't respond by screaming in pain, she'd take that bath. Catherine winced as her hand hit the warm water. No full body emersion in her future. Sighing deeply, she opened her bedroom window enough to call Bullet in from the yard.

She picked up the pain pills from their place next to her bed. Looking at them, she briefly thought about taking one, hoping it would bring a deep, dreamless sleep. Her stomach heaved.

Holding the bottle, she walked into her bathroom. Lifting the seat on the commode, she opened the pill bottle and poured in the contents. She flushed and waited to be sure no residue remained in the bowl.

Lying down in bed, she patted the empty space alongside her. "Come on, Bullet, hop in next to Mommy. You deserve a soft bed too." Clutching the dog's fur, her eyes grew heavy as sleep overtook her.

* * *

Catherine tossed in her sleep, dreaming of a barbeque in her back yard. Jerking her eyes open, she woke disoriented, surprised to find it dark. Stretching, she sniffed the air and smelled smoke. This was no dream. Where was Bullet?

She yanked both her gun and cell phone from the bedside table. Glancing past the open curtains through the window next to her bed, she saw a brightly burning mound in her backyard. Dropping the phone, she raced from her bedroom, slapping the panic button on the alarm panel as she passed. The wailing of the siren filled the air instantly. Casting a quick glance over her shoulder to be certain she had not turned on any lights, Catherine yanked the back door open and heard the slapping sound of the doggie door. Her heart sank. She realized she forgot to lock it when she called Bullet in before she lay down.

The acrid smell of burning cloth choked her. Taking a shooter's stance in the now open doorway, she held her gun level pointed in the direction of the flames, and called out over the wail of the alarm, "Halt, I'm armed and I'll shoot." Behind her, the phone rang. The alarm company or a neighbor she didn't know. The sound of sirens filled the night air.

In the light of the fire, Catherine saw the small body of a burning animal near her porch steps. Venturing out from around the door jam, her gun still at the ready, she stepped into the yard and toed the smoldering mass.

It was a stuffed dog.

CHAPTER 27

"Catherine," Mike called softly to her, "I'm here. Put down your weapon. The fire department is on the way."

Out of the corner of her eye, Catherine saw Mike, gun in his hand, advancing toward the bonfire. Billy LaMotta, weapon also drawn, walked slowly behind him. Catherine felt the air go out of her, leaving her like a rag doll. She slowly lowered her weapon, walked over to the garden spigot and turned it on. Playing the water over the fire, she hoped neither man noticed the tears running down her face. Bullet was not at her side.

Mike took the hose as firefighters raced through the rear gate. A blast from their hoses doused the smoldering remains of the fire. Mike returned to stand alongside Catherine. He held his silence. Billy stood a few feet back, surveying the smoking heap in the middle of the yard.

"Have you seen Bullet?" Catherine's voice trembled. "Oh God, Mike. He can't be buried under in that bonfire." The lump in her throat nearly choked her. "Please tell me he's not in there." Her voice broke and tears slid down her face. "I forgot to lock the doggie door. I felt so sick. I had him in bed with me. He's gone. Oh God, Mike, he's gone." Mike caught her as she crumpled.

Billy came closer and stared at the steaming heap. "They're all toy dogs. It's a burning pile of stuffed animals." He picked up one that escaped the fire and brought it over to Mike. "German Shepherd it looks like, LT." LaMotta used the familiar term for his Lieutenant. They all look alike, as far as I can tell."

Mike helped the now sobbing Catherine to the porch. He kicked the door open and assisted her to sit on the Florida room couch. "LaMotta, did you see her dog?" He asked as he squatted down and inspected the hard plastic flap inserted in the lower part of the door. Catherine replaced the standard issue butterfly turn bars with sliding bolts at the same time she installed the door. Bullet was big, even for a German Shepherd. If he could get through the door, so could children, or small adults. The bolts, when locked, prevented anyone from entering.

Billy shook his head. "No, I didn't see any dogs. I was two blocks over when I heard the alarm. I wasn't even sure it was Catherine's. I called you, just in case, given the recent problems. Then I smelled the smoke. I didn't see any cars either, not in my direction, at least."

Ann Moffat, Catherine's next-door neighbor ran over the damp grass in her nightgown. "Officer, officer, I saw someone run and get into a car. Where's Catherine? This is terrible. I don't know what's going on in this Village. All this crime. I want to move. Go someplace safe."

Mike looked from Catherine to her neighbor and back to his officer. "LaMotta, would you take a statement?" He asked.

LaMotta glanced over his shoulder. "Happy to. Who should I call for crowd control?" Billy cocked his head in the direction of the gate, reached for his shirt pocket, unbuttoned the flap with one hand and pulled out a notebook. Fingering through to a blank page he faced the neighbor and said, "Exactly what did you see?"

Ann rocked from foot to foot and craned her neck in Catherine's direction. The more Billy moved to block her view, the more she sidled over toward Catherine's porch.

Sobs still wracking her body, Catherine saw Ann's attempts to make eye contact through the large windows of the room. She waved off Mike's attempts to keep her on the couch. Groping in her pocket for a tissue, she blew her nose and tried to wipe the tears off her face with her hands. "Ann," she called. "Did you see Bullet? Is he in your yard?"

Billy followed Ann to the Florida room.

"She lives next door," Catherine said by way of introduction although it was unlikely LaMotta didn't know Ann, at least by sight. Looking at the woman, now seated on a chintz covered wicker chair she asked again, "Did you see Bullet?"

"Are you all right, Catherine?" Ann responded. "You look sick."

"Mrs. Moffat. Just tell us what you saw." Billy tried to get the interview on track.

"Wait a minute, officer. I'll answer your questions in a minute." Ann waved a hand in Catherine's direction and continued, "This woman is my neighbor. I have a duty to check on her first"

Catherine recoiled at the naked avarice she saw in Ann's eyes. It disgusted her to realize her neighbor was looking for information, not offering any. Still, she was their best hope to find Bullet. If she had seen something, they needed her testimony. "I'm fine, Ann, thank you so much for asking. I'm really worried about Bullet though."

Billy glanced back at Mike and rolled his eyes. He wasn't getting anywhere with their only witness so far.

Though the buzz of conversation going on outside Catherine heard the sound of someone, probably another officer, trying to secure the scene, attempting to get the looky-lous to go back home. The medley of sounds terminated with the blaring announcement "You don't tell me what to do. I'm the mayor of this Village, and if I want to come in, I will."

Arnie Cunningham forced his way past the frustrated officers and onto the back porch. He stopped short of pulling open the door to the Florida room.

Catherine shot a helpless look at Mike. She'd gone from persona non grata to Cunningham's best friend in the space of two disasters. It confused her, and made her suspicious.

"Reardon, don't you think you should help secure the scene here?" Cunningham asked.

"Actually, Mayor, I'm not on duty tonight." Mike responded.

"Mr. Mayor, have you seen my dog? A big German Shepherd?"

"Don't you think a fire is more important than a dog, Catherine? I know that's how you make your living now, but it's a matter of perspective. Your safety comes first. I'm sure your dog will be back once things calm down. He probably ran off. You've had a rough few days. The dog is probably confused."

Catherine's blood boiled. How dare this man accuse her dog of cowardice? She'd put Bullet up against anyone at any time. That dog had a protective instinct a mile long. He was the only reason Catherine felt safe staying in her house after the first attack. Now he was missing. The cocoon of security and safety Catherine normally felt behind her closed doors didn't exist without the dog. Not after two attacks. Holding her temper she replied, "Right now, the only thing I'm worried about is my dog. I can't do anything about the fire, it's over."

Mike looked over at Ann. "You said you saw someone running to a car. Did you get a description?"

Ann sat back in her chair and crossed her legs. She looked from Billy to Mike and then through the window to the Mayor still standing on the porch.

"I saw a man. At least I think it was a man. It was dark and he got into a car, a big car, like yours Catherine."

Mike looked at Catherine who gave a slight shake of her head indicating this was new information for her. The car that tried to run her over the other night was small. More Japanese than General Motors.

Sighing deeply, Billy asked, "Did you get any description at all?"

"No. It was dark." She said unnecessarily. "But he did come from back here. I'm sure of that."

Catherine thought she heard Cunningham sigh. She wasn't sure if it was in relief or frustration.

"If you have a photo of your dog, give it to Mike." Cunningham said. "We can post it on the Village board." When he turned to go, Catherine noticed some type of dusty cement-like dirt sticking to the cuffs of his jeans. He turned back and said, "I'm glad the Jackman thing worked out the way it did. I never thought you'd murder anyone. Of course, we're looking into his wife."

Catherine felt her mouth fall open in amazement. She couldn't believe he'd say anything so senseless. She was about to ask Mike what he meant when Ann spoke.

"I may have heard Bullet, now that I think about it. But I didn't see him. Whoever ran out of your yard did it like something was chasing him. I suppose it could have been your dog, chasing I mean, not running." Ann shot a quick glance at Catherine as if seeking support.

"Where was the car parked?"

"Over across the street. The streetlights are out, I've been complaining about that for weeks now. I could just make out a shape."

"But no dog?"

"Well, no. But then I smelled smoke, and I went to look. I thought it might be my house. I had a barbeque last night. I thought that maybe I sacked the charcoal before it was all out. I thought that maybe it lit something in my yard. I could have missed a dog chasing him, I suppose. Since the dog would have followed..."

Billy waited a while and when the woman didn't offer any additional details he said, "You said you didn't hear any barking, or you did?"

She shook her head. "I don't think so, but maybe. I can't be sure."

Ann swung her top leg back and forth and chewed on the side of her thumb. For the first time, Catherine realized why some people found the swinging leg motion so irritating.

"Ann, I appreciate your coming over, but I'd like to try to find my dog." Catherine's eyes looked out the window to the remains of the smoldering mound in her back yard. One of the firefighters raked through it. She prayed silently that he wouldn't turn up any dog bones. Catherine knew she couldn't stand it if the dog's remains turned up in the fire debris.

"There's something more." Ann said. "I'm trying to picture everything in my mind. The guy was tall. I thought it was Mike at first." Her voice trailed off. Catherine gave the woman her full attention, willing her to say something about Bullet.

The neighbor looked at Mike and smiled. "But he was bulkier, hunched over kind of."

"But you said he ran like someone was chasing him." LaMotta said, flipping back to the page in his notebook.

"Yes, he was moving fast but he was struggling with something too. I remember now, he opened the back door of the truck and shoved something inside. That's when I smelled smoke and went to check my yard."

"Door, or tailgate, or did it lift up?" Billy asked.

"Didn't the light come on at the same time the door opened?" Catherine asked.

"No. No light. But I think there was a head in the back."

"A head?" LaMotta looked up from his notebook. "You saw a head?"

"Well, maybe. I mean, it was dark. I thought, I don't know. I saw the runner shove something in the back, and I saw a shape pop up. I think."

Mike looked at Billy LaMotta. "Did you smell an accelerant? He could have been carrying a gas can."

Billy shook his head. "No gas, no kerosene and no lighter fluid, nothing but the smell of smoke."

"Chief." The firefighter raking the remains of the mound called out. "Come look at this."

Mike grabbed for Catherine as she sprang up from the couch and raced for the door.

CHAPTER 28

The fire marshal had uncovered a hunk of gold bracelet that meant nothing to Catherine. Billy had dutifully collected it when it was cool enough to handle. He'd asked Catherine if she recognized it as hers. The lump of gold was hard to identify as anything. On closer examination, she noticed a broken lobster-claw catch, and a melted blob clinging to a link. Catherine made a mental note to follow up with the crime scene examiner. She wanted to know about the blob, it could be a charm. If it was, then it could give a clue as to who had her dog.

Catherine was beside herself, she had exhausted every avenue she could think of to find Bullet. Yesterday she personally visited every vet in a ten mile radius and every animal shelter and humane society to leave photos, and both her and Mike's contact information. She'd taken a quarter page ad in the Metropolis and put up countless posters. No one she called or spoke to had seen the dog or heard of a stray German Shepherd.

Nancy called Catherine early in the morning to ask if Bullet had come home yet. When she heard the dog was still missing, she rounded up an impromptu breakfast and called Vicki and Susan to meet her at Catherine's house. The three women listened to every detail of the dog's disappearance and even offered to divide into search parties, but most of all, they wanted to make sure someone was always with Catherine.

Catherine chewed her lip. Her biggest fear wasn't her safety. It was Bullet's. She couldn't shake the image of the intruder shoving something in the back seat of his car. Was it Bullet, and if it was, had he killed her dog? Why hadn't Bullet barked? He should have barked his head off if someone tried to carry him away and he was alive. Was he muzzled? Was he unconscious?

"I don't get it Nance. It's been two days. Where's Bullet? Nobody's seen him. Sue, what about you? You know more people here than anyone else. Have you heard anything? Anybody say anything about a wandering German Shepherd?"

"I still think we should divide the town and search," Nancy said.

"The town's already searching." Sue replied. "There are signs everywhere."

Paddy Whack jumped up on Catherine's lap.

"She misses her canine brother." Vicki said.

"If only she could talk, she'd tell us what happened." Nancy responded. "Cathy, how did you sleep through Bullet barking? That's the part I don't understand."

Leaning back into the pillow behind her, Catherine noticed her physical discomfort seemed to be abating. She picked up the glass of lemonade and rolled it over her forehead, the cool moisture felt refreshing. Despite air conditioning, the room seemed humid. "I've asked myself that a million times. I'd taken a pain pill the night before. I blame that for my agreeing to Oliver's interview." She rolled her eyes at the group. "He's freelancing these days. Trying to anyway. Wants to quit the paper."

"Back to sleeping through Bullet's warnings," Sue said. "Are you sure you didn't take one and forget. It's easy to do."

Irritation flashed through her. No matter how far she'd come from her wild drinking days, it would never be far enough, for these women to forget. Recent history didn't help increase their comfort zone. The call to Gavin demanding her dog-sitting pay sprang directly from a bottle. Now it seemed that the girl power group feared once an addict, always an addict, and worried there'd been a change in the drug of choice.

"Positive. I flushed them. They made me sick. Really sick." Her face reddened at the admission.

"From one pain pill?" Nancy asked.

"Yeah, nauseous, blurry vision, headache, chills the whole works.

"Sounds more like poison. How did you feel that lousy and sleep through Bullet?"

"Only if I poisoned myself with my own coffee. I don't think Bullet barked. I called him up into bed with me. I remember grabbing on his scruff before I fell asleep. I think he went silent on me. Identified a problem and went out to deal with it." She felt tears sting beneath her lids. She buried her face in Paddy's soft fur, using the distraction to get control of her emotions. If anyone hurt that dog, I'd better not find out who. I swear I'll kill him."

"Catherine." Nancy's voice held a warning. "Don't say that. Don't even think it. Someone might believe you."

Catherine nodded, smiled, raised her glass and said, "They should. We're talking about my dog."

"What's going on with the Rivera's case? Anything?" Vicki asked.

"Ted thinks he can make it go away. I can't fathom how they're blaming me for a miscarriage. God, I'm a disaster lately. Let me touch it, and it will turn to mud." She raised her hand in front of her. "My business is a total loss. No one will trust me with their dogs..."

"Not true. Didn't you say the Kents asked you to take care of Pugsley?" Vicki interrupted.

"Have you seen the construction they're doing, Suze? Alvarez must have signed off on their plans for the pool house," Vicki said.

"Impossible." Sue replied. "They may have fired me, but I still know the Zoning Committee hasn't met yet, and it won't until the third week of the month. Then it takes two meetings. That's in the Village Charter."

"Catherine, you're not getting dog walking business? Have you figured out a new career yet?" Sue asked. "Going back to real estate seems out.

There must be fifty houses in foreclosure in the Village alone. Ask Mike. It's getting scary. Some are becoming crack dens."

"This is South Florida. The high-end stuff is still doing well. I'm scared though, Sue." Catherine looked back over her shoulder directly into her friend's eyes. "I don't know where I fit in anymore. I don't know where I belong."

Sue strode over to her friend and gave her a quick hug. She took the dog figurine from Catherine's hands, replaced it on the mantle and held Catherine by the shoulders. "We love you Cathy. Don't forget it."

"Isn't that Ashley's car pulling up?" Nancy pointed out the window to the road.

Following the direction of Nancy's gesture, Catherine stood and opened the door to admit the newcomer. "I'm sorry, I didn't mean to interrupt." Ashley paused before crossing the threshold. "Can I come back later, when it's just you?" She included Nancy in the request with a wave of her hand.

Sue rose, tugging lightly on Vicki's hand as she stood. "We were just leaving, Ashley. I stopped by yesterday to see how you were doing. I'm sorry you weren't home."

Ashley looked startled. "I'm sorry. I don't mean to be such a pig. Sue, Vicki, please, don't go because of me. Catherine, you can throw me out if you like."

"No, seriously, we need to go." Vicki said. "Catherine, I'll drive the perimeter of town, Susan, will you check for Bullet along the running route near the canals?"

"I don't throw anyone out, Ashley, before I offer them food and drink" Catherine replied, pouring a glass of lemonade from the pitcher on the coffee table and placing it in front of the dark haired woman, Catherine looked at her closely. "How are you, Ashley?"

Ashley bit her lip and looked from one woman to the other. She seemed to shrink in her chair. Then she looked up, and her eyes swam with tears.

"I feel like I've been through a ringer. My husband dies. Is it suicide or murder? I'm the prime suspect in murder and/or considered the cause of his suicide. My lawyer, by the way, says not to relax on the murder charge. He thinks the police could be waiting for me to make a mistake, admit some guilt or something. Then I got a call from the Village attorney. He wants me to turn over all of Gavin's financial records."

"What!" Nancy exploded. "Tell them to get a subpoena. Don't give them anything without one."

"He's especially requested any personal accounts of Gavin's. They're trying to pin missing money on my husband! There's a lot missing." Ashley's voice broke, and she pulled a tissue from her purse. "It's ludicrous to think Gavin embezzled money. He didn't have any access to Village accounts. None! He's dead, and he can't defend himself. Well I can defend him. They won't get away with this!"

Catherine moved toward the sobbing woman when the phone rang. "Nance, would you get that for me?" She asked as she put her arm around Ashley.

"It's Dannie. She's found Bullet."

CHAPTER 29

Motivated by the surge of adrenaline that raced through her, Catherine shot up from the chair, ran to the door, flung it open and charged outside. She stopped her forward progression so quickly she nearly tripped. Then she turned and came back to the house.

"Did she say where she found him?"

Going to her friend and giving her a hug, Nancy said, "Yes, she saw him in the cul de sac near the Kents. Meg was calling him and tempting him with a treat. She asked Dannie if she knew the dog, or his owner. They managed to get him into Meg's yard."

"But he knows Dannie. He'd go to her in a heartbeat. Damn, why didn't I grab the phone instead of running out the door at half cock?" Catherine bounced from one foot to the other. Gulping down rising panic, she asked, "Is he hurt? Did Dannie say? Is that why he didn't go to her?"

Nancy shook her head. "No, Cathy, she didn't say, and I'm sure, knowing Dannie, she'd have told me."

Unable to wait any longer, Catherine said, "I'm sorry. I've got to go. I want my dog! I'll be home soon!"

On the short drive to the Kents, Catherine wondered why Meg didn't recognize Bullet. Not only did she see him often, but the entire neighborhood knew he was hurt in the attempted break in. And Oliver saw him, complete with bandages, day before yesterday. Did the dog wander over? Why didn't he wander home? He knew the route, they ran it often enough. Did someone abandon him, someone who drives a large SUV? While she drove, Catherine kept a sharp eye out for any vehicle that might fit the description. Funny, she'd never realized how common large SUVs still were despite gas prices and the financial crunch. She spotted an even dozen on her trip to the Kents.

The sound of a siren and the sight of blue lights in the rear view mirror brought her to the present. Sighing deeply, she pulled over and watched Billy LaMotta get out of his unit.

He strode to her rolled down window. "Do you know how fast you were going, Catherine?"

Blushing, she replied, "No Billy, I don't. Bullet's found. I wasn't paying attention. I deserve the ticket. Can you drop it off later? I'd really like to pick up my dog."

"Where'd you find him?"

"I didn't, Dannie did. Wandering near the Kents. They have him in the back yard."

Billy chewed on the end of his pencil. Catherine thought she saw his expression clear. "Follow me," he said.

Muttering under her breath, Catherine waited until the patrol unit pulled in front of her car. What the heck is he doing? Running me in for speeding? She fumed. A sense of relief washed over Catherine as Billy failed to make the turn to the police station and continued in the direction of the Kents' house.

From two blocks away Catherine thought she heard Bullet's joyous barks. If it weren't for the police escort, Catherine would have happily run the stop sign on the corner. Bullet's face pressed into the ironwork on the gate. His tail wagged so hard it shook his entire body. Defying all logic, Catherine comforted herself with the belief the dog smelled her coming.

A wave of relief so intense it caused physical pain washed over Catherine as her car rolled to a stop. Slamming the vehicle into park without taking the time to turn off her engine, Catherine bounded out of the driver's seat and raced toward the closed gate. For a brief moment, woman and animal were the only two living beings in Catherine's universe. Bullet's paws rested on the top rail of the gate, his red tongue washing over his mistress's face as she fumbled to find the latch with one hand and pet her dog with the other.

A second hand, long-fingered and cool, brushed Catherine's away. The gate swung inward and Bullet leapt into Catherine's arms. Looking up from the dog's neck, Catherine smiled thanks to Meg.

"I can't thank you enough, Meg. Where did you find him? Did he look hurt? I'm so close to him now, I can't see!"

"Yes, I'd like some answers to those questions too."

Catherine stiffened at the sound of the masculine voice behind her. Then she relaxed. In the excitement of greeting her dog, she'd forgotten all about Billy LaMotta. Carefully lowering Bullet to all fours on the ground, mindful of his still bandaged body, she said, "Billy was kind enough to give me a police escort to your house. I really appreciate your help."

"I wondered how you got here so fast." Dannie came down the steps from the porch and stood next to Meg.

"Hey, Danno, I didn't see you. I thought Meg and Oliver were sitting on the porch. I was so intent on Bullet. I'm surprised I saw anyone besides my fur baby!"

"Well good, I guess I can drop that Atkins thing I've been on then," Dannie chortled.

Billy cleared his throat and riffled the pages of his notebook. "Is there someplace we can sit and be comfortable?" He handed Catherine the keys to her car. "I shut it off, waste of gas to leave it running."

Meg stepped back and indicated a small sitting area in the side yard of the house. Since their home sat on a double corner lot, they'd set part of the side yard up as an outdoor sitting room. "Oliver's on deadline, he likes the house completely quiet, but let me get some lemonade."

Torn between staying to hear the story and getting her dog home, Catherine asked Billy, "Do you need me to stay for anything?"

"Yes, I want to make sure the dog's acting all right before you leave. Ms. Gutierrez, I'd like you to stay as well. You helped find him, I believe."

"Had you seen the dog before today?" Billy asked Meg, nodding his thanks for the drink she placed in front of him.

She shook her head. "No, and I knew he was missing, but I didn't make the connection with a large German Shepherd in the cul de sac."

"What made you decide to round him up?"

Meg looked confused, "He was running without a collar. Nobody was around. I figured he'd escaped his owner. I worried he might get hit by a car, or jump into my yard and hurt Pugsley. What would you expect me to do?"

Catherine sipped her lemonade and watched Billy as he avoided the question. She hadn't thought Meg hadn't recognized Bullet. Given his size, it surprised her that anyone would try to corral him if they didn't know him and his temperament. Thoughtfully, she chewed her lip.

As the silence grew at the table, Meg endeavored to fill it. "I saw Dannie. She stopped her car and yelled out 'Bullet.' The dog ran toward her, and I felt much better. He shied away from her though, didn't go directly to her. Then I noticed the bandages that covered him. That's how I recognized him, and we gave chase."

From the corner of her eye, Catherine saw Billy look in Dannie's direction. Before he spoke,

Catherine said, "He shied away from you, Dannie? He knows you."

Dannie's curls bounced as she nodded. "Yes, it surprised me too. We've always been the best friends. Well as good as we could be, considering I have four cats!"

"How'd you get him in the yard?" Billy asked.

Dannie and Meg looked at each other. Shrugging Dannie said, "I whistled him up like you do. He came then, I grabbed on his scruff, Meg opened the little gate between the end of her yard and the cul de sac, and I brought him in. I had to drag him a little." Dannie looked at Catherine apologetically. "I was careful, I didn't want to hurt him, but I think the backhoe spooked him."

"He's been missing for two days now. You're telling me he hasn't been in the neighborhood before this morning. Did he look…?" Billy broke off in mid-sentence and stared at Catherine sitting next to him.

Catherine plucked at Billy's sleeve. Her face had gone putty grey. She felt the world spin around her. She wasn't sure if she was going to faint or vomit.

In one motion, Billy pulled back her chair and forced her head down between her knees. "Call 911." He barked at Meg.

Struggling to get her head up, Catherine said, "No, I'll be fine. It's the excitement. No need for 911. Honest, I'm fine. And I'm not going to the hospital so there's no point in calling rescue out here."

The officer must have heard something in her voice. He released his hold on her head and helped her to a full sitting position. "You look better." Meg stood next to the cop, a phone in one hand, a glass of water in the other. He took the water and held it to Catherine's lips. She took a small sip, then, grasped the glass in both hands and drank so deeply she nearly choked. Catching her breath, she rolled the chilled glass across her forehead, before she handed it to Meg.

"I'm better. I'm sorry." She looked from Meg to Dannie who'd put her arm around Catherine's shoulders. "Too much excitement lately." She smiled ruefully. "I thought I wanted more excitement in my life. Now I think I'll look for a nice quiet job someplace. If only I could think of one." She swallowed hard. Her throat felt like dust. She reached for the glass of lemonade and noticed it Meg had picked it up and held it and her empty water glass between her fingers by the rim.

Billy glanced at his watch and fingered the radio on his shoulder. "I'll call the LT to come get you."

Catherine's protest died on her lips as Billy placed his hand over hers and said, "He'd have me docked if I didn't. So it's either the LT or 911." Looking up at Meg who still stood next to him he said, "Can you take her inside? This heat can't be helping her."

As Meg led her away, Catherine heard Billy speaking. She glanced back and saw him talking to the microphone attached to his epaulette.

247

Oliver came out of a room off the kitchen that Catherine supposed served as his office. He looked at each of the women and the police officer in turn. His gaze finally coming to rest on the dog at Catherine's feet.

Meg sighed audibly when Billy took his notebook out again. "More questions?" She asked.

"Just one, Mrs. Kent, then I'll be on my way. Did the dog seem hungry or thirsty when you brought him in?"

Meg looked at Dannie again and said, "No. I didn't think so. I brought him water of course, and he drank it, but not in great gulps like Pugsley does when he knocks over his water bowl and goes without during the day. Dannie, do you agree?"

"Yes, in fact, it surprised me that he didn't seem thirsty. We didn't feed him though. I never thought about it."

"Poor baby," Catherine said, stroking his fur. "You must be so hungry. Mommy will get you home soon."

Billy stood at the same time a knock sounded at the door. Oliver handed Catherine a second glass of water and continued on to open the door. Mike stood on the front porch.

"Hi, LT, I've taken statements and I'm just leaving. Do you want a copy after they're typed?"

Mike nodded but his eyes never left Catherine. He strode into the room and squatted down taking her chin in his hand and gazing directly into her face. "You OK, Kit Kat?"

A comfortable warmth flowed through Catherine. Muscle knots in her neck relaxed at his touch. Nodding she said, "Yes, take me home, Mike."

"Kit Kat, I'm taking you to my house. There's been too much excitement at your house lately. I think we both could use the break."

Straightening up, Mike turned and looked at the Kents and Dannie. "I can't thank you enough for finding Bullet and taking care of Catherine."

Meg rose from her seat. "It was my pleasure, Lieutenant, but won't you stay for a few moments? Just to be certain Catherine's feeling better. She nearly passed out in the yard."

"I'd better go." Dannie said as she got up from the chair.

"Us too." Mike added. "In a few minutes. And Kit Kat," his jaw tightened and a slight pulse beat in his cheek, "I'm driving you." He sat.

Oliver and Meg glanced at each other, and sat. It amused Catherine to notice that their demeanor was more like students in the principal's office than homeowners in their living room.

"These two have had one heck of a week," Mike said, indicating Catherine and Bullet. "I'll be glad when they both go three consecutive days with no adventures."

Oliver seemed to relax back into his chair. "I can imagine. Do they know anything about who broke in or who started the fire?"

Catherine, freed from participation in the conversation that ranged over current Village topics including the end of the investigation of Gavin's death and the beginning of the investigation into embezzlement, directed her gaze around the room.

249

She noted Oliver's brag wall. Getting up she walked over and looked at the framed, autographed photos from Miami-Dade dignitaries, a number of Judges, including Nancy's boss, Phil inscribed 'a long way from Freshman year.' Toward the end of the wall, hung a plaque with an empty penholder honoring ten years with the paper.

"You work with Ashley. How do you think she's holding up?" Catherine asked.

Startled, his mouth pulled back in quick grimace. "I don't know. We work together but the Metropolis is a very large place. The arts and gardening sections are on different floors. From what I've heard though, she's doing much better than most people think."

Catherine sat in the chair next to the end table. "Meaning?"

Oliver shrugged. "As I said, we don't work together. We sometimes car pool, but that's rare, usually after hurricanes before the street lights have power restored. I've picked up on some undercurrents. That's all. Gossip really. Probably means nothing, but there have been comments about her returning to work full time so quickly."

Mike glanced at his watch again. "We'd better go, Catherine. You look tired."

Oliver and Meg rose to take their guests to the door. Bullet lifted his head from between his front legs and thumped the floor with his tail. He came over to Catherine's side, giving both Kents a wide berth.

CHAPTER 30

Catherine studied Mike's strong profile as he drove her to his house. The intense relief she felt at having him sweep in and take over forced her to realize that the ambivalence she had been claiming to feel was little more than a cover for her own fears of what it meant to love him. It was time she owned her own feelings in this relationship. A fair amount of guilt laced her understanding. Not just about the true nature of their relationship, but about persuading him to withhold information about Gavin's finances. She wondered if the omission was eating at him. Did he know about the Village attorney's request for Gavin's financial records? If Ashley turned over the documents, that was one thing. If Ashley turned over the documents and it became known Catherine had them, then that could taint Mike. She couldn't let that happen. He didn't deserve it.

Mike's hand snaked over across the center console and gripped Catherine's thigh. "Hey, Kit Kat, you're so far away. Everything will work out. You'll see. Don't worry. I want you at my house for a few days. You, Bullet and Paddy Whack if you think she'll come." He shot her a quick glance as if checking her reaction. "Give someone a chance to get some repair work done at your house, too."

"It seems as if the whole world's gone crazy, Mike. I used to think I was so competent." She gave a snorty laugh. "This always happens to me, I hit a comfortable place, I think I know what's going on, and then wham, my life goes to hell. I don't know if God's sense of humor is that good or if I'm cursed!" She dropped her head back against the leather headrest.

She'd been so intent on feeling sorry for herself that she hadn't realized they'd stopped in front of Mike's trim mission style home. Glancing out the window, Catherine did a double take. Nancy sat on the front steps, knees tucked under her chin like a child.

Catherine pulled up on the door handle and sprung out of Mike's truck before he could get around and open the door for her. Her feet hit the grassy area alongside the driveway only seconds before her hands. The sudden movement caused a wave of nausea and dizziness, and she lost her footing. Mike and Nancy reached her at the same time. Sitting on the grass, she held up a hand, opting instead to grip Bullet's neck and use his bulk to lever herself off the ground. Mike's arm wrapped around Catherine's waist, he helped her up the stairs and into the cool of his house. With his free hand, he motioned to Nancy to follow.

"You are going straight to bed."

"No. Damn, I don't know what's wrong with me. I promise. I'll stay flat on my back on the couch."

Mike's first renovation after he'd bought the house had been to break through the walls between the living room and the enclosed front porch. The change served to open up his living room to the street and bring light into the previously dark space. His second renovation had been to install impact resistant glass throughout his house. Catherine looked out the nearly floor to ceiling arched windows and realized if she'd had impact glass, the brick would have bounced off or at worst, crazed the glass. The trouble she found herself in would never have happened.

Settled on the couch with Bullet lying on the floor in front of her, she looked expectantly at Nancy.

"Guess you know I have friends in the law biz." Nancy began.

Catherine rolled her eyes and looked at Mike. He gave Nancy his undivided attention.

"There's a motion pending before Court, filed by the Village attorney, for an injunction freezing Gavin's assets."

"Ok, Ashley pretty much knew something like that was coming. You told her to demand a subpoena before she turned over any financial information." Catherine pointed out.

"There's more, isn't there?" Mike asked.

Nancy nodded. "Yeah, and this is harder to say. Catherine, there's been an Information filed against you."

Catherine's jaw dropped to her chest. She knew the filing of an Information preceded the request for a criminal warrant. "By whom? For what? How do you know? Never mind, don't answer the last one. I don't want to know who compromised themselves." She looked up at Mike. "Did you know about this?"

The tips of his ears reddened in anger and he shook his head.

"Chief filed it at the request of the Village attorney." Nancy responded.

"For what!" Mike exploded as Catherine raced for the bathroom.

Mike was waiting in the hallway for her after she got out. He tried to direct her into the bedroom, but she brushed off his hand.

"It's just a virus." She lay back down on the couch, her skin clammy. She shivered despite the heat. "Nancy, what's in the information?

"I haven't seen it. And there's no way I can get it. I heard it's for withholding information, interfering in a police investigation, and complicacy in murder."

Catherine's head spun in Mike's direction. "Is this about Gavin's death? Or is it about Maggie's unborn child?"

"I don't know. But Chief wouldn't care about Maggie. That's out of his jurisdiction."

"Murder," Catherine breathed.

"Complicity, Not murder." Mike said. "If you're complicit, there has to be another party. If there's another party, why not conspiracy? And who's the other party?"

"Ashley. They're going to go after Ashley again too. It makes sense in an odd and sick sort of way." Nancy said.

"You know a lot of folks in the Village were happy having Ashley as suspect number one. I've heard some talk that even if the death was a suicide, Ashley should have to answer for it because she forced him into it." Nancy rose from the chair where she sat and walked over to stand beside Catherine. "It seemed, the more Ashley tried to keep out of politics, the more the Village disliked her. I never understood that."

"I do," Mike said. "Too many people hoped to influence Gavin's decisions by cultivating Ashley. Because she wasn't open to it, they resented her. Simple self-interest. I've seen it a lot with cops. Nobody wants to get to know the cop, but a lot of people want to know his family, at least while they think the association can gain them something. Happens all the time."

Thinking back to her own days on the force, Catherine realized the truth of the statement.

"Nancy, my brain is full. I don't know what to do now."

"Wait, and get some rest, and get over the flu. That's all you can do. Just because they filed an Information doesn't mean there'll be any action on it. You know that. Oh, yeah. I meant to tell you, Sue got a call before she left your house. She's been reinstated."

"What!" Catherine's head shot up from the couch. A sheen of sweat dappled her face and wave of nausea made her lay back down.

255

"Yes, pending the hearing of her grievance. The Village attorney has been a very busy boy.

"Good," Mike said. He wiped Catherine's forehead with a tissue. "She deserves the job, she's great at it."

"Where's your car, Cathy?" Nancy asked.

"In front of the Kents." Mike answered. "If you'll stay with Cathy, I'll go pick it up and get it off their lawn."

"Nah, I'll go." Nancy replied. "I'll drive it to your house, Catherine, and I'll feed Paddy Whack at the same time."

Nancy hesitated at the door. She turned, gripped the knob, then turned back again. "I didn't want to tell you this Catherine." Nancy paused. "Vicki's house was broken into today."

Another wave of nausea washed over Catherine. "When?"

Holding up her hand, Nancy continued, "While she was with us. Nothing was taken, but something was left."

"Did she call the office?" Mike asked.

"What was left, Nance?" Catherine said.

"A note. They left a note. It said, 'Don't back a looser.'"

CHAPTER 31

The bed heaved under Mike's weight.
Through a gauzy veil of sleep, Catherine felt him
leave her side. She snuggled her head deeper into
the pillow, hoping to return to her dream of floating
over the waves in a little boat, relaxed, and without
a care in the world. A small smile curled her lips.
The sense of peace was like a warm blanket on a
cold night.

She rolled over on her side, tucked her hand
under her head, and floated off. A loud pop split the
night air, followed by the squeal of tires on
pavement. Still lost in that womblike world between
sleep and wakefulness, Catherine wondered how a
backfiring car got into her water dream.

Bullet lifted his head up over the side of the
bed and nuzzled his mistress. She tried to push him
away. The sound of a groan came from the living
room. Confused, Catherine called out for Mike.

Hearing no response, Catherine sat up and
concentrated on the sounds of the night. Mike's
impact resistant glass provided an excellent sound
barrier. All she heard was the cycling off of the air

conditioner and the ticking of a clock. Then, more faintly than before, she heard another groan.

Bullet growled. His nails click clacked on the wood floors as he cantered out of the bedroom. Catherine, her bare feet making a slapping sound, followed behind him. In the moonlight, she could make out Mike's body curled in a fetal position on the living room floor in front of the window. The flashlight he must have picked up to keep from disturbing Catherine illuminated the floor from under the couch. Bullet, as if sensing that he should stay back, sat in the hallway opening, his fangs bared.

The pounding of her heart drowned out any sound. Acting on training and instinct, she rushed to Mike's side.

"Mike. Come on baby, say something." She begged and pressed her index and middle finger to the artery pulsing in his throat. His pulse beat a strong and steady tattoo beneath her fingers. Relief washed over her. Leaning down, she kissed his forehead.

Her gaze fell on a small puddle of blood darkened the floor under his left side. Confused, she remembered her dream. The pop she heard was no backfire. It was a shot. It took all Catherine's training to leave him where he lay. Instead, her left hand groped for the afghan she'd crocheted for him as a Christmas present their first year together. Grasping its stretchy folds, she yanked it off the couch and covered him hoping its warmth would help ward off shock. Mike needed paramedics on the way, and then she could worry about first aid.

She levered herself into a standing position and raced for the kitchen counter. Grabbing his service radio from its place in the charger, she keyed the device on.

"Officer down," She barked into the hand held. "1535 Oleander Lane. Shots fired."

The crackling sound of the static as the radio came alive was music to her ears. While she listened to the dispatcher's demands for additional information, she gathered up kitchen towels, ice, a large bottle of water from the refrigerator, and started back to Mike. Putting the items on the floor next to him, she realized she'd scooped up his 38-caliber service revolver with the kitchen towels. He'd long ago stopped carrying the weapon he'd gotten at the time he completed training in favor of the greater firepower of a 40-caliber Glock. He kept the revolver in the towel drawer calling it his 'just in case' weapon. She slid the small gun into the pocket of her baggy sleeping shorts. Carefully lifting the afghan, Catherine saw the dark stain of blood had grown only a little in the short time she'd been in the kitchen. Checking again for his pulse, she thought it might be a little weaker. She rocked back on her heels and checked again. Yes, definitely weaker. Dropping her head into her hands she tried to will the ambulance to arrive faster.

"Stay with me, Mike, please. Stay with me."

Catherine blinked back tears. Mike's skin was growing clammy and his color paling, despite the slow-growing puddle. He looked like he was going into shock. She debated rolling him over and trying to elevate his legs. The blood seemed more a trickle than a flood, she didn't think the bullet hit an artery, but if it had, then his body position was applying sufficient pressure to stem the flow. She didn't want to take the risk moving him could bring. He groaned again. She poured water from the bottle onto one of the kitchen towels, and used it to wipe down his face.

"No, babe. You stay quiet. Don't move. Help's on the way." She shushed him not wanting him to talk or move toward the sound of her voice. In the distance, the sound of sirens approached.

She tried to see if she could determine where the bullet struck. If the wound looked bad, she intended to use one of the towels to apply pressure. If it looked like a flesh wound, then she'd cover it with ice to slow the bleeding. It wasn't protocol but she'd learned it in a field survival course, and it could work. He had no marks on his body that she could see. His arm, the one he lay on, was bloody, but she couldn't determine if the round entered there, or in the side of his chest. "Stay with me, sweetie," she whispered.

His pulse was getting thready and his breathing shallow and quick. She looked at the Grandfather clock in the corner. If the paramedics didn't arrive in the two minutes it took the clock to chime the quarter-hour, she'd roll him and take action to try to stop the deepening shock and get some pressure on that wound. In the meantime, Catherine kept a hand on his shoulder to keep him still and continued stroking his face with the wet towel. "You're doing great, Mike. I love you. Damn, why didn't I tell you before? I love you.

It seemed like hours before blue and red lights washed the living room in a kaleidoscope of color, but the clock hadn't yet chimed. She got up and yanked open the door to Chief and Officer LaMotta.

Calling to her dog to sit, stay and be quiet, she said, "He's there. I haven't moved him, but he's going into shock, and I'm afraid he's losing more blood than it looks like on the floor. I think he was shot in the arm he's lying on, but it could have been the chest."

Before the officers entered the house, the ambulance pulled up, coming on the front lawn right to the door. In the distance, more strobing lights lit the night. An officer down call brought every officer on the frequency. Not for the first time, the brotherhood of the badge awed her. The hollow aching she felt when she thought about it made her realize how much she missed it. Shaking her head, she watched as the paramedics took charge. This was a crime scene, but officer survival came first.

"LaMotta, take photos, we can't wait for the Crime Scene people. And stay out of the way of the medics." Chief barked.

The flash of the camera illuminated Mike's fallen body, adding to the chaos of lights and sounds in the room. Catherine felt the start of a migraine.

"What happened?" Chief asked.

"I'm not sure. I was half-sleeping, half-awake, I thought I heard a bang and the sound of a car peeling away, but at the time, I thought it was a backfire." She could see by the look on Chief's face that he didn't believe her. Troubled, and mindful that this man filed the Information on her, she searched her memory to dredge up any other details.

"And you, a trained officer, didn't recognize a gun shot?"

Looking him square in the eye, Catherine replied. "Yes, I did. It sounded like a small caliber weapon. More of a pop than a blast. No glass broke. That, and the car noise, translated to me as a backfire."

"A backfire?"

"Yes, but Chief, with all due respect, this isn't about me. Mike is the important person here."

"Uh huh. I agree. And I don't like having my officers hurt. What did you touch?"

Catherine broke away from the man as Mike groaned again. The paramedics were rolling him over onto the gurney. His left arm was a bloody mess. The fresh flow of blood rolling down confirmed this was the injury site. Silently she thanked God that the wound wasn't worse. His eyes were open. He looked at Catherine. "Why?" He asked.

She rushed to his side, brushing away the paramedic who tried to stop her, and grabbed his good hand. "I don't know, babe. I love you."

Mike smiled faintly and closed his eyes.

"Are you taking him to DePew Trauma?" At the paramedic's nod she asked, "Can I ride along?"

Catherine felt Chief come alongside her. He put a hand on her arm and said, "No. I have more questions for you, and we need to process the scene.

I want you to stay while we do it." He dropped his hand at the same time she turned toward him. The motion caused his hand to brush against the sagging pocket in her baggy sleeping shorts.

A red haze of rage obscured her vision. How dare he treat her like a suspect? Again. Was he going to try to pin every incident in the Village on her? She opened her mouth to argue, but Chief interrupted her.

"What do you have in your pocket, Catherine?" Chief asked in a voice that could freeze hell.

"Take it out. Carefully. Butt first. Hand it to me."

Her hand closed over the cold steel. Everything in her training rebelled at pulling the weapon out by the snout and giving someone else control over the trigger. The gun was loaded, and good to go. She couldn't imagine Chief or Billy drawing down on her if she handed it out snout first, but given Mike's wound, she decided to cooperate. Slowly removing the weapon from her pocket, she handed it, butt first as requested, to Chief. He pivoted away from her, held the revolver at eye level, pushed the barrel release and counted the rounds. Flipping the chamber closed, he grunted.

"All there. LaMotta, I want her swabbed for gunshot residue."

"Miami-Dade is sending crime scene over ASAP." LaMotta responded. "There's the slug." He pointed to an object lying near the far wall. "Passed right though his arm. Looks like a 38-caliber to me." He placed an orange numbered cone beside the spent bullet.

"I'm sure there's more than one weapon in this house, and I'm sure Catherine owns more than one weapon of her own, given that I've never known a one-gun cop. And I'm sure there're enough rounds in this house and hers to reload. The question is who owns this particular weapon, and has it been fired recently." Chief responded. "What do you suppose Reardon meant when he asked you why?"

"I think he meant exactly that Chief. Why? Why did this happen? Why was he shot?"

"Why didn't you defend him? Why did you shoot him? Why did you stand by and do nothing? Why do you have a gun in your pocket?" Taking her by the arm, chief led her to the dining room and pulled out a chair.

Catherine knew he was removing her from the scene to a place where she couldn't contaminate evidence. Her migraine worsened. She felt removed from her body, as if she was watching events from outside. "You can't believe I shot him," she said, knowing the gun in her pocket told the cops exactly that she could have. "Why would I call 911?"

"Remorse." The corner of the man's lip curled in contempt. "You, the master investigator without a badge, see my point of view, right."

Billy's voice called from inside the living area. "Chief, the glass isn't broken but it's hurricane resistant stuff. There's spider webbing. You can see the shot came from outside. Reardon sure bought the primo glass. There's very little webbing, just about 3 inches on all sides of the hole.

"Crime Scene's here, Chief. Strange, nobody else called in a gunshot."

"Even stranger, Billy, none of the neighbors are gathered outside. We've got this place lit like Christmas, and somebody should have heard something."

"Maybe that's why no one is outside," Catherine said.

"What do you mean, Catherine?" Chief asked.

"Maybe they're afraid they'll get shot. They don't know what's going on." The excuse sounded false as she said it. Fear never stopped looky-lous. It attracted them. Made them feel lucky someone else was the target. Billy and Chief looked at her incredulous.

Chief turned in his chair as the Crime Scene officers entered. Standing, he strode toward the living room. "Swab her." He pointed at Catherine sitting at the table. "LaMotta, go wake our fine citizens, ask them if they heard or saw anything…" He keyed the mike on his shoulder. "Dispatch, what time did the shots fired call come in?" He tucked his ear closer to the microphone to decipher the reply. "Around 2:30 AM, LaMotta, see if anyone heard anything then."

Catherine held out her hands for the technician to swab, hating the cold feel of the chemical against her skin as it tested for gunshot residue. She kept her range credentials updated. The last time she'd fired a weapon was two weeks ago.

On a range, signed in and legal. The swabbing didn't worry her. The time spent doing it did. She wanted to get to the hospital and Mike.

CHAPTER 32

By the time she got to the hospital, Mike lay in the recovery room. Bed after bed of groaning comatose bodies, partially wrapped in white sheets, stretched down the long cold room. IV poles, festooned with blue boxes flashing red numbers, stood alongside the beds. The high-pitched alarms beeped out of sync. Catherine swallowed hard. This was the first time she'd been in a recovery room without being the patient. When she asked at the emergency information desk if she could see Mike, she'd expected someone to point her in the direction of his room. Not take her to this place.

Mike opened his eyes and looked at Catherine standing alongside his bed. His unfocused gaze told her he was still under the influence of the anesthesia. He smiled, groaned and asked for water. Uncertain if he recognized her, she brushed her palm over his forehead and grasped his hand. His eyes closed again.

"Mike, I'm so sorry." Catherine whispered. "This is all my fault. You're shot. It stinks, and it's my fault."

The sound of someone clearing her throat brought Catherine out of her soliloquy. She looked over the bed and saw a nurse in green scrubs. Hot color flooded her cheeks.

"That's OK, honey. They say they can hear you. It never hurts to talk to them. He'll be fine. It's a through and through wound. Lots of blood loss, but no real damage." The nurse checked Mike's vitals. Catherine winced as she tapped him on the nose. "Time to rise and shine sugar," the nurse said in a southern drawl.

Mike opened his eyes again, and groaned. Staring directly at the nurse he said, "Where's Catherine?"

Laughing, the nurse looked over Mike's bed toward Catherine and said, "Are you Catherine?"

At her nod, she continued, "See, I told you. Sure hope you weren't making promises you aren't gonna keep!" The green clad woman looked back down at Mike. "You sound like you're ready to go to your room. How are you feeling? Any pain?"

The nurse toed off the wheel locks on the gurney. Mike mumbled something Catherine couldn't catch. Her relief mixed with uncertainty. Should she follow Mike up to his room, bringing up the tail of some sort of medical parade, or return to the waiting room?

As though she sensed Catherine's confusion, the nurse said, "Why don't you sit in the surgical waiting room? It should only be for a few minutes, and it's closer than going back to ER waiting. The doctor is still here. He's going to want a look at your man, and we'll get him settled.

"I heard there'll be an officer outside his door. I thought that only happened on television." The nurse looked expectantly at Catherine. "Our gunshots usually go to the criminal ward."

Catherine smiled and nodded her head.

"He's a cop. He needs protection from the shooter."

"Thought you just said that was you, sweetie. Wasn't that your apology?"

Her heart sank as the nurse bared her teeth in what looked like a grin. Pain gripped her stomach. The last thing she needed was this barracuda spreading rumors. Her hands knotted into fists so tight that her fingertips went numb.

Catherine followed the signs directing her to the surgical waiting room, sat down, and tried to tune out the whispered conversations of other people around her. The television suspended on the wall looped some endless news program every fifteen minutes. She felt naked every time Mike's police identification photo flashed up with the caption 'BREAKING NEWS Officer shot, suspects at large.'

After two cycles of Mike's story, she got up and headed for the parking lot. Her migraine was worse. Every thought hurt. Squinting at her watch, she saw it was after five in the morning. Not wanting to be alone a second longer, she dialed Nancy's number. The sound of her friend's sleep slurred voice brought Catherine to tears.

* * *

Nancy slid into the seat next to her friend. "I saw a photo of Mike on the TV just now. Don't you want to hear what they're saying, Cathy?"

Catherine shook her head. "No, I finally snagged a seat under the damn television so I don't have to watch it. At least here, I'm not constantly reminded."

She looked her friend full in the face. "Oh, Nancy, there was so much blood." Catherine dropped her head to her hands and shook with silent sobs.

"He's OK, though. You told me the nurse said it was superficial."

"Yeah, the bullet wound is. What about Mike's emotional wound? Every shooting leaves one, no matter what side of the gun you're on. Will he ever forgive me?"

Taking Catherine by both shoulders, Nancy pivoted her until the two women were face to face. "You did not shoot him. This is not your fault. This isn't about you." Nancy deliberately spaced each word out as she spoke.

"Damn it, Nancy." Catherine slumped forward, rested her elbows on her knees, and stared at the floor between her running shoes. "I was having such a wonderful time being Nancy Drew. I told myself I kept up the investigation to clear my name. Then, since it looked like I was in the clear, to help Ashley." She cast a glance toward Nancy. "In my fantasy, I charged in to Chief's office, solution in hand, and in a blaze of glory he begged me to rejoin the force. Do you know how heady it is to be able to have access to information because you don't have to play by the rules!

"Now look at me. My business is in shambles, the cops hate me, I'm the queen of the rumor mill, and I've single-handedly polarized the Village all because I wanted to belong again. I sure blew that."

"You're forgetting you've paid a price too. Your tires, the break-in, and the fire all happened at your house. Catherine, this happened at Mike's house. I don't know how else to say this, so I'll just say it again. It's not about you."

Catherine slumped in her seat, her long legs stretched out in front of her, sneakered feet crossed at the ankles. She felt as if a large weight lifted off her chest. Nancy might be right. It wasn't about her, not this time.

Mentally she ticked off who might be responsible for the havoc in her life. Who had the most to gain by Gavin's death? Ashley? Sure, but she had more to gain by him staying alive. Some disgruntled Village resident? Killing someone for denying you zoning seemed a little extreme. The embezzlers? That would point to another Commissioner. Cunningham over the loan? He struck Catherine as a coward. He would probably do the political thing and expose Gavin, not kill him. The Riveras? Well, Juan or his brother-in-law, Tomas. They fit, and they fit with the pattern of violence against Catherine. They were outsiders. Their only access to her was at her house. An angry husband or jilted lover? Maybe, but the death didn't seem an act of passion. Those usually involved a lot

271

of blood. Catherine winced at the memory of Mike's blood.

Whoever went after Mike, knew where to find him, or knew how to use resources to get his address. Even to Catherine, that sounded like a lot of trouble just to get at her.

She must have nodded off. A tap on her shoulder brought her upright. A police officer stood before her. "I'll take you to Lieutenant Reardon if you'd like to see him."

"Stay with me tonight, Catherine," Nancy said. "They'll probably keep Mike overnight. Don't go home alone."

Catherine hugged her friend. "I'll think about it."

"Good. I'll stop by the cop shop and ask if I can pick up Bullet from Mike's house. I'll get Paddy Whack from your place, and bring both kids to my house. You won't have any excuses not to stay with me."

Raising both hands in defeat, Catherine said, "OK, unless they send Mike home today.

"Even then, both of you come to me. I insist."

A chair occupied by a Metro officer in uniform sat outside Mike's door. The young officer looked at Catherine as if he were memorizing her features. Then he rose and rapped on the closed door and swung it open for Catherine to enter without waiting for a reply from inside.

Mike struggled upright up in the bed at the sight of her. "How are you holding up Cathy?"

"Me! You're the one in the bed. How are you? Can I get you anything while you're on your little vacation?"

He smiled and rested his head back against the pillow. "I'm fine. Still flying on whatever they gave me. Catherine, I want you to listen to me." He propped himself up on his good arm and looked her square in the face. She could only guess at the pain that the effort cost him. "I want you to have protection. I'll arrange it with Chief."

"What! Why? Mike, I talked this over with Nancy. She's right. This isn't about me, this happened at your house!"

Mike's mouth drew into a hard, straight line. A spot of color touched each cheekbone. "There's a clear pattern of escalation. First vandalism, then breaking but no entry, then arson. Everyone knows we're a team. You don't understand. You were right, Cathy. You are a target." He sucked in a deep breath. "I was wrong, Gavin was murdered. Now they're after you."

The air flew from her chest. As much as she believed his words, she wasn't ready to hear them. Not now. Not at this cost. And especially not when he was in the hospital. The pain of her migraine was slowing her thought processes. "What about Vickie?" She grasped at the only straw she could think of. "The break-in at her house didn't have anything to do with me."

"Didn't it?"

His head fell back against the pillow. She could see his exhaustion. Catherine put her hand on his forehead and smoothed back a shock of hair.

273

"Go to sleep, Mike. We'll work this out somehow." She whispered.

"What are the odds that no one saw anything at your house when someone set the fire?" Mike's smile looked more like a grimace. "In Summer Hill, people live at their windows barely concealing themselves behind their curtains. Why hasn't anyone come forward? You have to listen to me Kit Kat."

"Ann did."

"Ann wanted information more than she wanted to share it. No, Cathy, too many people think you're getting what you deserve for playing cop. I need to know if something else happens, someone will be there to help you."

"I have my friends. I'm not going home tonight."

"Have you heard from Vickie since the break in?"

Shaking her head, Catherine struggled to figure out where he was going with this.

"So you're being isolated."

Catherine's heart plummeted to her shoes. "That makes no sense," she said. Fear bubbled up in her again. Then guilt slammed into her at the thought that Mike took a bullet because of his association with her.

"Who do you think killed Gavin? Who do you think is after me?"

"You asked me that once before. I wasn't ready to answer then. Now, I'm not sure." He looked up at her with tears in his eyes. "Forgive me,

Cathy. If I had listened to you from the beginning, maybe I would know by now."

The tears she saw behind his eyes moved her more than anything else did. She was lost and she knew it. There was one more possibility he had to face, one she just thought of, before she could agree to protection. "Mike, if I agree, who would want to protect me? I think I'd be in more danger from the cops than from anyone else. Have you considered that everything that happened could have been someone on the force protecting you? One of your fellow officers could have slashed my tires, tossed the brick or created the bonfire? Think about it. If I spotted them, they had the perfect excuse. They'd seen something strange, and were investigating. Who's to dispute that? Remember, you asked them to step up patrols."

"I want you to have protection. No matter what you may think, the officers assigned will do their jobs. And I can't imagine anyone of them shooting me."

Catherine looked down at her hands. She clenched her fists and then opened them again trying to fight over the top of the pain of her migraine. Fear made her want to say yes, caution and a desire to continue investigating made her want to say no. There didn't seem to be an effective compromise. Looking up at Mike she said, "Ok." She stroked the soft spot on his wrist.

"Good. Now go to Nancy's. Promise me you won't go home."

CHAPTER 33

The sound of Bullet barking his greeting nearly drowned out the trilling of Nancy's phone. Catherine pushed the door open, dropped her overnight bag on the tile floor, scratched her dog behind the ears and debated answering the call. Deciding to let voice mail take it, she brought her bag into the guest room, opened it up and fished out her running shoes. After the long night at the hospital waiting room, Catherine needed a run to clear her head, and hopefully drive away the vestiges of her migraine.

She leashed up Bullet and set out. Her thoughts kept pace with the sound of her sneakers on the pavement.

On one hand, Mike's demand that she accept protection made sense. On the other, she knew the Village force didn't have the manpower to make it effective. The best she could hope for would be increased surveillance. Catherine also knew the boys in blue were holding her accountable for Mike's shooting, and they considered her involved in Gavin's death.

Surveillance might make sense, but Catherine thought it would inhibit her from looking into things on her own. Any further investigating she did would have to be by the book, and shared. No more instinct and lone wolf leaps of logic. The time for that was over. It was too dangerous.

Sweat rolled off Catherine as she rounded the corner in the direction of the Jackmans. The sticky air clung to her like a sweater, and she struggled for every breath. Roscoe barked his usual greeting to Bullet as Catherine's feet pounded their tattoo. She pulled up short, jerking Bullet back on his leash, as Ashley's front door swung open and Roscoe bounded out. Ashley looked older, her hair a mess, grey roots showing.

"Hey Ashley, is everything all right?" Wondering if cancer treatments or Gavin's death were taking the worst toll.

"I found what they were looking for." She said bleakly.

Wiping sweat off her face with her arm, Catherine waited, hoping Ashley would explain what she found, and who was looking for it.

A look of confusion crossed Ashley's face. Still Catherine held her silence. "The extortion you talked about. I found payments to that girl's brother, the criminal, Tomas Lopez. Small ones, Gavin paid him $1,000, every month for four months. Then they stopped. I guess that's when he went to prison."

"Is there any indication Lopez tried to get back in touch with Gavin? Any payments made in the last three or four months? Any payments after Tomas got out of jail?"

Shaking her head, Ashley replied, "No, there were two other checks written to cash right before he got out. Random dates, not in the same pattern. The amounts were the same, but I don't know what they were for, not like Gavin to take out that amount. Anyway, Lopez was still in jail then. Had to be something different." Ashley sighed deeply. "Maybe I didn't know my husband well at all."

"Or he paid Maggie directly. Maybe she called and asked. Would Gavin have done that? Especially if she threatened to release the Affidavit to the press."

She shrugged. "I don't know... maybe. Gavin always wanted to help people. Add his guilt over seducing her into the equation." A curtain of dark hair covered her face as she looked down. "And a desire to protect me." Ashley looked back up at Catherine. "Maybe."

Catherine watched Ashley nibble on a fingernail.

"There's something else. I've got an estate open. The bank told me that Gavin called the day before he died. He authorized them to turn information about the $50,000 deposits over to the Village attorney after they determined what they could about who authorized them. The account was still in the research process when he died. Once they froze the account, they froze the request. The information was never released."

"You have to tell the police. They need to know. Call Chief directly. Better yet, make copies of the statements, and then take them yourself. If Gavin called the bank, he may have spoken with other Commissioners. If you hold back on this information, you're putting yourself at risk. Especially if someone did kill Gavin to keep him quiet..."

Ashley blanched and turned her face away. Her hand twisted a strand of hair into a tight corkscrew. When she looked back, Catherine saw sheer exhaustion on her face. "I hoped you'd give it to Mike, let him decide who should see it."

"You don't know?" Catherine asked.

"Know what?"

"Someone shot Mike last night. He's in DePew."

"My God!" Ashley's hand groped for support as her knees buckled beneath her.

Catherine made a grab for the woman and managed to keep her from hitting the pavement.

"Whoa, steady there. Roscoe, come on, let's get Mom home."

"No, I'm fine. Really, it's, well, oh, Catherine. I'm so sorry. Will he be all right?

"Yes, he'll be fine. Are you sure you're okay?" Catherine studied Ashley closely, and saw the color return to her face.

"I couldn't stand the thought of someone else dying. It's too raw. I'm fine. Thanks, Catherine." Ashley gently extricated herself from Catherine's grasp, turned back to the house and shut the door.

* * *

279

The violence of Ashley's reaction stunned Catherine. For a moment, she didn't know if she should stay or go. Finally, she turned and continued her run. She reflected that Ashley's reaction was honest, and the woman was nearing the end of her emotional rope. She decided to run past her own home and pick up her mail before going back to Nancy's. Scrubbing her palms on the back of her running shorts, she wondered why the Village telegraph hadn't been more effective. What was it about Mike's shooting that kept it off the gossip wires? The sheer number of police and rescue vehicles should have caused some talk in the town. The information might be inaccurate, but you could generally be sure some story would be in circulation. The fact that no one seemed to know anything struck her as frighteningly unnatural.

A strange dark sedan sat on the swale in front of her house. Catherine crossed the road to run past her house on the opposite side of the street. If anything happened, she had Bullet with her. Despite his cuts and bruises, he'd defend her at all costs. As she drew closer, her stomach clenched. There was a man sitting on her porch. Anger and fear warred with each other. Anger won and Catherine slowed her pace, grabbed Bullet by the collar, and approached her house.

"Can I help you?" She asked. Bullet's hackles rose. He wasn't liking this.

"Catherine Swope?" The man asked.

With a sinking feeling, Catherine saw the badge at his waist and the envelope in his hand. This guy was a process server. Now what!

"Yes," she sighed, and held out her hand.

The seal on the Tyvek envelop fought her attempts to rip it open. The process server pulled a small pocketknife from his keychain and sliced through the top. The envelop contained a subpoena for her deposition in the matter of Rivera vs. Swope. The date was ten days away. Sighing, she looked down at her dog. "Damn, I should have let you eat him," she muttered.

The process server paled at her words and raised both his hands in surrender. "I just deliver them, lady." He reclaimed his knife and sidled carefully past the dog on his way to the car.

Bullet looked up at her and opened his mouth to let his tongue loll out. Catherine burst into hysterical laughter. Her dog seemed to smile at the thought.

Watching the man leave, Catherine decided running was bringing her bad news. She opted to walk the rest of the way to Nancy's house.

The cold-water shower sluiced down on Catherine's overheated body. She'd called Ted as soon as she'd gotten back to the house. He'd been unable to take her call so she called Nancy. The timing of the deposition bothered her. Falling on the heels of Mike's shooting, she didn't think she could prepare in time. She wondered if there was some Statute that she could invoke to put it off for a little while longer. Nancy assured her she could reschedule, but expressed surprise that Ted hadn't called her to check dates. Attorneys apparently didn't usually schedule depositions without speaking to the client.

Wrapping herself in a towel, she wondered what Nancy meant when she said she had some information for her that she didn't want to discuss over the phone. A hollow feeling in the pit of her stomach warned her that the information wasn't good.

The ringing of the phone pulled Catherine from her reverie. Deciding it might be Nancy, calling to tell her what she'd meant, Catherine picked up the receiver.

Ashley's voice greeted her. "I did what you asked. I went to the Chief with the information. He treated me like a criminal! Took me off into that little room behind the kitchen and asked me questions."

"What kind of questions?" Catherine asked, and grimaced, she'd forgotten she'd forwarded her own calls to Nancy's house. She'd have to remember to check the caller id before she picked up.

"Who, what, when, where and why questions. Again. The same one's they asked before. He didn't seem in the least bit interested in the bank statements, or anything else about the bank. They suggested I get a lawyer. As if they don't know I have one! He also 'suggested'," sarcasm dripped from Ashley's voice, "that I stick around. That really got my back up. I live here. Where does Chief think I'm going! My attorney says they're shooting in the dark. "Catherine, I can't go through this again. I followed your advice. It blew up in my face. My husband is dead. I'm trying to help them find out why."

"Ashley, I know it's small comfort, but we'll work this out. You'll see. We'll get peace for Gavin." Catherine gulped as she heard her own voice refer to 'we'. Was this what she wanted? To do it herself? "Gavin fought with someone before he died. That's all Chief is looking for."

No, she'd share. She promised herself. She'd share information with Mike. Ashley's voice continued in her ear.

"I'm sorry," Catherine pulled herself back to the conversation. She hadn't been paying attention. "What did you say about a deposition? Someone served you? When?"

"Not me, you. That Rivera man called me today. He said he'd drop the whole thing against you if I gave him $100,000."

CHAPTER 34

She sat with her feet propped up on the back porch rail overlooking Nancy's back garden. Bullet rested in front of the chair under her legs. "You're home early, Nance, what's up?" Catherine called as she heard the front door open.

When no one replied, fear bubbled through her veins. She patted the belly pouch containing her weapon. Slowly she turned her head and looked in the direction of the sound. Nancy stood in the doorway, her face so pale it looked grey. "Nancy?" Catherine swung her legs down avoiding her dog. She stood, walked to her friend, and pulled her into a hug. "What's wrong?"

"Phil put me on administrative leave. With pay, but leave. Catherine, that's like getting fired."

"Why?"

"The Clerk's office told him someone was repeatedly accessing the State Attorney system. Wanted to know why in case someone got his password. I didn't know they monitored access, I thought they just monitored printing. I'd been keeping watch on the status of your Information, and checking to see if anyone filed anything else about the Riveras, or Ashley, or you." Nancy's voice ended with a hitch. She stopped talking and drew in a shuddering breath.

Catherine's heart plummeted to her feet. Her friend was in danger of losing her job because she tried to help. Catherine hadn't asked, but that didn't matter. Nancy's problem was her fault. "Oh, Nance, I'm so sorry. Is there anything I can do?" Even as she said it, Catherine knew it sounded stupid. Clearly, she'd done enough.

Nancy moved to one of the wicker chairs on the porch and sat down. Tipping her head back, she rested it against the seat cushion. "There's more. You got served today?" Nancy looked over at Catherine who nodded her head. "I found a complete inquiry into the shooting years ago, when you were on the force."

"Who pulled it?" Mentally Catherine counted the years since the investigation. More than three but less than the five it took for most of the record to move to microfilm and off easy request access.

"Chief. There was a second request from the Rivera's lawyer. That's still pending. And Rivera's lawyer filed a subpoena today, for your bank records."

Catherine slammed her fist into the porch rail. "What the hell do they want with my bank records?"

"According to the subpoena, they want to 'prevent you from moving money in such a way to deny the plaintiff relief.' And he's filed notices of deposition for me, Mike and Ashley. They filed those requests today. We'll probably be served Monday."

Catherine's mind churned. She understood Ashley's deposition, but Nancy and Mike? Those two made no sense. Or did they? Asking for bank records meant the suit was all about money. Juan's call to Ashley indicated the same thing. Mike only figured in if the attorney was trying to find out if his client was a suspect in Gavin's death. A preemptive strike to acquire information. How the hell did Nancy figure in though? Made no sense, not given the information Catherine had now.

"I'm picking Mike up Monday morning. "Maybe we should stay at my house. You've got enough going on without houseguests."

"Don't be silly. I offered, and besides," Nancy looked over at her friend, "I don't want to be alone right now. Maybe, now that I've got time and you and Mike'll be here, we'll come up with the key to this whole mess."

Catherine walked to her friend's side, took her hand and squeezed it. "No matter what, I'm not going to let you down, Nance. I mean that. I don't know how I'll do it, but I'll make it right with Phil." She followed her friend into the kitchen. Something about the lay-off bothered her.

"Doesn't Phil have unlimited access to the State Attorney site? He's a criminal Judge for Pete's sake! Don't you have all the access he has? Why the monitoring."

Pulling a beer out of the refrigerator, Nancy twisted the cap off and drank deeply. She rolled the cool bottle across her forehead, and then returned to the porch. "Don't know." She shrugged. Maybe because it's not his case."

The two friends sat in silence staring out over the yard. Every now and then, a breeze wafted the scent of jasmine toward them.

No matter how she turned it over in her mind, Phil's reason for putting Nancy on administrative leave made no sense to Catherine. He knew Gavin. Ashley said they went to high school together and the two men stayed friends even after Gavin left the firm and Phil got on the Bench. She pressed her head back into top of the cushion and watched the interplay of light in the edges of the tongue and grove boards overhead. Why was Phil trying to stop Nancy from helping a neighbor? Or was he trying to stop her from helping Catherine in particular? Ashley told her he'd been generous to her with his time and advice. Sure, it was an election year for him. Phil traditionally ran on a tough on crime platform. Did he know something he wanted to keep from Nancy? Did he believe Catherine was guilty? Now that the Affidavit was in the open, and Nancy knew he authored it, was he worried about the fallout?

Catherine pitched her body forward and stretched out a kink in her back. No. Nancy knew where the bodies were buried in Phil's past and she'd never betrayed him. It didn't make sense for him to worry about her loyalty now.

* * *

Mike opened the door of Catherine's Tahoe, stepped on the running board and reached up with his left hand to pull himself up into the seat. "I'd have brought your pick-up," Catherine quipped, "but you don't have a running board. I thought jumping start, for a man with your disability, might be dangerous."

"Very funny, Kit Kat. I guess I'll be healed by the time I stop trying to use my right arm. Either healed or permanently tangled in this sling. Can they surgically remove these do you think?"

Catherine brought Mike up to date on everything that'd been going while he was out of commission. She downplayed her surprise at the deposition, and, as with Nancy, decided not to reveal the content of Ashley's phone call from Juan Rivera. She wanted more time to think that through, and try to figure out how to turn it to her advantage before she mentioned it.

"Holy Hannah, would you look at that." Mike exclaimed as Catherine drove past the Kents' house on her way to Nancy's house. "They've got a foundation poured and wall forms up. I thought they'd given up on the pool house."

Craning her head to see around Mike in the passenger seat, Catherine nodded. "Me too. Wonder what Sue has to say about the construction."

"Sue? She got fired."

"No, they reinstated her. Don't you remember, Nancy told us before you got shot. She's got the grievance and the Village attorney said she has to stay on the payroll pending the outcome. Are you having senior moments? Must be the stress."

"Brat. Well, her hands are tied then." Mike said. "No, wait, I take that back. Knowing Sue,

she'll be more vigilant. Makes her husband crazy."
At Catherine's surprised look, Mike clarified, "Cop
shop talk."

"Did you check out Oliver's glory wall?"
Catherine asked. When Mike shook his head, she
continued, "I think he has a photo with every
dignitary that ever visited the city and a bunch of
Judges, Phil included. Add to that the awards from
the paper, and I'm not surprised the guy has a high
opinion of himself. Wonder why he left the
Courthouse beat for gardening. I didn't know
garden writing held such cache."

"Me either. Did you know he used to
wrestle?" Mike asked.

"You're joking! Where did you hear that?
He sure doesn't have the build." Catherine shook
her head. The mental image of Oliver Kent in
wrestling shorts and singlet was not one she wanted
to keep.

"LaMotta told me. They went to the same
high school. I guess wrestlers were wirier on his
team. Simms and Cunningham too. Simms was a
couple of years ahead of Billy. They were all
Cathedral grads."

"Amazing. I never knew half the
Commission went back that far."

"Yeah, Jackman too. Only he was on the
honor roll."

"Stay there," Catherine ordered as she
pulled up in front of Nancy's house. "Let me get the
door for once. You're going to strangle yourself if
you keep pulling that sling every time you try to do
something righty.

"Mike, I've been thinking," Catherine began as she tried to help him balance his way out of her truck. "I know Chief's looking to file charges against me, and that he's filed an Information, but I still think something is missing in the puzzle of Gavin's death."

Feet firmly on the floor, Mike lifted Catherine's chin with a crooked index finger, and she looked into his eyes. "I think it's time I stopped being an amateur and remembered how to be a professional. I know I have information Chief needs. I'm just not sure what it is. Will you help me, while you're on leave?"

"Help you how, Kit Kat?" He asked softly. "I'm out of commission, and I don't want you in the line of fire."

She shrugged. "You know, listen, and help me put it all in order. I know I'm missing something. Worse, I'm missing something I know I discovered before."

"Hey lovebirds, are you two coming in?" Sue called.

Dressed in her running shorts and singlet, Sue propped her well-worn running shoes on Nancy's coffee table. "I came to offer my sympathy to the wounded man." Sue laughed.

"Wounded man!" Mike erupted. "Me? Wounded. Well, my friend, at least I've been doing my job. What's up with the Oliver's walls? Sure looks like a pool house going up to me."

Sue's face darkened with an emotion Catherine could only term hatred. The corners of her mouth turned down, and she grabbed for her fanny pouch sitting on the table. The zipper sounded unnaturally loud as she ripped it open. "How the hell do I know? Maybe a garage for those cars. Nobody is talking to me, except by e-mail." Sue pulled out a wad of folded paper and thrust it at Mike. "I don't suppose some of these would explain anything."

"Have you shown these to Nick?" Mike asked. He rapidly flipped through the pages from front to back as he read them.

Shaking her head, Sue replied, "No way. He's not only a cop, but he's my husband. I blew them off before Gavin's death. Then they stopped." She shrugged. "Now they've started again."

Catherine stood and walked behind Mike's chair so she could read over his shoulder. "Didn't you tell us girls that someone left poison bait for your pups after you got one of these e-mails? You told Nick about those, didn't you?"

"Yes, and he hit the roof and wanted me to quit my job. I would have if I'd thought it would help and protect my dogs. I was considering it. I mean, threaten me, but go after my dogs? That's about as low as anyone can be."

Mike looked up at Catherine. "You never told me about that. You told me Gavin got death threats, you gave me the e-mails, but you never said anything about Sue getting them."

"I never thought about it, or I never made the connection once Gavin died. That's what I mean, Mike. I need your help. What other connections did I miss?"

291

"I turned in the copies you gave me. They're part of the case file. Were they originals or did you make copies?"

"Originals, why?"

"I want to get them back. I'll call LaMotta. Have him bring me the case file. Sue, I'm going to have to turn these over. You should have done the same. I can't keep this from Nick either."

Sue nodded. "Ok, he's going to make me quit but you know what? I'm not sure I care anymore. Mike, what about this one?" She took the sheets from his hand and flipped through them, selected one, and handed it back.

CHAPTER 35

"Don't forget Gavin's accident." Mike read aloud from the e-mail he held in his hand.

"Ok, that seems pretty clear, but is it a confession or a warning?" Nancy asked.

"Either way, it's not comforting." Sue replied. "I kept telling myself that whoever wrote it had as much information as anyone else, and they were trying to tell me to back off in the most effective way they knew how."

"Let me see the rest of them." Catherine picked up the sheets of paper Sue laid on the coffee table, and then jerked her hand back and looked at Mike. "Can I take them out of order?"

He shook his head, the corners of his mouth tugged up as if fighting a smile. "I'm sorry, Kit Kat. I'm being a hard ass. I don't want anything happening to you. We're a team."

Crossing her eyes at him, she teased one of the e-mails from the stack. "That one," she cocked her chin in the direction of the page Mike still held, "has IP information after the sender alias. At least I think it does." She turned to Mike. Doesn't that look like a computer number to you?" At his nod she turned back to Sue and asked, "Do you still have these on your computer?"

Sue nodded. "The ones that come in on that account always print those numbers. I never figured out how to change it."

"Let's see if any of the IP information matches. Wow, are these all of them? Just these ten?" Catherine asked.

"Eleven." Mike said.

"They cover nearly a year. The first four are all in a clump, days apart, ten months ago, then these six, again days apart, but a month before Gavin died. Then there's nothing." Catherine looked at Sue again.

"Yes, nothing since Gavin died, until this one this morning." Sue swept out her arm. "I keep the e-mails in a password-protected file on my home computer so Nick doesn't see them."

Mike spread the sheets out on the coffee table in chronological order. "Three have the same IP address, this latest one and two from the group of six. Two others in the group of six have the same address, so that's five e-mails that have two repeated addresses. They came from the same computers. The other six don't seem to be the same. We need to compare them to the ones Gavin got. For timing and for IP address."

"Can those addresses be faked?" Nancy asked.

Mike sat back, cradled his injured arm, and looked at Nancy. "I'm not really sure. Metro has a team that works exclusively with Internet crime.

From what I know, you can't fake the constant IP that identifies you to your internet provider. There's another IP, though, that changes every time you log on. If you know what you're doing," Mike shrugged. "You can disguise your sending machine at first glance. Since we have some similar ones, they probably did come from the same machine."

"Is Billy going to cooperate with you, Mike, about turning over Gavin's e-mails?" Catherine asked. Now that she and Mike were staying together, he might balk at helping even his revered LT. "The investigation is closed. Is this sufficient to re-open it?" Remembering Chief's words to Ashley and the Information his department filed against her, Catherine sucked on the inside of her cheek. "Or is it still open? Given recent events." She smiled ruefully.

"It's closed. At least as far as murder is concerned. The investigation is separate from your obstruction charge. Clearly, Chief is still looking into collateral actions he can take that could shed light on Gavin's death. The Information against you, that's a way to continue an investigation and not re-open it. Unless something substantive turns up, then he'll join the two matters."

Catherine slammed her hand down on the coffee table. "Great - so I'm nothing more than an excuse. He's ruining my life so he can keep an open mind on the investigation instead of investigating."

"As for the e-mails, no, they're not sufficient." Mike laid a hand on her shoulder and squeezed. "They would be another matter too. Even though part of the information to re-open the case could come from Gavin's file. We'll get to look at the e-mails because there's a closing protocol for all case files, and it includes physical evidence presented. I can offer to keep myself employed during my off time by closing the file. Not like you, Kit Kat not to make copies."

"Yeah," Catherine used both hands to push her hair behind her ears, "if you remember, you took the file before I'd been through it."

"I've got to go." Sue rose from her chair. "Nancy, you've been really quiet, is everything all right?"

"Yes." Nancy stood to walk her friend to the door. "Just some junk at work I'm trying to work through." She leaned against the door as she closed it on her friend.

"Well, troops, what do we really think?" She asked as she came back to the group.

"I think we need to look for who murdered Gavin." Catherine responded. "Let's get you settled in bed, big guy. Tomorrow is soon enough for you to start back to playing cop." Catherine helped Mike to his feet and led him in the direction of Nancy's guest room. She'd already unpacked her things, and they sat comfortably around the room like old friends.

"You're comfortable that Gavin's death was a murder?" Catherine asked Mike as she helped him untie and remove his shoes.

"I don't think there's a question. And whoever it is, they're willing to kill again. It's not over, and it won't be until we really know what happened to Gavin."

Catherine pulled her knees up under her chin and wrapped her arms around her legs. Looking at Mike, she spoke slowly, rolling the words over in her mind before she said them. "I know you never thought Gavin committed suicide. I know you had no choice except to go along with Chief's findings. I know you can't re-open the investigation on your own. What I don't know, is what you know that I don't about Gavin's death. I also don't know what happens if you re-open the investigation on your own, unofficially."

Mike pulled the Velcro strips on his sling, freeing his right arm. He dropped it gingerly to his side, then lifted and flexed it, grimacing as he did so. Catherine knew he heard her, but she wasn't sure if he'd respond. Finally, he said, "They pretty much shut me out of the investigation after you got so involved. You know that. In a department as small as ours, and given my position as the sole lieutenant, I saw all the reports, but I couldn't be actively involved as an investigator." He swung his legs up on to the bed and leaned back against the pillows. "I did try to keep you informed whenever I could, and I can re-open the investigation if I have new evidence. Chief won't fight evidence." He glanced over at Catherine. "He's a good cop, Cathy. Really, he is."

"Were there any surprises in the case file compared to what I know?"

"No. Not that I can think of. We'll both look at it tomorrow, when I'm more awake."

"Why was Chief in such a rush to close the case, call it a suicide?"

Mike adjusted the pillows behind his back, and turned to look at Catherine. She saw exhaustion in his face and regretted asking the question. The man needed sleep, not interrogation.

"Arnie Cunningham pressured Chief daily to bring the inquiry to a conclusion. From what I heard, he never said how that was supposed to happen. I don't think he cared if it was murder or suicide, at least not at first. He'd already decided that no matter the cause of death, either you or Ashley was responsible. Then…"

"What, I can see Ashley, but…"

"Let me finish, Catherine, and then I'm going to sleep."

Catherine nodded, put her crooked index finger into her mouth and bit down on it.

"Good, now keep the finger there 'till I finish." His tired smile resembled a grimace. "Then Hank Simms and Thom Moore got into the act. LaMotta got the brunt of their interference, and the Chief too, to some extent."

Catherine removed the finger from her mouth to ask a question. Mike raised his eyebrows and waited. Catherine reinserted the finger in her mouth.

"Good. Simms and Moore claimed they were concerned that no one would accept the zoning vacancy while the murder investigation was open. Who knows, they may have been right. In any event, they wanted the investigation closed before the Charter required a replacement's appointment. There wasn't enough evidence to file an Information for a homicide warrant. He determined the case needed to close and let the cause of death stand as suicide. In truth, he had no other way to go, except accidental, but he couldn't make that work in a hanging case. Not with a noose. Now, I'm going to sleep. You too?"

Catherine got up and kissed Mike. "Nope, not yet. I'll be in soon though."

"No questions?"

She laughed. "Sure, but it's hard to ask them with my finger in my mouth. Mike, I realize my biggest mistake was trying to be a lone wolf. I guess I hoped I'd solve the case all alone and Chief would beg me on bended knee to join the department."

Mike rolled his eyes and said, "Good night, Catherine. Oh, did I happen to mention I love you? Even if you are totally nuts."

"Well, big fella, you're stuck with me now." Catherine turned and started for the door. Then she turned back and said, "Have I told you I love you too?" She blew him a kiss and left.

Catherine found Nancy in the living room, curled up in an oversized lounge chair, a glass of chilled white wine on the table beside her. Bullet lay at her feet.

"I think you peeved your dog, closing him out of the bedroom," Nancy said. She ran her finger down the side of the chilled glass, collecting the condensation on her finger. "He's my new best friend now." She leaned down and scratched his ears.

Catherine took in the scene and laughed. "Don't count on it. That dog is true blue. I'm sorry. I haven't been able to talk to you much today. I know you must feel like hell over what happened with Phil. I also know it's my fault. I wish there was something, anything, I could do to make it better."

Catherine watched her friend closely. She and Nancy met in grade school. They'd been mortal enemies in the second grade. Somehow they'd become best friends. The friendship lasted through high school and endured through college in different states. Catherine considered Nancy the sister she never had. There were times she could almost read Nancy's mind. She stared at her friend now, trying to read the depth of the hurt.

"You didn't hold a gun to my head, Cathy. I did this to myself. I knew better. I went ahead and abused my position. It's that simple. Phil's not going to fire me. Don't worry about that. If that were what he wanted to do, he would have done it. We've been together too long. He is giving me a strong warning though. And you know what…" She lifted the glass and took a long drink. "He's right. I screwed up.

"Nance…"

She waved her glass, and said, "I need to work this through alone. I think I'm more hurt than anything else. I see his point, but I thought he'd support me. He wants to know what happened to Gavin too. How's Mike doing?"

"Well as can be expected I guess. He's uncomfortable, of course."

Nancy got up and went to the kitchen and came back with two tall glasses of lemonade. She handed one to Catherine and said, "Tart, just the way you like it. What do you think about Sue's e-mails?"

Catherine took a long pull on her drink. She made a face and said, "Well, there's no sugar like no sugar. This is really good, once you get over the initial bite." She took another sip and licked her lips. "I think we need to see the ones Gavin received. I think Mike's right. I need to work with the cops, not instead of them."

"Meaning?"

"Nance, this investigation is going in three directions at once."

"Ok, what three directions, Cathy?"

"The Affidavit, we know blackmail was involved, at least initially. I saw Ashley the other day when I was running. She told me there were two more payments, after the regular payments ended. Made to cash, but for the same amount as the blackmail money."

"Recent?"

"Immediately before Tomas's release."

"What else?" Nancy asked. "That's one direction, what's behind door number two?

"Embezzlement. The bank told Ashley that Gavin questioned the payments into the account. They were in the process of investigating the payments when he died, and the bank froze the account. Suppose he told someone else about them too. Someone who knew what was going on, maybe even someone involved in the theft."

"You can't hope to get information about that, Cathy. The Village attorney is involved, there's no way you can get close to that one."

Catherine shrugged. "Maybe you're right, but it's all public information under the Sunshine laws, isn't it?"

"No, not until there's something that can be made public. It's a criminal investigation, there's no requirement to make the process public until they're ready to bring charges."

"Cunningham, Simms and Gavin knew each other in High School. Do you think Gavin's death goes back to an old rivalry somehow?"

Chewing on her ice cubes, Catherine gnawed on the ramifications of the Sunshine laws and old friendships. There had to be some way for her to find out the status of the investigation, and whom the Village Attorney was targeting. Surely, he couldn't keep the information from law enforcement. She shelved the idea for later discussion with Mike. "Did you know Cunningham owed Gavin money? And the note was due. That gives him motive.

"And who's behind door number three?"

"Disgruntled resident. Someone denied a variance. Tempers were out of control at the last meeting Gavin attended. Someone there could have decided to take advantage of a room full of suspects."

"The affairs?"

"Sure. Same thing, Village husband angry, Village lady scorned."

"You really think it was premeditated?"

"Given the death threat e-mails? I think it's a possibility."

"Are you forgetting Ashley?" Nancy asked.

"What do you mean?"
"Isn't she behind door number four?"

CHAPTER 36

A week later, driving to her deposition, Catherine reflected that in the past ten days, no one had shot at her, tried to run her down, off the road, steal her dog, or set any fires. She wasn't sure if she missed the action or welcomed the rest. Her biggest concern was her business setting all-time low records. If that didn't turn around soon, she knew she'd have to decide whether to go back to real estate, or begin applying for law enforcement jobs. Right now, she had a deposition to get through. The thought made her throat dry.

She handed her driving license to the security guard in the lobby of the downtown office tower and walked toward the double bank of elevators. Although grateful that Mike's arm was healing and Nancy's job restored, she couldn't shake the feeling that a giant anvil balanced over her head suspended by the slenderest of chains. She wouldn't feel safe until this ordeal ended.

She checked the suite number on the deposition. The attorney was on the 54th floor. Looking at the flashing lights on the elevator panel, she noticed this elevator topped out at 25. She'd have at least one more elevator ride. Moving from one side of the elevator lobby to the next, she entered the high-speed second set of elevators. Waggling her chin, she cleared the pressure the swift rise created in her ears. She wished she could clear the pressure in her life as easily.

The receptionist sat behind a huge oak desk in the pseudo-English lobby of the Fowler, Adams and Silversmith firm the Riveras hired. Catherine gave her name and appointment time and wondered just how much money the Riveras and their lawyer were looking for. Unable to resist the view, she walked to the bank of floor to ceiling windows and looked down. This building, perched on a spit of land jutting out into Biscayne Bay, was the tallest in Miami. Given the current state of the local economy, it was likely to retain the title for some time. About a foot in front of the window, it amused Catherine to realize she was inching her feet along to get closer while simultaneously making sure her feet were on solid ground. From where she stood she looked out at the Bay, Port of Miami, Fisher Island, Miami Beach, and beyond to the Atlantic Ocean. She watched fascinated, as little toy-sized boats created tiny wakes in the Bay water. From up here, she thought, you can see everything and nothing. Being far away created as much distortion as being too close.

Catherine turned from the window, took a seat on the leather sofa, and glanced over the magazine offerings. Not seeing anything that appealed, she pulled a notebook from her briefcase and reviewed the information she and Ted decided were likely to be the topics of the deposition. The sound of someone clearing his throat caught her attention. Catherine smiled, rose, and greeted her attorney with a hug.

"You ready for this?" Ted Reardon asked.

Shaking her head, Catherine noticed again how much alike Ted and Mike looked. "Nope, but then, I've never felt ready for a deposition."

Ted sat beside her, took the notebook from her hands and glanced at her notes. After what seemed like hours, the door dividing the office area from the lobby swung open with a hiss, he folded the notebook closed, handed it to her and said, "Show time, Cathy. You'll be fine.

"Remember, just answer the questions and don't offer anything extra. Pretend you're on the stand. You've been there before. Pause before you reply to anything. It will give me time to object if I have to. If you don't want to answer a question, or don't know the answer, say so." He grasped her elbow, helped her to her feet and seemed to shepherd her into the inner corridor.

Juan and Maggie sat beside their attorney in the conference room. Catherine and Ted took the only vacant remaining seats on the opposite side of the table. They faced spectacular views through the full-length windows. Remembering interrogation techniques, Catherine knew facing the windows meant the sun blurred her ability to read the expression on her opponents faces. She glanced at Ted wondering if she should suggest they move to the far end of the conference table.

"Do you mind if we lower the blinds a bit?"
The Court reporter asked. "It's hard for me to see
the type screen."

A look of reluctance flitted across the
Riveras' attorney's face, but he nodded in response
to his paralegal's questioning look. She rose and
brought down the blinds plunging the room into
semi-darkness.

Ted looked behind him in the direction of
the bank of light switches. He got up and flicked
them all on. "That's better," he said.

Bracing herself, Catherine listened to the
familiar explanation of a deposition and instructions
from the Riveras' attorney. She'd been through this
part before, but never on her own behalf. The first
questions were standard and easy, designed to relax
the deponent. Catherine answered them almost
without thinking. Her self-preservation antenna
went up as the attorney shuffled his papers and
picked up what looked to her like a large-type
checklist.

"So," the Riveras' attorney said, "you expect
us to believe that you went to the Riveras home just
to ask Maggie a few questions?"

"Is that a question?" Ted asked. "Or are you
looking for a conclusion?"

"This is a deposition, not a trial," the
Rivera's attorney picked up a sheet of paper and
made a show of running his finger down to the
bottom, "Mr. Reardon."

Juan's smirk made Catherine want to reach
across the table and wipe it off. A stab of sympathy
for Maggie shot through her. The dark-haired

woman seemed uncomfortable and twice interrupted trying to revise her attorney's questions.

Glancing at Ted for an indication of whether or not she should answer, Catherine squirmed in her seat. In response to his faint nod, she replied, "That's correct."

"You'd had a confrontation with Juan, isn't that true?"

"No. I had no interaction with him…"

"You weren't at the restaurant?"

"Yes, of course."

"Thank you."

"Just a minute. Let my client finish her statement." Ted said. "As counsel has so aptly pointed out, this is not a trial."

"She answered my question." The attorney reached in a large file box on the table and pulled out another file folder. Flipping it open, he reviewed the contents, looked up at Catherine and said, "What did you hope to gain by…"

"I'm sorry if I'm out of line, Mr.…." Catherine let the statement hang in the air hoping he would fill in his name. Although he'd stated it in the beginning of the deposition for the record, he hadn't bothered to introduce himself to either Catherine or her attorney.

"My name is on the bottom of your subpoena, Ms. Swope." The attorney responded. "And I'd like to move this along."

"Fine." Catherine replied hotly. "I have better places to be too. However, I did not take part in any confrontation with your client at the restaurant, and I want that perfectly…"

The sound of raised voices bled into the conference room from the hallway just beyond the door. "You can't go in there. Somebody tell security to hurry up!"

Everyone in the room turned toward the conference room door as it swung open. Ashley stood, outlined in the doorway. Her face looked wild. "Did you tell them?" She demanded of the room.

Ted rose, as did the Riveras' attorney, and advanced toward the distraught woman. "Did you tell them, Maggie?" Ashley shouted again.

Juan clenched and opened his hands. Catherine wasn't sure if he was attempting to control himself, or if he would rise from his chair swinging. Beside him, Maggie's face paled, her eyes turned into huge dark pools. Catherine read fear in their depths.

Ashley's voice pitched higher, and she said, "Your brother blackmailed my husband. Tell them."

The Riveras' attorney was on his feet. He lunged for Ashley as two guards appeared behind her. The uniformed men each grasped an elbow and pulled her back from the doorframe. Ashley's hands grasped metal jambs, "Did you tell them, Juan that you told me you'd drop this whole charade for $100,000?" Ashley screamed.

"You bitch!" Juan Rivera yelled. He stood up and pounded a callused fist down on the table.

Maggie leapt from her seat and grabbed her husband's arm with both of hers. "Juan. Stop. Please. What did you do?" Juan shook her off like a terrier with a rat. She reeled into the chair she'd just left, tangling her feet in the base and pitching into the edge of the conference room table.

"What business is it of yours? Your husband started this! It's his fault, and yours. If you'd been half a woman, he would have left Maggie alone. You owe me. And you owe me big!"

Juan's attorney struggled to get his client back into his seat. Juan shoved him aside into the glass of the 54th floor window. He hit with a sickening crack. "I wish I had killed your husband." He screamed at Ashley. "Tommy wanted to, but I thought the Affidavit would embarrass him. Make him pay us, Dead men don't write checks. We should have killed him.

"Getting that damn thing in the paper didn't do anything, except embarrass Maggie. That cold-blooded son of a bitch you were married to never cared about anything. You should have heard him when I called. He laughed." Juan's finger stabbed into his chest, his face purpled with rage. "He laughed at me!"

The suddenness of Ashley's appearance temporarily froze Catherine to the chair. Her hand slid to her hip seeking the solace of her weapon. Emptiness met her fingers. The last explosion of shouting brought her to her feet. She put a hand on each of her friend's shoulders. "Ashley," she said shaking her lightly. "It's fine. You shouldn't be here."

Behind her, Catherine heard Juan's attorney groan, "You furnished the Affidavit? Then you asked this woman for money to drop a suit against another woman?"

Catherine didn't hear a reply, but she heard the closing of a file folder. Ashley's eyes seemed to clear. The woman shook her head and looked Catherine full in the face as if seeing her for the first time. "I'm sorry." She rolled her shoulders. "I couldn't take any more."

Looking at each of the security guards, Catherine nodded. They seemed to sense the crisis was over, and they released their hold on Ashley's elbows. Catherine enfolded a sobbing Ashley into her arms.

"Should we call the police?" One of the guards asked the attorney.

Craning her neck backwards so she could see the man's face, Catherine saw him shake his head. "No. No harm done. I want a security review though. She's harmless, but how did she get past the receptionist and into the hallway? Clearly, some of our procedures aren't working."

The attorney made his way around the conference room table to Ted. "Thanks Ted." He said and extended his hand to the attorney. "This case is over for me. I had no idea my clients were trying to get payments to stop the case. I don't know what they're going to decide to do, but they're going to have to do it without me."

He spun around and faced Juan. The attorney's fingers balled into fists. He held his arms stiffly at his sides. "You will drop this suit, now," he hissed. "I'll tell any attorney you approach that the case is poison."

"Fine." Juan spat out. "You bastard."

Catherine's jaw hurt from her clenched teeth. Pressure built in the top of her head and the tips of her ears felt hot. She curled her toes in her shoes.

Ted slipped his arm around her and led her from the conference room. Ashley, her hand over her face, followed them to the lobby and the elevator bank beyond.

While Catherine retrieved her driver's license from the security guard in the lobby, Ted stood off to the side. His eyes seemed to be boring a hole into her back. Unable to fight the feeling any longer, she turned, license in hand, and walked to him.

"You want to say something?"

"Yes, you'll wonder about this too, once the adrenalin wears off."

Arching an eyebrow, Catherine cocked her head to the side and replied, "You mean about how Juan and Tomas got the Affidavit to someone at the Metropolis and got it published?"

"Precisely. Whom do they know?"

Slapping a hand to her forehead Catherine groaned. "I feel so stupid. I never thought about talking to whoever wrote the article that accompanied the Affidavit. Who did write the story?"

Ted shrugged in reply. Ashley joined the little group. Her eyes still red and her face blotchy. "Two new journalists," Ashley said. In fact, two brand new journalists who'd just graduated from intern status."

"Why?" Catherine asked her.

"I tracked them down after the story appeared. It was the first thing I did after I went back to work. They were horrified. They'd collaborated on the story. Done extensive background checking, enough to satisfy their editor. They were petrified of a lawsuit because of Gavin's death. They wrote the story because they wanted to make a name, break new ground."

"A Woodstein for a new generation. OK," Ted said. "That makes sense, they're new, and they want to win Pulitzers their first year on the job. How did they get the story? Sounds like neither of them are dry behind the ears. What tipped them to an old story and a private document?"

"According to them, the Affidavit arrived in the mail. It went to the Political Editor."

"So they were assigned?"

"No, that's the funny part. They're too new for an assignment like that. They said they found a copy of the Affidavit in each of their interoffice mail cubbies."

"So the political editor turned the story over to newbies and didn't give them any guidance. Mrs. Jackman, I'm sorry. That makes no sense." Ted picked up his brief case and escorted the two women to the parking garage. "And why did the paper care?"

"They didn't think so either, but they decided not to ask any questions. They plowed ahead, and after they turned in the story, the editor decided to go with it." Ashley looked away. Ted followed her gaze. "Slow week. That's what the editor said. Slow week and he needed a story. He wanted to slap the local reporter, too. He'd sent the guy out for a story on the Commissioners months ago, and he'd come back with nothing. Now, two new kids on the block…"

"Did you put the story in their mailbox?" Ted asked.

Ashley stopped short. Her head snapped around to face him. Her nostrils flared, her chest heaved with a deep breath. "Don't be stupid. Even if I wanted to do that to my husband, why would I embarrass myself?" She shook off the hand Catherine placed on her arm.

"Sorry, Mrs. Jackman. The story seems weak to me. Someone needs a bigger axe to grind with this kind of story. I'm not buying the slow week, or the local reporter. There has to be more of a payoff."

"Cathy, will you give me a ride home? I'm kinda shaky. I don't trust myself to drive back." Ashley's crystal blue eyes glittered, her face mottled with red splotches.

"Of course." Catherine bit her tongue. She'd been looking forward to a solo drive to try and sort out what happened before she got home. The three stood side by side in the parking garage elevator and concentrated on the changing numbers. When the cabin stopped at the third floor, Catherine smiled her thanks to Ted, took Ashley's elbow and led her out into the garage.

The two women seemed lost in their own thoughts as they found Catherine's car.

Catherine smiled as she pulled open the passenger door, helped Ashley in and then rounded

the car and climbed into the driver's seat. They
traveled in silence while Catherine negotiated the
downtown traffic. Constant construction,
jaywalking pedestrians and roads not widened since
the nineteen twenties made downtown driving an
adventure that required full concentration. As
Catherine pointed the car north on I-95, she turned
to glance at her passenger. Ashley had her face
pressed up against the glass of the passenger door
looking for all the world as if she'd never seen the
city before.

"What's so interesting out there?"

"Nothing. I'm trying not to think, and when
I can't stop that, I'm trying not to cry."

"Ashley, what kind of fact checking would
the Metropolis do before they published an article
like the one they did on Gavin?"

"That's just it, Catherine. They'd do a lot.
The piece was investigative, not breaking news.
They had time, it wasn't a deadline 'bleed it leads'
piece."

"So, would the Riveras information alone
get the piece published?"

Ashley shook her head. "No." She
whispered. "They'd have talked to both sides. They
couldn't and wouldn't risk a libel suit, especially
not from a lawyer, and presumably his former firm.
Someone from Gavin's firm talked to them. And
someone else gave out personal information the
firm wouldn't know."

Catherine chewed on this information while
the cars slowed around where the Airport
Expressway merged into the main road. She

expertly negotiated the knotted mass of vehicles enjoying the sheer challenge of it before she turned to her passenger again and said, "Yeah, Ashley, who besides Gavin would have personal information?"

CHAPTER 37

As Catherine turned off the Interstate at the Summer Hill exit, the air in the car seemed to thicken, and she felt Ashley's tension ratchet up. Puzzled, she wondered whether to prod further into the woman's reasons for crashing the deposition. So far, nothing Ashley had told her made any real sense, at least not as Catherine understood it.

"I'm not sure I'm clear on why you put yourself at risk that way, Ashley. Given all the security in high rises and law firms these days, you ran one hell of a risk of being tasered at best, arrested at worst."

"I wanted the ruse to end." Ashley replied. She tilted her head down, and her shining cap of dark hair hid her face. Her voice sounded exhausted to Catherine's ears.

"They wanted money from Gavin, money from me, and finally, from you."

Catherine chewed on her cheek and wished she had more answers. The hospital report Ted subpoenaed cited genetic defects in the fetus as the cause of Maggie's miscarriage. The child was not viable. Sad, but not my fault. The Riveras's suit was bound to fail for its own lack of evidence. No way they'd get any money, at least not from her. Catherine shook her head. Looking back wasn't going to change anything. Tiny tentacles of understanding began to weave their way into her thoughts. Was Ashley confessing? Did she have something to do with her husband's death? Or the Affidavit? Was that the ruse she wanted to end?

"Are you going to be OK?" Catherine asked. Out of the corner of her eye, she watched Ashley twist and release the corner of her jacket. A pulse beat a steady tattoo in her rigid jaw.

"Can we go to your house for a while, Cathy? I don't want to be alone just now. I know it's asking a lot. Especially after my little blow-up, but I promise, I'll be good." Ashley's smile looked more like a three year old's begging for ice cream.

From down the street, Catherine spotted four familiar cars. Sue, Vicki and Nancy parked on the grass swale in front, while Dannie parked in her driveway. "Looks like a crowd has gathered. Do you still want to come in or shall I take you home?"

"Home please, if you don't mind. I wouldn't want to crash the party."

"No party, unless they're having one without me, but I'll take you home if you're sure. And Ashley, call if you need me, I'll come over." Catherine said as she drove past her own house.

When they got to the Jackmans', Ashley climbed down. After thanking Catherine, she held the car door open a fraction of a second longer than necessary. In the interim, Catherine watched a series of emotions chase across the other woman's face. She waited, ready to listen to whatever Ashley wanted to tell her. The dark-haired woman stared toward the far window behind Catherine's shoulder, and then she shook her head. The car door closed with a soft click.

Vicki's car had left in the time it took Catherine to return home. Mike pulled open the front door, and Bullet shot out to greet her, placing his paws on either shoulder and covering her face in doggie kisses.

"I'm telling you Cathy, it was like Grand Central Station in here today. I think nearly every resident of the Village came by to see how I was doing. We have enough casseroles to last us until the next millennium." Mike chortled. "Everybody from A to Z showed up, Alvarez to Zimmerman that is."

"Oh God, Mike. Think of the thank you notes that need writing now. I sure hope you're up to it!"

Mike waggled his right arm in its sling at her. "Nope, I'm gonna need your help!"

Nancy poked her head through the gap between Mike's body and the door jam. "You don't sound so good, girlfriend. What happened at the depo?"

"Let me get out of my monkey suit. I'd forgotten how hot pantyhose are in the summer. I don't know what possessed me to wear them in the first place." Catherine lifted her face for a quick kiss from Mike and then walked into the cool of the air conditioning. She sketched a brief salute to Sue and

Dannie sitting on the couch and hurried off to her bedroom to change into shorts and a tank top.

"What's going on?" She asked returning to the living room.

"You first," Sue responded. "Did we see you drive past the house and then come back? Vicki thought she saw you, and that you didn't want company, so she left."

"I took Ashley home. I think they've dropped the case. Ashley barged in and informed everyone that Juan asked for money in return for his dropping the suit, and she confirmed that he'd asked Gavin for money too. At about that point, their lawyer quit." Mike handed her a tall glass. Catherine looked at it and said, "God, I could use something stronger than lemonade!"

"Well, if they've admitted to blackmail, maybe they did kill Gavin." Nancy responded.

"Unlikely step." Mike said as he sat on the floor next to Catherine. "Blackmailers rarely murder, except on TV. They're basically cowards and bullies. They want something for nothing, and they don't want to get their hands dirty."

Catherine leaned her head against Mike's shoulder. "Yeah, I agree with that. Besides, he admitted to planting the Affidavit. And he admitted that he wished he had killed Gavin, the way Tomas wanted to." She took a long pull on the lemonade, and then looked at the glass and frowned.

"Seems like today was a day of word wars," Sue said. "I went toe to toe with the Kents over their pool house. Those people wear me out!"

"What happened?" Catherine asked.

"Dannie here sort of rescued me. Meg was screaming at the top of her lungs about how dare I tell them what they can and can't do. Luis is the Zoning Commissioner or ZC as she refers to him." Sue looked over at Dannie and smiled. "I thought she'd have a stroke for sure, didn't you?"

Shaking her head so that her curls shook, Dannie rolled her eyes. "Nah, but I don't know what she was getting so uptight about. You gave her a warning. If they get a variance, then the whole thing will be dropped anyway and there's no fine."

"Beats me. Maybe they're having other troubles." Sue continued. "All I know is I'm sick of being everyone's favorite target. Moreover, I got another threat. This one said I'd better back off until I get fired or I'd be sorry."

"She took it to Chief." Mike answered Catherine's unasked question. "If looks are anything to judge by, Meg makes a really tasty macaroni casserole."

"God, have you no pride? You better get that casserole tested! I don't think the Riveras had anything to do with Gavin's death." Catherine said, rotating the glass between her palms.

"Do you think someone from the Village did it, Mike? There were plenty of folks at the last Commission Meeting that were steamed enough to take action."

"Like?" Dannie asked. "I was there. I saw how riled people were but it's a long step from screaming in a crowd to killing someone in a garage."

"What about the Commissioners themselves?"

"Catherine, that's a real long shot," Mike said.

"Is it? We know money's missing." Catherine rested her hand on Mike's thigh. "We know Gavin blew the whistle. We know Cunningham owed him money and his house was in foreclosure, we know Simms just saved his house from foreclosure. Where did all that money come from? Cripes, Mike. Look around you, all the for sale signs. What would you do to save your house?"

"Gavin had money problems too. In fact, now that the suicide verdict is in, Ashley can probably collect on the insurance," Nancy said.

"On suicide?" Dannie asked.

Nancy nodded. "Yeah, a lot of policies pay on suicide, as long as you've had them a while."

"Speaking of garages," Sue chimed in, "did you see the two new vehicles the Kents bought? What did they do, hit the lottery? Maybe I should quit before they fire me. I'm really getting fed up with the attitude of everyone in this town."

Catherine shrugged. "Don't do that Sue. That's letting them win. You lose the unemployment benefits, and it looks like they're right.

"I guess so." Sue replied.

Suicide. Everyone seems content with the suicide theory. Catherine bit her tongue to keep silent. If no one else pursued the loose ends, Catherine resolved she and Mike would do it together.

"You going to tell Chief about the deposition?" Mike asked.

"Already ordered a transcript for him. I don't think he ever considered the Riveras as suspects, but this should answer any questions he might have about them."

"Don't bet on it, Catherine. In going through the files, I discovered that he was considering asking them if they'd come in for questioning. He's also been in touch with Tomas's parole officer. There's a warrant out for Tomas, incidentally. He hasn't been reporting. Was he at the depo?"

Catherine considered this new information. So, Chief might finally agree that Gavin's death wasn't suicide after all. Either that or he was dotting the "i"s and crossing the "t"s for some other reason. She never bought Chief's theory that Gavin had jumped from the workbench. After all, if he went to all the trouble to make a noose, and hang it from a rafter, where was the stepladder? How did he secure the rope without one? And if he had one to secure the rope, why didn't he put the noose around his neck and jump from the stepladder? Catherine scratched her nose and crossed her eyes at Mike's questioning look.

"No, Tomas wasn't there. Last I knew he lived with his sister. Sue, how many open cases do you have that you've continued with after your reinstatement?"

Sue made a sound closer to a snort than a laugh. "About twenty-five, some more egregious than others, but there are at least twenty-five people out there that could be mad at me."

"Some more than others?"

"Sure, but I should mention that this IP didn't match any of the others. I'm thinking these e-mails are random, and meaningless."

"Remember your pups." Catherine cautioned.

Nodding, Sue said, "Believe me, I am. I told Nick about the e-mail, before Chief told him. I know how that 'brotherhood of the badge' thing works. Chief's stepped up early morning patrols past my house."

"Sue," Catherine said, "I know it sounds strange, but do me a favor. Make a list of the infamous twenty-five. In addition, if you can, tell me if they also had a beef with Gavin. Or if Gavin got nasty e-mails from them."

CHAPTER 38

Closing the door on the last of her guests, Catherine thought about suggesting dinner out. Mike sounded jovial while the girls were there. Looking at him now with his head resting back against the seat of the couch, his face pinched and drawn, she doubted he'd taken any of the prescribed pain medication in the week since the shooting. She leaned back against the closed door, and in a flash of insight, realized she felt like he looked.

"If I heat up one of those casseroles, do you think we can talk a bit?"

Mike rolled his head over and looked at Catherine. She read exhaustion in his eyes.

"But if you're too tired, then we'll skip it, and I'll tuck you into bed."

He dropped his head back against the couch. "Nah, Cathy, you had a lousy day too. I must be getting old. All this company and chitchat's worn me out. Let me grab a nap, and then we'll talk. I found some stuff in the file. My notes and the e-mails are there." Mike levered himself off the couch and walked over to stand in front of Catherine. He awkwardly lifted her chin with his left hand until she looked directly into his eyes. "Chief gave the file to me to review with an eye to new information. I think, now that you're not trying to be the Terminator, your input could help."

"Should I add the last bits of information I got from Ashley?"

"No, keep it separate, but we'll see if it ties in. You said she dropped off the private account statements?" He returned to the couch and tried to adjust his six-foot frame amid a variety of throw pillows.

"Yeah. I wish we could get more information on the embezzlement investigation." She hoped he felt more comfortable than he looked stretched out on the couch.

He pulled up the corner of the throw pillow he'd used to cover his face and looked back at her. "That's not going to happen. We can try to construct a scenario from the information we have. See if it fits what we know."

Catherine grabbed the pillow from his hands and pushed it playfully down on his face. "You have an hour. Get all the sleep you can!" She laughed.

She made her way to her office to pick up the latest financial information Ashley had given her. Opening the file cabinet, she riffled through the slim stack of folders until she came up with the one marked 'G – personal account'. Catherine's instruction to Ashley to turn the information over to the Summer Hill police resulted in Ashley's questioning. When the distraught woman arrived at

Catherine's house bearing copies of the statements, she'd practically thrown them in her face. Tired of always being the bad guy, Catherine had put them into a file folder unreviewed.

She grabbed the folder, a legal pad, and a pen and walked out to the living room and settled herself crossed-legged on the floor in front of the coffee table. Tapping her front teeth with the end of the pen she let her memories roll back to where she thought it began and again heard the angry shouts of the residents at the commission meeting. She began to draw an incident report based on her memories and the results of her investigation. Mike woke with a groan before she'd finished.

"Are you all right?" She shot up from her place on the floor to come to his side.

"Yes, I must be getting old though. This pain won't quit. I keep waiting for it to go away. You look like you're lost in deep space."

"I think we need a trip to the doctor."

"No. I think I need to stop being a pig head and take my meds."

Smiling, she shook her head. "Have you taken any?" Seeing his blush she laughed. "So, paybacks are hell. You are taking one now." She got up and headed for the kitchen returning with a pill bottle and a glass of water, watched him swallow the pill and put the glass on the coffee table.

"You better talk fast before I fall asleep."

"Don't worry, I'll talk fast, and feed you, too. Check this out." Catherine knelt on the floor between the coffee table and the couch, leaned over, and picked up the legal pad, holding it in Mike's field of vision. "I've listed everyone I could think of from the Riveras to the people who spoke at the commission meeting. Everyone has at least one blank beside their name. The Riveras and Lopez," Catherine's pen followed their names across the lines and continued, "sure, they had motive and alibis but did they have the means? Probably not."

"Err, Cathy, didn't you exonerate them today?" Mike rubbed his eyes and took the pad from her hands.

"Yes, the Riveras, but I'm not so sure about Lopez. He has a violent streak, and he did demand money."

"Sure, but where does that fit with releasing the Affidavit? Dead men don't pay"

"Why are you so sure the two are mutually exclusive? The Riveras were the ones who got the Affidavit published. For a man of action like Lopez, he might not wait until Gavin decided what to do. No, I can see him confronting Gavin the day the paper came out." Catherine shrugged. "Don't you agree?"

"I think the real question is how they got the Affidavit published in the first place."

"Anonymous tip?"

"Cathy, it's old news, why would the paper care? It could embarrass Gavin, but it couldn't destroy him. It got to those rookie writers somehow. Check with Ashley, maybe she can find out something more."

Mike ticked the pen down the list of suspects Catherine compiled from the Village residents. "Juan was in jail, I can't see his wife hanging someone. As for the rest, too far-fetched. And you know you'll never break the alibis."

"What about Chris and Terry? Catherine asked. They live next door, they hated Gavin, they made no secret of it, and they could come and go as they pleased between the two properties without anyone else seeing them."

Mike lay the tablet down on the floor beside him and tipped his head back against the arm of the couch. "Maybe, but unlikely."

"Why?"

"Because they still hate him. They haven't changed their story one iota. As far as they're concerned, Gavin needed to be out of office how ever that had to happen. No, either they're sociopaths, which I seriously doubt, or they're innocent."

"The Commissioners?"

Mike's hand closed over Catherine's. He lifted her fingers to his lips and kissed them. "Cathy, have you looked at the financial information?"

"No, not yet, I wanted to clear my thoughts first. Besides," she shrugged, "I'm not sure it's going to tell me anything other than list the deposits and withdrawals. There's not enough information." She flipped open the file folder and looked at the statement on top.

"This has been one hell of a roller coaster ride, Mike. I'm finally realizing that my neighbors don't hate me or suspect me. Pretty strange, don't you think?" She smiled and looked directly into

Mike's eyes. "Now that Chief is starting to look closely at me."

"You've got a blank next to your name too, Kit Kat. Right there, at alibi."

"Yeah, I know. Mike." Catherine dropped her head to her hands. "I feel like I'm about to go into battle without ammunition. I've got more questions than answers."

He propped himself up on his good elbow and looked at her. "Well then, you've either not asked the right questions, or you haven't found the right suspect. You know that." He took the folder of bank statements out of her hand, dropped them on his chest and awkwardly flipped the folder open with his left hand.

"These two deposits don't amount to a drop in the bucket compared to what's gone."

"Is there some way they could have been made in error? You know, the Commissioners salary for their service. What is it? Ashley said Gavin took a minimum amount, $1,000, $5,000, everybody else gets the rest of the money we vote for divided up. Maybe someone put the payola into the wrong account."

Catherine laughed as she watched him try to flip through the statements.

"Here, let me. You're going to hurt yourself! What are you looking for?"

"The salary deposit from the Village. If it's there, then you might have something," Mike said.

The color drained from Catherine's face. "Here. Five thousand dollars from last year."

"Any chance the $50,000 was an incorrect payment? A typo in the wire amount? The clerk deposited the salary and accidently gave the order for $50,000 not $5,000? Easy to do."

"I don't know. Maybe, but then, why two payments? There were two $50,000 payments, not one."

"Mistake on the correction? Someone from the bank double credited what should have been a withdrawal?"

"So unlikely, Cathy"

"Is it? One wrong keystroke and it's in the system. How can we find out?"

"Easy," Mike replied. "Ashley. Cathy, no matter what you say or how you say it, all the roads lead back to Ashley."

CHAPTER 39

While Mike dozed after supper, Catherine decided to take his advice. Lacing on her running shoes, she jogged over to the Jackman residence hoping for some answers. Through the sidelight windows, Catherine could see Ashley's shadow moving in the house, but there was no response to her knock. Catherine was about to turn and leave when the door opened and Ashley invited her in.

Catherine let her gaze wander around the Jackman Florida room. She understood why Ashley and Gavin considered it the best room in their house. The way the tinted light blue glass walls cascaded, each rounding out and building on the one below, they almost looked like a waterfall. The space was immaculate, the white furniture unsullied. No easy trick with an active and pampered dog in the house. Based on what she had heard, building this room put the Jackmans into deep debt and threatened their house. Catherine wondered if the beauty justified the price.

Ashley seemed more nervous and upset than at the deposition. Bustling around in the kitchen, she seemed almost hyperactive, moving for the sake of movement.

"Damn, damn, damn!" Ashley's swearing accompanied the sound of pottery smashing against tile. "Damn!" She shouted again, and swept her arm over the countertop hurtling canisters, cream and sugar to the floor.

Startled and a little frightened, Catherine bolted out of the chair she sat in and raced around the divider into the kitchen. Ashley's hysterical sobs filled the room. Avoiding the broken crockery, she approached Ashley from behind. The woman supported herself with both arms leaning heavily on the granite countertop. Catherine grabbed her, careful to encircle her arms in a bear hug to limit her mobility, and took her full weight as Ashley's legs seemed to buckle beneath her.

"I'm sorry, Catherine." Ashley wailed. "This is one hell of a way to get someone tea." Taking in great gulps of air, she managed to help Catherine duck walk her to a club chair in the Florida room.

Using her training, Catherine turned the still sobbing woman while keeping her under physical control. Until she knew what was going on, she did not intend to release her.

"I told you I can't take any more of this. Catherine, I wasn't kidding. I spend half my nights lying awake wondering how I'll look in prison orange and the other half wondering why no one is trying to find out who killed my husband. He didn't commit suicide. He couldn't do that to me. Leave me with nothing. No insurance, huge debt, nothing. Not even a roof over my head. I watch cop shows

on television, and I know I'm the first suspect."
Ashley wiped her eyes with her fists like a child. "I
didn't do it. I don't know who did. I want to know."
She took in great gulps of air. "I'm sorry." She
repeated. "You must think I'm nuts."

Her dark head rested against the back of the
white chair, and she closed her eyes. When she
opened them, her tears had stopped and the wild,
unfocused look was gone.

Loosening her grip, Catherine squatted in
front of the chair. "Where's a broom and dust pan?
I'll get the broken dishes off the floor before you or
Roscoe gets hurt."

A faint smile crossed Ashley's face.

"You didn't come over here to make me tea
and clean my kitchen." Ashley looked directly into
Catherine's eyes. "Leave the mess. Roscoe's
outside, I'll clean it before I let him in, he won't cut
his paws. Why did you come, Catherine?"

Sighing, Catherine rose, grateful to be out of
the squat. She walked back to her chair, turning her
head as she went, trying to read Ashley's
expression. "I thought you wanted to tell me
something when you got out of my car earlier."
Pausing, she debated whether to continue. Realizing
that things had escalated beyond the kid gloves
stage, she bit her lip and decided to be blunt. "And I
hoped you'd help me with some information about
the bank statements you gave me."

For what seemed like forever, Catherine
held the dark-haired woman's gaze with her own.
She watched Ashley's face, seeking clues to her
thoughts. Hoping to find answers to questions she

didn't yet have the words to ask. Ashley finally broke the eye contact, and Catherine felt exhaustion ripple through her body.

"Ok." Ashley whispered. "What do you want to know?

"About the deposits, there were two, right? Each for $50,000."

Ashley lifted her legs, crossed them on the ottoman in front of her, and dropped her head back. "Yes, two deposits. $50,000 each. I gave you copies of the statements."

Pulling her legal pad and the statement folder out of the tote she'd brought, Catherine fumbled further looking for a pen. "Ok, what about Gavin's salary?"

Ashley's head came up from the back of the chair. "Salary, are you kidding me, the $5,000 stipend the Village paid him? I have no idea. I think it went into our joint checking. Why?"

"Can you check that?"

"Catherine, do we really have to go through this exercise now? I don't even know what time of the year they paid him." Ashley's dark cap of hair flowed forward as she propped her elbow on the arm of the chair and cupped her chin in her hand. "OK, mostly, he either turned it back or gave it to someone."

"Who?"

"I don't know, Catherine. Anyone he thought needed it. This mortgage thing is out of hand. Gavin, my husband, saved more than one person from losing their homes. He never thought he'd have a problem saving his own."

335

"How'd that happen, Ashley?"

She reached for a small box on the end table next to her, removed a cigarette and lit it. The match burned down nearly to her fingertip before she shook it out. "Same way it happened to everyone. The stock market tanked, the house value tanked and the real estate market tanked." She leaned her head back and blew smoke rings toward the ceiling, then tipped her head down.

Watching Ashley's eyes gaze up at her through the curtain of bangs, Catherine saw no subterfuge, only tiredness. Did you get any answers from the Bank on the inquiry Gavin made?"

"You mean about who made the deposits? The Village did. Both deposits. They're asking for it back now. At least Hank is. He said they were illegally made."

"Who authorized the wires? Who signed the requests? Someone has to have that information?"

"Sure, but they're not sharing it with me. The signature on the transfer order was Hank's. He said it was a forgery. The Village attorney has to figure that out. In the meantime, they've subpoenaed all my bank records, any bit of financial information in Gavin's name, and in my name, to see if we've gotten more." Ashley skewered Catherine with her eyes. "I'm not giving you that kind of access."

Catherine squirmed in her seat, hoping she didn't look as uncomfortable as she felt. Talking about finances was never easy for Catherine. Asking about someone else's was more difficult. "No one ever requested a reversal of the deposit?

The second deposit, could that be a misrouting and should have been a debit not a credit."

"If it was, no one ever said anything to me."

Ashley rose from her chair. She went back to the kitchen, Catherine heard the whooshing sound of a broom as Ashley swept up the pottery shards. Coming back to the Florida room, she sat on the ottoman in front of Catherine. "Look, Catherine, I made that whole scene today because I want this to end. I want it over and done. It's too much drama for me."

"I understand, but…Catherine struggled with how far to stretch the truth. Deciding she had nothing to lose, she continued, "Chief is looking for a reason to look at Gavin's death as a murder." Catherine searched the face of the woman in front of her, looking for any emotion, guilt, rage, surprise. She didn't see anything. To buy time and busy herself, Catherine made a quick scribble on her legal pad.

The sound of Ashley clearing her throat broke the silence. "I never doubted his death was murder. Gavin wasn't the type to kill himself, and certainly not because the newspaper story embarrassed him. Our marriage was solid. He'd never leave me with nothing."

"You got no benefits from the firm?"

The harsh sound of Ashley snorting startled Catherine. "He cashed in his life insurance policy two weeks before he died. Talk about lousy timing. Hundred Thou. Oh, it had loans, I know. But sheesh."

For the first time since she arrived at Ashley's house, Catherine thought she had some answers. "That could explain the deposit. The life insurance, he put it in the bank." Her heart plummeted when she remembered the deposit came from the Village, not John Hancock or whomever.

"Not likely. The check hasn't arrived. Gavin wanted to use it to cover the balloon payment."

"Oh, Ashley, I'm so…."

"Yeah, and his partnership income died with him." Ashley looked down at her hands, knotted in her lap, and then gazed out the window before turning back to Catherine. I told you, the cancer is back. They are still trying to shrink the tumor with chemotherapy before they hopefully remove it. The chemotherapy isn't working. The tumor may be inoperable." She stubbed out the cigarette and ran her hands through her hair. "I may be a bag lady who dies on the street from cancer. Now there's a pretty picture. God, my life sucks right now."

"Oh Ashley, I am so very sorry!"

"Well, Catherine, this whole little episode has got to end. Right now, I have to take care of myself. I thought about flying to Chicago, for more treatment. Be near my family. I have no one left here."

"Ashley, you do have friends here. I know it doesn't seem that way now, but it's true."

Snorting, Ashley replied, "Yeah, friends. Sure. Catherine, I have people who try to be my friends, I know that. I probably do have some real friends, but the fact is I've isolated myself from nearly everyone. And I did it deliberately. I

immersed myself in Gavin and our relationship.
Once he became a commissioner, I avoided making
friends in the Village. I have friends at the paper,
but even there…" She shrugged. "It's a competitive
atmosphere. No. I want someone close. When my
hair falls out again, I want to be able to walk around
bald and be comfortable."

"Are you going to Chicago then?"

"They won't let me." She grimaced. "My
lawyer says there's not enough evidence to warrant
a warrant." She smiled at the pun. "But Chief
doesn't want me to leave South Florida."

"So, if you leave for medical reasons, so
what. Ashley," Catherine took the woman's hands
in hers. They were so cold she nearly dropped them.
"I was a cop. Trust me on this. Chief's words are a
suggestion. They're to intimidate you. He can't
enforce them. Tell him you're leaving, and tell him
why, or don't tell him why. He can't hold you. You
need to get treatment."

"I am getting treatment, Catherine. The
bottom line, my doctors are here. The ones I'm
comfortable with, the ones who saw me through the
first bout. My history is here, but my heart isn't."

"Can your sister come?"

"Sure. The point is my doctor says I need to
end this. It needs to go into the past. There are
studies that link stress and cancer. Alleviating the
stress won't cure the cancer. I know that. But it can
help my state of mind, and that can help make the
treatments more effective. Stop now, Catherine. I
want you to stop investigating. I want you to stop

asking me questions. That's what I wanted to tell you before. I wanted to beg you to back off."

"But…"

"No, Catherine. I pray to God that Chief finds who killed my husband now that you say he's finally looking. I know it won't be me. If he charges me with something, I'll deal with that, but right now, I need peace."

Catherine rose, tucked the pen between the pages of her legal pad and stuffed it in her tote.

"My pen," Ashley said.

Pulling out the legal pad, Catherine pulled the pen off, "Oh, sorry. I didn't mean to…"

Ashley shrugged, "It was a gift."

CHAPTER 40

The door made a swishing sound as it closed behind her. Catherine looked over her shoulder and wondered whether she should return and try to offer Ashley a deeper form of friendship. Shaking her head, she realized it wouldn't matter. Friendships are born of time, not desire.

Salsa tones cut through the air announcing a call from Mike on Catherine's cell phone. Cursing she dug in the tote, and retrieved the phone before voice mail took the call. Grabbing it in the middle of the third ring, she flipped the phone open and shouted 'just a second' into the bowels of the bag as she pulled the cell out and put it to her ear.

"Hello." She bellowed hoping the caller hadn't disconnected in the while she searched.

"Cathy," Mike said. "Where are you? Now. You need to get home. I've called Ted."

"Slow down, cowboy. What's going on? Why have you called Ted? What do I need a lawyer for?"

"Where are you?" Mike repeated, spacing each word to emphasize them.

"Just leaving Ashley's about two minutes away by slow walk."

"Ok, good. Billy called me. Your prints turned up on a shovel in the Jackman's garage."

"So what, I grabbed the shovel to clean up after Roscoe. What's the big deal?"

"You used it that morning?"

While she moved steadily toward her house, she tried to picture what she'd done when Roscoe did his business near the Payson window. She remembered grabbing the shovel. Did she use it? Catherine shook her head trying to bring the image into focus.

"Yeah. I think so. Maybe. I'm not sure." The haze of memory cleared and she saw herself put the shovel back. "No, wait. No. It seemed so out of place, scooping up after the dog while Gavin hung in the garage. No. I picked it up, and then put it back down."

"But you touched it."

"So what! Where are you going with this?"

"The shovel is consistent with the contusion the medical examiner identified on Gavin's head. Where did you get it?"

"Damn." She stopped in her tracks and raked her hand through her hair as if clearing it from her forehead could clear her thought process.

"Catherine, Chief can place you at the scene, and in possession of a potential murder weapon."

A sheen of sweat that had nothing to do with the weather covered her face. Catherine bounded up the steps to her front porch, pulled the door open and threw her cell phone at the couch. She slammed the door behind her and stared into Mike's ashen face as he stood in the opening to the kitchen. She felt a cold sweat trickle down her spine. Black spots danced in her vision. How in God's name could this get any worse?

"Gavin died of suffocation, asphyxia."

"He did."

"The bump was there, we knew that, but a shovel?"

Catherine watched as Mike looked at his hand and closed his phone. He'd been talking into it while he talked to her standing in the living room. She let out a breath she didn't realize she'd been holding. "Ok, then. He died of suffocation. The shovel wasn't the murder weapon, and it may or may not have been the instrument to cause the internal bleeding."

Striding across the floor to the couch, Catherine picked up her phone. "Were my prints the only ones on the shovel? And if it didn't kill him, how is it a murder weapon?"

Nodding, Mike said, "Billy's on his way back to the Jackmans. You know how this goes Cathy. This is the part where all the cards get tossed in the air and the pattern when they land, well, that's usually correct."

"What's Billy going back for? Any evidence would have been compromised long ago."

"We thought Gavin hung himself. No one made the connection between the bruise and the hanging." Mike cleared his throat and hung his head. "He was so close to the motor for the garage door opener, in the photos, the ME thought he might have struck his head when he jumped."

"Sounds like poor investigative technique to me. I was there. This is bogus. You figure out what's really going on and let me know. That scene was preserved. You treated it as a homicide, not a suicide." Catherine spun on her heel. "I'm going for a run. You need to figure out who wants to get you for shoddy police work."

"Catherine?" He watched while she scratched her nose.

"I'm ticked, Mike, that you didn't share that information with me. We were sharing, at least I was."

He strode toward her, but she shook off his intended embrace and moved toward the door. As her hand rested on the knob, she turned her head and said, "Now, here I am, in the position of chief suspect because of a bruise and a shovel. This stinks. I want to think. Her hand reflexively stroked the scar on her thigh. "Bullet, come to Mommy, we're going for a run."

The look in Mike's eyes impaled her to the wall. She'd clearly missed something. Running her mind back over the conversation, she tried to see another avenue. Something to explain Mike's look.

"Don't you want to know what Chief wants to charge you with?" Mike asked.

"You mean this conversation hasn't been about a murder charge?"

"No. It's about an obstruction charge. The same one he filed the Information on."

"Obstruction. Because of fingerprints?" She said, incredulously. "Are you going to tell me not to leave town?"

"Don't be stupid. I'm telling you so you can mount a defense." He said through gritted teeth. "Catherine, I know you didn't have anything to do with Gavin's death. And while we're on the topic, what did Ashley say?"

A peel of thunder sounded. Catherine cracked the door open and looked out. The sky had turned ominously dark and streetlights blinked on. Her avenue of escape cut off, she went to the kitchen and poured herself a cup of coffee instead. Carrying the cup to the kitchen island, she put it down and walked over to Mike. Wrapping her arms around him, she hugged him hard. "I'm sorry. I'm being a spoiled brat. This came out of nowhere. You've been with me on this every step of the way." She looked up at him. "Did you see this coming?"

His good arm tightened around her, and she felt a kiss brush the top of her head. "No. I didn't have a clue. And you're not being a brat, you're in shock."

"Mike, tell Ted to stand down I need some time. I need to think. How long will it take to get the warrant? Did Billy say if they were going for an emergency one, or going through the channels?"

"Channels, I think. You're probably not looking at before Wednesday."

Catherine relaxed. "Ashley fired me, in a manner of speaking. Her cancer has come back, with a vengeance. Her doctor thinks everything that's happened is a contributing factor. So she wants to let things take their own course with respect to Gavin and deal with whatever comes when it comes."

"God, she's had a rotten time of it."

"Yeah. That's an understatement." Catherine pulled back from the circle of Mike's arm and looked him directly in the eyes. "She says the bank confirmed the deposits came from the Village. Hank's saying the signatures on the authorizations were forgeries."

"So, there were two deposits?" Mike asked.

"Seems so. But Mike, why didn't someone ask for a reversal of the deposit? Why wait until things got to this point? OK, I can understand Hank, or whoever really balances the checkbook, not knowing about the mistake until the statements came in. However, it makes no sense to go more than a month out and not ask for the money back." Catherine drew a shuddering breath. "I'm going to try calling the bank. I mean, they can't tell me it's none of my business until I ask them."

"Aren't you giving this way more importance than it needs to have?"

Catherine chewed her lower lip. "Probably, but I might as well try. Where's the file with the statements?" Was she grasping at straws here? Why did it matter? Would someone kill Gavin rather than simply having the deposit reversed? If it were an innocent mistake, then no. If the mistake opened the door to a problem, and someone knew Gavin was looking into it, then maybe. If the mistake weren't innocent, well, then it would depend.

Her heart pounded as she dialed the Bank's number. Telling the woman who answered, that Ashley asked her to call to confirm the details of the transactions, she asked if a request to transfer the funds out had gone through, and the date of the transfer.

Mike's eyebrows shot skyward. He mouthed that Catherine should ask for the bank manager.

Catherine shook her head and put a finger to her lips. Hearing the familiar classical hold music, she whispered, "I want to try to catch someone off guard enough that they'll give me the information. The bank manager gets paid to be on guard."

"That's gonna blow up in your face, Cathy. Do it right if you're doing it."

Twenty minutes and at least four conversations later, Catherine finally spoke to the bank manager. He informed her that she had no right to the information and not so kindly told her not to call back.

Rotating her head to try to ease the crick in her neck she smiled ruefully at Mike. "Ok, I give up."

"Kit Kat, it was worth the try. Now, give it a rest before Chief finds out. I'm telling you, girl. You can be your own worst enemy."

"I know Mike. I guess if he did find out, he'd have more ammunition to level his charge of obstruction." Shrugging, she said, "I can't take anymore." She craned her neck in the direction of the window. Water dripped from the eaves, but the storm had abated. "I'm going for a run."

She grabbed the dog leash, called Bullet and jogged out the front door.

Catherine's mind was in turmoil as she headed in the direction of the bike path that bordered the canal. Midday in high summer is a lousy time to run, even in tree shade. She usually avoided it, but it was the only way she knew to clear her mind. The humidity following summer storms climbed to new heights as puddles evaporated. The canal might offer the hint of a breeze.

Off in the distance, a small clot of people gathered in a driveway. Catherine briefly considered changing her route. The last thing she wanted at this moment was to stop and make small talk.

Pushing the neighbors from her mind and using techniques she'd learned in the academy, she tried to conjure up a mental image of the morning Gavin died. Glossing over finding Roscoe outside and her tour of the vacant house, she fast-forwarded her memory to the point where she approached the back door of the garage.

"Oh, if it isn't Miss Speedy running from her sins."

The sneering tone broke into her reverie. Nearly tripping as she skidded to a stop in the still wet roadway, she looked into the face of Terry Payson. Catherine's thoughts so engrossed her, she hadn't realized when she drew abreast of the group in the driveway.

"Excuse me?" Catherine said, jogging in place. Looking each person in the face, she noted Rosita and Luis Alvarez, were also in the group. "Is this an informal meeting of the future Summer Hill Commission?"

"Are you finally through playing cop? You've managed to polarize this entire Village. All because you want to cover up what you did."

Terry's smooth face showed no emotion as she spewed her venom. The dichotomy disturbed Catherine more than the accusations. The response from the majority of the Villagers since Mike's injury demonstrated to Catherine that she wasn't the cause of any polarization. She might, in fact be a target of it.

Luis stepped forward and put a hand on Terry's arm. "This isn't the time, Terry." Smiling at Catherine, he continued, "Emotions run strong. Too much is going on, and there are still too many questions."

"Come on, Mr. Politician," Terry said. "We all know someone helped Gavin to his death. And we all know who made the threats, who found the body..."

"Err, Terry..." Catherine began. She knew the woman considered her a busy body. Terry made that clear after Gavin's death. Time apparently hadn't softened her stance.

"Who has the knowledge to obscure the evidence, and who sleeps with the investigator?" Terry continued despite Catherine's attempted interruption.

"Terry." Luis's voice held a warning note. "That's enough, I think."

Pulling her arm out of the newly appointed Zoning Commissioner's grasp, Terry continued.

"I'm waiting for her to point her fickle finger of fate at me. I live next door to Gavin. Doesn't that make me a likely suspect in her parade of who other than me did murder?"

CHAPTER 41

Bullet sat at Catherine's side, tiny ripples under his coat revealing the tension coiled tightly in his body. If anyone in this group of irate neighbors made a move toward her, the dog would bare his teeth and growl. Worse would follow the warning, if necessary. Conducting a mental review of her liability policy made Catherine shorten her hold on the dog's leash to a point where she could control a lunge but give him space to act to protect her. Although he'd been her pet for years, he'd been trained as a K-9 and she still practiced hand and voice control with him.

Behind her, the sound of jogging feet beat a steady tattoo. Adrenaline tensed her muscles. A familiar copper flavor filled her mouth as she prepared to deal with a threat from the rear. Trusting her dog to cover her, she maintained eye contact with the group in front hoping to read someone's impression of the approaching runner. Beads of cold sweat broke out on her forehead and mingled with her run-induced perspiration.

351

"Hey there, neighbors!" Susan's voice rang out clear and strong. "Are you guys having a party without me?"

Susan jogged up and stopped beside Catherine. Bullet hunched between them. Glancing over at Susan, Catherine read understanding in her eyes. Susan may have happened to be running past, but she knew something wasn't going well.

"Oh, no, Susan." Luis replied. "We'd never have a party without you. What fun would that be? Are you coming to the meeting tomorrow?"

The atmosphere thickened. Tension crackled between Susan and Luis. No longer the center of attention, Catherine watched the small group carefully, trying to understand the relationships among them. Gavin's death no longer seemed important to any of them.

"What meeting?"

"About your grievance. The Village attorney hasn't called you yet? I'm sure he's tried to reach you."

"Not yet, but I'll be glad to have all of this wrapped up in a neat package. I guess everyone else will be too."

"Why do you want to stay and work where you're not wanted?" Terry asked. "I'd think you'd have better ways to spend your time than jogging and pissing people off."

Susan's face tightened, her eyebrows lifted high on her forehead. From her reaction, Catherine realized Susan knew about the meeting and relished it.

"Wow, Terry, I know we're never going to take a house by the sea together, but you're really getting a little out of line here. Look, whatever is going to happen tomorrow, is going to happen." Susan shrugged and grabbed Catherine's arm. "Come on, let's hit the road."

"You okay, girlfriend?" Susan asked after the two women and Bullet had put a block between them and the disgruntled group.

"Ya, glad you came along when you did though. I thought I was through with that kind of vitriol."

Susan tossed a glance over her shoulder. "Yes, I did too. I know they hate me. I couldn't resist pretending not to know about the meeting. I wondered how much trash Luis talked to Terry. You know she's my successor."

Catherine tripped at the news. "I thought for sure that wouldn't fly. She wasn't too successful in her brief tenure replacing you. Then, after you were reinstated..."

"Yep. Oliver Kent, of all people, let it slip when I went over to his place yesterday. I hate to be a bitch, but you know, sometimes it feels so damn good."

"How are you feeling about the termination?"

"To tell you the truth, I'm more than ready to leave the Village workforce. The new magnate school that's opening next year asked me to teach civics and first year history. Nick really wants me to do it."

The tone of the Waltzing Matilda split the air. Distracted, Catherine reached for her cell phone and waved Susan on ahead of her. As she noted her neighbor, Ann's, number on the display she reflected that this summer is that one that has everyone deciding whom they want to be when they grow up. Flipping the phone open, she spied Sue half a block ahead and jogging in place. Pointing to the phone and shrugging, Catherine waved good-bye and blew her friend an air kiss of thanks. Sue returned the wave and jogged away.

"Catherine," Ann hissed into the phone. "You're not going to believe what I just saw. You have to come home. Are you in town?"

"Hi, Ann." Catherine rolled her eyes. Ever since the fire, Ann declared herself a one-woman crime watch. Unfortunately, her last call resulted in a police challenge to the meter reader. "Yes, I'm about five blocks away. Are you all right?" Catherine resumed her jogging in place to keep her heart rate up.

"Hank Simms is over at your house."

Catherine waited through what she could only describe as a pregnant pause. What the heck was the finance commissioner doing at her house? She barely knew the man.

"He has a gun." Ann continued. "I wasn't watching your house, of course, I was out pressure cleaning my back patio, I saw him pull up through the open gate. He slipped it into his pocket."

"He slipped the gate into his pocket?" Catherine asked.

"No." She responded curtly. "Not the gate, he slipped the gun into his pocket."

"And you're sure it's a gun?" Catherine asked.

Ann sniffed. "Well of course I'm sure. I'm not stupid. I mean I don't know what kind, but I know what it was. He took it out of the glove compartment of his car. He spun the little barrel thing while he was looking at it, and then put it in his pants pocket." She finished this speech with a note of triumph in her voice.

Catherine felt chilled despite the heat. Ann probably didn't know a gun from a tire iron but then again, she was giving a good description of a revolver.

"Are you there?" Ann asked. "This guy looks like the one I saw the night of the fire. You know…"

"I'm on my way." Catherine interrupted. "Ann, this is important. Go into your house. Do not come out. Do not try to see anything. Do not let anyone know you saw anything. Do you understand me?"

"You bet. You coming now? I'll call 911"

"No!" The vehemence in Catherine's voice must have made the point. The last thing Catherine wanted was Hank firing on Mike because he heard sirens. "I'm coming home. I don't want you in the line of fire. Mike is at my house. I'm sure he can handle anything that happens. Ann. Do. Not. Call. 911."

Fear leant speed to Catherine's feet. The faster she ran, the slower she felt she was moving.

Frustrated at what she perceived as her lack of progress, she wished for once she were in her car. Finally, after what seemed like an eternity, her house came into view. Sure enough, there was a huge SUV parked on the swale in front.

Crossing the street, Catherine tried to see into her front windows. She didn't want to overreact and burst in like some unarmed superhero. Not seeing anything, she jogged around to the street behind. Years before, at the time her neighbor got her first dog, they put a gate into the rear fence between the two properties. The dog was long gone, but Catherine was grateful they'd never taken the gate out.

The rain made the grass beneath her feet slippery. She carefully lifted and placed her feet, looking for bare spots and going through the flowerbed planted near the gate. Holding her breath, Catherine pushed, keeping her hand on the post and ready to stop at the first sign of a creaking hinge. Much to her relief, it swung open silently. Putting a finger to her lips, she tried to tell Bullet to be quiet. She didn't want to leave him behind. She might need his bite, or his bark.

Cautiously, dog and woman crept toward the back of the house. Obscured by lace but still visible, she saw Mike and another man in her bedroom. Mike's arms rested at his side. It took Catherine a moment to realize he wasn't wearing his sling. Straining, she tried to make out the identity of the visitor. She watched in horror as his arms came up shooter style, and a weapon showed clearly clasped in his hands.

A low throaty growl rumbled in Bullet's throat. Catherine lifted a hand in the stop position and signaled him to be silent. Then she pulled her cell phone from her pocket and dialed 911. Whispering, she gave the dispatcher a brief synopsis of the situation and then tucked the phone, still open, in her waistband, hoping the dispatcher would be able to hear and report on whatever happened next.

Mike's mouth worked as if he were shouting. The impact resistant glass didn't transfer any sound. Silently, Catherine cursed herself for upgrading the broken window after the brick incident. Instinct led her to the back door. Hand on the knob she prepared to open the door.

"Damn!" she hissed and pulled her hand back as if burned. No matter how quietly she opened the door. The telltale beep of her house alarm would give away her entry. The system offered a silent mode. She remembered the installer tried to convince her to get it. Now she wished she had listened to his advice.

Bullet looked at her expectantly. Then he nudged the flap of his doggie door, with his nose. The flap moved inward. Catherine couldn't believe she'd forgotten to secure the doggie door, not after everything that happened. No matter how it happened, she was grateful for the oversight. With quick motions, she thanked the dog directed him to him to sit and stay. Crouching down she folded herself into a small enough package to slither through the dog's access. It was all she could do not to cry out in pain as she scraped skin from her thigh forcing herself through.

On silent feet, she made her way to the door connecting the Florida room to the kitchen. Slowly turning the knob, she thanked God she hadn't wired this, or any interior door to the alarm.

"Simms, if you fire that weapon, you'll have the rest of your life to regret it." Mike said.

Catherine couldn't hear any indication of fear or trepidation in his voice, only the flat tones of a law enforcement officer facing danger.

"What the hell do you care? You won't be around to know about it." Hank Simms shouted. "Neither will I; not around here anyway. I have enough money to get the hell out of the country before anyone knows what happened to you. I don't have as much as I wanted, thanks to Jackman spewing his trap to our esteemed Village attorney, but I have enough."

The edge of hysteria Catherine heard in Hank's voice made her blood run cold.

"Then you don't need to be here, Hank," Mike said. "Why not get on a plane and leave?"

"Shut up Reardon. Don't interrupt me. It was such a beautiful plan. Nobody would have known anything until we were gone."

"We?"

"I told you to shut up! What gave you and your girlfriend the right to interfere? You can stop investigating now. You'll never tell anyone anything ever again."

"If you have all this money, why is your house in foreclosure?"

"I paid it off you stupid idiot. The last thing I wanted was someone looking at my finances. I paid it off, obscene mortgage rate and all. Had to leave the wife something. I'm done Reardon. You can take that to the grave."

Fear leant speed to her hands. Catherine slid the towel drawer open and grabbed her .357-caliber revolver. Flicking the well-oiled barrel open, she checked to see each chamber held a round. Closing the weapon, she hugged the wall, making her silent way down the hallway to her bedroom door.

A flicker of recognition flashed in Mike's eyes. Catherine shook her head slightly at him and watched his eyes flatten again while her body flowed into a shooter's stance. Without thinking about it, she turned slightly to the side, spread her feet hip width create a solid center of gravity, and let her arms form a tripod to support the weight of her weapon. Then in one fluid motion, she aimed, and extended her finger alongside the trigger.

"Drop the weapon, Simms, or I'll shoot."

Simms spun around at the sound of her loud, clear, voice. Holding his gun in his right hand, Catherine saw his finger curl toward the trigger. The sound of the blast was deafening.

CHAPTER 42

"You have the right to remain silent, anything you say may be used against you in a court of law, you have the right to an attorney, if you cannot afford one, an attorney will be appointed for you at no expense to you. Do you understand these rights?" Billy intoned as he read the Miranda warning from the plastic card he held in front of him.

The cadences were as familiar to Catherine as her own name. Never in a million years did she expect that she'd hear them read to Hank Simms, the Village Finance Commissioner. Huddling deeper into the curve of Mike's arm, she felt goose flesh rise on her body again. In near shock, she picked at the splintered wood in her bedroom doorjamb. Every time she relaxed her mental guard, she heard the sound of the bullet and felt its hot breath blow past her face before it splinted the wood and came to rest in the hallway wall.

"You OK, Kit Kat?" Mike asked.

Catherine nodded into his chest. She didn't want him to turn her around. If he looked at her, she feared she'd lose the thin veil of distance, and scream her terror aloud. Her emotions and memories caromed and collided like a cue ball on a pool table. One moment she was in her own house, the next painful memories had her lying on the sun-heated sidewalk in North Pinehurst holding her smoking gun tightly in both hands watching the life bleed from the man she shot. The discharge of a weapon, Catherine recalled her instructor saying, has consequences on both sides of the gun. Concentrating hard, she pulled herself back into the present.

"You stupid pig, you have no idea who you are arresting." Hank hissed as Billy double locked the handcuffs behind his back. "I approve your pay rates. I could buy you on one corner, sell you on the next and not care about the change."

"Yes, sir." Billy replied automatically.

The sound of a knock startled Catherine. Zombie like, she moved from the security of Mike's arms to the front door. Cracking it open, the afternoon sunlight nearly blinded her. Through the heat haze, she made out the figure of Chief in the doorway. For some reason Catherine couldn't fathom, he wore shorts and a tee shirt.

"Are you going to let me in, Catherine?" Chief asked gently.

Mutely, she pulled the door fully open and stood aside. She tried to smile as Chief looked back at her as he walked down the hallway, but the effort made her face hurt.

"Reardon, your girlfriend is in shock. Don't leave her alone. She really looks rocky," Was anyone hurt?"

Catherine tiptoed back down the hallway, giving Hank Simms as wide a berth as she could in the narrow space. The fog in her brain dissipated and anger took its place.

"Chief, I don't think I've ever seen you dressed this far down on duty," She said.

She didn't miss the glance he directed at Mike.

"Well, she's back, Reardon. Too bad, I almost preferred quiet Catherine."

A serious look settled on Chief's face. "We've never arrested a Commissioner before. This one pulled me away from a barbeque. I'm not thrilled either, but I'll be damned if I'll lose a murder collar because the 'i's aren't dotted or the 't's crossed. No offense Billy, but with me and Reardon both here…"

"No offense taken, Chief. I'm grateful for the backup. I Mirandized him. Metro wants to know whose taking him downtown. Are we questioning him here first?"

"We'll transport. We've got enough men on to cover the shift if you take him."

"Do you mind if I ask him a couple of questions first, Chief?" Catherine asked.

Not waiting for an answer, she strode up to face the man and said, "Why? Why in God's name did you kill Gavin, and why stalk me."

Bullet bared his fangs and growled.

"Did you take my dog? You set the fire too! You bastard." Catherine lunged at him and Chief lunged for her.

She watched as Hank curled his lips and seemed to roll his tongue in his mouth. A nanosecond before the glob of spit left his lips, Catherine realized what the motions meant, and stepped aside.

"I want my lawyer." Hank Simms said. He smiled at Catherine. "You're still suspect number one. I didn't do it. None of it."

Billy handed Chief a heavy box punctuated with holes, some with wire ties protruding. It contained Simms's .38-caliber handgun. He gripped the Finance Commissioner by the elbow, and looked at his Chief.

"Downtown, Billy." Chief shook his head and sighed. "Much as I'd like to question him now, get him booked and wait for his lawyer. Don't even ask him how he feels. Get him the hell out of here."

Nodding, Billy marched the Commissioner out of Catherine's house and into the waiting cruiser.

"It all fits, Chief. He was an embezzler. He knew Gavin went to the Village attorney. He told Mike that. He confronted Gavin. They fought. He hung him. He had the strength. He came after me, he shot Mike, he stole my dog! Look at the truck outside, a big SUV. Ann said it was a truck like mine."

Chief seemed to weigh the gun box he held in his hand as he followed his officer out. Just before he got to the doorway, he turned and looked back at Catherine and Mike as if he had something more to say. Raising an eyebrow, he looked at Mike and said, "Don't let her strain anything jumping to conclusions."

Falling more than sitting on the coffee table behind her, the brief adrenaline surge left her muscles cramped and her emotions more drained than fear had. She grimaced at the copper taste in her mouth. "This is too much," she whispered.

Mike came over and squatted in front of her. Taking her hands in his strong ones, he looked deeply into her face. "I think you need a brandy and a hot bath."

She snorted, her eyebrows shot in the air and her eyes widened to the point they nearly hurt. "Are you suggesting I have a drink? A real booze drink?"

"Yep. I think in this case, it's medicinal. Besides, I'll be here with you. No worries."

Catherine wriggled one hand out of Mike's grasp. "I'd love one," she said, brought her hand to her mouth and folded her lower lip, pushing the vee of flesh under her upper teeth.

"I know that pose, my dear. You are lost in thought" Mike laughed, and levered himself up from the floor. "Brandy still under the sink?" He asked. "Catherine? Is the brandy still under the sink?"

"Oh, sorry, yes. Something's wrong, Mike"

Handing Catherine the brandy snifter, Mike seated himself on the recliner chair facing the coffee table where she still perched. Holding out his drink, he clicked the glass against the one she held and said, "Congratulations. You not only arrived on time, you caught the killer."

Shaking her head she said, "I'm not so sure about that. For the record, I didn't do anything. Ann called me. I had no idea Hank came here, armed or unarmed."

Leaning back, Mike sipped deeply from the glass he held in his hand. Catherine set her untouched drink on the coffee table beside her.

Silently, she reviewed everything she knew about Hank Simms. It wasn't much. Uncomfortable, she pushed herself off the coffee table and sat cross-legged on the floor. The wooden table-edge bit into her back just under her shoulder blades. "What's Hank charged with?"

Mike propped his elbows on his knees and bent forward. "You were here, Kit Kat. Don't you remember?"

"No. I think I zoned out for a while there."

"He was charged with breaking and entering, assault with a deadly weapon, attempted murder of a police officer and unlawful restraint. That was for starters. I'm guessing once Chief gets the information, criminal mischief for the rock incident at your house, arson, animal cruelty for kidnapping Bullet. Grand theft charges are pending for the embezzlement."

"Only if they get evidence supporting those charges."

"Do you doubt it?"

"Simms couldn't have done the embezzlement alone. He had to have co-conspirators, at least one. Who else was in the car the night he took Bullet? What about Gavin's murder? Do you think he killed Gavin?"

"You sure thought so, and you let Chief know about it."

"Yeah, but now, in the cold light of day, do you think he did it?"

"Yes. I do. The whole case hangs together."

Catherine's head shot up. "When did you think it? How did he do it?" I don't think it does. Why kill Gavin? Why come after me? Why go after you? Make a case so I can believe it."

"Why don't you make one against it, Cathy?"

Hearing the warning note in Mike's voice, Catherine considered her options. "I can't, but neither can you."

"Ok, yes, I can. Simms was embezzling. Someone made a mistake and deposited $100,000 into Gavin's account. Gavin alerted the Village attorney, the Village attorney started looking into it. Simms got wind of the investigation. This is a small town. It has more leaks than a colander. He probably went over to Gavin's to confront him, they argued, fought, and he killed him."

"And hung Gavin? Why? Who would think of that?"

"Given the publication of the affidavit that morning, and Ashley's absence – Simms probably thought Ashley left him. A despondent Gavin hangs himself after he finds her car gone."

"Weak, Reardon. Then why come after me, and you."

"Because…" the trilling of Mike's cell phone interrupted him. Pulling it from his pocket, he looked at the display. "It's Chief," he said to Catherine and flipped the phone open.

Catherine watched the play of emotions cross Mike's face. The quick rise of color to his cheeks told her that something wasn't right. His half of the conversation consisted of little more than grunts interspersed with the occasional 'yes, sir.'

She watched Mike slowly close the phone. "The rounds don't match. The gun Simms had here wasn't the gun that shot me."

CHAPTER 43

"I love waking to the smell of coffee perking in the morning." Catherine smiled and looked up at Mike standing alongside the bed holding a steaming cup out to her. She hoisted herself up from under the sheet, piling pillows behind her back and accidentally upending Paddy Whack. The cat's loud yowl brought the sound of Bullet's nails clicking on the floorboards.

"Sheesh, nobody wants to be left out." Catherine blew on the hot liquid to cool it. She sipped and said, "Elixir of the gods. You'll make some woman a fine houseboy. What are you doing up?" Putting down the coffee, she tipped the alarm clock face up so she could read it. "Cripes, it's only seven in the morning!"

Mike cocked his head to the side, turned and sat on the edge of the bed. "I thought I'd go in today."

Catherine' jaw tightened and blood tingled through her arms. Visions of yesterday's attack came flooding back. Much to her chagrin, she realized the thought of being alone frightened her.

"It's too soon, Mike. The wound's still raw. I know. I changed the bandage last night."

He rotated his right shoulder, and lifted the arm and sling. "True, but I'm feeling a lot better. It won't be a full day. Just part time until the doctor releases me. I'm on desk duty, so the most motion I'll get is answering the phone." He grimaced, making Catherine laugh.

"Ya, action boy. Well…" She swung her legs down to the floor and picked up her coffee cup. Taking a deep breath, she decided the best way to hold Mike, was to let him go. "I think you're scared to stay here. Too much action!" Using the cup as a shield, she lifted her eyes over the rim in time to catch him returning his tongue to his mouth.

"I talked to Chief this morning"

"About going back?"

"Yes, and about Hank. He's being held on a no bail."

Raising her eyebrows, Catherine tried silently to encourage him to continue. Questions bubbled to her lips, but she knew if she pushed, he'd shut down on her. They'd been up late into the night sparring about Hank's guilt or innocence. Catherine was adamant. The man deserved prison for what he tried to do to Mike, and for what he may have done to her. She finally conceded he might be her harasser, but she insisted he didn't kill Gavin.

"Cathy," Mike scrubbed his face with his left hand, "it fits. I know you don't agree, but it fits."

369

Taking a deep sip of the coffee, Catherine let the liquid roll over her tongue using the time to frame her question. 'So, Chief told you something new?"

The bed heaved as Mike stood quickly and strode to the door. Stopping, he brought his hand up to touch the scar on the doorjamb where the bullet shattered the wood. He turned to face Catherine still seated on the edge of the bed and said, "Just some details about the theft. Hank rolled on Cunningham…"

"Arnie Cunningham?" Catherine squeaked.

Nodding, Mike continued, "They each have large accounts in a Bahamian bank. Details of the funds are hard to come by. The Bahamas won't cooperate citing their privacy laws."

"But it's a crime!"

"Yeah, well, they don't seem as moved as you are. Anyway, Hank had Sassy do the transfers while he was on vacation. He'd pre-signed the transfer orders, reimbursements to the Commissioners for personal funds they'd paid out, general stuff. He gave a stack to her with a pile of bills and invoices she normally paid."

"That's really dumb. He had the Village clerk make the transfers. Did she do all of them?"

"No, just the last one. Hank got careless, he was on vacation, remember? He was in the Bahamas setting up his escape, and probably Cunningham's too. It was salary time for the Commissioners. She misread the line and transferred $50,000 to Gavin's account."

"Misread or typo. She had to know a commissioner's salary."

Mike answered with a shrug. "Doesn't really matter." He ruffled Catherine's hair.

"There were two transfers, Mike."

"Yeah, dumb luck on her part. The second deposit was a typo. The Village records show that transfer should have been $50.00. Reimbursement for postage, Gavin went to the Post Office for stamps."

Surprise made Catherine swallow her coffee down the wrong pipe. "What! No way," she finally managed to sputter.

"Yeah." Mike slapped her on the back with his good hand. "Go figure."

"Where's Cunningham now?"

"Downtown. Chief arrested him last night, after Hank cut his deal on the embezzlement. Said it was all Cunningham's idea and fault."

"What about Thom, was he in on it too?"

"They all say no. Oh, Hank took Bullet. Cunningham was in the back seat."

"Why?"

"The financial records. Remember Ashley told Chief you had records. Hank wanted them back, before someone fingered him."

"And Gavin's murder?"

Mike shook his head. "Hank says if anyone killed him, Cunningham did. He was Special Forces in 'Nam. Could have killed him, accidently or on purpose, with his bare hands. Didn't want to repay the loan. Yada, yada point the finger, yada, yada point, yada." He ran his fingers through his hair.

Catherine read tiredness in his eyes. "Funny thing, Kit Kat. I believe him. He didn't kill Gavin. Neither did Cunningham."

Catherine curled her lower lip between her fingers and shoved the resulting vee under her upper teeth. She looked at Mike, while she considered what she knew versus what he told her. "Nope. I'm still not buying it. He died by hanging, not hand to hand."

Resting his head on the damaged doorframe, Mike sighed deeply. "Let it go, Cathy. It's over. The hanging was to fake suicide. Cunningham couldn't let him live. Not after the confrontation."

"Cunningham said that?"

"No, of course not, but it makes sense, don't you think."

"I think the same thing you've been screaming at me. Where is the evidence? The gold hunk under the fire rubble? What about that?"

"Base metal, Cathy. It was a medic alert bracelet. Simms has Graves disease."

The sharp intake of breath caused Catherine to choke. Graves disease. An adrenal disease. She searched her memory and couldn't recall a time that she'd seen him wear a bracelet. Was it Simms? Even at this late date, was he covering for someone? "What time will you be home?' A chill chased tiny fingers up Catherine's spine as the small muscles of Mike's face tightened.

Emotions chased themselves across Mike's rugged features. His sky blue eyes seemed to darken to a stormy grey. He took the mug from her hands, placed it on the bedside table, raised her face and kissed her hard. "Should be early afternoon, unless I start hurting too bad."

Relief flooded Catherine, and a little pride, this living together was still so new. She listened until she heard the door click and the lock turn. Then she flopped back on the bed, and tried to box her fear into a tiny corner of her mind. The sound of her front door re-opening brought her bolt upright, beads of sweat breaking out on her hairline. She swung her legs over the side of the bed, her hand groping in the nightstand drawer for her weapon.

"Just me, dead-eye." Mike sang out from the living room. "I walked Bullet already, and fed both critters, I forgot to tell you."

Catherine smiled and lay back down. Yesterday had taken more out of her than she wanted to admit. An extra hour or so of sleep would be wonderful.

Bullet woke her by jumping up on the bed. Eyes still heavy with sleep, Catherine stroked his soft fur. "Come on, fella," she mumbled, just another few minutes. I have it on the highest authority that you got walked." Rolling her face away from his soft fur, Catherine heard the sound of a key in the front door followed by the familiar boop of the alarm indicating an open zone. Fully awake, she looked at the clock. "Shoot, it's one o'clock. Why didn't you get me up earlier, big dog?"

Muffled voices sounded in the living room. Straining her ears to make out the voices, she stumbled out of bed and grabbed for shorts and a tee shirt. She smiled as she identified Mike's voice talking to Nancy. Shoving her feet into her puppy slippers, she padded down the hall and greeted Mike with a kiss.

He leaned into her body, wrapping one arm around her waist, and with his free hand reached awkwardly and tousled her hair. "I'm glad I went, in." He said fondly. "Looks like you needed the sleep."

"Hey Nance, want some coffee? What are you doing here?" Catherine said.

Catherine felt her friend's eyes travel her body taking in the sheet wrinkles that still adorned her thighs, face and arms. "Want me to take Bullet out for a quickie?"

Looking at Mike, who nodded, Catherine said, "That would be great. I gotta admit I need way more coffee than I had this morning to make me human!"

Visibly forcing her tongue into her cheek, Nancy mumbled over the bulge, "Let me leave you two love birds alone, at least until Master Pooch does his business." Reaching for Bullet's leash, she snapped it on his collar and announced, "But then I want some coffee too! Ashley's talking about going back to Chicago now that Simms and Cunningham are in jail."

Arm in arm, Catherine and Mike headed for the kitchen, she arched an eyebrow at Mike. "Any more news."

"About."

"Why the break-in, why the arson? Who's gonna win the World Series, come on Mike!"

Exasperation tinged her voice and her hands gripped the edge of the marble countertop.

He unscrewed the top on the thermal carafe and looked inside. "Still hot. Why don't you go sit on the couch, I'll bring some over."

"Mike." Drawing a shuddering breath, Catherine struggled for control. Through clenched teeth she said, "Why would Hank throw a rock through my window. What could I have that he wanted so badly that he'd risk getting arrested?"

"Sit."

Catherine felt the couch dip behind her as Mike sat down and put the steaming cup on the coffee table. He placed his good hand on her shoulder and proceeded to do a one handed massage. "Kit Kat," he said softly, "Cunningham gave him access to the first file of information I got from you. It had the phone message notes from Gavin's call to the bank, about the $50,000 deposits. Your notes were in there too. You had a note about getting the rest of the statements for the account."

"So?" Catherine turned her head to face him. "So why did he try to break in?"

"To get the rest of the information, Catherine. This isn't a mystery. Stop and think." Nancy replied.

"So you're on his side?" She snapped.

"I'm not on anyone's side here, Catherine, but it makes sense."

Irritated, Catherine got up from the couch, walked to the mantle and grabbed the antique dog.

"Does the foot print fit too? The one they found in my flower bed?"

"There's no information on that Cathy," Mike said.

"Why not? You got the ballistics back on the gun fast enough. Why not on the….? You bastard. I recognize that tone. You know, you won't tell me."

"The ballistics haven't come back yet. Simms allowed the lab to do a comparison of the test shot he said he got at the time he bought the gun. The lab pushed it through because I'm a cop. They still haven't finished the FBI database comparison of the round they recovered from my house. We only know that the round Simms provided does not match."

Shaking her head and rapidly passing the china dog from hand to hand, Catherine continued as if Mike hadn't spoken. "Arson, why that, and why take my dog?"

"Catherine," Nancy began.

"No, you're just supporting him. Don't say anything Nance. You don't have the information to speak."

She heard more than saw Mike rise from the couch. "Come on, Nancy, I'll drive you home. I think Catherine needs to be left alone right now."

Catherine continued to stare into the maw of the fireplace and rotate the dog between her hands. "I'm sorry. It's just…"

"It's just you feel like your glory's been eclipsed," Mike said. "Catherine, I know how much you wanted to find the killer, but he's been found. Just because it doesn't fit with your theories, doesn't negate the evidence. Anyone who would shoot at a cop would shoot at anyone. It was all about protecting himself from the blame."

Slowly, she replaced the dog statue on the mantle.

Nancy came up behind her and touched her gently on the shoulder. "It's an antique, you know." She leaned over Catherine and settled the statuette further back on the shelf. "Be careful with it."

Hot tears slid down Catherine's face. She hugged her friend to her and said, 'I don't deserve you. I don't deserve either of you."

She put both hands on the mantle and leaned heavily into it resting her forehead against the hand-hewn slate edge. "Mike, are you coming back?" Every fiber of her being tensed waiting for his response. Her emotions were in a free fall, and Mike seemed to be her only touchstone.

He walked over, placed his good hand on her shoulder and massaged gently. Then he kissed the top of her head. "Yeah, let me get Nancy home, pick up some extra clothes and see what's in my mail. I want to swing by the cop shop again. Check on the footprint. We are in this together, Catherine. I am not holding out on you, but I can't manufacture evidence to fit your theories."

"Nancy, will you wait for me in the car? I want a couple of seconds alone with Catherine."

"Just a sec, Mike." Catherine heard Nancy say over the creek of the door hinge closing, followed by a thin clunk. "Hey Cathy, this is for you, Ashley said it wasn't hers."

The door clicked shut before Catherine could ask Nancy what she meant.

His large hands scrubbed his face and exhaustion seemed to ooze from every pore. "The Kents didn't find Bullet wandering around the neighborhood. What Dannie saw was Meg trying to coax Bullet back into the house after he escaped. Simms figured dognapping Bullet would be the perfect way to shut you up in case you knew anything about the embezzlement. He doesn't know anything about the murder. The bonfire was supposed to scare you. All those stuffed toy German shepherds burning. You forgot to lock the doggie door, when Bullet ran out, Simms took advantage of the situation."

A frisson of fear ran through Catherine's veins. Simms could have gotten into the house through the same door Bullet used to get out. What then? Would the fire have been in the house? How far was Simms prepared to go that night?

"Frankly, you're damn lucky Simms didn't decide to try to crawl in through the door. I've told you to get that thing replaced with one of the new ones. Bullet ripped off Simms's Medic Alert bracelet. Since Simms only recently started wearing one, he wasn't sure where he'd lost it, or even if he had it on at the time he set the fire."

"How did Simms, Cunningham and Kent get together? That makes for strange bedfellows. Kent's not on the commission."

"Much as I hate to say this, so far it's co-incidence. They all hated Gavin. Kent saw Cunningham wrestling with Bullet in the car that night. Simms lives across the street. Kent agreed to take the dog to help Simms out. He intended to dump Bullet in the 'Glades and leave him to die out there in the sawgrass."

Waves of nausea nearly overcame Catherine at the thought of her dog abandoned in the 'Glades. "Why? Why would Oliver want to do that? He wasn't involved in any of this. He didn't murder Gavin and he certainly couldn't be involved in the embezzling."

"No. Something's missing. I don't know what it is, and that's what I'm trying to find out. What ties Oliver to all of this?"

"Cunningham had grey mud on his jean cuffs the night of the fire. Like you would get at a construction site." Catherine looked at Mike. "From the Kents construction?

"Well, that could put him at the Kents, and he came to your house for damage control. See if anyone saw anything. That would make sense."

"My poor dog. He got hurt because of me."

"No, it was their fault." Mike pulled Catherine into his embrace. "They did this, Catherine," he whispered into her hair, "not you."

"Why did Hank go after you? If he wasn't involved with Gavin's murder, why not stay out of it? You weren't investigating the embezzlement."

"The bank statements. He knew I had them, in the Jackman file." Mike replied.

"So what!" Catherine exploded. "The Village attorney had that investigation. Why didn't Simms leave town, go to the Bahamas? He had enough money. Why come after evidence that wasn't going to matter?"

"If criminals made sense, Little Bits, we'd be out of business. Hank claims he was afraid it would somehow tie him to Gavin's murder, and although he didn't think the Bahamas would give him up for an embezzlement charge, they might for a murder charge."

Mike glanced at his watch and then out the window to his car. Nancy sat patiently in the passenger seat. "I gotta go, Kit Kat." He leaned down and kissed Catherine gently on the lips.

Exhaustion flooding every fiber of her body, Catherine shuffled to the front door. She opened it and propped herself against the jam watching until Mike's car rounded the corner and went out of sight. Sighing, she pulled the door closed. When she turned to go back to the couch, her gaze fell on the hall table. Next to a hand-thrown mug and her cell phone lay a pen, Ashley's pen.

She picked it up and rolled it between her fingers.

"Damn it!" She exclaimed, and raced down the hall to pull on her running shoes.

CHAPTER 44

The pen, that had to be it. Only two people had access to both Gavin and that particular pen. At least only two Catherine knew about. The memory of Oliver's complaints about his lost pen returned with the force of a freight train. The pen Catherine now remembered picking up from the floor of Gavin's garage. The pen she found when Terry decked her. In one fluid motion, she scooped up her cell phone and the commemorative pen from the Miami Metropolis from the hall table and shoved them in her back pocket of her shorts. "Damn," she muttered. "I had the answer all along. I never saw it."

Closing the door in Bullet's face, she shouted. "Mommy will be right back. Tell Mike to come get me if I'm not."

"OK," she mumbled as her feet found their rhythm, "Now I'm leaving messages with my dog. That's a new low." Her hand swung back without interrupting the steady rhythm of her feet and pulled the cell phone from her pocket. Flipping it open, she pressed Mike's speed dial code and heard the sterile sound of dead air. Not wanting to stop and look at the display, she pushed the red end call button and dialed the number fully. Silence. Slowing, she saw the phone and crossbar icon displayed in the corner. "Damn," she hissed. "No service."

At the intersection, Catherine briefly considered running to Mike's house first. Hank didn't kill Gavin. Mike was right. She knew who did. But Mike was wrong about something else. There was a connection among Gavin, Hank, the Mayor and Oliver. High School. They all went to High School together. How far back did school spirit, and hatred, go. A sudden frisson of fear kept her from involving Mike. Better to be sure. Arcing a curve in the middle of the street, she reversed her direction and headed for the culprit. If she was wrong, then Oliver's wrath and embarrassment was her only punishment. She'd avoid jeopardizing Mike's job.

Buoyed by her decision, Catherine forged ahead. Stopping long enough to slide the bar on the gate open and carefully close it behind her, she jogged up the steps and rang the bell.

"Hi Meg, Oliver home?"

"Yes. He's on deadline. I don't want him disturbed."

Pushing past the woman, Catherine headed for the office. As she passed the glory wall, she stopped at the ten-year plaque from the Metropolis. Pulling the pen out of her pocket, she fit it on the prongs. "Perfect." She smiled as she said it.

Meg followed behind Catherine and made a grab for her arm. "Stop right there, you crazy bitch."

Looking over her shoulder at the dark-haired woman, Catherine gave her the flat-eyed cop stare she'd perfected in her days on the force and pulled her arm out of the other woman's grasp. She felt her skin rip as Meg's fingernails tore into her bicep. Wincing, Catherine spun around and simultaneously pulled her cell phone from her back pocket while pushing open the door to Oliver's office.

Oliver stood from behind his desk. The look on his face more confused than fearful. "Catherine? Is something the matter?" Judge Phil Brandon, seated across the desk from Oliver, glanced in Catherine's direction, a small smile played on his lips.

Relief flooded through her and the icy knot around her heart relaxed a bit. Nancy's boss tugged his pant leg and casually crossed one leg over the other. At least she had an ally until Mike arrived. She tossed a quick smile in his direction. "Glad to see you, Judge," she said while her fingers finished punching 911.

Catherine's heart skipped a beat. The feeling of cold steel pushed into the soft spot at the base of her skull just where it joins her spine. She cast a desperate gaze at Phil Brandon who rewarded her with a half-smile. The still open phone dropped from her bloodless fingers to the floor where Meg's flip-flop clad foot kicked it under the desk. Phil Brandon, he went to high school with the rest of them. A member of the fraternity from hell. Think Catherine. No one in this room is going to help you.

"Why the gun, Meg?" Catherine asked loudly, hoping that the 911 call had connected and the phone line was active. "I thought the Kents had more class than that." She looked over at Phil again. His position remained unchanged the smile a bit broader. What the hell was going on? No way he could be involved.

"Meg, what are you doing?" Oliver asked. "We didn't do anything."

"She knows, Oliver. I saw it in her face when she barged her way in. She has your pen, the one you lost the day… I should have killed the bitch when I had the chance, that night in the rain. I told you.

"Summer Hill is too small a town to keep secrets. Isn't it Judge Brandon?" Catherine all but shouted. Maybe if he heard his name it would pull him out of a stupor. What was wrong with him? This woman had a gun on her.

"Someone is on the other end of that phone. Would you get it Margaret?" Phil stood and shoved Meg out of the way reaching for the gun as hc did.. The gun flew from her hand, Catherine and Phil each scrambled to retrieve it. Phil managed to grab Catherine spinning her backwards and trapping her next to his chest. His arm cut across her ribs like an iron band making it hard to breathe. "You're not going to shout anymore are you, Catherine?" He hissed into her ear. With is foot, he prodded Meg, "Go get something to tie her up. Duct tape, rope, anything." He bent, doubling Catherine's captive body in half, to pick up the gun from the floor.

"Goddamn it." Meg spat out. She bashed her shoulder on the desk overhang as she stood. "I don't see that damn phone."

"Forget the phone. Get something to tie this bitch up with." He pushed the gun muzzle deeper into Catherine's temple. "Do it Now. If anyone were on the phone, we'd already hear sirens. Go." Phil ordered.

"There's stuff in the pool house, Meg. Duct tape at least." Oliver's voice broke with emotion. "Phil, what are you going to do? We don't want any part of this."

"Christ, you are a wuss. Like it or not, you have a part. You killed Gavin."

"Goddamn it Phil, that's not…"

With lightening like speed Phil spun around to face Oliver, Catherine held in front of him like a shield. The motion caused him to relax his grip slightly. Using the opportunity, Catherine managed to maneuver her hand up and grip his thumb. With all the strength she could muster, she pulled down on the digit. The sound of a loud crack followed by Phil's scream rewarded her effort. Spinning around, she knocked the injured man off balance as Meg dove for her. In slow motion, Catherine heard the weapon fire, and she collapsed to the floor under Meg's weight.

Immobilized by Meg's body, Catherine lay sandwiched between the Meg and Phil.

"That bitch," moaned Phil, she broke my thumb."

"Shut up you wuss." Oliver hissed, using Phil's words against him. Worried that one of the neighbors would call the police because they heard the gunshot, Oliver had found a roll of gardener's tape in his bottom drawer. "Let me finish tying her up, and then we'll deal with you. Meg, get the hell out of here. Whatever happens, I don't want you involved." Oliver wound tape around Catherine's hands as he spoke while she balled her hands into fists trying to make space between her wrists for slack. Phil sat with his back against a bookcase grasping his injured hand and moaning pitifully.

"You can't keep her out of it." Phil's voice sounded like a breathy whimper. "You don't think I'm going to lie to cover for you, do you? "You put that story in the Metropolis. She whacked the poor guy. You choked him."

Now Catherine understood the shovel. Meg hit Gavin with the shovel. That's how they managed to hang him without a struggle. But the choking. When did Oliver choke Gavin, and why? Why choke an unconscious man. It still didn't make sense. And how did Phil know. He had to be there. Was Phil the murderer? Catherine ran over the events from the morning of the murder. Nothing indicated Phil was in the garage.

A jolt of pain shot through Catherine's side as Meg's bare foot jabbed into her rib cage rolling her on her back taking the pressure off her bound hands. "Shut up Phil, You know I hit him because he tried to attack Oliver. All we wanted was a zoning variance. You saw it, but I thought you just

said you weren't there. You can't have it both
ways." Roll over, Cathy. Where's the gun, Oliver?"

"I have it, Meg" The calm in Phil's voice
sent chills down Catherine's spine that had nothing
to do with the air conditioning. "It doesn't matter
what she knows now. She won't have anyone to
tell. Yes, I saw you. And I saw him fall when Oliver
grabbed him from behind because he went for you
after you hit him. So what if I was there. The only
people who know that are in this room. I want this
bitch dead, But first," Phil grunted as he leaned
down and shoved the gun butt between Catherine's
bound hands. "I think this bitch is going to have to
commit a little murder of her own."

Struggling to turn her head to the sound of
the Judge's voice, Catherine saw a hard coldness in
his eyes. This man had nothing to lose. He was the
one who gave the order to hang Gavin. Gavin was
the one who could keep him from being re-elected.
Gavin knew about Phil and Maggie. Catherine was
sure of it. Time slowed to a crawl. Unable to move
much more than her eyes without attracting
attention, she studied everything in view, seeing if it
afforded her any opportunity to live.

"Don't you want to know what happened,
bitch? You and that little bitchette who works for
me have been trying hard enough to figure it out."

Phil's right thumb hung at an awkward
angle forcing him to cradle the weapon he now held
in two hands. Her experienced eye noted a slight
shake, probably caused by the pain. Still, she knew
a good aim didn't always count for as much as luck.
From the living room, Catherine heard Pugsley

growl. Hope flooded her. If her call had gone through, someone should have figured out her location by now. Even if the operator couldn't hear all the words, they could triangulate the signal.

"See if someone's out there," Phil ordered Meg. He shoved Catherine at Oliver. He yanked Catherine upright and began to drag her to the office's back door. "Get her out of here."

Oliver's voice pitched an octave higher as if sensing a reprieve from death. "I'll take this bitch to the pool house, they haven't covered the well. No one will find her."

Catherine drew a deep breath and shouted, "I'm in here."

The sound of splintering wood flooded her ears. Meg screamed. Mike shouted her name. Oliver threw Catherine's body at Phil and bolted for the back door.

Phil caught her and pressed the muzzle of the gun to her head leaving enough space, Catherine realized, so the discharge of gases from the muzzle wouldn't deflect the trajectory of the round. "Guess we won't need your fingerprints after all, sweetie."

She felt him shaking, whether from fear or pain, she didn't know, and she offered up a silent prayer that his finger wasn't on the trigger. In her brief glimpse of the gun, she'd seen Glock emblazoned on the barrel. She knew the weapon had fired once. It would take very little pressure to get off a second round, what effect the lack of balance from his broken thumb would have would be a wild card. Pulling in a deep breath, she brought both her hands up and drove the gun Phil was holding into his chin. The sound of the weapon discharging deafened her.

Catherine's world shrank to the tiny bit of real estate her bound feet rested on. She felt vibrations in the floorboards indicating a commotion in the living room, but it didn't seem to concern her. So this is what it's like to be deaf. Or maybe dead. Each beat of her heart sounded so loudly in her ears that she couldn't hear anything else. She saw Mike's mouth moving, but no words seemed to come out. Her skin tingled as she felt the blood flow in the veins beneath it. Her brain cried out to say something to Mike, but her training kept her silent. Gradually she heard a loud buzzing sound and beneath the buzzing, she heard whispered words a loud keening sound.

Slowly Phil's body slid down hers. Inch by inch it crawled down her body leaving behind a bloody trail where Phil's face moved from her breast to her knees before finally losing contact and hitting the floor. Phil's eyes blinked. His mouth seemed frozen in a large o as he screamed in pain. The shot had blown off his nose and part of his right cheek, stopping just under his eye and cutting a deep gouge in his scalp.

Catherine, off balance and left with no support pitched forward. She twisted her body to try to protect her face and struck her head hard against the wooden arm of the wing chair.

From her place on the floor, she saw two pairs of high gloss duty shoes stop inches from her nose.

"Got him, Mike." Billy's voice said.

Catherine heard the sound of zip tie cuffs pulled tight. She felt a familiar hand grasp her taped wrists.

"Hand me a knife, Chief."

As soon as the pressure released from her wrists, Catherine levered herself to a sitting position and took the knife from Mike's hand, slicing through the binding on her ankles.

"That's gonna hurt coming off, Kit Kat. You alright?"

Nodding, Catherine bit her lip and felt hot tears course down her face. Vaguely, she felt Mike's arms circle her as she cradled her face in his shoulder.

It wasn't until he asked if she could speak that she realized she hadn't spoken a word since she screamed. That seemed like hours ago.

"How did you know?"

"Emergency operator traced your cell phone. They called Summer Hill, and patched it to us. I heard you say something that sounded like "cans.""

"Cans?"

"Yep, then I heard Meg's voice and knew you said Kents. We came looking here first."

"What were you doing at the office?"

"Long story, does it matter?"

Catherine sat in the wing chair and rubbed her head. Mike leaned over and pushed back her hair.

"Ouch, that's going to leave a mark. You sure you're all right?"

"Yeah, I hit it when you rushed Phil."

"How's Meg?"

"She'll survive. We have the slug."

"Slug?"

"The shot went through the wall."

"How did you know it was Phil?" Mike asked. Billy came to stand beside him as two Metro officers guided the cuffed Kents and Judge Brandon out of the house to the ambulance. Chief came back into the room, dangling a set of keys in his hand.

"I didn't." Catherine whispered her throat sore from emotion. "I thought it was Oliver."

"Catherine, you up to some questions while we process the scene?" Chief asked. He looked down at his feet. "Would you rather come back to the station? On the other hand, I could come to your house later.

"No, Chief. This is fine. There isn't much to tell." She saw him nod to Billy who flipped open his notebook in response.

"It was the pen, and a hand thrown mug that tipped me off. But I was wrong. Well, part wrong." Seeing confusion on their faces, Catherine looked at Mike and pointed in the general direction of the Kents' living room. "Remember the glory wall?"

He nodded and she continued, "I looked at it while you and Oliver chatted. There's a plaque there, an empty plaque. I found a pen in Gavin's garage and picked it up."

"Catherine," Chief interrupted, "you know better than to tamper with the evidence."

"Your people processed the scene and released it before I went back. I picked up the pen then. When I went back to the garage, Terry Payson was already inside, and she was staring under the workbench. That's where I found the pen." Her face heated with the rise of a blush. "Actually, I picked it up without thinking. I needed to make a couple of notes. "

Chief's amused smile startled her. "Yeah, we've all been there," he said, "and it's never good."

Returning his smile, Catherine continued, "Ashley took the pen from me when she saw it. Thought it was hers. Nancy dropped it off today. I saw it sitting next to the mug, then I remembered Meg asking if Gavin's kiln was for sale. How did she know about the kiln? They weren't close, and the kiln was in the garage." Rubbing her wrists, she picked at the duct tape that still encircled them. "I didn't know they had a kiln until the morning I found Gavin hanging, and I took care of their dog. I'd never been in the garage before. Why would Meg be in the garage?"

"Why? What motive did the Kents have?" Billy asked.

"I don't know Meg said they only wanted a variance. I don't know why Phil was involved either except I think it had to do with Maggie. The girl in the story in the paper. Oh Gavin was too, but I think Phil had a real thing for her. And I think I was unwelcome. When I met with her, she said some things that didn't make sense at the time, but do now. Phil said Oliver planted the story in the paper. Juan and Tomas claim to have put it in the paper too. They couldn't have gotten it to anyone who could have published it though. Oliver could do that. When I think about the timing — it's the only thing that makes sense."

"That fits," Chief said. "He worked there. Both cub reporters," Chief glanced at Mike and winked, "do they still use that term Reardon, you're the one who's had TV watching time lately, agree, the Affidavit appeared in their mailboxes at the Metropolis."

"Yeah, but for some reason Oliver and Meg went to Gavin's house the morning after the Commission meeting." Catherine continued. "Judge Brandon…"

"Don't call him a Judge," Mike broke in. "He doesn't deserve the term if he was involved in this."

Catherine shrugged. "Well anyway, Phil then, said Meg hit Gavin with a shovel and Oliver choked him to death. The whole scenario made it sound like all three were there, but why? There's a photo of Oliver and Phil on the wall. Oliver covered the Courthouse beat, I went to high school with a ton of people I wouldn't know if I saw today. So, were they friends, close enough for this kind of thing? I've never seen Phil around here except at Nancy's parties sometimes. Why would he go bad? It makes no sense."

Catherine looked over at Mike. She read concern in his eyes. Her stomach plummeted. Motive. All she had were rumors and innuendos and unless the cell phone line stayed open, an unsubstantiated confession of sorts. Did that put this whole thing back in her court?

CHAPTER 45

The next morning Catherine pulled up in front of the police station in her SUV. For once, she'd decided to drive, not run. The call of coffee and donuts seemed louder than the call of exercise today.

Mike waited for her in Chief's office. The two men quickly brought Catherine up to date on the various confessions Meg and Oliver made the night before. Phil still claimed innocence. Oliver and Meg refused to let him off so easily. Especially since the ME's report suggested they'd hurt Gavin but Phil's actions murdered him.

"The whole thing was about a pool house! That makes less sense than anything I've heard or thought of. It really was about the zoning. Meg wasn't kidding." Catherine sat perched on the corner of Chief's desk. Mike took the leather armchair off to the side, the good cop chair the officers jokingly called it. Chief's feet were propped on the file cabinet, his arms crossed over his chest. The leather of his chair creaked as he swiveled to face the doorway as Billy entered the room.

"And an election, Catherine," Mike said.

"Pull up a piece of real estate, Bill. It's just us chickens here." Chief nodded in the direction of the straight back wooden chair in front of his desk.

Catherine watched the officer carefully. She knew from cop shoptalk that this was the bad cop chair.

Billy looked down at the chair and around the room. Grimacing, he said, "No thanks, Chief, I'll stand. Besides, I have to get back downtown. I want to get these statements typed and signed."

"Let me guess," Mike said, "Meg talked."

Nodding his head, Billy replied, "Yep, and Oliver. They cut a deal."

A frown creased Catherine's brow. "Why about Meg? I don't believe she killed Gavin."

"No, not directly. She's being charged with accessory, Oliver with manslaughter and Phil, murder one." Chief swung his feet down, looked at his sergeant and said, "Correct me if I get anything wrong, Billy.

"The part about Phil we've had to piece together from what the Kent's told us." He shot a quick salute in Catherine's direction. "And most of it accords with what you told us based on your investigation and your hunches, Catherine." Chief settled back in his chair, picked up a pen and stared at it as if it held the answers to the questions of the universe.

Catherine felt her lungs expand as she fought to breathe. She watched Chief struggle with his next words. After what seemed like an eternity, he put the pen down and met her eyes.

"We wouldn't have solved this case without you, Catherine. Good job."

Spots dappled her eyesight. Tears that she prayed would not fall burned the back of her eyes, and her throat tightened. She wanted to say something but her mind was empty. His words were the same ones she'd heard in her dreams a thousand times. Now that they were spoken, she didn't have a reply.

"You told us Tomas called Phil. What you couldn't know was that Phil had an affair with Maggie as well. You were right when you guessed it was closer to rape than consensual. Maggie told her brother that Brandon was crazy jealous that she'd picked Jackman and not him. It happened once in Brandon's office. Brandon ran for Judge right after that and Tomas was afraid to blackmail a Judge."

"That's disgusting."

"Yeah, and probably no one ever would have known about it either. Except this is an election year and Tomas Lopez got out of jail and needed money. Gavin turned him down flat. Said he didn't care who he told it was old news and he'd already told his wife. Tomas called Brandon and threatened to go public with it. Brandon not only saw his career going down in flames, he saw his life going down as well..."

"So that's why Brandon met with Gavin. He wanted to control the situation. Let him know the whole sordid thing might surface again." Catherine interrupted. "Sounds like he didn't know Gavin paid Tomas off in the past."

"Yeah, so Brandon figured if he managed to get the paper to release the Affidavit, then if someone pointing a finger at him after that, would look like sour grapes. So he encouraged Tomas and Juan to send the Affidavit to the Metropolis, and he got Oliver to get it to someone who would run with the story hoping it would get used. There was a problem though. Gavin knew about Phil's involvement with Maggie and he was pissed that somebody was dragging this whole thing up again and he was being played for the fall guy."

Little things that happened around the time in question suddenly fell into place. Gavin began getting vindictive in commission meetings and blowing up. Nancy mentioned that Phil seemed to be worried about something, but she'd written it off to campaign jitters. That was the same time Gavin was so nasty about paying her for the dog sitting too. Telling her to get a real job and stop trying to pretend that she was doing something of value. Looking back, it was easy to see when the seeds of this particular disaster were planted.

"So Gavin threatened to go public?"

"We're not sure. But suddenly Phil wasn't sure leaking the Affidavit was a good idea, and wanted Oliver to pull it back but it was too late. The reporters were hip deep in research by then."

"So how did everyone get to Gavin's the day he died?" Mike asked.

"Sort of a perfect storm. Phil wanted to talk to Oliver to see if there was some way they could take advantage of the situation to morally discredit Gavin further. The Kents were just leaving to walk their dog as Phil pulled up. He went along. When they passed Gavin's house that morning, they found Gavin in his garage, putting something in his kiln. Phil wanted to test the waters, the Kents wanted to talk zoning."

"So that's how Meg knew about the kiln," Catherine said. "I'm listening, Chief. What's the rest? You had me for prime suspect for a while."

"Oliver claims Jackman became livid at the sight of them. Began to rant and accused him of being responsible for the Affidavit and the story. Blamed Phil for standing by and letting it happen and not trying to stop it, then Gavin said he was going to tell his side for the first time ever, and he would tell the whole truth.

"Then the Kents started ranting about getting their pool house built. It got physical. Kent claims Jackman took a swing at him. He struck back, but using a wrestling move and going for the knees. Jackman fell. That's probably when he hit his head. Since the skin didn't break, there was nothing external for the crime scene folks to find."

"He didn't die of head trauma, Chief, and the shovel with my prints was wiped clean." Catherine pointed out. She looked over at Mike who seemed too relaxed, and realized none of this was news to him.

"Cool your jets, Catherine. You conducted your investigation in your way. Let me tell the story in mine! Chief rocked back in his chair. "Billy, you've got the quotes, why don't you take it from here."

Billy looked at the notebook in his hand and thumbed the pages forward. He cleared his throat and said, "Jackman lunged for Meg."

"For Meg?" Catherine interrupted. "Gavin went for a woman? Why? Seems to me, he would have gone for the guy who hit him."

"We'll never know for sure, Cathy, but I'm guessing that Jackman never fell, I think Oliver went for Jackman, and Meg joined in and smacked Jackman with the shovel. Don't forget, Oliver wrestled in high school. It's likely he would attack with a legitimate wrestling move and try to get Jackman to the floor. In a real fight, play fair doesn't come into the equation. Jackman probably got free, went for Oliver, and that's when Meg grabbed the shovel and hit him.

Either way, it won't matter. As you say, he didn't die of head trauma. It would explain Gavin going for Meg. Kent swears he didn't strangle him, just grabbed him from behind in a chokehold to protect his wife," Chief said. "That right, Billy?"

"Carotid-sinus-stimulation." Catherine mumbled. She looked over at Mike. "We learned about that at the Academy. It's why they banned chokeholds. Death can occur very quickly."

Billy looked down at his notes and nodded. "Pretty much.

"That's also what Phil and the Kents said when I was tied up. But the question is, what was Phil doing all this time? Standing around filing his nails?" Catherine asked.

"According to the Kents — looking superior. Since they were the ones fighting about zoning, he stayed out of it. But when Jackman passed out, Brandon panicked. Afraid someone might have seen him go into the Jackman garage and remember him. Jackman was unmarked, and dead. Meg claims Brandon felt for a heartbeat and breath, but he didn't detect any." Billy paused, thumbed his next page over and looked at Chief who nodded, "This is Oliver talking now, 'Phil was the one. He said to hang him. Make it look like suicide'

"He was alive though, wasn't he?" Catherine asked.

"Yeah, but he probably wasn't breathing or if he was it was so shallow a scared man couldn't feel the breath, we'll never know if Brandon really did feel a pulse before he ordered the murder. In a chokehold death, breathing stops, but true death, brain death, follows later. In this case, the hanging was overkill, he was dead either way, but it was the immediate cause of death." Chief said.

"Meg said if Ashley wasn't home at six-thirty in the morning, she'd left Gavin because of the affidavit." Billy flipped his notebook closed.

Catherine gazed at Mike for a long moment before finally asking, "Did either of them have anything to do with Mike getting shot?"

The sound of Mike clearing his throat broke the silence. "When we searched Phil's house, we found a .38. We also got back the ballistics report. The test fire comes back to the gun."

"Why go after you?" Catherine asked.

"He wasn't. He was after you. You were the one who could tie in the Riveras. You had contact with Maggie and Juan."

"Come on Mike, it was your house." Catherine chewed the inside of her lip thoughtfully, images of Mike shot and bleeding on the floor flashed into her mind. "But we'd pretty much told the Kents the day they found Bullet that I'd be at your house, didn't we."

Meg was the one who tossed the rock through your window. She wanted to scare you off the investigation. Oliver claims he found out about that later." Chief said.

Billy flipped some more pages in his notebook. "She claims Oliver threw the brick, wonder why they don't agree on that point."

Chief rose and stretched. "Impossible. The print we found was a woman's foot. Let me tell you, that girl has her feet firmly on the ground. She wears a size eleven. The same size as the one we cast at the scene after the brick went through your window."

"Guess that's what the trial's for. To tell us who did what and how." Catherine yawned. "Sorry. It's been a long couple of weeks.

"I suppose Terry was in Gavin's garage that morning to borrow a cup of sugar?"

Billy laughed. "Just snooping, Catherine. Same as you! Oh, one other thing, remember you got sick after Kent was at your house?"

"Yeah, and after I was at his house too."

"Meg says he put eye drops in your drink. You're lucky it didn't kill you. It's what he wanted.

Figured it would look like you drank yourself to death."

Catherine looked at the condensation dripping from the glass of soda she held in her hand and slowly replaced it on the desk.

Chief walked to the tall file cabinet and removed a small box. He turned and came to face Catherine where she sat on the desk.

Catherine felt a flutter in her stomach as he gave her a hard stare and thrust something in her direction. Slowly she reached for the flat blue box. Afraid to open it, she looked first at Mike and then at Chief. "Is this a proposal?" She asked, trying to joke.

The silence dragged on until it became uncomfortable. Finally, unable to think of anything else to do or say, she thumbed open the lid.

"Your certification is current, I checked." Chief said gruffly.

In the box was a shiny new sergeant's badge.

A flood of emotion washed over her. Catherine's eyes misted as she looked from Chief, to Mike, to Billy then at the shield in the box. She had a mental image of herself in a blue uniform; badge pinned over her heart, gun resting heavy at her hip and knew it wasn't the life she wanted. She watched the events since Gavin's death clack past like a line of dominos tipping over, one into the other. She realized she had a chance to make a family for herself this time based on love and respect. Not on a profession. A family that included Mike. Catherine squirmed in her seat. She liked this rebuilt life, and didn't want to risk it. Silently she closed the box and handed it back to Chief.

"Not yet, Chief. Maybe not ever."

www.ingramcontent.com/pod-product-compliance
Lightning Source LLC
Chambersburg PA
CBHW060141260626
47160CB00001B/76